It was the first time she had really been in his arms in four years. For all that time they had looked at each other, and wanted, and dreamed, and turned away. But now the longing was greater than ever, and they swayed toward each other, their lips almost touching.

"I understand you and your husband don't get on so well nowadays," he said.

"And that means I'm ready to fall into the arms of the first man who asks me," Constance said. "Is that what you think?"

"No, I'd hate to think that. It's just that I have an idea I'm in love with you, Constance."

Then she was in his arms and he was kissing her. She felt his fingers moving from her shoulders down her spine, reaching her bustle and sliding past to hold her buttocks and press her against him.

As waves of desire spread through her, she sank to the grass, feeling him kneeling with her, his fingers gently plucking at the buttons of her blouse . . .

# THE CRIMSON PAGODA

☐ EMERALD'S HOPE by Joyce Carlow. (123263—$3.50)*
☐ THE IMMORTAL DRAGON by Michael Peterson.
(122453—$3.50)*
☐ HOME OF THE BRAVE by Joel Gross. (122232—$3.95)*
☐ THE BOOKS OF RACHEL by Joel Gross. (095618—$3.50)
☐ MAURA'S DREAM by Joel Gross. (125932—$1.95)
☐ SEVENTREES by Janice Young Brooks. (110684—$3.50)
☐ NEVER CALL IT LOVE by Veronica Jason. (093348—$2.25)
☐ WILD WINDS OF LOVE by Veronica Jason. (119118—$3.50)*
☐ THE KISSING GATE by Pamela Haines. (114493—$3.50)
☐ CALL THE DARKNESS LIGHT by Nancy Zaroulis.
(092910—$2.95)
☐ THE CORMAC LEGEND by Dorothy Daniels. (115554—$2.25)*

*Prices slightly higher in Canada

---

Buy them at your local bookstore or use this convenient coupon for ordering.

THE NEW AMERICAN LIBRARY, INC.,
P.O. Box 999, Bergenfield, New Jersey 07621

Please send me the books I have checked above. I am enclosing $_____
(please add $1.00 to this order to cover postage and handling). Send check
or money order—no cash or C.O.D.'s. Prices and numbers are subject to change
without notice.

Name_____

Address_____

City _____ State _____ Zip Code _____
Allow 4-6 weeks for delivery.
This offer is subject to withdrawal without notice.

# THE
# CRIMSON
# PAGODA

## CHRISTOPHER NICOLE

Ⱶ

A SIGNET BOOK

**NEW AMERICAN LIBRARY**

TIMES MIRROR

PUBLISHED BY
THE NEW AMERICAN LIBRARY
OF CANADA LIMITED

*PUBLISHER'S NOTE*

This novel is a work of fiction. Names, characters, places, and incidents are either the product of the author's imagination or, if real, used fictitiously.

NAL BOOKS ARE AVAILABLE AT QUANTITY DISCOUNTS WHEN USED TO PROMOTE PRODUCTS OR SERVICES. FOR INFORMATION PLEASE WRITE TO PREMIUM MARKETING DIVISION, THE NEW AMERICAN LIBRARY, INC., 1633 BROADWAY, NEW YORK, NEW YORK 10019.

First Printing, December, 1983

2   3   4   5   6   7   8   9

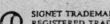 SIGNET TRADEMARK REG. U.S. PAT. OFF. AND FOREIGN COUNTRIES
REGISTERED TRADEMARK · MARCA REGISTRADA
HECHO EN WINNIPEG, CANADA

SIGNET, SIGNET CLASSIC, MENTOR, PLUME, MERIDIAN and NAL BOOKS are published in Canada by The New American Library of Canada, Limited, Scarborough, Ontario

PRINTED IN CANADA

COVER PRINTED IN U.S.A.

# CONTENTS

# I

## The Young Ladies

# 1

# The Wife

"China!" said Mrs. Bunting reverently. "The greatest country in the world. The most people. The most history."

She spoke with authority, as if she had lived all of her life in the Celestial Empire, and had the presence to defy argument, being at once tall and plump, with an aggressive nose and chin. The other passengers grouped about her at the rail of the steamship *Edward Collier* listened attentively, peering forward for their first glimpse of this famous land.

As indeed did Constance Baird, even if she knew that Mrs. Bunting had obtained all of her knowledge from books; they had, in fact, spent much of the voyage from San Francisco sitting together, exchanging their reading materials and the knowledge they had gained from them, and practicing their Chinese on each other—with less success.

It would never have occurred to Constance to pretend to such a knowledge of China. Partly because of her age; she was just nineteen, and in fact Mrs. Bunting, more than twice her age, had become rather a mother to her during the long weeks at sea. And also partly because this was the first considerable journey she had ever undertaken, much less alone. And also partly because she was too excited.

So she clung to the rail just like anyone else, and she stared into the morning mist with a certain feeling of disappointment. As the ship had steamed around the southern islands of Japan and past the rugged cliffs of the Liaotung peninsula, which formed the southernmost arm of Manchuria, the scenery had

3

grown increasingly dramatic, increasingly suggestive of the immensity of the land she was approaching. But now there was nothing in front of her except, so far as she could see, an area of mud-colored water, very still and calm, on which there were several ships at anchor, mostly warships, flying the flags of Great Britain and France as well as the United States, and then an even larger area of flat, obviously swampy land, with the rooftops of a town situated several miles inland.

"There's a bar at the mouth of the Pei-ho," explained Lieutenant Wynne, leaning on the rail beside her. "So deep draft ships can't get up to Tientsin. That's the port for Peking, you know, Mrs. Baird. That town you can just make out."

"Oh, yes, Mr. Wynne?" she asked politely, although he wasn't telling her anything she did not already know from her books.

But he was a handsome young man, tall and dark, with aquiline features and a flashing smile which went well with his lively brown eyes, while in his tropical white uniform he made a dashing figure.

"Is your ship lying here?" she asked.

Because Franklin Wynne was a Marine officer, seconded to the China Station. His first appointment, as he had graduated from Annapolis only a few months before. Thus he was as excited as she, and the fact that they were by some distance the youngest passengers on board the *Edward Collier* had naturally thrown them together. Mrs. Bunting had not approved, and in her heart Constance had not approved either; since her marriage she had come to regard men from a totally different point of view than six months ago, and while Frank Wynne was only just twenty-two, he *was* a soldier, even worse, a marine, and undoubtedly had all the disturbing thoughts men apparently enjoyed most of the time.

But he was such splendid company. He had learned about China at the Academy, and he was also busily teaching himself the language, for he had been told that in this year of 1890 it was in China and Japan, in the entire seaboard of eastern Asia, that the future lay for a serving American officer. This was the promised land, and also the promise of future crises, as the aging, almost moribund Empire of the Dragon seemed to lie helpless before the nibbling bites at its territory of the trade-hungry Western powers, while the equally old but for so long isolated Empire of Japan was just beginning to square its shoulders and enjoy the feel of the power that could be gained from Western technology and Western weapons. Thus he was constantly interesting, and thus his obvious admiration for her was flattering. But equally, thus he had to be kept at the arm's length of polite conversation, in view of her position.

Now he nodded. "That's her over there." He pointed. "The cruiser *Alabama*. But I'm not due to report for another week. I'll be able to see a little bit of the country before going aboard. I'd be happy to escort you out to Chu-teh, Mrs. Baird. I've heard all China is nothing but a hotbed of bandits and robbers." He met her gaze, and flushed. "But I imagine your husband will be in Tientsin to meet you."

He could tell how excited she was. Because the excitement had been growing with every day, since she had stepped onto the train in Richmond and steamed out of Virginia for the first time in her life, with Mother waving and weeping on the platform. Father had stayed at home. He did not care for emotional occasions, because his entire life was an emotional occasion; as a young man he had watched *his* father's house burned by Federal soldiers. Twenty-six years after Sherman's army had disemboweled the Confederacy, Father still brooded, embellishing his memory with copious drafts of whiskey, muddling his way through life thanks to the support of his family and friends. The marriage of his only daughter—who was also his only child—had been a sufficiently distressing event. That she should have become the wife of a missionary, and be doomed to spending the rest of her life in some remote corner of an even more remote country, was more than he had been able to stand.

Mother, on the other hand, had been delighted, because Mother's solace had always been religion, a direction in which Constance had also very naturally gravitated. Thus the Reverend Henry Baird. Marriage had in fact been in Constance's mind for some time. She wanted to be married, desperately. It was not merely a means of escape from the depressing atmosphere of the Drummond household. It would be the beginning of her life; she had spent her girlhood feeling very much in limbo, aware of a hundred and one things she wanted to *do*, and equally aware that not one of them was practical while she remained at home.

She had never considered the possible personality, or even the physical appearance, of her eventual husband very deeply. It was the *act* that interested her. She had assumed he would be considerably older than herself, and of an old Virginia family—Mother was a distinct snob. She knew lots of such men, several of them distant cousins, had been aware for several years that masculine visitors to the Drummond household were admiring her. It was difficult to decide exactly why. She was, by all accepted standards, a shade too tall, and she was several shades too thin. Her face fitted the pattern, and was somewhat long, and solemn in repose, and her nose was a trifle pronounced. She had brilliant white teeth, and thus could support a flashing smile, the more attractive because it was rarely in evidence, and she had magnificent pale blond hair, very thick and straight, to go with her light blue eyes. But she had been educated at home, and had absolutely no hopes of inheriting any money. Without wealth or beauty or voluptuousness, it was sometimes difficult to imagine *who* might decide that she above all others was *the* one for him. Reflections like these would leave her deeply depressed.

That her eventual savior should be a man of the Church was therefore not altogether surprising. But that he should live and work in faraway lands, and be handsome and gravely charming, with a sparkling wit and a superb aura of universal knowledge, that he should be able to speak Chinese as fluently as English, had all combined to make her convinced that this had to be the best of all possible worlds, whatever the miseries of Father's existence.

Nothing that had happened since the wedding had made her change her mind, although events had certainly encouraged her to some deep reflection on subjects she had never dared consider before. She and Henry had been able to enjoy only the briefest of honeymoons, four days at a small hotel in Yorktown, before he had had to leave again, without her. They had spent most of the time talking about China, where she would be living for the rest of her life. Henry had approached the subject, and her, with a distinct air of "What have I done?"—as if he were only just realizing, having put a ring on her finger, that he had taken on a total innocent fifteen years his junior. But he had been reassured by her eagerness to learn, by her utter acceptance that he must know best about all things.

Certainly in the matter of sharing a bed, an area of which she knew absolutely nothing. Mother had never discussed it with her, and Constance had no idea whether her parents had ever indulged in anything quite so disturbing. It was not the fact that Henry, having turned down the lamp, had folded the skirt of her nightgown back to her waist—she had kept her eyes shut so she did not know what he had done about his nightshirt—nor what he had then proceeded to do with her body, because he had explained that sexual intercourse was ordained by God as a means of procreation, and that it was their duty to indulge it until she became pregnant, which was *her* principal duty as a wife.

All of which she had accepted without question, and if she had braced herself for a long bout of agony, it was entirely because she could not imagine such an act, which seemed to be essentially violent in its nature, would not also be intensely painful.

But it had not been. That was the disturbing part. Not only had it not hurt, but it had aroused the strangest sensations, slivers of feelings she had only glimpsed before, in her bath or on her horse. These had always been immediately rejected. But with Henry on her and then inside her they could no longer be dismissed. She had been impelled almost to cry out in delight, but had not. Certainly she had been drawn toward expressing herself in *some* way, and on the third night of their honeymoon had actually, quite without intending to, moved her arms from her sides and held him tightly against her as he had surged into her—but he had raised his head in such evident concern that she had hastily released him. Sexual intercourse was a duty, not a pleasure. He had told her so. Thus such feelings must still be repressed.

She had in fact been rather relieved that their honeymoon had been so short and should have ended in a temporary separation. Henry had not come back to holiday in Virginia with any idea of getting married, and therefore he had not considered that the mission, in the village of Chu-teh, quite close to the capital city of Peking, apparently, was a suitable place for him to take his bride back to, until he had had a chance to prepare it. Some eyebrows had been raised in Richmond at his decision, but Henry was not the sort of man anyone argued with. He merely announced what he intended to do, looking over anyone present as he might regard his congregation, and that was that. And the separation, which had now lasted several weeks, had given her the time to think, and understand, and make some decisions of her own. Because Constance Drummond was quite as decisive as her husband, even if she had only hitherto been able to order her own private affairs, her own thoughts, and her own relationship with God. This last was the most important thing in her life, as it should be, for any Christian young lady, above all the wife of a Methodist missionary. But it was not something she had ever discussed with either Mother or her husband—heaven forbid the latter. For Constance's God was a very pragmatic deity, and thus it was quite easy to determine that Henry, for all his vast knowledge and total certainty, was in this instance utterly wrong. Of course sexual intercourse was designed by Him purely for the procreation of children; there was no other possible reason for such a basically obscene act. But just as, if eating was essential for the maintenance of life, it was not only possible, but *necessary* to enjoy one's food, without of course making a display of it or a glutton of oneself, so clearly the same rule had to apply to sex. She did not know whether or not Henry enjoyed sex with *her*, and she had no intention of ever asking him. But there could certainly be nothing wrong, or immoral, or unchristian in her enjoying *his* lovemaking, brief and utilitarian as it was.

And after several weeks away from him, she knew she was going to enjoy it more than ever. It was, in fact, what she was looking forward to more than anything about their reunion. So her eyes shone as she smiled at the handsome young soldier. "Oh, yes, Lieutenant," she said. "My husband will be there to meet me."

To Constance's total disappointment, however, Henry was not in any of the sampans—manned by shouting, flat-hatted, pig-tailed Chinese wearing red-and-blue shirts and pantaloons and soft ankle boots—which swarmed about the *Edward Collier* as the steamship dropped anchor.

"He'll be on the dock, my dear," Mrs. Bunting said reassuringly. "I'm sure he had no wish to get himself all grubby. Ugh"—as she gingerly descended the accommodation ladder, and declined the assistance of a Chinese arm to seat her amidships in the bobbing little boat. Constance, immediately behind her, nearly overbalanced, and was very glad indeed for the help of a brawny arm before she collapsed beside her friend, anxiously gathering her yellow silk traveling coat to prevent it from trailing in the bilge water which surged over the floorboards. Bought for her by her mother just before she had left Richmond, it was her proudest possession—after her wedding ring and the Bible Henry had given her as a present.

"You be all right now," said the large yellow-skinned man with a drooping pencil-thin mustache who had helped her, and was now speaking remarkably good English. "But you must have these."

He handed them each a brightly colored parasol. "For the sun," he explained, and began giving parasols to the rest of the passengers as they arrived—even Lieutenant Wynne. Yet his gaze kept returning to Constance, or rather, she realized, her coat; he seemed quite fascinated by it.

Mrs. Bunting raised her eyebrows, but obediently opened the sunshade. "When in Rome, my dears," she said. "When in Rome."

The sampan was cast off, and rowed toward the distinctly turbulent bar.

"Nothing to be afraid of, Mrs. Baird," Frank Wynne said. "Just the river meeting the shallows." He pointed at the fortifications which lined the mouth of the river, from the embrasures of which the muzzles of cannon poked at them. "And those fellows are friendly today. They weren't always, you know. Those are the Taku forts. The British had to storm them before they could march on Peking, back in the sixties. There was some pretty hard fighting."

"I do assure you that I am not in the least afraid, Mr. Wynne," Constance lied, watching the bubbling water as it seemed to gather speed, and the rowers responded, the bows of the sampan lifting to the surge. But in truth, she thought, "uncomfortable" would be a more accurate word. It was by now late in the morning, and the sun was already high, and distinctly warm; she was sweating. She was also becoming aware that parts of her body beneath her clothing were itching, which she had not experienced on the ship, no matter how great the heat. Presumably it was the lack of air, because it was very still down on the water, with the promise of bad weather to come, for great purple rain clouds were banking over the land in front of her, and the sampan was not moving very fast against the current.

"China!" Mrs. Bunting said reverently. Her husband was in business in Peking, and she too had been separated from him for some time; although they had been married for several years, this was the first time he had apparently felt sufficiently sure of his place in this strange land to send for his wife. "Do you realize, my dear Constance, that this empire has proceeded, virtually unchanged, through history for four thousand years? It was a civilized land when our ancestors were still painting themselves blue."

But she also was uncomfortable; she was squirming in a restless fashion quite unlike her normally sedate self.

Now they were in the river itself, and the water was again calm, a vast turgid mass of liquid yellow mud, it seemed, bordered by enormous reed beds, which hid any sight of the surrounding country, but was quite a busy little thoroughfare, with other sampans plying up and down, while here for the first time Constance glimpsed a seagoing junk, sufficiently flat-bottomed to negotiate the bar, with square sails set as it made its way downstream with both the current and the light land breeze to assist it.

"Will it rain, do you suppose?" she asked Lieutenant Wynne, watching the clouds still building.

"I think it will, Mrs. Baird," he said. "Let's hope it doesn't do so until we make Tientsin."

"There," Mrs. Bunting exclaimed with great relief as they rounded a dogleg bend and came in sight of houses and wharves. Tientsin was suddenly larger than Constance had supposed it would be, with some attractive large houses on its eastern side, many of them flying European flags, and beyond, the heavy clay walls enclosing the old Chinese town. The sampan was directed toward one of the wharves in the European district, where there seemed a large crowd of people was waiting to greet them; farther upriver, toward the Chinese city, the waterfront appeared as nothing more than a mass of small boats, each boat equally a mass of people, cooking and washing and generally living as if they were in houses. The wind was from the west, and a sickening smell of effluvia drifted toward them.

But they had arrived. Constance looked up at chattering Chinese coolies, wearing pigtails like the crew of the boat; at Manchu mandarins, standing quietly and surveying the scene, arms folded into the sleeves of their green tunics, straggly white beards lying on their chests; at armed bannermen, the descendants of the Manchu warriors who had swept out of the north to capture this immense empire two and a half centuries before, and who were prevented by law from assuming any job except that of a soldier, even if it was more than twenty-five years since they had had any employment; and at several Europeans.

"William!" Mrs. Bunting was shouting. "William!"

Mr. Bunting was a small man, hardly half the size of his wife, who wore a neat little mustache and a sun topee, and seemed as delighted as she was at their reunion. Mrs. Bunting was first ashore, to fold him in her arms. Constance never moved, as she looked from face to face and could not find Henry, and became aware of an enormous weight seeming to gather in her stomach. Frank Wynne had gently to urge her to her feet and up the wooden steps to the dock, where she was assailed by heat and odors, and by tremendous interest, once again centering on her coat.

"Mrs. Baird? You must be Constance Baird."

The woman projected an air of efficiency, and was perhaps in her early forties, Constance estimated, handsome enough although rather stout, clearly a European for all her suntan, and equally British, from her clipped accents. "I'm Joan Mountjoy, and this is my daughter Kate. Oh, welcome to China. But, my dear, that coat . . .''

Constance was uncertain whether or not to curtsy. She had no idea who these people were. But she liked the girl Kate on sight. Catherine Mountjoy was about her own age, she decided—like her mother, of medium height and inclined to plumpness. Her hair was a delightful deep auburn in color, worn up, although she was clearly not married, in a tight little chignon beneath her ribboned straw hat, while her face, the sharply pretty features contrasting with the soft contours of the rest of her, was a glow of good-humored welcome.

But even as she shook hands, Constance was looking left and right, the lead in her stomach seeming to grow. ''Henry . . . ?''

''Couldn't come, my dear,'' Joan Mountjoy said. ''He is terribly busy. But we'll deliver you to him, safe and sound, if . . .'' She glanced at a sun-helmeted white man, wearing a starched white suit, who had approached them, and who, Constance discovered the moment he spoke, was another Englishman.

''Good day,'' he said stiffly. ''Mrs. Baird?''

''I am she,'' Constance said.

''You must go through customs, madam,'' he explained, gesturing to the large shed where the other passengers were already entering. ''But, madam . . .'' He stroked the end of his mustache. ''You are an American, I believe?''

''Yes,'' Constance said, wondering at his embarrassment.

''Ah . . . you have no connection with, ah . . . European . . . ah, with any, ah . . .'' He looked at Joan Mountjoy in despair.

''You don't happen to have any royal blood, do you, Mrs. Baird?'' Joan asked.

''Me? Good heavens, no.''

''Ah,'' Joan said. ''Then, my dear, you simply must take off that coat. Only members of the imperial family may wear yellow in China.''

The coat was hastily removed and given to Joan Mountjoy to fold away, while the Chinese onlookers continued to chatter among themselves, and Constance wished the earth would open and swallow her up. Of all the embarrassing situations. And whatever would Henry say when he learned of it?

But where *was* he? How could he possibly be too busy to meet his bride? She wanted to weep, but they would be at least partly tears of indignation.

''Absurd people,'' remarked Mrs. Bunting with reassuring contempt. ''How were you to know, my dear?''

"I really wouldn't give it a thought, Mrs. Baird," Lieutenant Wynne said. "All these Oriental places have strange customs. But . . ." He glanced at Mrs. Bunting. "When in Rome, eh?"

Customs clearance was hardly more than a formality, and then they were out in the street and walking toward the hotel—"It's not far," Joan Mountjoy explained—while a procession of Chinese coolies followed, balancing their various boxes precariously on the tops of their heads. These apart, there were in fact few natives to be seen, once the docks were left behind. "Because this is the European city," Catherine Mountjoy explained. "The Chinese city is over there behind the wall." She gave a little giggle. "A terrible place."

"Oh, but . . ." Constance bit her lip. She had been going to express a desire to see it; as she was destined to spend the rest of her life living among these people, she wanted to know *all* about them, at the earliest possible moment. Besides, the only possible real reason for Henry's not meeting her was a fear she might let him down with her gaucheness and inexperience; thus these were faults which had to be eradicated as rapidly as possible.

Perhaps Joan Mountjoy could understand something of her feelings. "The Chinese city is really *no* place for a white woman, my dear Mrs. Baird," she said. "Anyway, I'm sure you'll be wanting a bath and a change of clothing."

"A bath?" Constance asked in amazement. In the middle of the afternoon? And she had put on her gown only a few hours before.

"You'll want to get rid of the fleas," Joan Mountjoy explained, and ushered her through a gate being held open by an elderly Chinese gentleman before she could express her astonishment at the remark. "This is the hotel. You'll be quite comfortable here."

And indeed it was a substantial three-story building, with verandas on the two lower floors, and wide-open windows, and scurrying Chinese servants—all male—and delightful gardens in which the willow and the banyan trees dominated with massive, shady dignity. But . . . fleas?

And yet, she *was* itching all over now.

"It's the sampan," Joan Mountjoy told her, coming with her into the bedroom, where a tin tub had already been placed in the center of the floor. "Like all things Chinese, they are crawling with fleas. Shall I send someone to you?"

"Someone?" Constance asked cautiously.

Joan smiled. "A girl, to help you."

"Well . . ."

"It would be best," Joan said, and went to the door. "She will be here directly."

The door closed, Constance took a long breath and threw her hat on the bed, gazed at the yellow coat already lying there, and suddenly found herself scratching her head. Fleas? That was absurd. And disgusting.

She watched the door opening again, and four coolies came in carrying ewers of obviously very hot water. These they proceeded to empty into the tub, gazing at her with enormous eyes, bowing as they saw her noticing them, their pigtails flopping over their shoulders, and then withdrawing, their floppy boots seeming to scour the floor as they never raised their feet. And they wore blues and reds, in various faded shades.

Too late Constance wondered if she should have tipped them, and was then distracted by the arrival of a young woman, a girl who she suspected was younger than herself, pretty and pert, and wearing a pale blue tunic and matching trousers, with her black hair in the inevitable pigtail, who bowed before closing the door. "I am Tao-li," she said in almost perfect English. "My father is cook here. I help you, eh?"

"That would be very kind of you," Constance agreed.

"You strip, eh?" Tao-li suggested, and proceeded to do so herself, taking off her tunic and her pantaloons to reveal that she wore nothing underneath. She did not remove her boots. Constance could only stare at her with her mouth open. She had never actually seen any other naked human being before in her life—Henry had always taken care to be up and dressed before she stirred, and had invariably left the room whenever she had been changing her clothes—and she felt she should be horrified at the girl's insolence and vulgarity. But it had happened so quickly, and so naturally, she could not help but feel that to express her displeasure might put *her* in the wrong, and besides, Tao-li was possessed of an entrancingly miniature figure, into which her little button breasts and slender thighs fitted perfectly.

Yet the suggestion that she should do the same remained impossible to consider.

Tao-li smiled. "I help you," she said, and advanced. Constance wanted to push her away, but could only think of Frank Wynne and his "when in Rome," and immediately was utterly embarrassed by the idea that he might know what was happening to her, and then wanted to laugh as she thought of Mrs. Bunting being faced with a similar situation.

Before she could again concentrate on her own plight, her sweat-wet blouse had been gently but firmly removed and thrown on the floor, to her concern, and she was being urged out of her skirt. Three minutes later she also was naked save for her boots, and these Tao-li knelt to unlace. "You sit in tub," she commanded. "You sit and soak, and fleas drown. All fleas. I wash your hair. Such hair . . ." She allowed the golden strands to drift through her fingers as Constance cautiously lowered herself into the near-boiling water. "It is royal hair."

Constance was still holding her breath. But the heat soon became bearable, and she found that she did enjoy the feeling of utter relaxation which spread through her body while Tao-li continued to stroke her hair, driving her fingers into it to search her scalp, and withdrawing them again, always to the accompaniment of a little snapping sound.

"But it is not real, eh?" Tao-li inquired.

"Not real?" Constance opened her eyes, which had drooped shut with a combination of heat and fatigue.

"It is different color," Tao-li pointed out, and Constance looked down at the brown silk on her groin, and hastily brought her legs together again.

"Have you not seen a yellow-haired woman before?" she asked.

Tao-li shook her head. "Is real?"

"Of course it is real," Constance snapped, hugging her knees and gazing in consternation at the little black dots which were floating all around her, some from her hair, certainly, as Tao-li dropped them into the water after snapping them . . . between her *teeth*, she realized with total consternation. To imagine where the others might have come from . . . She felt it very necessary to gain control of the conversation. "All white women have dark . . . well, like you," she said, and realized that she had made another blunder, for the Chinese girl had almost no body hair at all. Desperately she determined on another attempt. "Why do you wear *your* hair in a pigtail? It's such lovely hair. Or do you keep off the fleas that way?"

Tao-li's fingers tightened, and Constance nearly exclaimed with pain as her hair was pulled. "It is what the Man-chu say," Tao-li said. "The Man-chu," she repeated contemptuously, again carefully splitting the word into two parts. "We must do what they say, and humble ourselves. Because they say. Because *she* say."

"She?" Constance asked.

"The empress," Tao-li said. "The empress decrees all things, and all men must obey. All men." She gave a little sigh. "And all women, too."

\* \* \*

"The dowager empress, Tz'u-Hsi," Joan Mountjoy explained. "She is the aunt of the present emperor, but really controls the country. I have only seen her from a distance, but from all accounts she must be a remarkable woman. Just an ordinary wellborn Manchu girl, taken as concubine by the then emperor, oh, thirty-odd years ago, and not even as chief concubine, I've heard, and yet who by sheer force of personality has assumed control over the entire empire."

They sat in another sampan, the two Mountjoys, the Buntings, and Frank Wynne, as well as Constance, now making their way slowly upriver. It had rained very hard during the night, although the skies had cleared with the dawn, which was when they had left Tientsin, and momentarily it was quite cool, but the atmosphere remained heavy, and once again, as the sun soared into the heavens, the clouds were building, while, as with yesterday, down on the river it was impossible to see anything of their immediate neighborhood over the huge reed beds which banked to either side; the entire country seemed utterly flat, and only the rooftops and pagodas of Tientsin remained visible in the distance. Yet the river continued to be interesting enough. Apart from the constant boat traffic in either direction, they had just passed the entrance to what had appeared as another large river entering the Pei-ho from the south, but which Mr. Bunting told her was not a river at all, but the end of the Grand Canal, an immense waterway, the largest manmade one in the world, built thousands of years earlier to connect the huge Yellow River with the Pei-ho.

It was all too absorbing for her to feel the slightest embarrassment about any of yesterday's episodes, even if, Constance thought sadly, she was presumably accumulating a new army of fleas which would eventually have to be removed. Which made her think again of Tao-li. "And do the Chinese really hate her?" she asked.

Mrs. Mountjoy shrugged. "I sometimes think the Chinese hate everybody. They hate the Manchu, of course, because they are the ruling elite. But they hate us equally. . . ."

"Us?" Constance asked in alarm.

"Oh, indeed, Mrs. Baird," Frank Wynne said. "Well, they hate the British and the French, more than us Americans. . . ." He glanced apologetically at Mrs. Mountjoy.

"Oh, quite true, Lieutenant," she agreed. "Supposing they ever trouble to differentiate between nationalities. To them, a white skin is a foreign devil."

"A foreign devil?" Constance cried.

Kate Mountjoy squeezed her hand. "It's just an expression, really. The Chinese always used exaggerated expressions."

"But . . . why?"

"Well, my dear," Joan Mountjoy explained, "as the lieutenant says, it really was the fault of the French and the British. They forced their way into China about fifty years ago, demanding treaty ports and trade concessions, and when the Chinese tried to fight, they defeated them by using modern weapons. It was all most unfortunate. And now, of course, the Chinese regard all Christians as their natural enemies. Which does not make the task of your husband or mine any the easier."

"But . . ." Constance wanted to say: Then why are we here at all, if we are hated? Hated! It was a terrifying thought. She had never been hated by anyone in her life. Nor had she ever hated anyone. But could that charming girl Tao-li have hated *her*?

"That's why we don't go into Tientsin itself," Kate Mountjoy said. "Because of the massacre."

"The massacre?"

"Kate!" her mother remonstrated.

"Well, Constance may as well know about it," Kate said. "She will, anyway."

Joan Mountjoy sighed. "It really was quite ghastly. Only a few years ago, the mob in Tientsin murdered an entire convent of French nuns."

"Murdered the nuns?" Mrs. Bunting cried. "How terrible."

"Now, say, Mrs. Mountjoy," Frank Wynne protested. "I've read something about that. Wasn't the trouble started by a French consular official shooting a Chinese?"

"That is as may be, Lieutenant Wynne," Joan Mountjoy said severely. "But I am sure he had a very good reason for what he did. And certainly that was no possible excuse for butchering fifteen white women."

"Butchering?" Constance had a distinct feeling that she was going to faint.

"The things they *did* to them," Kate said.

"Kate!" her mother snapped again.

"Oh, all right," Kate said, but she leaned close to Constance to whisper, "I'll tell you all about it when we get to Chu-teh."

I don't want to go to Chu-teh, Constance thought desperately. Not even if Henry is there. I want to go home. Oh, I want to go home. I don't want to be hated, and then perhaps butchered, by a Chinese mob.

But the sampan was nearing the shore, where there were a

dock and people . . . and a puffing locomotive engine. "Yang-tsun," explained Mrs. Mountjoy. "Here's where we join the train."

They disembarked into the midst of a group of Chinese soldiers, apparently. As the men wore no uniforms and carried a motley assortment of ancient rifles, they made Constance think more of Mexican brigands than disciplined troops, and in view of their conversation on the boat, she stayed very close to Frank Wynne, who had prudently worn civilian clothes for the journey. However, the soldiers seemed friendly enough, but they poked and prodded the white people's baggage to the accompaniment of much shrill humor and comment, spoken at such a speed that Constance's carefully learned Chinese was useless.

"Just smile at them, my dear," Joan Mountjoy recommended. "And they will not harm you."

But suppose I don't feel like smiling? Constance wondered, even as she arranged her mouth into the best semblance of a vacant grin she could manage. And felt even that fade as they went toward the station and came across a man lying on his back at the side of the road, with his legs held in the air by a kind of wooden framework into which his ankles had been fitted, rather like pictures she had seen of the stocks in old America, only upended. The man's shoes had been removed, and his feet were cut and bleeding, while he was clearly half-mad with thirst, as he twisted his head to and fro, trying to lick up moisture with his lolling, swollen tongue from the mud left by the night's rain.

"My God!" Constance cried. "We must help him."

"Sssh, my dear," Joan remonstrated. "And do please ignore him."

"But . . ."

"He has been sentenced to the bastinado," Mr. Bunting explained. "Obviously the fellow is a criminal of some sort. Or has offended the military commander of the town. The bastinado is a dreadful punishment."

"They beat the feet with bamboo canes," Kate Mountjoy told her. "Hour after hour after hour. Why, some of the poor wretches can never walk again. And some even die."

Constance became aware that Frank Wynne was holding her elbow, for which she was intensely grateful. But even his normally good-humored face was unusually grim. "I'm afraid you will find Chinese standards of civilization somewhat different from ours, Mrs. Baird."

Constance gained the carriage, and collapsed onto the seat,

fanning herself vigorously, while the coolies piled their boxes in the corridor outside, and Joan Mountjoy opened the hamper provided by the hotel and poured lemonade. "I always thought China was the *home* of civilization," Constance said, still feeling able to hear the moans of the poor wretch outside, especially as she tasted the deliciously cooling liquid.

"It is, historically," Joan agreed. "But differences of religion . . . they have no use for the Christian virtues of meekness and forgiveness and charity, my dear. And where a country so teems with humanity, they have little concern for the sanctity of life, either. Yet it will change. People like your Henry and my James will make it so. That is why we are here. We must never forget that."

Until the day we are murdered by a mob, Constance thought. But the train was moving, and they were proceeding through a vast flat plain, covered with cultivated meadows, and obviously very fertile.

"Wheat and oats, mainly," Mr. Bunting explained.

"But who owns a farm this size?"

"Why, the neighboring village, my dear. It is common land, to which each family gives its share of labor, and from which each family draws according to its need." He smiled at Joan Mountjoy. "That at least bears some resemblance to primitive Christianity."

"If it were true, Mr. Bunting," Joan argued. "But you know as well as I that in every Chinese village there are very wealthy people and very poor ones."

Mr. Bunting sighed. "I suppose that is the way of the world. And it is not altogether unfair, you know, where some people are prepared to work harder than others. There is the village, Mrs. Baird." He pointed to a cluster of houses rising around a splendid red-lacquered pagoda, from which a roadway led to the railway track and where several Chinese were waiting to board the train as it slowed to a stop. Close by was a large well, not built up with stone or roofed as in America, but just a hole in the ground, which was overflowing from the recent rain. Here there were several cows drinking, several naked children playing, several dogs urinating—and several women drawing water.

"Ugh," Constance remarked. "That doesn't look very clean."

"It isn't," Joan Mountjoy said.

"But don't they get ill from it?"

"My dear, they die like flies. Their ideas of hygiene are utterly primitive."

"But then, they breed like flies as well," Kate said with a giggle.

Constance watched a woman coming down the path from the houses. Or rather, being brought, she realized, for the lady sat in a sort of cart, which was yoked to a man, who was running, and drawing her at speed over the rutted surface, bouncing and jolting. And she was clearly a wealthy woman, for her clothes looked expensive and her boots had leather tassels and various intricate designs in leather worked on the calves. She was also quite young, Constance observed, as she came up to the train. But when she stepped down from the cart to board, she hobbled in a most painful fashion, and had to be assisted by two men.

"That poor girl," Constance remarked. "Whatever can be the matter with her?"

"The lily foot," Mr. Bunting said.

Constance looked at Joan, who smiled. "It is a practice among the Chinese, the well-to-do Chinese, anyway, to bind the feet of their female children, compressing the heel as close as possible to the toes, until they are quite deformed. That girl can hardly walk. But she is perfectly healthy otherwise. And to have a lily foot is a sure sign that she comes from a wealthy home, as poor people need their daughters to work, and cannot have them half-crippled. That girl's father is probably mayor of the village."

"But why do they do it in the first place?" Constance asked.

Joan Mountjoy shrugged. "Chinese men find it attractive, my dear."

The poor girl was clearly at once attracted and repelled by the country and the people, Frank Wynne thought, surreptitiously watching her across the compartment as the train chugged into the afternoon. He didn't blame her; he was rather appalled himself, and he had been briefed on what to expect.

Her vulnerability made her even more attractive, if that were possible. To which was added the poignancy of their coming separation. He had boarded the ship for the long, slow voyage across the Pacific anticipating total boredom, and instead had found *her*. As she was married, and he was an officer and a gentleman—and as she was very obviously under the aegis of the fearsome Mrs. Bunting—they had done nothing more than smile at each other, although the smiles had grown warmer as week had succeeded week, and by the end they had found it quite natural to wait for the other to promenade after luncheon. He felt he knew her as well as any of his own sisters, and had constantly to remind himself that she had to remain nothing more than a sister.

And yet, being a romantic, he had been unable to stop himself dreaming, of a shipwreck, perhaps, from which they would be the only survivors, to reach a desert but fertile island, where they would commence a perpetual, naked, erotic idyll.

Guilty thoughts, which even now could bring a quick flush to his cheeks. Because that was over. Like everyone who had anything to do with China, he had heard all about the Reverend Henry Baird. If a missionary's quality could be measured by the numbers of his converts, or by his reputation, Henry Baird had to be the most successful of all. And in addition, he was widely known for his courage and probity. He no doubt deserved a bride like Constance, and it was difficult to imagine Constance, married to such a splendid man, ever having guilty thoughts of her own. Only the fact that Baird had been too busy, or not sufficiently interested even *in* his bride, to make the journey to Tientsin to meet her, suggested that perhaps, one day . . . But what was he *thinking*? He was still an officer and a gentleman, and she was still Mrs. Henry Baird . . . even if she was also the most attractive woman he had ever met.

He realized with something of a shock that he had fallen in love; fallen in love with a woman he could never have.

He discovered she was gazing at him, and gave a nervous start, followed by an even more nervous smile, which she reciprocated.

He was dreaming again, once more guiltily. But he knew he was going to continue dreaming about Constance Baird for the rest of his life.

China was a country, Constance decided, that was going to take some getting used to. The trouble was, she was no longer sure she *wanted* to get used to such barbarism that she could speak of it in utterly matter-of-fact tones. And yet, a country of endless fascination, as well. The railway proceeded across the plain for some sixty miles, with never a hill in sight—''When, as happens quite regularly, the Han-ho and the Pei-ho burst their banks,'' Mr. Bunting said, ''there are the most frightful floods''—until suddenly they saw a huge forest of trees rising to their right.

''The Imperial Park,'' Joan Mountjoy told her.

And beyond, the afternoon sunlight gleamed from the gilded roofs of innumerable palaces and pagodas in the far distance. ''Peking,'' said Mr. Bunting in almost reverential tones. ''You must come and visit us there, my dear. It is an unforgettable sight.''

For the train was slowing again, to enter the junction town of Feng-tai. Here the railroad bifurcated, one arm swinging right, toward Peking itself, and the other left toward Hankow and the great Yangtze River, although this left-hand fork, in the course of construction by a firm of Belgian engineers, was apparently not yet completed. Neither branch of the line continued northward, however, toward the Great Wall and Chu-teh, and so the Mountjoys and Constance had to exchange the comparative comfort of the train for the jolting *dis*comfort of a bullock cart.

Thus here, also, Constance was forced to say good-bye to her two companions of the past three weeks. She felt quite weepy as she hugged Mrs. Bunting, who repeated her husband's invitation, and then shook hands with Frank Wynne, who was going to have a look at Peking. ''Although I'd surely like to come on with you,'' he said. ''I mean, . . .'' He flushed. ''I hate to think of you three ladies out there with just those fellows.'' He looked at the bullock drivers and the coolies, who were waiting for them.

''Ah, but, Lieutenant,'' said Joan Mountjoy, ''we are nearly in our own backyard. These carts are from Chu-teh. Those fellows, as you call them, are good Christians. So don't worry about us, now.''

''Well . . .'' He squeezed Constance's hand. ''It sure has been a pleasure meeting you, Mrs. Baird. I'd like to think we might meet again one day.''

''I'm sure we shall,'' Constance said, now wanting to burst into tears.

''Yes . . . well . . . say, do you suppose I could write to you, from time to time? I mean, I wouldn't want Mr. Baird to suppose . . . well . . .'' He realized he was digging himself a conversational pit, and his flush deepened.

''I would love you to write to me, Mr. Wynne,'' Constance said. ''Just whenever you can.''

''Not that I suppose he will,'' she confided to Joan as they settled themselves in the back of the cart as best they could.

''I've an idea he might,'' Joan said thoughtfully. ''He seems an awfully nice boy. But, well, he *is* a marine, you know, Constance. I don't think you should get *too* friendly with him.''

''I'm sure there can be nothing wrong in receiving the odd letter,'' Constance said. There could be no doubt that Joan, being well over twice her age, was setting up to be a mother to her rather like Mrs. Bunting, and she had no intention of permitting that. Besides, she was quite sure Henry would not wish it, either. If he was making his way, successfully, in such remark-able surroundings, he would need the support of a mature woman, not a scared little girl. She had allowed the strangeness of the people, their apparent callousness as much as their peculiar ideas on sanitation, to upset her. But that must be put behind her now, and she must assume the responsibilities, as well as the prerogatives, of being Mrs. Henry Baird.

Yet once again she felt her resolution slipping as the cart bounced and banged and rattled its way into the evening, and as she saw, rising suddenly and starkly to her right, the bulk of a large pagoda, painted a brilliant crimson, seeming to hover above the cart and the track from a shallow hill.

"That has been there ever since I can remember," Joan Mountjoy remarked. "But no one ever goes there."

Now the sun, huge and round and red, sank into the Gobi Desert to the west, as insects whirred and buzzed about them, mosquitoes which needed to be slapped and which left bloody splotches on her arms, and fireflies which glowed almost as brightly as the lanterns lit by the drivers, and as a wind arose across the plain to howl and whine and blow dust into their faces—and as the brief twilight left them plunged into an enor-mous darkness. She could not help but reflect that they were, as Frank Wynne had said, three white women entirely at the mercy of the eight Chinese men, and while these might profess to be Christians, well . . . Dear Frank Wynne, she thought. Of course, he was just a boy. She thought of him as the brother she had always wished to have. He was so young and innocent and eager, it was impossible to consider him as an adult, certainly in the sense that she was already a woman or that Henry, with his masterful knowledge and certainty and confidence, was so clearly a man. And his transparent admiration for her had been as embarrassing as it had been flattering. But she did hope he would write.

Amazingly, she dozed, while every bone jolted and banged against every other bone. And dreamed that she was being chased by an entire army of Chinese soldiers, all intent upon turning her upside down and beating her soles until they turned into deformed lily feet. She awoke with a start when Joan Mountjoy shook her shoulder. "What's happening?" she asked in alarm. "Oh, where *are* we?"

Joan pointed through the darkness at a cluster of lights. "Chu-teh, my dear," she said. "You have reached your home."

*       *       *

Constance realized that the bullock cart had slowed, because the ground was rising, and that in fact the village of Chu-teh actually stood on a distinct hillock. "The site was carefully chosen, by your husband and by Father Pierre," Joan Mountjoy explained, "so that Chu-teh would always be safe from the floods. They really do happen quite often, but we have never been troubled."

"Father Pierre?" Constance inquired.

"We are all Christians here," Joan told her.

She did not understand, but was too interested in the approaching village to pursue the matter. Here were houses, strangely European in design, and a church, the first she had seen since landing—and no pagodas at all. And here were crowds of Chinese, dressed in European-type gowns or shirts and trousers—although she observed that none of them wore yellow—and very obviously much cleaner and healthier than any of the people she had seen by the coast. And here too were several gray-kirtled nuns, gentle, pink-cheeked Frenchwomen, anxious to chatter at her in broken English, and Father Pierre Laclos, tall and thin and dignified, to bend over her knuckles as if she were entering Versailles, and the Reverend James Mountjoy, shorter than his wife but equally plump, and very red-faced and jolly . . . and Henry Baird, waiting until all the others had greeted her.

In the darkness beyond the glow of the lanterns, Constance had not appreciated he was there, until he stepped forward. Then her knees felt too weak for her to move, and she could only wait for him to approach her. In seven weeks she had forgotten how big he was—three inches over six feet, with a physique to match—and the hugeness of his black beard, as well as the glow of his dark eyes, the height of his forehead, the thrust of his nose, the supremely confident manner in which he moved. He was the handsomest man she had ever known, or would ever know. And she had actually been preparing herself to be angry with him for not coming down to Tientsin to meet her. As if it mattered now. He was her husband. And she was his wife. The long weeks of waiting and wondering were over, and now she was again in his arms.

"I have missed you so, my dearest Constance," he said. "I have missed you so."

"We did not really expect you before tomorrow," said the Reverend James Mountjoy. "And really, my dear Joan, you should not have come on in the darkness. Why, it is almost midnight."

"I did not suppose Constance would wish to spend the night at Feng-tai," Joan Mountjoy pointed out. "Especially with Chu-teh only a few more hours away. Feng-tai," she explained to Constance, "is really a most ghastly place. Far worse that Tientsin."

As it was so late, dinner had already been served, but now a supper was produced for the three travelers, eaten in a communal restaurant, apparently shared by all the missionaries, Constance gathered. But she would not have cared if it had been served in the open air; she sat next to Henry, and his words of greeting still filled her ears, even if she wished he had been slightly more demonstrative in his physical greeting. But that was Henry's way, and the meal would soon be over. After her nap on the way, she felt not the least tired, had no desire to sleep again this night.

"Nonetheless, it is not good," Father Laclos said. "Not in the dark. There is rumor of revolutionaries in the north."

"Revolutionaries?" Joan inquired. "Up here?"

"Two men were in Feng-tai itself last week, we've heard," her husband told her. "Handing out pamphlets against the dynasty. They only just escaped the military."

"They come from the south, actually," Henry told Constance. "From Canton, and around there. Down there is a hotbed of sedition and revolt. Because it is so close to the British settlement at Hong Kong, I suppose."

"The poor old British carry the can for everything that happens around here," Mountjoy observed.

"Not entirely," Henry argued. "I regret to have to say it, but most of these young revolutionaries, people like that fellow Sun Yat-sen, have been educated in the United States. That's where they get their ideas of revolution from."

Constance decided it was time she stopped mentally anticipating what was going to happen after supper, and took a part in the conversation. "But what do they want to rebel against?" she asked.

"Why, the Manchu," Mountjoy said.

"But didn't the conquest take place over two hundred years ago? Surely everybody's used to the idea by now."

"One would think so," Henry agreed. "And had the Manchu any sense, it would have *been* so. But they have carefully preserved their ruling-caste status. Rather like us and the Indians in North America. Unfortunately, while the white man in North America completely outnumbered the Indians, of the population of China, which is estimated at about four hundred million people, you know, only five million or so are Manchu. Yet they rule everything. They have the pick of the provincial governorships, of all the army commands, of any position worth having. Only Manchu girls may be imperial concubines, at least officially. And one has to say that they are on the whole a much tougher, stronger race than the native Chinese, and less hidebound by tradition. They don't practice any absurdities like the lily foot, for instance.''

"Thank heaven for that," Constance said.

"But they've still landed themselves with quite a problem," Henry went on. "One day, perhaps one day soon, there could be a big explosion in China."

"Like the Taiping," Mountjoy suggested. "We don't want that to happen again."

"God forbid," his wife agreed. "Do you know, Constance, that it is estimated that twenty million people died during the Taiping revolt. Twenty *million*."

"It sounds terrible," Constance acknowledged. "But if these people have a legitimate grievance . . ."

"We stand for the Manchu dynasty," Henry said. "And must continue to do so."

"Because they are Christian?"

"Good heavens, no, my dear. His Celestial Majesty and his court regard Christianity with total contempt. But they do provide at least a modicum of law and order. Were they to go, China would relapse into complete anarchy. Now, I know you are tired after your journey. Here are Peter and Elizabeth."

Constance smiled at the Chinese boy and girl a trifle uncertainly. She supposed they were about sixteen years of age, and looked very alike, both romantically handsome, with intelligent black eyes and ready smiles. Like everyone else on Chu-teh, they wore European clothes—but as Chinese they also wore the shaming pigtail decreed by law, the plaits lying awkwardly on the boy's starched collar and the girl's neat dress.

"Peter and Elizabeth are twins," Henry explained. "And will be your servants. They asked for the position. Didn't you, Lizzie?"

"Oh, yes, sir, Mr. Henry," the girl said. "You come, Mistress Constance?"

Shades of Tao-li in Tientsin, Constance thought. But this girl had none of the other's pert conversation, her suggestion of insolent equality. While Peter toted her boxes into the bungalow which was to be her home, Elizabeth remained at her side, showing her where to go and where the household offices were.

Then she prepared Constance's bath. But again unlike Tao-li, she did not remain to assist. She had also adopted Western standards of modesty.

Constance was relieved about that, just as she was delighted at once with the size of the house, for it contained three bedrooms in addition to a large drawing room and a spacious dining room, and with the furniture, which was mainly made of rattan cane with cushioned backs and seats, and was splendidly comfortable.

"It is a paradise," she told Henry as she sat up in bed in her new and previously unworn pink nightgown. "I had no idea it was so lovely."

"Tomorrow I'll take you on a tour of inspection," he promised, standing by the bed and looking down at her. "If you're not too tired."

"Tired?" she cried. "I'm not in the least tired. Henry . . ."

They gazed at each other, and she wanted to hold out her arms. But he was obviously feeling the same as she, because he went into his dressing room, carefully closing the door behind himself. But he would be back in a moment. After seven weeks. She was so excited she could hardly keep still, slid down the bed and up it again, and then decided to discard the nightgown. She threw it on the floor, sat up, arranging the sheet across her waist, but low down so that her navel and just a wisp of her pubic hair showed, while the cool breeze seeping through the open windows was doing delightful things to her nipples. She wanted him to find her irresistible, to leap on the bed . . .

"Cover yourself up, woman," he said from the dressing-room doorway, his voice brittle. He wore a nightshirt.

Constance hesitated, then drew the sheet to her neck. "I wanted—"

"Christian women do not want," he said. "Things like that. Your body is your own affair. That I have the use of it is but to perform a service required by God. Now, I will turn down the lamp, and then you may kneel and pray for forgiveness." The room was plunged into blackness, and Constance rolled across the bed to kneel beside him. "On the other side," he commanded. "Would you confuse lewd thoughts with prayer, woman? I am ashamed of you. On the other side. I understand that you have been alone too long," he said in a softer tone when she was kneeling opposite him on the far side of the bed. "But there will also be occasions when I must leave you alone here. Thoughts of the flesh should never be indulged or even permitted. Sufficient that we do what we have to do. Now, let us pray to God for forgiveness and for the strength to perform our duties without lewdness or obscenity. Let us pray.''

Constance clasped her hands together as she knelt against the bed, rested her forehead on the clenched knuckles, and discovered that her fingers were wet with the tears rolling down her cheeks.

# 2

# The Empress

Following which, they did their duty, as Henry conceived it. It occurred to Constance that all was not yet lost, because he was very eager, and for that reason very quick and totally unsatisfying or even arousing—but he must have been anticipating her arrival. And next morning, when she awoke, it was to find him standing by the bed, gazing at her breasts; the moment he saw her watching him, he turned away and hurried into his dressing room. She wanted to follow him, but dared not. Whatever she was going to achieve would require patience; the worst thing she could do would be to embarrass or anger him.

So when she was dressed, she sat patiently and endured his lecture. "I am not at all sure I have done the right thing," he said. "In marrying you at all, much less in bringing you out here. I sought to obey God's will, to procreate, as is a man's duty, but I allowed my sinful nature to lead me into unrighteousness. A man should not choose a wife for her beauty, but for her goodness. You are very beautiful, Constance."

She raised her head in delight, but immediately realized that he had not intended a compliment.

"And beautiful women," he went on severely, "are the source of almost all the evil in the world. Think of any crime you wish, it can be traced back to the desire of a man to possess a beautiful woman."

This was too much. She had to keep her temper with an effort. "But you do possess me, Henry," she said. "Legitimately, and before God. What can be wrong with that?"

"Simply that you make my mind turn to lewdness," he said. "Which is a sin in itself. And you yourself . . . I had not suspected it of you, Constance. Now I wish you to understand something very clearly: never again must you come to bed unclothed. Indeed, you must never be unclothed at all, at any time. The surest protection for any man, or any woman, against the sins of the flesh, is to be fully clothed at all times."

Now her anger could not be contained. I wonder we do not have separate rooms, she thought, and was about to say so, when he continued.

"Suffice it that we shall continue to do our duty until God in his wisdom sees fit to grant you the mercy of conception."

Which means you get to mount me every night, she thought, while *I* must lie there like a dummy and never allow myself to feel, or even, presumably, to think about it. That had to be wrong. Wrong, wrong, wrong. But she knew it would be a mistake to attempt to convince him of that on her first day here. And she *was* here, and was apparently going to stay here for a very long time. There would be opportunities when he got more used to her company.

"Now, come," he said. "And I will take you on a tour of the mission. And show you your duties."

In fact, the mission was sufficiently interesting to end both her anger and her disappointment, at least for the time being. To begin with, it was considerably larger than she had supposed or anticipated, covering some twenty acres, the full extent of the miniature plateau on which it was situated. In this area lived some two hundred and fifty people, in neat little houses built in very close proximity, but the Chinese did not seem to indulge in private gardens; the area they cultivated, down the slopes to either side, was of course much larger, another three hundred acres, and was watered by a bubbling stream which was apparently a distant tributary of the Han-ho.

The industry was tremendous, because Chu-teh was not only separated from the nearest town, the railhead of Feng-tai, by some thirty miles, but because it was deliberate policy on the part of the missionaries to make their community as self-supporting as possible, not only to protect it from the periodic famines and waves of resulting unrest which afflicted the country as a whole, but also to wean the young converts from Chinese traditions and ideas—no Christian parents, for example, were allowed to practice binding the feet of their girl infants. In the pursuit of a sufficient food supply, therefore, apart from the inevitable wheat and oats—Constance was interested to discover that the rice with which she had always associated Chinese diet was confined to the south of the huge country—there was considerable pasturage for the cattle and pigs, as well as a large hen run and a duck pond, and out of this arose a dairy industry, as well as a tannery.

But there were also a haberdashery and a furniture workshop. "Everything you see on Chu-teh, even the houses, has been built by the converts themselves," Henry explained with some pride.

She very quickly realized that he had a great deal to be proud of, not least his remarkable achievement in bringing the three very separate religious denominations into one community. "It seemed the only sensible thing to do," he told her with characteristic modesty. To a certain extent, of course, this was true. The first Christian missionaries to enter China, some fifty years before, had been well received, their doctrines listened to and analyzed with true Chinese gravity. Unfortunately, the rebellion inspired in 1850 by the mystic Hung Hsiu-ch'uan, known as the Heavenly Kingdom of Great Peace, or the Taiping, had assumed many of the outward characteristics of Christianity, one reason for the phenomenal success it had first enjoyed. But when Hung and his aides had proved themselves as cruel and corrupt as any other Chinese rulers, they had lost support and eventually been crushed, although not until, as Joan Mountjoy had said, there had been a quite unbelievable loss of life, more than the entire population of Great Britain, in fifteen years, as much from disease and starvation after the Taiping had swept across the countryside as from actual battle. And the Taiping might have been crushed, but the suggestion that they were Christianity-inspired had lingered. That the missions were tolerated at all was only because the dowager empress, studying the example of China's neighbor Japan, was beginning to understand that there was much to be learned from Western technology and Western ideas. The problem was, as Henry explained, that Tz'u-Hsi was incapable of pursuing any policy consistently, being entirely at the mercy of her mood and her current favorite adviser, and so the Christian communities teetered on a knife edge which varied from state protection to being regarded as public enemies, with possible ghastly results like the Tientsin massacre of ten years before.

Thus it certainly paid them to band together. The entire concept had been Henry's. Chu-teh had originally been a Methodist mission pure and simple, founded by himself. But to it had fled both the neighboring Anglican and Catholic missions four years earlier, the last time there had been a really severe flooding of the North China Plain. And Henry had invited them to remain. This was a revolutionary, and, to Constance, a distasteful concept, at least at first sight. Much as she liked the Mountjoys, and could not help liking Father Pierre and his hardworking, jolly nuns, she could not but abhor the idea of Roman Catholicism and even the Anglican communion, as she had been brought up to do. But Henry pointed out that the three services never clashed, as each denomination had the use of the church at different times of the day, and if undoubtedly most of the converts were a trifle confused, and were apt to attend whichever service took their fancy on the day, he had no doubt at all that in the long run they would settle for the simplest and most faithful, in his opinion, version of the Word, Methodism.

This Constance was inclined to doubt, as the Catholic and, to a lesser degree, the Anglican masses were obviously far more physically attractive than the stark Methodist service. On the other hand, there could be no doubting Henry's place in the community. Quite apart from the fact that it was *his* village, he was the unquestioned leader. Younger than either Mountjoy or Laclos, he possessed an energy and a sublime confidence which they lacked, and presumably they were quite unaware of the torments of the flesh which he suffered, and which it was her duty to alleviate, briefly and unhappily, every night.

For the rest, Henry was here, there, and everywhere, with a fund of knowledge, supported by his divine certainty, which carried the converts through every problem. Nor did he confine his efforts to Chu-teh alone, but would frequently take tours through the surrounding countryside, speaking and preaching, and gradually adding to the Christian community. Constance would have loved to accompany him—sometimes he went as far as the Great Wall, only fifty miles to the north—but he refused, saying that he traveled too rough for her to experience. The disappointment was bitter, but while he was away she was at least allowed to sleep in peace, with neither sex nor lectures to leave her tossing in discontent. Her principal problem was that, as Henry was so obviously right about everything else he did, and so respected by every member of the community, she could not help but feel that *she* had to be wrong about their sexual relationship, whatever her instincts. And she could not help but respect him herself, and even feel a growing admiration for him, and a pride in being married to so dominant a personality. Thus, before long she adopted his point of view, refused to consider "lewd thoughts" at all—even when he was actually entering her, she thought resolutely of other things—and prayed for the day when she might become pregnant, and their "duty" be fulfilled.

Her other duties were sufficiently onerous to keep her fully occupied. With Peter and Elizabeth she was expected to maintain Henry's house and his wardrobe in spick-and-span condition, while as Henry's wife she was also required to play the fullest part in the communal kitchen, a direction in which Henry was keenly aware that he had been benefiting for too long from the skills of the nuns and Joan Mountjoy. In fact, Constance was a good and interested cook, even if she found the conditions, the wood-burning range—in Richmond they had naturally used coal—and the strange vegetables, not to mention having to supervise the slaughter of her own meat, somewhat difficult to get used to. She also anticipated some resentment, at least from Joan Mountjoy, at having a nineteen-year-old girl pushing in to such restricted areas as menu planning and actual cooking, but Joan could not have been kinder, and went out of her way to make her feel at home, with a true Christian spirit.

A spirit which, Constance reflected sadly and often, *she* lacked too much of the time. Chu-teh, she felt, should be an utterly serene and peaceful place, for the individual spirit as well as in physical fact, an island of contentment in the seething hotbed that was China. But she could only feel that she was suspended in a sort of limbo, waiting, she was not quite sure for what—she could not even regard pregnancy as an absolute goal. Even when she played the organ in church of a Sunday, another of her duties, or conducted the Sunday school in the afternoons for the young Chinese converts—a great occasion for the children, and for many of their parents as well, who adored sitting around the strangely yellow- and thus imperial-haired young American lady, and stared at her with their mouths open throughout the lesson, obviously not taking in a word she was saying (or perhaps not understanding her Chinese well enough, she sometimes feared), but all obviously disappointed when she announced the lesson was finished—she wanted only to get on to the next thing, as if there was an actual end to the work she must perform, and then a reward. Henry's physical love, perhaps. Or even his mental love. For she could not overcome the feeling that to him she was not a human being, but some kind of finely wrought object, miraculously sent to him by God for his use, but in which it would be a sin to take pride or find pleasure. But then, he seemed to regard all pleasure as sinful, an unnecessary intrusion upon the serious business of working, and regularly lectured her on the errors of "frivolity" whenever he found her reading one of the half-dozen novels she had brought with her from Richmond.

On the other hand, he was not jealous when she received the promised letter from Franklin Wynne, and did not even wish to read it himself, apparently, although she left it on his desk. Frank had now joined his ship at anchor off the Taku forts, and was finding life unbearably dull. Thus he wrote an eleven-page epistle, which she found fascinating, because he not only described the city of Peking in all its tree-shaded, purple-walled, white-pagodaed beauty but also delineated the political picture as he saw it. His opinions, that there was really much less unrest in the country than was supposed by most European observers, including the missionaries, were derided by both Mountjoy and Henry when Constance chose to air them. But hearing from the young marine at all was like a breath of fresh air blowing through an overheated room, a reminder that there *was* a world out there beyond the unending plain.

"And actually," Kate Mountjoy confided, "I think Mr. Wynne is quite right. I think Mummy and Daddy and Uncle Henry are far too pessimistic." She giggled. "Although sometimes I wish there *would* be a revolution, or something, just so we'd have to leave. Otherwise I am going to die an old maid. You don't suppose, dear Constance, that you could ask Lieutenant Wynne to have one of the other officers on the *Alabama* write to *me*?"

The two girls had naturally become close friends. They were almost exactly the same age, and had, Constance soon learned, similar ideas regarding the social and religious straitjacket into which they were clamped. Kate obviously supposed that Constance was the most fortunate young woman in the world, in that she was actually married, and to a man like Henry, and was transparently disappointed because Constance refused to discuss any of the more intimate side of marriage. Because *she* had no boyfriend and no possibility of obtaining one, so far as she could see. The Mountjoys apparently had no relatives in England to whom she could be sent in search of a husband, and no contacts among the large British colony in Peking, who were mainly either legation officials or merchants, and equally regarded the missionaries as trouble-causing nuisances who made their task that much more difficult.

"So I shall undoubtedly die a virgin," Kate would confide. Although invariably her quite remarkable good humor would immediately come bubbling to the surface, and she would add,

"Unless I were to elope with a *Chinaman*. That would make them sit up and take notice."

She was a unique composition of ghoulish romanticism, Constance discovered. Almost the first occasion the two girls were alone together she insisted on regaling her new friend with a blow-by-blow account of how the French nuns had been raped and then mutilated, while still alive, by the vengeful Chinese mob, while from conversation with the converts she had unearthed a large number of amazing and disgusting facts about Chinese sexual habits. "They think, you see," she told Constance, "that the way white people do it is utterly stupid. They do it all sorts of other ways. Even backward and upside down." She pulled her nose. "I'm not quite sure how they can manage that. Do *you* ever do it any other way, with Henry?"

"Of course not," Constance snapped. It was not a subject she wanted to discuss anyway, even with Kate.

"Because you're Christian," Kate said. "I don't think Mummy and Daddy have ever done it any other way, either. I don't think they do it at all, nowadays," she added sadly. "Because *they're* Christian, you see. But the Chinese . . . I mean, the Chinese out there"—and she waved at the plain—"aren't Christian, so they do it all sorts of ways. Can you imagine being raped by a man who would do it . . . well, differently?"

"I should think to be raped by *anyone* must be the most horrible experience one can possibly have," Constance said, feeling as severe as Henry, entirely because she *was* being excited by Kate's rambling.

Catherine sighed. "It has to be better than never having it at all," she said, so dolefully that Constance had to forgive her and put her arms around her and give her a squeeze. In fact, she thought, without Catherine, she might well have gone stark, staring mad. But even Catherine ceased to be of importance when, three months after her arrival on Chu-teh, in the early fall of 1890, Constance discovered she was at last pregnant.

Everyone was delighted, not least Constance herself. It meant that the humiliating sham of making love every night was ended for a considerable period—Henry at once moved into the spare bedroom, to avoid any risk of either of them suffering an irrepressible desire. It also meant that their personal relationship improved enormously, for he was even more pleased than herself, ceased the unending lectures on lewdity and frivolity, and even relieved her of many of her duties around the mission so that she could protect the health of herself and the child; she spent her time knitting booties and vests against the severity of the winter which she was assured was coming, regardless of the fact that of course the babe would not be born until next spring.

Joan Mountjoy, as might be expected, was a tower of strength, as was Kate, and news having reached Peking, Mrs. Bunting sent her best congratulations, as did Frank Wynne, when it filtered down to Tientsin. In time there was even a letter from Richmond, an exceedingly rare event. Suddenly Constance was the pampered pet of every Christian, it seemed, in North China, which was in fact, she would admit to herself, how she had hoped to be regarded from the beginning. Joan and James Mountjoy had had Catherine before ever coming to China, so the baby Baird would be the first white child actually to be born on the mission. This aspect of things alone concerned Constance, as she feared there might be some Manchu hold on him, or her, but Henry was as ever massively reassuring.

Soon enough winter did set in, with very strong winds from the north sweeping out of the deserts of Mongolia and over the Great Wall, to howl around the mission, and with considerable falls of snow. Yet it was a happy time, for now more than ever Chu-teh was cut off from the rest of the country—with the cart tracks impassable, it was impossible for the converts even to reach Feng-tai to sell their surplus products—and thus they were also cut off from all the rumors of incipient revolution or natural disaster with which China apparently constantly abounded. To be entirely surrounded by a field of snow several feet deep for as far as the eye could see, and yet to know total comfort and security, for Henry had his slaughtering and reaping and preserving program carefully worked out, and protected sheds within the mission walls in which the animals could be bedded down in warmth and safety—Constance sometimes thought he would have been even more successful as a farmer than as a missionary—gave her a most pleasant feeling of contentment; for the first time, she thought, since landing at Tientsin the previous spring.

By Christmas her once slender body had become distinctly round, but now her very last duty was transferred elsewhere, and with the cold weather she did not feel especially uncomfortable. Christmas itself was a splendid occasion, at which all the white people sat down at the same table, along with the senior converts, and drank each other's health and to the safe delivery of the baby Baird, as the child was now universally known. But soon after the turn of the year, the temperature now having settled itself just below freezing, and the snow in consequence being very hard-packed, Henry decided it was time to undertake one of his proselytizing tours into the country to the north and west, where he was sure he was making steady progress in spreading the Word. Constance was appalled at the idea that he would wish to go out into the snow, but he smilingly assured her that he did this every January, as soon as the tracks were passable, and she was somewhat relieved when James Mountjoy decided to accompany him, without apparently causing Joan any concern. "It is the best time of the year for the men to be away," she explained to Constance, "as we are the least likely to be troubled by any nonsense from Feng-tai." What exactly she meant by "nonsense" she did not explain, but Constance immediately felt a pang of her old uncertainty.

"I'll be back for your delivery," Henry promised. "You may count on that." And he kissed her on the mouth with more warmth that at any moment since the night of her arrival. But she could not stop herself from weeping as she watched the small caravan of twelve men walking their horses across the snow, little black dots which kept dancing before her eyes even after they had disappeared and she had gone to bed.

After that it was a matter of waiting until they would reappear again, within about ten days, Henry had reckoned. She had not realized how badly she would miss him, for all the understanding that she was not in love with him and probably never would be, now. But he was her husband, and the father of her child-to-be, and whatever his private shortcomings, probably the finest man she had ever known. And Chu-teh was not the same without him, certainly in winter, when there was little outdoor activity, and without the daily round of duties which had kept her preoccupied during his summer absences. Her imagination played her all manner of silly mental tricks as she conjectured a hundred and one things that might have happened to him, traveling through the snow, and not even Joan Mountjoy's massive calm could truly reassure her, while Kate's overexcited company was no longer enjoyable, now that she was pregnant. When, about a week after the party had left, she heard someone calling, "Men come," she went running as fast as she could onto the veranda of her bungalow, looking to the north and west.

"Not Mr. Henry," Peter said, and pointed the other way. "Men from Feng-tai. Soldiers, we think." His face was anxious.

Father Pierre was hurrying across the compound separating the Catholic from the Methodist bungalow, waving a pair of field glasses. "I do not like the look of it at all, Mrs. Baird," he said. "Would you care to borrow these?"

Constance took the glasses, focused on the distant riders. Two of them were out in front, flogging their horses, which were clearly on the point of dropping from exhaustion, and floundered through the snow. Behind them, at a distance of perhaps half a mile, were a dozen very heavily armed men; the winter sun gleamed from their lanceheads, and occasionally one would obviously fire a rifle—as they were upwind, the people in the mission could not hear the explosions, but they could see the puffs of smoke.

"They are definitely making for us," Joan Mountjoy observed. She and Catherine had also come to the Bairds' veranda, much as it seemed the entire population of the mission was gathered beneath them, all staring out at the snow. Now all the heads turned to look at the white people.

But the white people's heads had also turned, Constance realized. To look at her. They were so used to looking to Henry for guidance in their relationships with the outside world, they were turning to Henry's wife, instinctively. She felt almost sick, even as her heart began to pound, and she could feel the flush in her cheeks. But she must do what Henry would do, say what he would say. "We must open the gate and let the first two in," she decided.

"Open the gate?" Father Pierre exclaimed.

"Those two men are almost certainly fugitives from the law," Joan pointed out.

"We do not know that," Constance said. "Only that they are fugitives. We must presume they are innocent until they are proved guilty. Oh, look there."

One of the horses had at last fallen, sprawling in the snow, and sending his rider sprawling as well. The second man drew rein, but the pursuers were now very close, and the man on the ground could be seen waving his companion away and pointing at the walls to the mission. The first man hesitated for a moment longer, and then again gave spur and made for the gate.

"Open the gate," Constance shouted.

The people stared at her.

"Those others are probably imperial soldiers," Joan said.

"They must prove that. And that they have a right to those men," Constance insisted.

"They *could* be brigands," Father Pierre muttered. He did not specify which group he meant.

"Then we will keep them out," Constance said, choosing to assume he was referring to the pursuers. "But we must save that man.'' Still no one moved, so she turned to Peter. "Peter," she commanded. "Open the gate."

"I will help you," Elizabeth said, and ran down the steps beside her brother.

"Wait for me," Kate Mountjoy cried, hurrying behind them.

"Kate, you come back here," shouted her mother. But the three young people were already lifting the massive wooden bar which secured the gate, and just in time, for the fugitive reached the wall exactly at the moment his horse also fell to the snow. But he landed on his feet, and kept on stumbling forward.

Constance gathered her skirts and went down the steps. "Constance," Joan shouted, hurrying behind her after a moment's hesitation. "Really, Constance, in your condition . . ."

"Close it again," Constance ordered as she reached the young man—and he was, very young; his legs had at last given way, and he knelt, panting, staring at the yellow-haired woman who stood over him. "He is done in," she said. "Some brandy, Father. And haste."

"Open the gate," came the call, in Chinese, from outside. "In the name of the emperor, open the gate."

Once again everyone looked at Constance, not least the kneeling young man. What have I done? she asked herself. And then reminded herself what Henry would have done. There is no need to be afraid of those men. Not here on Chu-teh, surrounded by friends. She went forward, determined to ignore the weakness of her knees, the throbbing of her heart, climbed the short flight of steps to stand beside Peter and Elizabeth and Kate on the platform beside the gate, and looked down on the soldiers. And on the other fugitive, whose wrists had been bound together in front of him, so that he could be tied to a saddle and pulled along behind his captors, stumbling and falling, being dragged over the snow.

"What crime has he committed?" she asked.

The commander of the soldiers was busily looking at her, with the expression of alarmed amazement most Chinese assumed when first meeting her.

"I am Mrs. Henry Baird," she told him. "Wife of the Reverend Henry Baird. If you wish to enter here, you must tell me what crime that man is guilty of."

The officer recollected himself. "It is no business of yours what he has done, devil woman," he said. "He *is* a criminal. So is the other. Open the gate and send him out to us."

"I will do no such thing," Constance said. "Until you show me a warrant or convince me of his crime."

"Crime?" shouted the officer. "He is a traitor to the emperor. He preaches rebellion. He is a villain and a scoundrel. I demand you hand him over to us."

Constance looked over her shoulder at the young man. Father Pierre had at last fetched him a glass of brandy, which he had drunk greedily, and looked much stronger. "Are you what he says?" she asked.

"I beg you," he said, to her amazement speaking English with a faint American accent. "If they take me, they will cut off my head, without trial."

Obviously she *had* to help him now, if he could speak English. But he was being absurdly melodramatic. "Now, really," she said. "That is ridiculous." She turned back to the officer. "If this man really is a traitor," she said, "you must have a warrant for his arrest. Show it to me. And tell me what his punishment will be."

"You dare to defy a captain in the Imperial Guard?" demanded the officer, his mustache almost seeming to quiver. "That man is an agent of the villain Sun Yat-sen. He preaches sedition against the empire. Against the emperor. Against the dowager empress," he added in a reverent afterthought. "There is no need for a warrant for such as he, no need for a trial. He is condemned to death by what he is. Bring that fellow here."

The other prisoner was dragged out in front of the horsemen. "This fellow will tell you his crime," the captain said.

Constance watched in horror as the prisoner had his hat torn from his head, his blouse pulled from his shoulders, exposing his naked chest to the subzero temperature; he almost immediately seemed to turn blue.

She became aware that Joan Mountjoy was standing beside her. "You cannot defy the empress, Constance," Joan said. "Surrender the man, and have done with him. You can be certain that he is not a Christian."

Constance's head jerked in disbelief. "Would that matter?" she demanded. "He is a human being."

"But he will endanger all of us," Joan wailed, her normal composure at last collapsing in fright. "The entire mission."

Constance stared at the shivering man in the snow beneath the wall, then at the young man who still knelt in the compound behind her. He did not speak again, but *he* stared at *her*, his lips moving silently, imploring her. And she had no idea what to do. If only Henry were here. If only he could appear now, riding over the horizon. How splendid that would be. What would he do? But could he really send a man to almost certain death, when his life could possibly be saved?

"I must see a warrant," she temporized. "Or hear a confession." And hated herself, as she realized she had probably just condemned the other man to mistreatment.

"Speak, devil, speak," shouted the captain, dismounting to kick the shivering man in front of him.

The prisoner fell forward into the snow, apparently trying to bury his face and inhale as much of it as he could, and suffocate. But two more of the soldiers had dismounted and quickly seized his pigtail to pull him upright again.

"You wish to hear him speak?" bawled the officer, also dismounting. "I will make him speak. I will make him scream. I will send his soul forever screaming around the entire universe, begging for mercy. Show the foreign devils how we deal with traitors," he commanded his men.

Two more of the soldiers dismounted, and while the first pair held the shivering captive's shoulders, these yanked down his breeches.

"Don't look, Constance, for God's sake don't look," Joan shrieked. But Joan was looking, as was Kate, and as was Constance herself, even as her mind seemed to have coagulated into a horrified mass. For one of the guardsmen had seized the prisoner's penis to hold it away from his body, while the other's razor-sharp sword was sweeping through the air, gleaming in the winter sunlight. Blood spurted, and the man shrieked his pain and shame and misery, as, released by his captors, he rolled in the snow, which turned red about him, while, most ghastly event of a ghastly morning, his bound hands sought his severed member, which had been dropped by his other tormentor, and which was now kicked away from his reach by the laughing soldiers.

Constance had a sudden feeling that she was going to faint, felt Joan Mountjoy's fingers closing on her arm, while a great wail of dismay went up from the watching converts.

"Now send the other man out," commanded the officer. "Lest we deal so with every man in there."

Constance had to swallow great masses of saliva that kept flooding her mouth. But at the same time she was aware of being angry, angrier than she had ever been before in her life. Slowly she got her breathing under control. "I would not give him to you if he were guilty of . . . of murder," she shouted.

"Constance," Joan begged.

But Kate shouted, "Bravo! You shan't have him, you shan't

have him, you butcher." Her cheeks were pink and her entire body was a mass of emotion.

"Break down that gate," commanded the captain.

Constance forced herself forward, leaned over the rail. "We have rifles trained on you," she shouted. "You will all be killed."

The captain hesitated, looking right and left. While Constance looked right and left as well. From their position on the slope below the wall, the soldiers could see only the heads of the converts looking out. And if the faces were registering only terror, there was a great many of them, and none of the soldiers could *know* that each man they counted did not actually hold a weapon and was prepared to use it. As the captain was slowly realizing. Now he signaled his men to withdraw. "You have defied the empress," he shouted. "Remember that." He waved his arm, and the cavalry turned and rode back for Feng-tai, their mutilated prisoner again being dragged at their horses' tails—it was difficult to suppose he would survive the journey.

"You have defied the empress," Joan Mountjoy repeated. "May God have mercy on all of our souls."

"You have saved my life," the young man said between mouthfuls. He ate greedily, consuming bowl after bowl of the chicken-and-corn broth placed in front of him by Elizabeth; Constance supposed that he might not have had a square meal in days.

While she still felt sick as she thought of that spurting blood, that mutilated belly. She had never actually *seen* a man before, in broad daylight, owing to Henry's modesty. And to be so callously destroyed, *as* a man . . . The amazing thing was that the young man's appetite did not seem to be affected by the ghastly fate which had overtaken his companion. *She* had to draw several long breaths to get her stomach under sufficient control even to speak. Eating was not a practical possibility. "How do you speak English so well?" she asked.

"I have been to America. To San Francisco," he said proudly. "I am Lin-tu."

She estimated he would be about twenty-five years old, with the flatter features of the true southern Chinese and the lively, intelligent black eyes of all his race. She had made Peter take away his soaking, freezing clothes and bring him others, a shirt, trousers, and woolen pullover, as well as a thick pair of socks, in which he looked incongruous, but not uncomfortable—he *had* worn such clothes before.

"And do you really work for Mr. Sun Yat-sen?" she asked.

"Dr. Sun and I work together," he explained. "For China."

"Then you admit to being a revolutionary," she said.

He gazed at her thoughtfully. But he was no longer afraid. He knew she would never give him to the soldiers now. "I am a patriot, Mrs. Baird," he said. "The Manchu are the enemies of all the true people of Han. And the dowager empress, Tz'u-Hsi, is the most evil woman in the world. Always, in history, when a woman has ruled in the Middle Kingdom, it has been bad for the people. But she is the worst. While she lives, and rules, the Middle Kingdom can only be weak and poor, because she is interested only in power and the wealth that it can bring. You have come here from Tientsin, Mrs. Baird, and you have read about my country, and heard of it. The way it is being carved up by the European nations. We are doubly invaded. The Manchu rule us, while the British demand concessions here, the French there, the Germans somewhere else, and the Russians . . . they wish it all. Those things must be ended, the foreigners must be expelled, before the Middle Kingdom can again be great. And to accomplish that, we must bring about the end of the Manchu. And the Dragon Empress."

The meal was finished. Constance rose from the table and went into the drawing room. Constance Baird, she thought, entertaining a foreign revolutionary at dinner. But she had already done more than that. What, she was not even sure. Joan seemed to think that she had endangered all of their lives. But there was nothing else she *could* have done.

She sat down. "Then you would drive us away as well?"

He sat on the floor, cross-legged, in front of her. "You do my people much harm, Mrs. Baird. Christianity may be a good thing, even a great thing, but here in the Middle Kingdom it leads to dissension. We must be united and strong if we are to drive out the Manchu."

He was so sure of his mission, quite as sure as Henry ever was. But she was equally sure that he was taking on an impossible task. "Does not Confucius say that it is the duty of every Chinese . . . I beg your pardon, I should have said, every man of the Han, to respect authority, and obey it? You *do* believe in Confucius?"

"Of course I do, Mrs. Baird. But Confucius also says that when authority *may* be overthrown, it no longer has the support of heaven, and then it is the duty of every man of Han to destroy it."

"I would say that is rather a convenient philosophy," Constance remarked.

"Philosophies, Mrs. Baird, are there for the use of man, not man for the use of philosophy." He smiled, the somewhat harsh lines of his face softening. "But you will never have cause to fear my people, Mrs. Baird. You have saved my life. And while you are pregnant, too. You are very brave. You will always be honored by Lin-tu, and I will make sure that your name is honored by all the men of Han. This I swear."

Once again they gazed at each other for several seconds, until she flushed and looked away. Because she had the strangest feeling that he could read her thoughts, and those thoughts had suddenly drifted down absurd and obscene channels, as she recalled Kate's rambling chattering. Somehow, the converts on Chu-teh had always seemed like children to her, and if, like children, they did not comprehend and perhaps even despised the ways of their elders, that was a state of affairs which would be corrected with more wisdom. But this young man had been to San Francisco, and seen the American way of life. He would know more about her, about what she wore and what she did in her private moments, than any convert to whom she was essentially the wife of their leader, a remote figure in a long skirt and black laced boots and a straw hat. And he used words like "pregnant," which she had hardly ever heard before; everyone on the mission referred to her "condition," or that she was "carrying her child," as if it was already born and being cradled in her arms.

But then, as he must be very like his unhappy accomplice, at least physically, she knew a great deal about *him*, as well. And could not stop herself remembering.

He *could* read her thoughts, because now he said, "I am sorry, Mrs. Baird, I did not mean to embarrass you. I wish only to honor you. Now and always. This is the word of Lin-tu."

"Well," Henry said, "you seem to have had quite an adventure."

He had been regaled with the facts of what had happened almost the moment he had come through the gate, by Joan Mountjoy—whom Constance was now positively beginning to dislike—as well as by Father Laclos and several of the converts. Now he added, "I am sorry to have left you to face such an experience."

She had half-expected him to be angry. But he merely looked

grave. Relief flooded her mind. "I tried to do what you would have done," she said.

He nodded. "Unfortunately, sometimes it is necessary to weigh the life of the individual against that of the community as a whole. This is not necessarily a Christian point of view, but it is a practical one. It is also necessary to be realistic. This young fellow, Lin-tu, where is he now?"

"I don't know, Henry. He stayed here for forty-eight hours and then he left. He said he was returning to the south." She hastily added, to prevent any misunderstanding—and just in case Joan Mountjoy had been malicious as well as critical, "He shared Peter's bedroom."

Henry apparently had not considered any possible alternative. "Perhaps he will go south," he said thoughtfully. "But soon he will be out in the villages again, preaching revolution, and will be taken by the soldiers, and executed. It is his way of life, and it is inevitable that it will end in his death. You have not *saved* his life, Constance. You have merely prolonged it." He looked out at the compound. "At the risk of how many others?"

"If you had *seen*," she said, "what they did to that other poor man . . ."

"I have seen some examples of Chinese notions of justice, in all its horror," he said. "And perhaps I am more sorry than anything that *you* had to see it. But it is not so wantonly cruel as you may suppose, although in another sense it is even more cruel than you can possibly suppose. It is a Chinese superstition, you see, that only a whole man may enter heaven. And when he is beheaded, as that fellow will certainly have been by now, his relatives often bribe the executioner to let them have back the head to place in the coffin, to ensure him everlasting peace. Thus by mutilating him, and then throwing away his . . . ah, member, the guard captain was seeking to condemn him to everlasting suffering. Which is why court eunuchs, for example, always carry their genitalia around with them in a bottle, to be buried with them when they die. But for you to see it happen . . . or to see him exposed at all . . . You have suffered no nightmares?"

She knew he meant had she suffered any lewd thoughts. But to tell him the truth of that would be merely to let herself in for a fresh round of lectures and reproofs. "Of course not," she lied. "But I swear I would act the same again."

"We shall pray to God that the occasion never arises," he said. "Or worse," he added.

"Oh . . . do you really think the empress concerns herself

with every little thing that may happen to her soldiers? Or to what two agitators might say of her?''

"As I say, we must pray that she does not. But be sure that what has happened here will be reported to her. And be sure, too, that she will know of you. All northern China already knows of you," he said. "Of your hair . . ." He stretched out his hand to touch it. "Your magnificent hair."

Constance realized that, whatever his temporizing, he *was* proud of what she had done. So there was nothing for her to fear. And as the weeks passed and no word came from Feng-tai, she soon even ceased to worry that the officials there might decide to take action against her. Besides, what action *could* they take? She was not a Chinese, and was therefore protected by the laws of extraterritorialism extracted from the Manchus by the victorious Western powers, that their nationals could be tried only by their own consular courts, no matter what their offense. The best the Chinese could do would be to demand that the American ambassador in Peking send her away from the country.

Strangely, it suddenly occurred to her that that would *be* a punishment, now. Because however much the converts and the other missionaries might feel she had endangered them by her actions, they too were very obviously proud of her. From being an ornament, the wife of their pastor, she had become, in a matter of seconds, a human being in her own right, and a human being on whom they must surely feel they could rely in any future crisis. And thus for her a feeling of belonging began to spread, a discovery that she might, after all, learn to be happy here on Chu-teh.

If only she could rid her mind of the crystal-clear memory of those few devastating seconds outside the gate. Of the feeling that so long as she remained in this vast and brooding cesspit, she might at any moment uncover something equally ghastly, equally breathtaking, equally—dared she admit it to herself—titillating. Or perhaps even experience it herself. Kate had told her endlessly how the nuns in Tientsin had been stripped naked and raped repeatedly, and then had their breasts cut off before being torn to pieces while still alive by the mob which had invaded their convent. That certainly titillated Kate, however much the thought of it might turn *her* stomach. But still, what had happened in Tientsin was remote, like something out of a history book, or the news of someone being burned to death in a fire. She had actually witnessed a man being castrated, and then had sat and talked with another man, who, but for her intercession, would also have been mutilated and then dragged away, still bleeding, to his death. Somehow she felt that between herself and Lin-tu there must be a tremendous if unspoken bond of intimacy, far more than if, for example, she had saved him from drowning or some other prosaic fate. A bond she was sure he had also felt, from the way he had looked at her. And he had met her when she was seven months pregnant.

But those were the lewdest, most obscene thoughts of all, as she remembered more of what Kate had prattled, about backward and upside down. What absurdity. But what if it were true? With a handsome young man like Lin-tu, who owed his virility entirely to her?

The idea that Henry might be able to read her mind, to understand that despite all his efforts, thoughts of the flesh were still creeping into her mind, terrified her. But Henry had other things on *his* mind, as the winter ended unusually early, to be followed by a brief, bright spring—but then by a series of tremendous rainstorms, which came booming down from the mountains in the north, soaking the plain day and night. "Depend upon it," he muttered. "This will be a flood year." And he immediately put the mission on three-quarter rations to hoard their food supply against the ruined crops he foresaw.

Not his wife, of course. She needed everything that was available as her confinement drew near. It turned out to be a very simple affair. Joan Mountjoy, however she might regard the young Mrs. Baird as a dangerous lunatic in her dealings with Chinese authority, proved an excellent midwife, and Kate and the nuns were also there to help. Constance went into labor at ten o'clock on the night of May 17, and little Charles was born at one o'clock the following morning. "Because you are made for childbearing," Joan said, placing the babe in her arms. "You will undoubtedly have a huge family." This last a trifle sadly, for *she* had apparently suffered so badly bearing Kate that she had never had another.

But her words were a salutary reminder that soon enough Constance would have to return to her "duty" of nightly submitting to Henry's brief entry; whatever the sexual content of her reveries, she could find no pleasure in *that* prospect. But there was still a spell of freedom left, as he would not resume relations with her while she fed the babe, and her milk lasted for several months. She was delighted, in fact, with the way her breasts had grown, and with the amount of milk they produced. The summer of 1891 was a suddenly happy one, one of the happiest she had ever known, as she was not required to return to *any* of her duties around the mission, while feeding, and as she also no longer had the burden of the child in her belly, but could sit day after day on the veranda of the bungalow, in a rocking chair, with Peter and Elizabeth always there to supply her with cooling drinks, and Charles on her lap, his face buried in the open bodice of her gown, and the enormously joyful feeling of his gums closing on her nipples spreading through her entire system.

Not even the rain could interfere with her contentment. And the rain was an ever-present factor. Soon tales spread up to them of flooding closer to the rivers, of whole villages being swept away, of crowds of refugees pouring into Peking and Feng-tai. Indeed even their own little stream broke its bank and turned into a series of miniature lakes. But on the hillock that was Chu-teh there were no immediate problems, although undoubtedly with their crops also lying drowned on the plain beneath them it was going to be a hard winter. But one with which Henry would be able to cope, Constance never doubted, especially when in early September the rains at last ceased, and the ground began to dry, and they were able to harvest at least a little of the wheat. Thus she was the more surprised when one day there was a flurry of activity from the gate, and a few minutes later he hurried up to the house, his face quite pale, his whole demeanor more agitated then she had ever known before.

"Whatever can the matter be?" she asked.

"There is a patrol of soldiers at the gate," he said.

"Soldiers? A patrol?" She sat up straight, jerking her nipple from Charles's mouth, which caused him to wail, while a huge lump of lead seemed to form in her stomach. She had forgotten all about the possible implications of last winter. "What do they want?"

"They are the advance guard of the empress's entourage. She has spent the summer, as usual, at the imperial palaces in Jehol, north of the Great Wall, and is on her way home. But now she has been informed that the Han-ho is still flooding and that the way to Peking is barred." He flung out his arm, pointing to the north. "She is on her way here, with all of her people. She wishes to wait here until the floodwaters subside."

# 3

# The Court

Constance's heart seemed to give a huge bound as if it would leap right through her chest. "The empress? Tz'u-Hsi coming *here*?" She looked left and right along the sweep of the veranda.

"Yes," Henry said. "She will have to occupy this building. But her entourage will require all of the bungalows. We shall have to move into the convent for the time being. The Mountjoys as well. I have already informed Father Pierre, and he quite understands. Our people will have to move out of *their* houses as well. . . ." He sighed. "It is the food I worry about. They will eat us out of house and home."

Constance looked past him at the soldier who had arrived from the gate at the foot of the steps, still mounted, but obviously taller than the average Chinese, dressed in the invariable tunic and breeches and boots, but in his case all were in deep blue, and very finely decorated with gold and black thread, and he wore a sword as well as, incongruous in such an un-Western garb, a revolver in a holster strapped to his black leather belt. He was a fine-looking man, with a high forehead and black mustaches surrounding a firm mouth and drooping beside a prominent chin. She felt quite weak as he gazed at her, and even weaker when he spoke. "The devil woman," he remarked in Chinese.

"Ah . . ." Henry seemed to have lost much of his usual incisiveness with the approach of this unexpected crisis. "I am afraid that is how they speak of you, Constance."

Constance stood up, handed Charles to the hovering and very

nervous Elizabeth, and went to the veranda rail. "I am Mrs. Baird," she said. She was aware that the bodice of her nursing gown was flapping, but refused to lower her gaze or fumble at the buttons, told herself that only boldness counted here, as it had been all that had saved them last February. "Her Majesty will be most welcome in my home."

The officer continued to stare at her for several seconds, and then nodded. "I am General Yuan Shih-k'ai," he said, and gave a brief bow, which allowed her to see that he wore the pigtail. Therefore he was a Chinese and not a Manchu. But he was already a general, and he was certainly not very old. And he was commander of the empress's bodyguard. She realized that she had to be in the presence of a remarkable man. Who now spoke again, raising his hand to point. "My men will search your house."

She opened her mouth to protest, and then thought better of it. Of course they would have to do that. So she bowed in turn. "They are welcome, General Yuan."

Her assurance obviously pleased him, for he dismounted and himself came up the stairs, to stand on the veranda and look left and right, while his soldiers, a somewhat more-disciplined-looking group than those Constance had encountered at Yangtsun, or those who had pursued Lin-tu, entered the drawing room and began rooting around, but very carefully, so as not to break anything, watched in the most utter terror by both Peter and Elizabeth. Yuan himself stood in front of the Chinese girl to look at Charles, while Henry at last realized that Constance was revealing far too much, and hissed at her, "Button yourself, woman. Button yourself."

Constance obeyed, while Yuan turned and smiled at her. "Your son?"

"Yes," she said, starting to be afraid again.

"Present him to the empress," he recommended. "When the moment is right. Her Majesty once had a son. He was our late emperor."

"How should I address Her Majesty?" Constance asked.

"You do not address her at all, until she speaks to you," Yuan told her. "*Should* she do so, you may address her as 'Majesty,' but you must not, under any circumstances, look at her." The smile returned. "Remember this, because I am sure that she will wish to speak with you, Mrs. Baird. Now, prepare yourself."

\*　　\*　　\*

There was so much to be done. And so very little time to do it, for now they could see, to the north, the huge moving mass of the imperial entourage, brightly colored parasols raised against the drizzle which had returned, a habit indulged even, Constance observed to her amazement, by the soldiers, and by General Yuan himself, who gravely allowed an aide to hold a blue umbrella over him as he stalked about the mission compound inspecting and ordering changes.

The converts were all hastily putting on their Sunday best, while obviously in a state of total terror, uncertain whether they would not stand more chance of avoiding the Celestial displeasures by wearing Chinese costume. Constance had no such problem, but there was hardly time to put on *her* best—her only—chiffon ball gown with its puffed sleeves and daring décolletage, and the ruby brooch Mama had given her, a family heirloom, and there was no time at all either to transfer her clothes from her wardrobe and chest of drawers—she reflected that the empress would hardly wish to use *her* bureau anyway—or to arrange her hair, for by the time she was dressed, the imperial bugles were already sounding at the gate. So she brushed it straight and left it on her shoulders, put on her widest-brimmed straw hat, had Peter and Elizabeth bring their parasols, and hurried outside, mud splashing over her boots and the hems of her petticoats, to take her place beside Joan and Kate Mountjoy and their husbands, as well as Father Pierre and his nuns, and the senior converts, and sink into a low curtsy as the huge procession came slowly through the gate, splashing water, kicking mud, staring around themselves with ferocious curiosity.

A squadron of bannermen came first, men of the Yehe Nara clan, whose emblem was the Bordered Blue Banner—these were the empress's own kinfolk. Then a group of mandarins, also mounted, and escorted by their servants and guards, men of importance, these, some of them of the very first of the ten ranks, and thus wearing the ruby buttonhole and the emblem of the crane if they held civil positions, or the emblem of the unicorn if they were of military rank.

Behind them came another group of men. Or *were* they men? These walked through the mud, turning their hairless faces and bland expressions to and fro, chattering among themselves in unpleasantly harsh falsettos. "The eunuchs," Kate whispered, and Constance's stomach rolled as she realized that each of these men, and there were nearly a hundred of them, had endured the horror she had witnessed, at some time in their lives; she found herself wondering if each carried his severed member in a bottle in his pocket, as Henry had suggested, and felt quite ill. But these were also important creatures, who understood their roles. Where the soldiers and the mandarins had formed ranks beside the converts to await the imperial party, the eunuchs proceeded directly toward the bungalows, beckoning the coolies who followed them carrying the chests of imperial linen and imperial food; the thought of them commandeering her neat little house was quite nauseating to Constance.

But she was now preoccupied with the arrival of the imperial princes, half a dozen nephews and cousins and uncles of the reigning emperor, and therefore all relations, at least by marriage, of the empress. For these it was necessary to sink into a yet lower curtsy, and by now the rain had returned even more heavily, and was soaking Constance's hat and trickling down the neck of her gown, which was certainly being ruined, from both ends, by the weather, despite the efforts of Peter to keep her protected.

"Thank God the emperor is not here himself," Henry muttered. "We should never be able to accommodate them all."

Constance, gazing down the slope at the small army of soldiers still to come, and at the huge shaded litter which was being carried by two dozen brawny coolies, immediately in front of the soldiers, wondered how he could be sure the emperor was *not* about to descend on them.

Kate understood her thoughts. "There are no concubines," she whispered. "The emperor never travels without at least some of his concubines." She giggled.

But now all the Chinese were kneeling, and performing the kowtow—resting their heads on the ground—despite the mud. The converts followed suit; the soldiers alone remained rigidly at attention, but allowing their eyes to roam left and right, still more in curiosity than in watchfulness, Constance felt; presumably it was not even considered that some maniac might dare wish to harm the dowager empress. She gave Henry a hasty glance, wondering if Europeans were also expected to kowtow, totally unable to envisage such an action while wearing a wide-brimmed straw hat, and saw to her relief that he was only preparing to bow. But even this meant that she had to sink into another low curtsy, so that she could feel her bottom brushing the ground and know that her skirt was irretrievably ruined, while she wondered if she would ever get up again, her thighs and knees were so exhausted with the unusual crouching, and at the same time endeavor to see under the brim of her hat without actually raising her head. For the imperial palanquin was now inside the mission, and being set on the ground. Soldiers formed a bodyguard to either side of the heavy yellow drapes which effectively concealed the occupants, and which the head eunuchs were hurrying forward to raise, yellow umbrellas held high entirely to blot out the gray of the sky, while others unrolled a yellow carpet across the mud to the foot of the bungalow's front steps.

There was only one occupant of the palanquin. Constance gazed at the smallest woman she had ever seen, scarcely five feet tall, and dressed in a heavy green gown which covered her from her neck to the ground. Her hair, which was black, was erected into an obviously elaborate coiffure on the top of her head, but was almost entirely concealed beneath a matching green headdress which spread to either side rather like an outsize nurse's cap, and which was studded with rubies and sapphires and emeralds—Constance did not suppose she had ever looked at such wealth at one time in her life. The face was small, the features regular, the expression remote, although the black eyes were lively. As the empress had been born, according to Constance's books, in 1835, she had to be fifty-six years of age, but she looked much younger, her complexion unmarked by any lines—or very cleverly made up. She carried a fan, in imperial yellow embroidered with a red dragon, in her left hand, and moved easily and with the grace of a woman used to an active life, unlike the Chinese females over whom she ruled. And as she walked over the yellow carpet to the Bairds' bungalow, looking neither left nor right, Constance saw that her nails were a full six inches in length, and superbly manicured—but only the last two nails on each hand. The first two fingers, those holding the fan with her left hand, for instance, were of quite ordinary proportions.

She understood that she was in the presence of probably the most powerful woman in the world. More powerful even, in terms of real ability to command, as well as in *numbers* to be commanded, than Queen Victoria herself. Lin-tu had described her as the most evil woman in the world. But there was little in the small, neat, compact figure which was now standing on the veranda, for the first time looking over the crowded compound, to suggest evil.

But now Constance also realized that Tz'u-Hsi was gazing directly at her. And speaking, in a very clear, slightly high Chinese voice, easy to hear, as the huge assembly was absolutely still, the only sound the dripping of the rain. "The devil woman," the empress was saying. "I would see the devil woman. Bring her before me."

\* \* \*

Several of the soldiers moved toward Constance, and she had visions of being seized and dragged toward the empress like some common felon. She looked at Henry in alarm, but he still seemed overawed by the very presence of the Great Woman, stared at the veranda as if hypnotized.

Fortunately, Yuan Shih-k'ai was there to wave the soldiers back, and himself gesture her toward the steps. She gathered her skirts and splashed through the drizzle; Elizabeth took a step behind her, holding the parasol, but was checked by a shake of the head from the general, so Constance was left to proceed alone.

She was chilled by the rain, but was yet aware that she was pouring sweat. And that she must look a sight, with her straw hat a soggy mess, her hair clinging damply to her shoulders, her hem stained with mud, and her boots all but disappeared beneath the cloying earth. She checked again at the foot of the steps, and stamped her feet, then proceeded up, uncertain whether she *should* look at the empress, despite Yuan's warning, or keep her eyes fixed on the floor, and opting for the latter, while feeling a distinct coward. When she had gained the veranda, she curtsied again.

"You are the devil woman?" asked Tz'u-Hsi in pretended astonishment, for she must have been able to identify Constance from her first look over the assembly—there was no one else present with yellow hair. "But you are only a girl."

Constance waited, feeling her thighs begin to stiffen and darts of pain driving through her knees, and listened to the soft hiss of the Celestial smile. "I, too, was a girl, once," Tz'u-Hsi said. "And I think I was considered something of a devil woman myself." She sighed. "I was thought beautiful then, too. But not so lovely as you, devil woman." She sat down, the eunuchs having placed a chair for her, and now she indicated the floor beside her chair. Constance hesitated only a moment, then half-fell onto the appointed spot. "Lemonade," said Tz'u-Hsi. "We shall have some lemonade."

Wearily Constance made to rise again, to prepare the drink, and realized that the eunuchs had already hurried off, having quickly familiarized themselves with the layout of the bungalow.

"Such hair," Tz'u-Hsi said. "Let me touch it."

Constance was happy enough to remove her sodden hat, but it was embarrassing to be watched by several hundred eyes as the empress took strands of her hair between her fingers to feel it and peer at it and even to sniff it.

"Truly Celestial hair," Tz'u-Hsi observed. "Are there many with such hair in your country?"

"Many, Majesty," Constance said.

"And a voice to match," Tz'u-Hsi remarked. "You defied my soldiers," she said, without changing her tone. "To aid an enemy of my nephew, and therefore of me. Do you know what happens to those of my subjects who defy me?"

Constance lifted her head to gaze into the soft black eyes. "I am not your subject, Majesty," she said. "I am the subject of President Harrison, in Washington, in the United States of America."

For a moment the features before her hardened, the eyes became like flint. "And you suppose that gives you the right to break my laws in my country?"

Constance flushed and bit her lip. "I—"

"You foreign devils are all alike," the empress complained. "You are arrogant. You presume too much."

"As a Christian, Majesty," Constance said, interrupting her, "as one who *preaches* Christianity, it is my duty to save life, wherever I can, and whatever the circumstances."

Tz'u-Hsi gazed at her for several seconds. "You are a bold young woman," she said at last, and half-turned her head as a eunuch presented a golden tray on which was a goblet of lemonade—a golden goblet, Constance realized. "The devil woman will have one also," the empress said, and sipped, looking at Constance over the rim of the goblet, but waiting for another to be brought. While the entire compound also waited, in the drizzling rain, hardly daring to breathe. As Constance dared not look at Henry or the Mountjoys. I must be dreaming, she thought. I cannot be experiencing this.

"You have a son, I am told," Tz'u-Hsi observed, once Constance had also sipped.

"Yes, Majesty."

"Let me see him."

"I . . ." Constance hesitated.

"Do you suppose I mean him harm, Mrs. Baird?" Tz'u-Hsi asked. "Why should I mean him harm?"

And suddenly Charles was with them, brought by a eunuch, and still half-asleep. Constance wanted to be angry, that her son should be held by a half-man—the empress made no move to take him, but merely regarded him with her invariable unblinking stare—was relieved when Tz'u-Hsi gave a nod, and the child was removed again. "A fine child," she said. "But he does not have Celestial hair."

"It is too early to tell, Majesty," Constance said. "But he may not. My husband has black hair."

The empress ignored the observation, looked to left and right, and then out at the compound. "These are fine houses," she said. "And fine people. They are well fed. Not all Chinese are well fed. You have done well, Mrs. Baird. And now you give an old woman shelter from the rain. That is Christianity, is it not? You have my thanks. But you must not defy my soldiers."

Constance drew a long breath. "I . . . I shall not do so again, Majesty."

"Of that I am sure," the empress remarked somewhat enigmatically. "Now, come, Mrs. Baird. I would have you talk to me of these United States of yours, and this President Harrison, that I may know whether he is to be considered a friend or an enemy."

"I am pleased," Tz'u-Hsi said. "Pleased with Chu-teh. Pleased with you, Mrs. Baird."

The empress ate alone, at the Bairds' dining table, served by the eunuchs who constantly surrounded her, and who apparently took the place of any serving women; Constance wondered if they would also undress the empress when the time came—the thought left her quite breathless. But she had been breathless, in any event, all day, at the way *she* had been singled out, for she was the only other *person* in the room, commanded to sit cross-legged on the floor—in her own dining room—and be served by Peter and Elizabeth. The empress had shown not the slightest desire to converse with any other of the missionaries—not even Henry, of whom she must surely have heard.

"One hears so many absurd tales of the crimes the missionaries commit," Tz'u-Hsi mused. "It is good to see for oneself, occasionally. Of course, you *do* commit crimes, do you not, Mrs. Baird?"

Constance hung her head. "Yes, Majesty."

"I am not thinking only of defying my soldiers," Tz'u-Hsi said. "You are not truthful. And truth is the greatest of human virtues, therefore it must follow that untruthfulness is the greatest of human sins."

"Not truthful, Majesty?" She raised her head in consternation.

"These things you have been telling me, of the wealth and power of these United States of yours, of this Mr. Harrison. How can they be true? You talk of this ruler of yours as *Mister* Harrison. How may a ruler be a mere mister? Were he even a usurping general, I might believe you. We have had sufficient of those here in the Middle Kingdom. But a mister . . . and one who gives up his throne and abdicates every fourth year? That is an absurdity. A ruler must be a prince or a king or an emperor, if he is to be a true ruler, and he should reign until he feels his powers waning. Only then may he abdicate. Even the Queen of England calls herself an empress, and England is only a small island in the middle of an ocean. But she has reigned for more than fifty years, I am told." She smiled. "Soon I will have reigned more than fifty years. And my responsibilities are much greater than hers."

Her ignorance of the world outside China was quite remarkable, and very irritating; Constance had a great temptation to remind her that it was the fleet of that small island in the Atlantic which had humbled her country fifty years before. But she was learning tact. "I did not lie, Majesty," she said. "Everything I have said of America is true. Our ruler is a mister because we have renounced kings and princes and emperors, and even usurping generals, for the happiness of all our people."

Tz'u-Hsi gave her another of her appraising stares, then said, "You have two delightful servants. What are their names?"

"This is Peter," Constance explained. "And this is Elizabeth."

"Those are not Han names."

"No, Majesty. They are Christian names."

Once again the long stare. "Tell me more of this land of yours," the empress said.

Her curiosity was insatiable, and therefore flattering. But she was an enormous strain. Of course Constance was proud, and relieved, to have been singled out, but she was also deeply embarrassed, and knew that Henry could not help but be offended, not to mention the Mountjoys. She was also constantly on edge, because the empress seemed capable of taking offense very quickly, for all her lavish praise, and because she required Constance's presence every waking moment. Throughout the imperial visit to Chu-teh she was not allowed more than a few moments with either her husband or her son, except when she collapsed exhausted into her borrowed cot in the convent. She could only be thankful that she had already started to wean Charles onto one of the convert women who had recently had a stillborn babe. Thus it was a great relief when, after two days, General Yuan's scouts reported that the waters had subsided far enough for the Celestial party to proceed the final thirty miles to Peking. But now came a fresh embarrassment, for as the huge column of soldiers and mandarins and eunuchs wound their way down the hill, Tz'u-Hsi once again summoned Constance to the veranda where she waited for her turn. "You have been good to an old woman seeking refuge, Mrs. Baird," she said. "I have given instructions that no longer are you to be known as the devil woman, and any man or woman so describing you will suffer the bastinado. I would also leave you some more tangible evidence of my esteem." She half-turned her head, and the chief eunuch stepped forward with a small casket, which he placed in Constance's hands.

"You may open it," Tz'u-Hsi said.

Constance released the catch, flipped up the lid, gazed at the largest emerald she had ever seen—or imagined to exist.

"But, Majesty," she protested, "it is too much."

"It is nothing," Tz'u-Hsi said. "For one friend to give another. Because we *are* friends, Mrs. Baird. I shall look forward to receiving you in Peking, in due course. When we may resume our conversations."

"*Well*," Joan Mountjoy remarked, gazing at the jewel and then down the hill at the slow-moving imperial entourage. "She certainly took a fancy to you, Constance."

"I think she was perfectly sweet," Kate declared. "I can't imagine Queen Victoria ever being as charming as that."

"Kate," her father reproved, "that is no way to speak of Her Majesty the Queen."

"I must say I find it difficult to understand why the Chinese hate her so," Constance said. "Why they refer to her as the most evil of women."

"As Joan says," Henry pointed out, "she happened to take a fancy to you, Constance. She was also grateful to have somewhere comfortable to rest. I do not suppose we have seen anything of her true nature."

Constance managed to get him to one side. "I am truly sorry about what happened, Henry," she said.

He frowned at her, pretending not to understand what she was referring to. "Sorry? About what? I thought it all went off rather well."

"I mean about the way she chose me to entertain her. I'm sure it was just the color of my hair. I told her that Chu-teh was all your work, your dream, your creation."

"I am sure you meant *God's* creation," he pointed out. "Believe me, I am not jealous of you, Constance. I only hope you made the most of your opportunity to convince her that we do good rather than harm here."

But he was not telling the truth, she knew. And there was

nothing she could do about it, save change the subject. "What do you wish me to do with the emerald?" she asked.

"I would put it in a safe place."

"But I can never possibly wear it."

"Who knows?" he asked coldly. "Down to this morning, I would have said you could never possibly *possess* such a thing. But now you do. So it would be a bold man who would state definitely that you will never wear it."

Constance bit her lip as she too gazed after the flags of the imperial party. Obviously he was going to require some time to recover from the slight he had received. Well, she would just have to sit it out. Meanwhile . . . She frowned as she watched a group of horsemen riding back toward the mission. "Looks as if they've forgotten something."

"The emerald." Kate giggled. Because even she was jealous of her friend's good fortune.

Henry did not look amused as he ordered the gate to be opened again, went to receive the soldiers. Constance waited on her veranda, the casket at her elbow. She hoped they *had* come back for the emerald. But she was sure they had not. The empress had genuinely seemed to like her, seemed to wish to be friends with her. And she was sure she knew why. Alone of everyone on Chu-teh, alone of everyone in all China, perhaps, she had not been obviously overawed by the mere Celestial presence. No doubt Tz'u-Hsi, being a human being herself, and surrounded entirely by fawning eunuchs and courtiers, longed to converse with someone on reasonably equal terms. But that was not a point of view she could put to Henry.

Who was now hurrying toward her, accompanied by several of the soldiers, and their captain, all still mounted. Henry looked grave. "A message from the empress," he said. "Peter and Elizabeth are to go to Peking immediately. I must inform their parents." He hurried off again, leaving Constance facing the soldiers.

"Peter? Elizabeth?" She looked left and right. Her two servants both seemed struck dumb by the summons.

"Now," said the officer in command of the squadron. "Haste."

"No," Elizabeth said, and fell to her knees. "I beg of you. No!"

Peter also fell to his knees, but seemed incapable of speech.

"Now," the officer repeated. "Haste."

"Please, Mistress Constance," Elizabeth begged. "Oh, please help us."

"Well, I . . ." Constance did not know what to do. She could well understand the two young people being taken aback by the suddenness of the summons, and it was gratifying to think that they did not wish to leave Chu-teh, even for the splendor of the Imperial Palace, just as it was gratifying that they should turn to her in the certainty that the final decision would be hers. But on the other hand . . . "I suppose you must go," she said. "I mean, summoned to the palace! Her Majesty told me how much she liked you both, when she was here. I am sure she means to make you her pages or something. Really, I cannot help but feel that this is a great chance for your advancement. I mean, you cannot intend to spend all your lives as servants on Chu-teh."

She paused in consternation, because Elizabeth was openly weeping, and Peter also looked close to tears. She wished Henry would come back, and listened to more weeping and wailing from across the compound. While the officer was growing impatient. "They come now," he said, and gestured to his soldiers, who immediately dismounted and seized the two Chinese by the arms.

"There is no need to be rough," Constance protested. "You must give them time to pack their things."

"No things," the officer said. "Things will not be necessary." Peter and Elizabeth were already mounted behind two of his men, and now the entire troop turned and rode for the gate. Just like the Chinese, Constance thought; such a slow-moving, indolent race normally, and then suddenly everything has to be done at a gallop. And she had not even said a proper good-bye. She gathered her skirts and ran down the steps and across the muddy compound to where several of the converts, including the twins' parents, as well as the Mountjoys and Henry, were gathered to watch the departing patrol. The Chinese were all looking utterly miserable.

"For heaven's sake," Constance protested. "I know it was very sudden, and I am even sadder than you to lose them. But that is the empress's way. I know they will prosper, and it has to be better for them than being my servants all of their lives."

Everyone stared at her, and she wondered what she could possibly have said.

"You don't understand, Constance," Henry explained. "I don't think you really understand anything about China. The imperial summons may mean advancement, but in the Chinese manner. Elizabeth is undoubtedly being summoned to service the emperor."

"To . . . ." Her jaw sagged, and she looked at Joan.

"I'm afraid that is true, Constance," Joan said. "The Manchu men often take a Chinese woman, if she is whole and healthy, as a mistress. But because she *is* Chinese, she can never be an official concubine, will merely be used and then discarded, as a menial about the palace.''

"But . . ." Constance dared not put her next thought into words.

"Oh, yes," Henry said. "As for poor Peter, he is undoubtedly to be required to take his place among the palace eunuchs.''

For a moment Constance could not believe what she had just been told. "But . . . you let them go," she cried, staring after the little group of horsemen.

"Well, what else was I to do?" Henry demanded. "They were sent for by the empress herself. I don't think she would take very kindly to being defied again. I told you that little old lady wasn't quite the dainty tea drinker that you imagined.''

"But . . ." Constance looked at the weeping parents. "Surely something can be done?''

"It is not quite as bad as you suppose, Constance," Joan explained. "It will be nothing as horrible as what we saw here. Peter will be drugged, and operated on while he is unconscious. Of course he is shocked and afraid, we all are, because here on Chu-teh we have taught our people different ideas of . . . well, of society. But it would be true to say that many Chinese families *encourage* their sons to go to the court as eunuchs. A successful eunuch can make a lot of money for his family. As for Elizabeth, well, it is very unfortunate, but there we are. And she, too, could be lucky, and attract some great mandarin when the emperor has finished with her.''

"Could be lucky?" Constance shouted. "Why, you . . . all of you . . ." She glared at Henry. "Just standing there, when you knew what was going to happen to them. Why, you *would* have let the soldiers take Lin-tu, wouldn't you? Just to avoid the risk of trouble. You'd have stood here and watched them chop him to pieces before your eyes, and said, 'Well, it could have been worse.' ''

"Now, really, Constance, there is no need to make a scene," Joan admonished. "You happen to be living in China, and you must accept the way the Chinese do things.''

"*Why* do we have to accept that?" Constance demanded. "I thought our business, our *mission*, was to change things, not to slink around the edges of this society like a pack of gutter rats, picking up crumbs which no one may notice have fallen.''

"Constance!" Henry snapped. "You are being quite remarkably rude to Joan and to all of us. We are merely trying to explain to you certain facts of life of which you are obviously unaware. But which, believe me, are very necessary to survival here in China. You think you can do anything you like because you got away with confronting the soldiers once before. Well, you merely have to reflect upon the number of Europeans, including missionaries, who have come to a very sticky end these last fifty years to understand how fortunate you have been. Now, I think you should apologize to Joan.''

"Apologize? I'll apologize to no one. I am quite disgusted with the lot of you,'' Constance declared, now thoroughly furious, the more so because she could understand there was a good deal of truth in what he was saying. But she could not escape the feeling that he and Joan were secretly pleased that she had been taken down a peg, even if it meant a ghastly fate for Peter and Elizabeth. And more than anything else, she was angry because Henry was proving himself just as pusillanimous as the others. The only thing their marriage retained was her complete respect for him, for his vision and his ability and his courage and his presence. But all the others rested on the courage.

"Then you are behaving like a stupid little girl,'' he said, going very red in the face. "And shall be treated as one. Go to your room, madam. Go to your room, and stay there, until you are ready to behave properly.''

Constance stared at him for several seconds, and felt the tears start to her eyes. They had never actually quarreled before, and to have it happen in public, and then to be told off like this . . . She turned and ran across the compound, hurled herself into her bedroom and across the bed, collapsed into tears, lay on her face for more than an hour, until she was alerted by a soft sound, raised her head and stared at Kate, climbing in through the window.

"Constance?'' her friend whispered. "Oh, Constance, what *are* we going to do?''

Constance pushed herself up. "Kate,'' she cried. "Oh, Kate. I thought, well . . .''

"I'm on *your* side,'' Kate said. "We must do something. We can't just . . . well . . .'' She rolled her eyes.

"Of course we must do something,'' Constance agreed. "We *shall* do something.''

"What?'' Kate asked with her usual disconcerting directness.

"Well . . . we shall write to the empress,'' Constance decided.

"It'll be done before a letter can possibly get to her,'' Kate pointed out. "If it ever gets to her at all. Poor Peter will have had his—"

"All right," Constance said hastily. She didn't even want to think about it, much less have it described with Kate's invariable graphic detail. "Well, then, we'll . . . we'll go to see her."

Kate's mouth formed an enormous O. "But . . . she's in Peking. In the Forbidden City. No one may enter the Forbidden City save a member of the court."

"Oh, bah," Constance said. "That law is meant to keep out the Chinese. No one is going to stop two white women. Anyway, she said she wished to talk with me again. I shall give her the opportunity." She glanced at her friend. "You aren't afraid?"

"Afraid? Of course I'm not afraid," Kate lied. "But . . . will *they* let us go?"

She was referring to her own parents as well as Henry.

"I don't suppose they will," Constance said. "So we won't tell them. We'll leave tonight, when everyone is asleep."

"To go to Peking? You and I? At night? Thirty miles across the plain?"

"We'll take someone to guide us," Constance said. "Yes. We'll take . . . William." William was a young convert who not only obviously worshiped the ground she trod but also had the practical value of working in the stables. "Listen. I'm not supposed to leave this room until I promise to behave or something. My God, can you believe it? You'd think I was some schoolgirl. So you go and see William and tell him not to say a word to a soul, but to have three horses saddled and waiting by midnight. Don't tell him where we are going. Say it is just a ride. Tell him I have ordered this and that I will be very grateful to him if he obeys without question."

"But . . . do you think he will? Henry will be very angry when he finds out."

"Henry will be as pleased as punch when we return with Peter and Elizabeth," Constance pointed out. "As for William, tell him I shall . . . I shall reward him."

Kate rolled her eyes again.

"I shall have him promoted when we come back," Constance said primly. "But don't tell him that. Just tell him I shall reward him. Now, off you go."

Kate turned to the window, then checked. "We shall be gone at least a whole day. What about Charlie?"

Constance wished she wouldn't call the baby Charlie, but now was not the time to argue about that. "I am sure he will be all right," she said. "Miriam is already feeding him, and she can look after him, too. Now, off you go. I'll meet you by the gate at midnight.''

She suddenly felt enormously happy and confident, wondered why she had bothered to feel miserable at all. The trouble with the white people on Chu-teh, she realized, was that they were constantly afraid, without actually knowing what they were afraid of. Perhaps the memory of those nuns in Tientsin still haunted them. But that was twenty years ago, and that had been an out-of-control Chinese mob, not the dignified and slow-moving imperial court. Besides, she and the empress were friends. The empress herself had said so. And she had the emerald to prove it. And they were friends because *she* had made them friends, because the empress, like all the Chinese or the Manchu she had observed, respected people who met her as an equal, and had only contempt for those who fawned and crawled about in fear. A class into which she had even to put Henry now, she realized to her disgust. And to her anger. When he came to her room that evening, she did not have to do any acting to convince him that she was just as recalcitrant as she had been in the morning.

"I really would never have suspected such moods of you, Constance," he said severely. "I wonder that I do not thrash you. Really I do." She suspected he was working himself up to it, but when he met her gaze he flushed and looked away. "But that would be unchristian. I shall leave you to come to your senses. There shall be no supper for you tonight. Miriam can care for the boy."

He might almost have been laying her plans for her. But she said nothing, just glared at him, and after another moment he turned and left the room. Then it was just a matter of waiting for midnight. And for praying that they would reach the Forbidden City in time.

The bungalow was silent by eleven. Henry had obviously resolved to let her stew in her own juice—and with that streak of meanness she was now beginning to discern in him, he did not even bring little Charles for a good-night kiss. But she was determined not to let this upset her tonight. Rather it hardened her own resolve. She would return in triumph once again. She was not prepared to look beyond his resentment then.

She dressed in the darkness, in her best green riding habit, pocketed her emerald, which she regarded as a passport to the imperial favor, and tiptoed from the room, her boots under her arm. These she put on while sitting on the front steps, before splashing through the mud toward the gate; it had stopped raining but the ground remained very soggy.

And there, to her great relief, were Kate and William, waiting for her with three ponies already saddled. "But where we going, Mistress Baird?" William wanted to know.

"Let's get outside," she told him. "We'll talk about where we're going later."

They could not close the gate behind them, but she did not see that this mattered; it meant that their departure, or someone's departure, would be noticed at dawn, but by then they would be in Peking. They walked their horses down the slope and then broke into a canter. "Peking, William," Constance shouted. "Take us to Peking!"

"Peking?" he cried in reply. "But that is thirty miles, mistress."

"Then we must hurry," she said. "We must be there by dawn."

Still he hesitated. "What you going do in Peking, mistress?"

"Ah . . . we are going to the legation, to tell them about Peter and Elizabeth. Don't worry, Mr. Baird and Mr. Mountjoy know all about it. But we must hurry." She saw that he was still doubtful, and rode close to him. "And I shall be eternally grateful, William. Eternally."

He hesitated for a last moment, sighed, and pointed. "That way."

They rode southeast through a seemingly unending night. How he knew for certain which direction to take, Constance was never sure; after a few minutes, when the lanterns which burned all night on Chu-teh were lost to sight, she had no idea at all where she was.

"Isn't it marvelous?" Kate shouted. "I've always wanted to ride across the plain at night." She looked the very epitome of an English gentlewoman after hounds, with her silk hat, gray habit, little whip, and flowing auburn hair. But that, Constance supposed, was all to the good; the more European and therefore beyond the reach of Chinese law or restriction they seemed, the better.

They splashed through puddles which were really miniature ponds, and waded brooks that were really miniature rivers. Constance understood where she was for the first time when the deserted pagoda loomed to her left, but they saw no one on the road, either; riding at night was not a Chinese pastime. They were caught by a brief shower of rain which soaked them to the skin and aroused fears that the rains might not after all be over and they were about to encounter impassable floods, but when

William would have halted, Constance urged him on again. And after what seemed an eternity the black began to give way to gray, and they found themselves in the midst of a thick white mist, which seemed to bubble out of the plain—but now too they could *hear*, an immense stealthy rustling from in front of them, the sounds of a great city awaking to a new day. And then, without warning, they beheld, rising out of the mist immediately in front of them, an extensive grove of white pine trees, and beyond, the walls of the most populous city in the world.

They drew rein, overcome with a sudden exhaustion, an awareness of their aching muscles—and of what they had done, as well. And a sudden realization, on the part of William, that it could *not* be done. "No one may enter the city without passports," he said.

"*We* shall enter," Constance said with a confidence she did not entirely feel, although her instincts told her that dawn was probably a better time than any other to take their chances. On the other hand, William had already taken sufficient chances. "But you must go back," she said. "Go back to Chu-teh and tell Mr. Baird and Mr. Mountjoy that we have gone into Peking to regain Peter and Elizabeth, and that we shall return, probably not by tonight, but by tomorrow night. Tell them not to be afraid. And tell them, too, that everything you have done has been at my express command."

He hesitated for a last time, then bowed and turned his horse, checked again, remembering that his task of guiding them was not yet over. "The Yun-ting-men is directly in front of you, Mistress Baird," he said. And galloped into the mist.

The two girls waited until he was out of sight. Neither in fact wished to take upon herself the responsibility of making the irrevocable move.

"I suppose," Kate said at last, "that we *could* go to the legation. They would help us."

"No, they wouldn't," Constance asserted. "They care even less for the missionaries than the Manchu. They'd be more likely to put us under guard and return us to Chu-teh. We cannot go back, Kate, without Peter and Elizabeth. You must promise me that. No matter what happens, we will *not* go back without Peter and Elizabeth."

The thought of facing Henry, a failure after having defied him, was not possible.

Kate's face was a comic mixture of fright and attempted determination. But she nodded. "I promise."

"Well, then," Constance shouted, rising in her stirrups. "*En avant.*"

They rode forward, and as they did so, the mist suddenly dispersed before the first rays of the morning sun, and in front of them they glimpsed the brilliant yellow-glazed eaves of the massive gatehouses of the inner, Tartar City, with beyond, the fantastic bulb, like an elaborately carved rook at chess, of the White Dagoba, the Emperor's Holy of Holies.

The rest of the city was hidden beneath the high mud walls, and the pine woods which clustered almost up to the gate were unutterably gloomy, dripping with the night's damp, and apparently the home of innumerable crows, which cawed to and fro, while the open spaces between the trees contained large numbers of sheep, plucking at the scanty grass and raising their heads with bemused wonder at the sight of the two white women cantering by. Then they were at the moat, and beyond, the Yun-ting-men, the South Gate. Here there were sleepy guards arguing and gossiping with the first travelers of the day, early farmers attempting to take their produce into the city to steal a march on their neighbors, and anxious merchants in a hurry to leave with their bullock carts full of goods, in order to gain the railhead at Hachiapo, a few miles to the west, in time to secure good places on the daily train to Feng-tai and thence Tientsin. But the gates were wide open. "Ride through," Constance shouted, and kicked her weary horse.

They rode at the opening, while people scattered before them, and chickens clucked and cattle mooed, and the sheep behind them watched with patient amazement. Their hooves clattered on the bridge which spanned the muddy mess of a moat which stretched to either side. The guards called at them to stop, but were as amazed as anyone else at the apparition of two white women riding toward them, and a moment later they were through and galloping straight up the Grand Avenue, while someone behind them fired his rifle into the air, to bring heads twisting and voices shouting—but no one actually attempted to stop their progress.

Now they rode between the vast park of the Tien-tan, the Altar of Heaven, some six hundred acres in extent, on their right, and the scarcely smaller Sheng-neng-tan, the Altar of the Inventor of Agriculture, on their left. Beyond these they entered the Chinese city itself, with houses and shops huddled to either side, but surprisingly few people as yet. In front of them rose the massive yellow-glazed pillars of the Tsien-men, the gate to the Tartar City, flanked to either side by the thick, high purple walls, much higher and more massive than the outer defenses, and here there were suddenly a great many people indeed. There were few guards on the gate itself—those on the Yun-ting-men were supposed to keep out undesirables—but beyond, where the street suddenly widened into an avenue sixty feet wide, there were booths and shops crowded three rows deep, each with a flag outside which by its color or shape denoted the type of goods to be found for sale within. Here also were groups of beggars, organized into gangs, seeking alms from any wealthy-looking passerby, and not above supplementing their pleas with threats. Behind them rope dancers and jugglers displayed their skills, and fortune-tellers sold almanacs foretelling the lucky days, on which children could be married and dead relatives buried without offending the gods. In and out of this throng, all scattered by the thudding hooves of the horses, went peddlers by the score, each beating a drum or blowing a pipe to his own tune, so as to inform the householders on either side that he was selling rice cakes or doughnuts, or toys or tea or fans, or household necessities such as needles, while behind everyone else the night-soil merchants were busy with shovel and bucket, gathering up the manure—human and animal—which had been deposited during the hours of darkness. And behind even *them* were the fixed merchants whose shops were permanent buildings; here were the barbers, busily making sure every Chinese wore the shaved forehead and the pigtail required by law; the porcelain painters bending over their exquisite art and apparently oblivious of the racket around them; the storytellers, surrounded by eager groups of children; and the quack doctors and dentists, often in the middle of a considerable operation, without benefit of hygiene or anesthetic. While the smell of roasting meats and ginseng and soy combined to remind the girls that they had not yet breakfasted— and in Constance's case, that she had not had any supper, either.

Yet she would not have eaten here, even if she could. For all the vigor and liveliness about her was laden with the stench of sewage and human excreta, as men and women urinated and squatted by the roadside with a complete lack of modesty; her horse splashed through inches-deep layers of mud and muck which sprayed over passersby but did not seem to disturb them in the least. The clothes of the people themselves were also filthy rags—she could only imagine the fleas that must roost in *there*— and the sight of children scrabbling for scraps beside mangy dogs in the gutters did nothing for her appetite. As they were forced to slow to a walk to avoid riding down some of these unfortunates, they had the time to look over the houses, to their right, and make out the imposing walls and rooftops of the European legations, only a few hundred yards away, and to identify the flags of Great Britain and France, of Russia and the United States, flying in what seemed almost a cluster, for the legation gardens in many cases adjoined one another. There was temptation. But one which had to be resisted. They *would* get no help there. The right of maintaining legations in Peking at all had only recently been conceded by the Chinese, and the various ministers were too aware of the delicacy of their position, their need not to offend the Tsung-li-yamen, the Manchu Foreign Office, in any way. Nor were any of them, Constance was sure, on as intimate terms with the empress as she herself. They would do better on their own.

But it was tempting to think of Harriet Bunting, no doubt still asleep in her bed over there—or of her going shopping in the midst of this nauseating mayhem.

Had she the time to think. For the decisive moment was at hand. No one had yet been sent behind them from the South Gate, and thus no one in the Tartar City had yet made any attempt to stop them. So far their boldness had been rewarded. But now, immediately in front of them rose the Ta-tsing-men, the Gateway to the Forbidden City itself.

From this gate it was only a short distance to the South Gate of the palace, looming before them, a huge area of gardens and pavilions and lakes and houses and pagodas and temples. This gate was known as the Gate of Heavenly Peace, and was in fact the one invariably used by the emperor to enter or leave his home, for south was the imperial direction—he always used southward-facing doors, would be buried facing south, and even slept facing south. Only when he performed his duty as emperor, and sacrificed at the Altar of Heaven, when he was suppliant rather than god, did he face the north. Thus here there was a large squad of guards, and no civilians at all in whose midst Constance and Kate could hope to hide themselves. But Constance's instincts told her that they would not be able to rush this imposing array as they had done earlier, even had their horses not been utterly blown.

She drew rein and dismounted, signaling Kate to do the same, while the soldiers goggled at them, never having seen two white women so close before. ''We seek General Yuan,'' Constance said, having decided that to announce they were going to the empress might be to alarm rather than reassure the guards. "We are in great haste."

"You have no business here, devil woman," said the guard commander. "Go back."

"I must see General Yuan," Constance insisted. "Look!" She took off her hat, allowed her hair to fall about her shoulders. "I am indeed *the* devil woman. You will have heard of me. I am the friend of the empress. Look . . ." She felt in her pocket and pulled out the emerald. "This was given to me by the empress herself. You will have heard of this, too."

Again they peered at her, their suspicion now tinged with uncertainty.

"Look more closely," Constance shouted, and held up the emerald for them to see. For the moment their attention was entirely distracted. "Run," Constance shouted, and dashed past the soldiers and along the narrow pathway, over a couple of small high-arched bridges, to the Wu-men, the Gate of the Zenith, the inner entrance to the palace. Here there were only two soldiers, but these were already alarmed by the sight of the women running toward them, as well as by the shouts coming from behind. Now one stepped forward and raised his hand; he had not drawn his sword.

"Don't stop," Constance gasped, and shoulder-charged him. She was at least as tall as he, and probably as strong as well; the force of her charge knocked him over, and she gathered her skirts and jumped over him, not daring to look behind her, but understanding that Kate was still at her heels from the mixture of gasps and giggles she could hear.

Inside the gate, for a moment they checked without meaning to, as they gazed at the beauty around them, for in complete contrast to the squalor of the city outside, here every building was made from the purest white marble, on raised terraces fringed with balustrades, surrounded by magnificent leafy trees, untrampled grass, and bubbling streams of clear and obviously clean water. But like the outer city, it was suddenly crowded with people, emerging from the houses to discover what all the noise was about.

"What do we do now?" Kate panted.

Constance pointed straight ahead. "Up there."

In front of them was the most splendid of the buildings, which she felt had to be the actual home of the emperor, and therefore no doubt of Tz'u-Hsi as well. And it was reached by a wide staircase, the marble of which was painted with an enormous

green-and-red five-clawed imperial dragon, so beautifully done
as to give the impression that the monster was alive and actually
slithering down the steps.

"Hurry!" she shouted, for people—mostly eunuchs, she
guessed, from their lack of mustaches—were beginning to con-
verge on them. They ran forward and up the stairs, to the
accompaniment of a great wail of consternation from their pursuers.
Pausing at the top, they saw that the eunuchs were coming after
them by a flight of plain white stone steps which mounted on
either side of the dragon stairs. "I think we've committed
sacrilege," Constance said. "Come on." Because only Tz'u-Hsi
could save them now. They ran on, and checked again as they
entered the throne hall, the largest room either of them had ever
seen, with a towering ceiling some forty feet above their heads,
with walls at least that distance away to either side of them, and
with, directly in front of them, the imperial throne itself, a vast
gleam of gold and precious stones. This was unoccupied, as
indeed the entire hall had been empty when they had entered.
But it was empty no longer. Every one of the many exits was
now crowded with eunuchs, gazing at the trespassers, chattering
at each other, and slowly advancing.

Kate's shoulder bumped into Constance's. "What are we to
do?" she cried. "What *are* we to do?"

Constance hesitated, chewing her lip, and then squared her
shoulders. "They aren't really men at all," she said, remembering how she had overthrown the soldier on the gate. "They'll not
stop us. That way." Again she pointed due north, behind the
throne. They gathered their skirts once more and ran, boots
clumping on the marble floor, and watched the eunuchs converging on them.

"Don't stop," Constance repeated, and swung her fists. But
she failed to connect and ran full tilt into one of them. Instantly
others closed on her, seizing any part of her body they could,
lifting her from the floor as she punched and wrestled and gasped
for breath, difficult, as she was now surrounded by their acrid,
unwashed body odors. She had the satisfaction of landing a kick
which made someone gasp, and then was hurled to the floor with
a force which knocked the air from her lungs. While she lay
panting, she was dragged back to her feet, to find herself facing
a mandarin with the badge of the Golden Pheasant, denoting that
he was of the Second Rank.

And very angry. "Defilers of the imperial presence," he
snarled. "Devil women!" His hand flashed out to strike Con-

stance across the face, bringing a start of pain and a sudden taste of blood into her mouth.

But she had got her breath back. "You . . . when the empress learns of this . . ."

"The empress!" He sneered and snapped his fingers. "Take these two devil women outside and cut off their heads. Haste! Cut off their heads!"

# 4

# The Proposal

His words were too impossible to be comprehended. Constance's head still swung with the blow on her mouth, and now her cut lips were beginning to smart. Dimly she realized that she was being dragged forward by the wrists, still surrounded by a crowd of eunuchs, who hummed at her like angry bees. Dimly she heard Kate screaming and begging for mercy. Kate was not, after all, made of very stern stuff.

But was being made of stern stuff going to save their lives? Because they were outside the palace now, on a grassy bank by a quiet stream, where there seemed to be an enormous number of people, and she was being forced to her knees and held there, while someone seized her hair—her hat had been lost in the fracas—and pulled her head one way while the two eunuchs holding her arms pulled her the other, so that she thought her neck would break, and another of the evil-smelling half-men stepped up to her and tore at the collar of her silk blouse, further to expose her neck.

And then she saw the sword, huge and gleaming, with space for two hands on the haft, being dangled before her nose. Tears were streaming down her cheeks and she ached all over, but yet she refused to admit to herself this was really happening, felt sure that if she could but gain her breath she could end it all with a shouted command, a reminder of who she was and what she represented. But would she gain her breath in time? For the sword was being moved from in front of her, while the chorus of chattering rose to a crescendo, and a moment later she felt the touch of cold steel on her exposed flesh as the executioner measured his distance.

Constance's courage gave way, as her muscles seemed to give way, and she felt her body sag, held up only by the grasp of the eunuchs. At last she could breathe again, but no words of command came to mind. "No," she screamed. "No! *Help* me!" she shrieked, so loudly she thought her lungs would burst.

The touch of the steel had left her neck. He would be raising the sword. "Help me," she moaned, no ounce of resistance left in either her body or her mind, and was suddenly released, so that she fell to the ground, every part of her plummeting downward in the same instant, to lie in a crumpled heap. I am dead, she thought. My God, just like that, I have had my head chopped off. I am dead, dead, dead, she wept, and listened to voices close by her, and to one which was familiar. She raised her head and blinked through her tears at Yuan Shih-k'ai.

There was no pleasure or even compassion in his face as he looked down at her. "Foolish devil woman," he remarked. "What have you done?"

Constance gasped for breath, looked left and right. The executioner, huge and bland-faced, leaned on his two-handed sword. Behind him, Kate had also been released, and also huddled on the ground like an abandoned rag doll. Around them the eunuchs clustered and chattered, pointed and gesticulated, but they had now been joined by several soldiers. And by General Yuan. Oh, thank God for General Yuan.

Because she was, after all, alive. She had entered the very pit of hell, and survived. She pushed herself up, found some breath, pulled hair from her face. "We came to see Her Majesty," she said. "We must see Her Majesty."

"And you suppose it is merely a matter of breaking into the Imperial Palace?" Yuan demanded. "Of defiling the imperial stairs, on which only His Majesty or the empress may ever tread? Of entering the throne room, where no female is ever allowed? Any of those crimes is punishable by instant death."

Constance got to her feet. She was *not* dead. Therefore it had only been a bluff. As she had known had to be the case, from the beginning. "If you will but take me before Her Majesty," she said, "everything will be explained."

Yuan nodded grimly. "I am indeed to take you before Her Majesty, devil woman. But not to save your worthless life. It is Her Majesty's wish to pronounce sentence on you herself."

\* \* \*

Constance looked at Kate, realized that her friend was utterly disheveled, her habit in a mess, her hair a gigantic tangled knot. And *she* had not been prepared for execution. She put up her hands, discovered that the entire neck and bodice of her blouse had been torn loose—and her hair could hardly be in any better condition, while she could still taste blood on her lip. As for what Yuan was saying . . . She tossed her head. "I am sure Her Majesty will be entirely sympathetic," she declared, "when she hears what we have come about. But we should like a few minutes in private, to attend to our toilettes, considering the treatment we have received from these . . ." She looked at the eunuchs in contempt. "These creatures."

"You will come with me now," Yuan said, "or I will give you back to them. That way." He pointed, and set off.

Kate glanced at the soldiers who immediately formed up behind them, at the eunuchs who waited to either side, still chattering and muttering at each other, clearly not yet convinced they had lost their prey. "I think we had better go with him," she whispered. "Anyway, we'll probably have more effect on the empress, looking like this."

Constance had already decided that it might be best not to protest *too* much at this stage, so they set off behind the general, holding hands now—Kate's idea—entirely like the two babes in the wood, Constance thought disgustedly. But the touch of Kate's hand *was* reassuring.

Yuan led them around the throne building and into another some distance behind it. Here again all was white marble, with exquisite light-colored tiles set into the floors, all pale blues and imperial yellows and delicate greens, with only the occasional harsh red design to catch the eye. And here, too, Constance observed to her relief, there were women, peering at them from doorways and behind pillars—she had feared they had entered a world inhabited entirely by men and half-men. But now great doors were being thrown open in front of them by two eunuchs, and Yuan was immediately sinking into the kowtow. "Kneel," he hissed at the girls. "Kneel."

Kate obediently knelt, and rather uncertainly inclined her body forward to touch the floor with her forehead. Constance remained standing. It was part of her predetermined attitude, and besides, she had not knelt on Chu-teh, so why should she kneel now? But she wished her knees would stop knocking, and thought that she would give ten years of her life for a cup of water, so parched was her throat.

She looked into a long room, in the main empty of furniture, although there were marble benches set against the walls, some distance away to each side. Up the center of the floor there was an imperial-yellow carpet, which led directly to a not-very-distinguished-looking high-backed wooden chair which occupied the exact center of the room. Here sat Tz'u-Hsi. This morning she wore blood red with green and yellow designs, and carried a matching fan. And this morning there was no softness in her face. Nor, Constance realized, was she alone, which was a disappointment; behind her chair there stood two more eunuchs—and from their clothes they were at the very top of their limited society—as well as several First Class mandarins, and also several women. None of them looked other than severe.

"Come closer, Mrs. Baird," Tz'u-Hsi commanded, her voice soft.

"Do not walk on the carpet," Yuan warned in another whisper. And this time Constance decided to take his advice. She advanced up the room, to the left of the carpet, until she stood immediately before the throne. What Yuan and Kate were doing, she had no idea.

"Is there no end to your insolence?" the empress inquired, still speaking quietly.

Constance refused to lower her gaze. "I must apologize, Majesty, for what has happened," she said. "And for the condition of my clothes. I was manhandled by your people. But the matter is most urgent."

"Urgent?" Tz'u-Hsi repeated. "What about *you* can be so urgent as to concern *me?* You have committed a crime in coming here. You have committed sacrilege in walking on the floating staircase, which is reserved for the Sons of Heaven alone. What can you say to me that can possibly prevent your instant execution?"

Constance drew a long breath. But she was sure that the only mistake she could make would be to collapse now or reveal in any way how terrified she was. "I came here to plead with you for the lives of others, Majesty," she said. "Not to sacrifice my own, although I shall do that if I must."

Tz'u-Hsi frowned at her. "The lives of others? Whose lives can possibly interest you, in my palace?"

"My servants, Peter and Elizabeth, Majesty. The twins you sent for after leaving Chu-teh yesterday."

"Their lives are not in danger, stupid devil woman."

Constance decided against reminding her that she had promised that title would not be used again. As Yuan had also called her by it, presumably she had forfeited her rehabilitation by coming here at all. But she refused to consider it as a strike against her. "Their very souls are in danger, Majesty," she said. "They have been baptized as Christians."

"And that is why I have taken them," Tz'u-Hsi said. "Because I was impressed with what I saw on your mission, because I wished to know more of this strange religion of yours. Because I wished my nephew to learn of it too, I will advance your servants, Mrs. Baird. You have sacrificed yourself for nothing."

Constance decided to ignore the last remark for the moment, and to suppress the panic which was lapping at her mind. "Can you advance a man by taking away his manhood, Majesty?"

Tz'u-Hsi raised her eyebrows. "How else may a male person advance in this palace, save he be a royal prince or a soldier?"

"Majesty," Constance said, "that is the Chinese way. But Peter, by adopting Christianity, has also adopted Christian values, and for a Christian, to be robbed of his manhood is a worse fate than death itself. As it is for a girl to be forced to submit to a man she does not love. Believe me, Majesty."

Tz'u-Hsi studied her for several seconds. "Love?" she asked at last. "What has love to do with it, when an emperor summons? But yet I must believe you, Mrs. Baird, as you have taken so considerable a risk to save these worthless creatures from what you must consider is a fate worse than death. But I do not know if it is possible." She half-turned her head, and the eunuch standing on her left whispered in her ear. Tz'u-Hsi smiled. "You will be relieved to know that it *is* possible, Mrs. Baird. The girl is still being prepared, and the boy . . . It is the custom of my executioners to provide a future eunuch with a last twenty-four hours of sensual experience before the operation. This the young man is now enjoying. Indeed, I wonder if he will be so pleased to have it terminated so abruptly. But it shall be done, as you have sacrificed so much to save them. I think you are very wrong, but the decision has been yours. They will be expelled from the Forbidden City and commanded to return to Chu-teh, within the hour."

Now Constance fell to her knees, great waves of relief sweeping over her to bring tears back to her eyes. "I knew you would be merciful, Majesty, could I but reach you and explain the situation to you. You may be sure of my everlasting gratitude. Of the gratitude of every Christian in China."

"Yours is indeed a strange religion," Tz'u-Hsi observed. "That you and your friend would die to save two people who were in no danger of death. I honor your courage and your self-sacrifice, Mrs. Baird. As you *must* die, I would offer you the use of the silken cord, instead of the ax or the knife.''

Once again the words were utterly incomprehensible to Constance's tumbling mind. ''Die?'' she whispered. ''You cannot be serious. I have done nothing to harm you. I—''

''Remember, General Yuan,'' Tz'u-Hsi said. ''The silken cord.'' She rose from her chair and everyone in the room bowed. The empress walked around the chair and to a doorway at the far end of the room, followed by her women. Constance realized that Kate and she were being left alone with the men. She ran forward, immediately had her arms seized by the two eunuchs.

''Majesty!'' she shouted. ''Majesty!'' she screamed as the door closed behind the last of the ladies. ''You cannot *do* this. I am not your subject to condemn. I am an American. Majesty!''

The door was closed, and tears were rolling down her face. General Yuan touched her on the shoulder. His face was sad, but there was a touch of contempt in his expression as well. ''That was unseemly,'' he said. ''Have you no courage, after all? Her Majesty has granted you a great boon. You should show gratitude, not shout like a fishwife. Come.'' He signaled the eunuchs to collect Kate, who had remained collapsed in the kowtow, quite unable to move.

''A great boon?'' Constance demanded, her brain a confused mixture of utter terror and teeming thought, teeming desire to understand what was happening. ''To be strangled is a boon?''

Yuan smiled as he escorted her through the doorway at the outer end of the hall and into the now brilliant morning sunlight. ''No one is going to strangle you, silly devil woman.''

Constance inhaled. She had been so overwrought. She looked over her shoulder at Kate, being half-carried and half-dragged by the eunuchs, boots scoring the grass. Poor Kate would never get over this morning, that was certain. But it would be something to laugh about when they were safely back in Chu-teh, in triumph, with Peter and Elizabeth beside them. ''I am sorry,'' she said. ''I had supposed . . . I am confused.''

''Of course you are, Mrs. Baird.'' Yuan escorted her up another brief flight of marble steps, and now he showed her into a small chamber, one in which she saw to her surprise there were no windows and no other door, and no furniture. Apart from the bare walls, there was only a single rounded beam of wood, which stretched across the middle of the room, about eight feet from the floor, with beneath it a single low wooden stool.

Hanging from the beam were six short lengths of yellow silken cord, each ending in a noose.

Constance checked in the doorway, and was given a gentle push by the general, which sent her staggering forward, so that her face actually brushed one of the nooses. Her head jerked away, and she turned to face Yuan, who was signaling Kate also to be brought inside. "The empress," the general said, "has granted you the privilege of ending your own lives, and in privacy."

Constance found that she was sitting on the marble floor—her knees had simply given way, and her thighs as well. Kate, released by the eunuchs just inside the door, had collapsed there, leaning against the wall, panting. But it had to be some form of Chinese torture, Constance told herself, alternately to promise them freedom and life, and then bring them face to face with catastrophe again. Some attempt to break their spirit.

"To be allowed the use of the silken cord is the greatest privilege which can be granted any criminal," Yuan said, standing above them. "And if it is done properly, it is quite painless, so far as can be judged. When you place the noose over your head, be careful to see that the knot is under your left ear. Then when you kick the stool away, your neck will snap. You will know nothing lasting longer than a split second, and you will have joined your ancestors. If you do not place the knot under your ear, you will dangle until you suffocate, and I would say that is extremely disagreeable." He glanced at Kate, who was now crying loudly. "Your friend has not your strength, Mrs. Baird; therefore I would suggest you assist her to depart first. Then you may attend to yourself. If you leave her, she may be unable to carry through the sentence, and then her fate would be too horrible to contemplate. And remember, you have but an hour. I will leave you now. One hour."

He turned for the door, and Constance at last realized that it was not either a game or a means of refined torture. They were genuinely expected to take their own lives.

The understanding brought her courage bubbling back, even if it was the courage of desperation. "Are you mad?" she shouted.

He checked, and turned, frowning.

"I am an American citizen," Constance told him. "Miss Mountjoy is a British citizen. Together our two countries are the most powerful in the world. If we are harmed, a British and American army will march on Peking and burn it to the ground, as the British and French burned the summer palace in 1861.'' She paused for breath.

''I understand the power of your great nations, Mrs. Baird,'' Yuan said quietly. ''Better perhaps than do most of my colleagues. Better even than Her Majesty, I think. But your people cannot help you here.''

''Perhaps not. But they can avenge us.''

''They cannot even avenge you, Mrs. Baird,'' Yuan went on. ''Because they do not know where you are.''

It was like a slap in the face. But she would not despair. ''Of course they do, or they will,'' she said. ''Do you not suppose my husband knows where I have gone? Do you not suppose Peter and Elizabeth will tell the world?''

''Peter and Elizabeth can tell the world nothing, save that they were sent home, no doubt because on closer inspection it was found that they did not, after all, measure up to the requirements of the palace,'' Yuan said. ''They have no idea it was your plea that saved them. As for Mr. Baird, he may well know where you *intended* to go, but it will be up to him to prove that you actually entered the Forbidden City, and he will never be able to do that. You are here, and here you will die and be buried. And do not suppose that Her Majesty is dealing harshly with you, or acting out of pique or anger. Her Majesty is above such emotions. But even she has to obey the law, and the law is written, and inviolable. She might even wish to save your worthless lives, but she cannot. You have committed sacrilege, and before the eyes of many of her people. Do you know what your fate *should* be? Death by a thousand cuts. Do you understand what that is?''

Constance could only stare at him, panting.

''It means that you would be publicly executed, by having a cut made in your body, a piece of your flesh removed, every hour for a thousand hours. And I can promise you, Mrs. Baird, that our executioners are so skillful that you would remain alive and screaming for an end to it *until* the thousandth cut. It is the most horrible of all ways to die. But were you Chinese, that is what would now be happening to you. That is what *should* be happening to you, even though you are white. The grant of the silken cord is reserved for those of royal blood or the most distinguished men in the empire. Believe me, Her Majesty could do no more. Now you have already wasted precious moments in which you should be making your peace with your god. I will leave you.''

It *was* happening. They were actually supposed to put those nooses over their heads, and stand on the stool, one after the other, and kick the stool away. . . .

"We cannot do it," she gasped.

Once again he checked in the doorway.

"It is against our religion," she said. "To take our own lives would be to condemn our souls to everlasting hell. We *cannot* do it."

Yuan faced her, his expression grave. "Is this true?" he asked.

A glimmer of hope? Constance's head bumped up and down as she nodded. "Yes. I swear it."

Yuan sighed. "That is sad," he said. "Very sad. For those given the option of the silken cord, and who refuse to use it, for whatever reasons, there can be only one punishment."

Constance clasped both hands around her throat. She knew that once again her mental stamina was about to be assaulted.

"The thousand cuts," Yuan said, "is at least reserved for men and women who it is anticipated will die with spirit. For cowards and cheats and liars, execution is by the bastinado."

"The . . ." She rose to her knees, remembering the poor wretch by the roadside in Yangtsun.

"For women," Yuan said, "it is one stroke upon the bare buttocks every tenth second until she dies. The sentence is carried out in public, and death sometimes takes a long time to come, if the woman is strong and well fed. I would estimate that you are strong and well fed, Mrs. Baird. So I would beg of you, for your own sake, try to come to some arrangement with your god, with your conscience, that will enable you to avoid such a painful and humiliating form of death. You have forty-five minutes."

The door closed behind him, and they heard the key turning in the lock.

The only sound in the room was Kate sobbing. Constance had no tears to shed. She had wept, in the confusion and physical misery of the manhandling she had received, the feel of the sword blade on her neck. Now she was aware only of anger, of outrage, that a bunch of hag-ridden Orientals should so presume to threaten her life, her existence, her place in the ordained scheme of things, and when she had committed no real crime against them.

But combined with the anger was the recurring theme that this had to be some game or some nightmare. That no people could be condemned to death so casually and so unemotionally and, indeed with such civilized courtesy. But then she remembered the way the rebel had been treated outside the Chu-teh gate.

Kate stirred, rose to her hands and knees, stared at Constance through a tear cloud, auburn hair hanging in straggling rat tails to either side of her face. Constance realized she could hardly look greatly different. In all the excitement of the past couple of hours she had not had the time to stop and feel more than terror or immediate pain. Now she knew only discomfort, dampness where the rain of the night had penetrated her clothing and where she had been equally soaked with sweat from fear and exertion. An awareness that her clothes—including her favorite habit—were torn and filthy, that her hat was lost, and that her hair must be equally a snarled mess. Henry thought she was beautiful. And she knew that the empress also thought she was beautiful. So did General Yuan, obviously, and the majority of the converts. If she was going to die, she wanted to die beautiful. She was seized with an absurd desire to take off all her clothes and comb out her hair with her fingers and *then* hang herself, so that she would surprise and astonish them with the beauty that was suspended before them and that they had so carelessly cast away.

But was that not just the first insidious suggestion that she *was* going to do as they wished? Not because the alternative was too horrid to be considered, but simply because the idea had been planted in her mind.

"Constance," Kate whispered. "Oh, Constance, what are we to do?"

Constance gazed at her. Although they were both twenty years old, the English girl's plump cheeks and figure made her look the younger, as her abject terror also made her appear younger. She was so afraid that Constance realized she would do whatever she was told to do. She would even hang herself now if Constance told her to.

And the Dragon Empire would have won another easy victory. Constance stuck out her chin. "We are going to do nothing."

"But . . ." Kate's eyes once again filled with tears. "They'll cane us to death. I don't want to be caned to death, Constance. Can you *imagine* being stretched on the ground before all those people, with nothing on . . ." Despite the tears, Kate's eyes were rolling, as usual.

"Oh, shut up," Constance said. "Your imagination is absurd. You should write books. Okay, so they'll cane us to death. But we won't give in to them. Not now, and not ever."

"Oh, Constance," Kate wailed. "Oh, Constance, I don't want to die. I didn't expect to die when I said I'd come with you. Constance, why should I die? Why should either of us die?" She fell on her face again, tears trickling across the marble tiles, her entire body racked by gigantic sobs. Constance held her shoulders and brought her close, stroked her hair into some semblance of order. "We just *have* to face it out, Kate," she said. "Don't you see? We can't just kill ourselves, even if it wasn't a sin. That would be to surrender, to accept that they are right and we have somehow done wrong. But we know we haven't done wrong. We've just broken one or two of their silly superstitious rules. We have to make them murder us, if that's what they mean to do, and hope that somebody gets to hear of it and makes them pay for it." She tried to smile. "Maybe, if we holler loud enough when they're beating us, they'll hear us in the legations. Anyway, I'm positive they can't execute two white women without *some* news of it getting out."

Kate only cried the louder. But the hour was nearly up. Constance stared at the door. She didn't want to think, to imagine, as Kate was too clearly doing. She wanted to shut her mind to everything save the present, to remain, if it were possible, sitting here on this floor for the rest of her life . . . but she could not stop herself wondering what *was* going to happen when the door opened. Would there be some sort of trial? Or would their next punishment follow immediately and automatically?

And would they be given anything to eat or drink? She had never been so thirsty in her life; she could not understand how Kate still had the moisture to weep. And her stomach seemed a great empty void, as if it had never received nourishment in her life. Her head hurt, and . . .

The door swung open, and she gazed at the eunuchs. Six of them, headed by one who had stood by Tz'u-Hsi's chair when she had sentenced them, and who had given her the information that Peter was still unharmed.

Constance rose to her knees, and then her feet, unsteadily, but dragging Kate with her. Somehow she had not expected the bastinado to be administered by *eunuchs*. That was too horrible to contemplate.

He glanced at the silken cords but did not seem concerned that they had not been used. No doubt he had been briefed by Yuan. Now he merely jerked his head. "You come," he said.

Constance hesitated, then squared her shoulders, tossed hair from her eyes, held Kate's arm, and walked out of the door into the morning sunlight.

\* \* \*

People—women and eunuchs—clustered to stare at them, and whispered to one another. Constance ignored them. She was concerned with the place of execution, where surely someone in authority would be present, either Yuan or the empress. But did she really wish to be stripped and spread-eagled before the empress? Or Yuan, come to think of it?

In any event, she could see no one she knew, and no indication of where the execution was to take place, either.

"In there," the eunuch said.

They were outside another, smaller dwelling. Their sentence was to be carried out indoors. There was a measure of relief. But when she went to mount the shallow steps, she found her knees would not move. It required an immense effort of will to go forward and upward again, still half-carrying Kate.

The doors at the top of the steps were open, and they entered . . . a bathhouse? The entire center of the marble floor was filled with bubbling hot water, an area not less than twenty feet square. Set around it were marble benches.

"You undress," the eunuch said. "And bathe."

My God, she thought. We have to be washed before being beaten to death. Or be subjected to fresh indignities. But having elected to die like white gentlewomen, Constance was determined that they would act the part to the bitter end. "Then you leave," she said.

The eunuch frowned at her.

"We will not undress before you," Constance said. "White women do not undress in the presence of . . . of men. You leave, and we will bathe."

He looked at his companion in mystification—only two of their escort had actually entered the bathhouse with them—but the other eunuch merely shrugged. They turned and left the house, closing the doors behind them. Constance felt quite cheated by the ease of her victory—but presumably it did not matter to the eunuchs if they now chose to commit suicide by drowning themselves.

"Constance?" Kate asked. "What is to happen? Why are we here?"

"God alone knows. I guess they like their victims to be sweet-smelling. But I'm going in. That water looks too good to be missed." She tore off her clothing, let it lie on the floor—she did not suppose she would be allowed to wear it again anyhow—and leaped into the pool. The water was even hotter than she had anticipated, but the more soothing to her exhausted and bruised muscles for that, and although it clearly contained some perfume, yet it was pure enough to drink. She sucked it into her mouth, holding it there and swilling it round and round to reach every parched recess, before swallowing it.

"Constance," Kate remonstrated, removing her boots and cautiously dipping one toe, "you'll make yourself ill."

"Not before tomorrow," Constance said.

They gazed at each other, and Kate suddenly burst out laughing. Her resilience was amazing. Now she stripped off the rest of her clothing, and also dived in. She really had a most splendid figure, Constance reflected. What in clothes merely appeared as plumpness turned out to be heavy breasts and strong, wide thighs; she might have been a Boucher model. They soaked, and gazed at each other, and then splashed water at each other, and smiled at each other, and then sank to their necks, and lower, allowing their entire heads to submerge, feeling the blessed heat seeping through their hair and across their scalps, feeling *clean* for the first time in a long time, it seemed, living the present, the glorious present, unable to believe that there was no future, that soon they would feel nothing but pain and shame . . . and turned with little gasps of dismay as the doors opened again, huddling together at the far end of the bath.

It was Tz'u-Hsi, accompanied by the two eunuchs, but also by several ladies. The empress stood on the edge of the bath, looking down at them. "Come out now," she said.

Constance instinctively stood up, then hastily crouched to her neck in the water again. "Send away your creatures first, Majesty," she said.

"Do you presume to give me orders?" Tz'u-Hsi inquired. "Are you ashamed of your body? God gave you what you possess so that you could be admired. To be ashamed of it is a sin. Come out, or they will come in and fetch you."

Constance hesitated, but realized the old lady meant what she said, and she had had enough manhandling for one morning. She stood up, climbed out of the bath; Kate followed her.

"So," Tz'u-Hsi remarked, "even your celestial hair is false."

Oh, Lord, Constance thought; not that again. "My hair is real, Majesty," she said, and watched a eunuch coming toward her, carrying a huge blue towel. He did not seem very interested in what he was looking at, and suddenly it seemed the most natural thing in the world to stretch out her hand and take the towel from him, although she felt a lot more secure when she had wrapped it around her, under her armpits. "All white women are like me, no matter what the color of their hair."

Tz'u-Hsi inspected Kate in turn. "Hers is lighter than yours," she pointed out.

"Because her hair is red, Majesty," Constance said.

"Bring them to me," Tz'u-Hsi said, and left the house, accompanied by her women. The eunuchs immediately produced voluminous robes, one in red and the other in blue, and little matching slippers.

"I suppose you had better wear the blue," Constance said regretfully. Red was not her favorite color, but it would clash with Kate's hair. How absurd that she should be allowing herself to be dressed by a half-man who would shortly . . . She refused to think about it, allowed herself to be led across the grass again, and into the empress's palace. Here they discovered Tz'u-Hsi alone, although the two eunuchs immediately took up their places behind her chair.

"Sit," Tz'u-Hsi commanded.

No chairs were provided, so the two girls sat on the floor, tucking up their legs in the Chinese fashion. The whole morning had taken on a totally unreal aspect, their emotions had been stretched to and fro so often it was impossible for them to think clearly, and they were in any event light-headed through hunger.

As Tz'u-Hsi apparently understood. For now one of the eunuchs brought them little bowls of food, roast duck which had been removed from the bone and dipped in some kind of rich sauce, and corn, and rice, all of which they were expected to eat with chopsticks. But this art they had learned on Chu-teh.

Tz'u-Hsi watched them eat for several seconds. Then she said, "So you have refused the silken cord. Because it is against your religion."

"Yes, Majesty," Constance said. She chewed very slowly, because it was almost painfully pleasant to feel the taste of the duck slipping down her throat.

"And are you aware of the penalty for those who refuse such charity?"

"General Yuan has told us what is going to happen to us, Majesty."

"But you are undisturbed at the prospect. Perhaps you cannot believe I would have two white women flogged to death."

"That must be your decision, Majesty," Constance said, meeting her gaze. "We are at least confident that we shall be avenged."

"You are a bold young woman," Tz'u-Hsi said. "As well as a beautiful one. But I formed that impression when I first met you. You remind me, as you did then, of myself as a girl. I have been studying your situation. To enter the Forbidden City uninvited is a crime which must carry the death penalty. I have no power to change the law. But it is possible to alter circumstances, and thus preserve your lives. Does this appeal to you?"

Constance opened her mouth, and closed it again. Beside her Kate seemed to have an acute case of indigestion. "It appeals to us, Majesty," Constance said.

"The circumstances I envisage," Tz'u-Hsi said, "are that it is put about that I brought you here as royal concubines."

Constance almost choked as her head jerked. Tz'u-Hsi, misinterpreting her reaction, smiled sadly. "I cannot send you to the emperor," she said, "because you are not a virgin, and in any event, I do not suppose it would be a good thing for him to take a white woman to his bed; you could have a son who might cause untold difficulties to the dynasty. But you can be of great assistance to me in a problem I have."

Constance swallowed, and got her breathing under control. She dared not look at Kate.

"I have a large family," Tz'u-Hsi explained. "I speak of myself, personally. Of course my sister and *her* family are not of royal blood, but they are nonetheless the highest in the land, after the princes of the blood, and they are also faithful supporters of myself. This is important," she said ingenuously.

Constance discovered that she was eating again, chewing even more slowly. Thought was utterly suspended. She *dared* not think.

"Thus when it became necessary to *treat* with the long-nosed hairy barbarians"—Tz'u-Hsi's expression twisted with contempt—"I sent one of my own cousins as ambassador to Great Britain and France. With him went his son, Prince Ksian Fu. I should have known better. The prince was of a young and impressionable age . . . ." She gazed at Constance. "And his father did not keep him under proper control. He returned a Christian."

Constance swallowed the last of the duck, licked her fingers clean, almost unaware of what she was doing.

"As such," Tz'u-Hsi said, "he is difficult to employ. A prince's duties relate mainly to the religious requirements of the throne, but Ksian Fu refuses to accept the gods of his ancestors, or indeed the importance of his ancestors themselves. He has become the most utter barbarian in his outlook. Nor will he fulfill his duty in the domestic field, either, as he regards concubinage as a sin, much as you do yourself, and declares that he will never take any woman merely for the procreation of children, but talks such claptrap as mutual love and respect, as if a prince has the time to consider such irrelevancies. It has been a source of great worry to me. But your presence here has made me evaluate possible solutions, at once to your danger and to his problems."

She paused, and Constance realized that she was expected to make some sort of reply. And obviously she had to keep talking, while she endeavored to think. "You spoke of concubinage, Majesty," she said. "But if Prince Ksian Fu is a Christian . . ."

Tz'u-Hsi shrugged. "*He* will speak of marriage, and claims to wish but one 'wife' throughout his life. Imperial princes of course may not take wives, only concubines. It would be quite impossible if on the death of an emperor before any of his heirs was old enough to rule—this happens too often—his 'wife' should arrogate herself as queen regent or some such thing. In those cases the regency is vested in the new emperor's mother, as is proper." She did not expand on how she, having acted as regent for her own son, had then managed to become regent for the present emperor, her nephew, and to retain such power even after the Kuang Hsu emperor had come of age. "But we are merely playing with words, as far as you are concerned. Ksian Fu will consider himself married, and his wife may also consider herself to be married. That is neither here nor there. It is my opinion that a woman with a personality like yours will be one to whom he may respond, and with whom he might discover these qualities of love and affection which he seeks. I may say, Mrs. Baird, that he has looked upon you, and found you physically desirable, so there is no problem in *that* direction."

"He has done *what?*" Constance shouted, rising to her knees.

"I used the opportunity to have him survey you as you bathed," the empress explained.

"But . . . Oh, my God!"

"You are being childish again," Tz'u-Hsi pointed out. "You would hardly expect a man to take a woman to his bed without being sure she is whole and undiseased? And if you are going to his bed in any event, what difference does it make for him to have seen you?"

"But . . ." Constance glanced at Kate, who was staring at the empress with her mouth open. Quite apart from the suggestion that the prince would wish to *see* her after they were married.

But of course that was an absolutely ridiculous concept. "I cannot marry your nephew, Majesty," she said. "I am already married. I have a child."

"Your marriage will have to be terminated, and your former husband will have to make arrangements for you to be replaced as a mother for his child. As I have explained, such a procedure, that of taking a *spoiled* woman to one's bed, is not a course practiced by us Manchu, or indeed by the Chinese, but it is apparently accepted in your society."

"Well, it isn't, really," Constance said. If only her head would stop spinning, and she could think. But coherent thought, after everything that had happened to her today, and after she had ridden all night, was next to impossible. Of course, what the empress was proposing was quite impossible. Quite apart from Henry . . . although why should she consider Henry, when she now knew that she positively disliked the man? But she *was* married to him. Yet it would be possible to obtain a divorce, especially if the Empress of China wished it. However, to live the rest of her life in this gloomy convent with some man probably old enough to be her father . . . What about all the tales Kate had told her of Chinese lovemaking, as far removed from Henry's perfunctory caress as it was possible to imagine? She had never met a single Chinese with whom she could possibly consider . . . There was a lie. She *had* considered it, however subconsciously, with Lin-tu. But Lin-tu was young and handsome and . . .

Anyway, there was Charles. She could never abandon Charles.

If she refused, though, would she not be losing Charles anyway, by means of the cane?

"I can see that this idea attracts you," Tz'u-Hsi said. "I think it would be best if you met my nephew. Again, this is not the Chinese or the Manchu way, but he has told me it is the Christian way. Fetch the prince, Chiang," she told the head eunuch, who obediently hurried out of the inner doorway.

"I . . ." Constance chewed her lip. "Your Majesty . . ."

The door was opening again, and Chiang had returned, accompanied by a man. Prince Ksian Fu was tall, only an inch or so under six feet, Constance estimated, and young, hardly twenty-five years of age. His face was solemn but handsome, his mustache European in that it was a brief wisp to either side of his upper lip. He wore Chinese clothes, but moved with European vigor, and he flushed as he came face to face with the two girls.

"Forgive me," he said in perfect English. "And forgive the

manner in which this affair has been handled. My aunt . . . well, she knows no other way. But you may believe that I will make up for all the misfortune that has been visited upon you, if you will but give me the opportunity to do so.'' He held out his hands—to Kate Mountjoy.

# 5

# The Bride

Constance, already rising to her knees, sank back on to her haunches. Kate merely stared at the prince while she slowly extended her hand; she hardly seemed to be breathing.

"You stupid boy," the empress said. "Have you gone blind?"

Ksian Fu turned his head. "Majesty?"

"This is the one," Tz'u-Hsi pointed out. "The one with yellow hair."

"But this is the one *I* chose," the prince said. "The one with *red* hair."

"She? She is nothing but a foolish scatterbrain," Tz'u-Hsi snapped. "I wish you to wed the American girl with the celestial hair."

"And I wish to marry this one, Majesty," Ksian Fu said. "I do not *care* if she is already married and a mother. She is the one I wish, and you said it could be arranged."

"I am not married, or a mother," Kate announced.

Constance attempted yet again to gather her thoughts, to stop merely thinking over and over that this delightfully attractive young man had just watched her cavorting in a bath . . . but he had also watched Kate cavorting in a bath—there was the trouble.

She tried to tell herself that she was not piqued or insulted, but rather relieved by his choice. On the other hand, the whole idea was just as impossible now as before. "There has been some mistake," she said.

"I can see that," Tz'u-Hsi said angrily. "My nephew and I appear to have been talking at cross-purposes. As we usually do."

"But if she is *not* married, Majesty, then she will be a virgin," the prince was saying.

"Of course I'm a virgin," Kate declared.

"Then nothing could be finer. What is your name?"

"Kate . . . Catherine Mountjoy," Kate said, allowing herself to be raised to her feet.

"Kate Mountjoy," Ksian Fu repeated, half to himself, as he might have repeated a verse from the Bible.

Constance also got up, unaided. "This is quite impossible," she said.

"Of course it is," Tz'u-Hsi agreed. "I wish him to marry you. I wish you to come and live here, with me, in the Forbidden City, to tell me about the world outside, and amuse me with your insolence and your courage."

"But . . . that is impossible too," Constance said.

"If I cannot marry Miss Mountjoy, I shall never marry at all," Ksian Fu declared.

The dowager empress glared at him, then at Kate, who attempted a bright smile, with considerable success.

"Oh, very well," Tz'u-Hsi said. "You may have them both, I suppose."

"No," Constance said.

"No," the prince said.

"Oh," Kate said.

"I wish only one wife," Ksian Fu said. "I may *have* only one wife."

"Yes," Constance said. "A Christian is allowed only one wife."

"I am surrounded by insolence," Tz'u-Hsi complained. "Nobody pays my word any heed. I should have let them cut off your heads and be done with it."

"Then would my life have been ruined," Ksian Fu said. "If I cannot marry Miss Mountjoy, I shall use the silken cord myself."

He looked so determined it was possible to suppose he was serious.

"Oh . . . marry whom you choose," Tz'u-Hsi shouted. "But do not suppose I wish to have *her* about the palace. I shall send her away. I shall send you both away. I shall send you to . . . to Manchuria. Yes, that is it. I will send you to Manchuria. I will make you viceroy in Port Arthur. Then I will not have to look upon your face, you stupid, disobedient boy."

"Thank you, Majesty," Ksian Fu said gravely.

"But Kate *can't* marry you," Constance cried. "I mean . . . the whole idea is absurd."

"Why is it absurd, Mrs. Baird?" he asked.

"Well . . . a white woman and a Chinese man . . . well . . . can you *imagine* what her parents will say?"

"They'll be horrified." Kate giggled.

"Exactly. And—"

"*Any* parents," Tz'u-Hsi said, "will be gratified to have their daughter marry a prince and be accepted into the House of Ch'ing. How dare you describe Ksian Fu as Chinese? Obviously you are angry that *you* were not the one chosen, Constance."

"I?" Constance flushed scarlet, and hated herself, even as her brain went into another spin that the empress of all China should have addressed her by her Christian name.

"Well, so am I," Tz'u-Hsi said. "But I will arrange for you to come to visit me from time to time. I have always been forced to settle for what pleasure I can get. Very well, Ksian Fu, take the redheaded one. I will see to an escort for Mrs. Baird to be returned to the mission." She smiled at Constance. "It will be put about that you came here as chaperon for your young friend."

"But . . ." Once again Constance could not believe the utter casualness with which these matters appeared to be settled in China. "Just like that?"

"What else would you have me do?" the empress asked.

"Well . . . don't you suppose the matter should be discussed with Mr. and Mrs. Mountjoy?"

"There is no need for that," Tz'u-Hsi said. "Their daughter has been summoned to a royal bed. I will see that they are informed. Indeed, you may inform them yourself, Constance, upon your return. They will be delighted."

"Delighted?" Constance cried.

"You may tell them that I will bring Kate out to Chu-teh," the prince said. "For a Christian wedding. In a very short time. You have no objection to that, Majesty?"

Tz'u-Hsi pointed at him. "You had better make haste. You are going to Port Arthur just as soon as it can be arranged. The very end of the earth, Port Arthur," she said with considerable satisfaction.

"You mean you'll consummate the marriage first?" Constance asked. "And *then* have the ceremony?"

"Is there something wrong with that?" the prince asked. "As long as the ceremony is held?"

Constance wanted to tear her hair out by the roots. She looked at Kate. "Don't you think someone should ask the bride what *she* feels?"

"Of course you are right," Ksian Fu said courteously. "Miss Mountjoy, will you come with me now?"

"Oh, yes, your Highness," Kate said. "Oh, yes."

The soldiers left Constance at the Chu-teh gate, which was swung open for her. Slowly she rode through, aware that everyone in the mission was gathered to stare at her, and not least because she was still wearing Chinese robes, as her own clothes were ruined beyond repair.

She had spent the night in the Imperial Palace, but had been forced to talk far into the evening with Tz'u-Hsi, utter nonsense about the world of the West, about the ships and the weapons used by the great powers, about education and political systems, and she had in any event been exhausted . . . and all the while knowing that somewhere in the palace, Kate was having the experience of her life. An experience which should have been hers.

Of course it could never have been hers. Even had Ksian Fu chosen her, she would have had to decline. She was Mrs. Henry Baird, and she was a mother . . . but how she wished he *had* chosen her. She *was* far more intelligent than Kate, and she was prettier too, she thought. But presumably Kate had the more attractive figure, simply because there was more of it, and equally presumably, to a Chinese, red hair must be just as fascinating as yellow. In fact, she told herself, she had had a very fortunate escape, because she might not have had the courage to say no, *had* he chosen her.

But if only he had. She had never seen so handsome a man. He had all of Henry's looks and personality with none of Henry's meanness, and obviously he would suffer none of Henry's prurient torments.

But it was Henry she now had to face. Henry and the Mountjoys. She felt unutterably weary. And it was at least as much a continuing confusion as lack of sleep. She still did not know how much of what had happened yesterday had been a vast charade designed at once to test her courage and weaken her resolution. She wanted to sit down and think about it all, and *try* to understand—but she was not going to be given the chance.

"Constance!" There he was, flanked by the Mountjoys, and, as usual in moments of crisis, by Father Pierre and the nuns. And there was no relief at seeing her in his face, no joy in his greeting.

"Where is Kate?" Joan Mountjoy asked.

Constance dismounted, handed her reins to William—a cowed

and distressed William. "Have Peter and Elizabeth arrived yet?" she asked.

"They came in last night," Henry said, not attempting to kiss her or even to take her hand. "Where did *you* spend last night?" He gazed at her Chinese gown.

"In the palace," she said. "Where is Charles?"

"Charles is having his morning nap," Joan Mountjoy said. "Do you really expect us to believe that tale, Constance?"

Constance shrugged. "It's true."

"Do you mean Kate slept at the *palace?*" James Mountjoy asked. "But . . . where is she now?"

"She has remained there," Constance said.

They stared at her.

"She is to be married to a Manchu prince," Constance explained. "She will be coming out to see you in due course, but for the moment . . . she is staying there."

"You left Kate at the palace?" Joan Mountjoy whispered. "Oh, my God!"

"You abandoned your friend to those Chinese devils?" Henry shouted. "You did *that?*"

"She can't marry anybody," James Mountjoy was saying, apparently to himself. "She's not yet twenty-one."

Constance looked from face to face. And realized that it made very little difference what she said. They had already made up their minds what must have happened. The trouble was, the reality was not so very different from their supposition of it— only Kate's happy acceptance of the situation saved it from the horror they envisaged. Certainly there was no explanation she could attempt which would not make matters worse. "You had best talk about it to Kate when she comes," she said.

"You left her," Joan screamed. "You left my daughter to be . . . to be . . ." She burst into tears.

"I think I left her to be happy," Constance said, and walked away from them to the bungalow.

Constance became aware that they were following her, straggling behind her like geese—and clucking like geese as well.

"But is she all *right?*" Joan Mountjoy asked.

Constance climbed the stairs to her veranda. "I imagine she is better than ever before in her life," she said. "Now, will you excuse me? I am very tired." She went inside, faced Elizabeth, carrying Charles. "Oh, Lizzie," she said. "I am so very glad to see you."

To her surprise, Elizabeth did not look equally glad. She

seemed almost embarrassed, while Peter, peering at her through the kitchen doorway, scuttled away the moment she looked at him. She sighed; no doubt Henry had been on at them. She took the baby from the girl's arms, went into her bedroom, sat down with Charles on her lâp, and raised her head as Henry entered.

"I do not know what to say," he remarked. "I really do not. I am quite astounded by the whole thing. Certain it is that no man can ever have made a greater mistake regarding the character of the woman he chose as his wife. I am astounded. Quite astounded."

"I am very tired, Henry," she said. "I should like to lie down and have a rest."

"Lie down?" he demanded. "Lie down? You have to pack your things."

She frowned at him. "Pack my things? Whatever for?"

"Well, obviously you cannot possibly remain here, remain in China, after this . . . this escapade. I shall send you down to Tientsin, with money for a fare back to San Francisco. Back to Richmond. Yes, you shall go back to Richmond."

She gazed at him, "You intend to send me back to Virginia?"

"Well, my dear girl, after your behavior, setting half China by the ears, spending the night in the Forbidden City, abandoning a young girl to the foul caresses of a Chinese lecher . . . no doubt submitting yourself to . . . well, I don't know what to say."

"You," Constance said, "make me sick."

He checked, completely taken aback.

"Tell me something," Constance went on. "When William told you where Kate and I had gone, what did you think?"

"I was astounded," Henry declared. "Quite astounded. So was Mountjoy. I can tell you—"

"Did you suppose we were in any danger?"

"Well, of course I did. Two white women, alone in that den of iniquity . . ."

"So what did you do about it?"

"Well, I prayed. We all prayed. And we wept, I can tell you that. We all wept."

"You prayed," Constance said. "And you wept. But it did not occur to any of you to ride into Peking and attempt to rescue us?"

"Well . . . ." He flushed. "We knew that would be impossible."

"Ah," she said. "You knew that would be impossible. So you prayed, and wept. Well, Henry, maybe your prayers were answered. I have felt the edge of an executioner's sword, right here.'' She touched the nape of her neck. "But he didn't actually chop off my head. As for the den of iniquity, or Chinese lechers, they are at least honest about their iniquity, their lechery. They do not dream and then become afraid to act out their dreams. Now, get out of my room. I wish to sleep.''

He pointed. "You are going to pack and leave Chu-teh. Now. Your coming here was the greatest disaster that has ever overtaken this mission. You will leave within the hour. You will—''

"Henry,'' she said, "I am going nowhere. Much as I would love to leave you and never ever see you again as long as I live, I am not allowing you to rob me of my child.''

"Your child.'' He sneered. "You have forfeited all rights to the boy.''

"He is *my* child,'' she said. "And I intend to be his mother. That is why I am here now. Do you know, I *was* offered a bed by one of those lecherous Chinese . . .'' Well, to all intents and purposes, she thought. "And I refused it, because I am your wife and Charles's mother. I think *I* am the fool, you know, Henry.''

"You are disgusting. You are nauseating. You are impudent. I wish you off Chu-teh within the hour.''

Constance gazed at him. "I am not going anywhere, Henry. I could not even if I wanted to. The empress has expressly forbidden me ever to leave China. She wishes me to attend her once every week in Peking, to talk. If you wish to send me away, *you* will have to go to the Forbidden City yourself and ask her permission. Would you like me to tell you what happens to those who enter the Forbidden City uninvited?''

"Gifts for the lady mother of the Princess Ksian Fu,'' explained Chiang, the head eunuch, appearing rather like the most unlikely of peddlers as he gestured his coolies to open the chest on the Mountjoys' front veranda. Certainly Joan Mountjoy stared at him as if he were a creature from the pit, on earth to suborn her soul.

Successfully. She could not stop herself exclaiming in bemused wonderment as he started to display his wares. "Best emeralds,'' he said. "From the mountains of Tibet. These rubies come from Mongolia, from the ancient home of the Ch'ing themselves.'' He brushed the jewels to one side, began placing the magnificent porcelain dishes and cups and saucers on the wooden floor. "Best cloisonné,'' he said. "Created by His Majesty's own craftsmen.'' Another chest was brought forward, and the bales of material unloaded. "Best silk," he said. "You wear, mother of the princess."

Joan gazed at him, then at Constance, flushed, and looked at her husband. "I cannot possibly accept all of this," she protested.

"For the father of the Princess Ksian Fu," Chiang said, and clapped his hands. More coolies hurried forward, to place on the floor a sporting rifle, the steel of which was inlaid with bronze and jade. "To shoot the fowl," Chiang explained. "And to find the game . . ." He gestured at the gate, where four magnificent horses waited, each held by its own groom, each as richly caparisoned as any mount in the Imperial Guard, in green and celestial yellow. "Tartar ponies," Chiang explained. "The fastest in the world. From the celestial hunting park, in Jehol."

"My word," James Mountjoy remarked. "I say, Henry, those are rather fine-looking beasts."

"They are yours, father of the Princess Ksian Fu," Chiang explained.

"Well," Mountjoy said, gazing at his wife in turn.

"I am sure Her Majesty would take it as an insult were you to return them," Constance said. She was present only because Chiang had refused to reveal the gifts until she had been summoned. But she thought this was as good a time as any to attempt to restore relations on Chu-teh to something approaching their old footing; for the past week she had quite literally been sent to Coventry. Even by her servants, which was the most amazing and distressing thing of all. Peter and Elizabeth could not avoid speaking to her, but her presence certainly seemed to embarrass them, while the twins' parents also appeared quite lacking in any gratitude. Nor could she discover why. Henry had not spoken to her at all since their quarrel, and slept in the spare bedroom, as he had done for the past year anyway.

And apparently she was not going to be allowed to return to the fold that easily, either. Joan Mountjoy gave a monumental sniff. "I am sure, Constance," she said, "that James is capable of deciding what is best."

"Well, of course," James Mountjoy said. "It would be improper to return the gifts. We shall put them to the best possible use. Oh, indeed. You may tell the empress that we are most grateful. Most grateful."

"If only we could learn some news of our daughter," Joan said. "We have heard not a word. We do not know if she is alive or dead, happy or weeping. Have you news of her, sir?"

Chiang grinned at her. "Your daughter, the Princess Ksian Fu, comes to visit you tomorrow," he said.

"Tomorrow?" Joan cried.

"Tomorrow," Constance breathed. Oh, thank God for that, she thought. A friendly face at last. And more than that; she was actually dying to hear all about it.

"Tomorrow," Chiang agreed. "She comes to you with her husband, the Prince Ksian Fu. She comes to have a wedding. You must prepare. For her wedding."

The bride wore celestial yellow. With her smile, and her red hair, and her personality, she seemed to fill Chu-teh with the aura of her presence. She was a stranger to them all, even Constance. Kate Mountjoy had always had a ready smile and an infectious sense of humor, just as she had always been a pretty girl. But to these basic assets she had suddenly, in the space of a week, added a *presence*, an awareness of who and what she was, which gave her somewhat pert looks a true beauty, made her seem older than her years—in the past she had always appeared younger—made her *glow*.

Her parents were clearly unable to believe their eyes. James Mountjoy could only stare at her—he kept staring at her throughout the entire ceremony, which he conducted—while Joan kept whispering, "But are you all *right*, darling?" by which Constance decided she meant "Have you actually lost your virginity yet?"—as if there could be any doubt about that.

But then, they were equally overwhelmed by the personality of the prince, who dominated them with his easy confidence and his flowing conversation. "Kate tells me you come from Cheltenham, Mrs. Mountjoy," he said. "I know it well. I spent a week there a few years ago. Do you know, I saw Gloucestershire play Surrey? I watched W. G. Grace make a century. I do not suppose I have ever beheld a grander sight."

Henry was so bemused he actually turned to Constance for an explanation, the first time he had looked at her, at least openly, during the week.

"The prince is talking about cricket, I think," she whispered. "Dr. Grace is a very famous English cricketer."

"Why, do you know, Mr. Baird," Ksian Fu was saying, "with that black beard of yours you look very like the great man himself. Indeed you do."

Henry was left obviously trying to decide whether or not he had just been insulted.

"I'm sorry to have to tell you that Kate and I will be leaving for Port Arthur at the end of next week," Ksian Fu was telling Joan Mountjoy. "I have been appointed viceroy of the city and port. Do you know, Constance," he went on, smiling at her, "your old friend General Yuan Shih-k'ai has also received an important posting. He is to be resident minister in Seoul, in Korea. And that is no sinecure, I can promise you, with the Japanese behaving so oddly. They'd like Korea, you know. Indeed they would."

"There's no danger at Port Arthur, is there, your Highness?" Joan asked anxiously.

"Of course there isn't, Mother," Kate said.

"Indeed there is not, Mrs. Mountjoy," Ksian Fu said. "Port Arthur is in Manchuria, not Korea. The Japanese have no business in Manchuria. Anyway, it is a place of immense strength. You must come to visit us there. I will be pleased to show it to you. And Kate will need you, as soon as she is pregnant."

"Preg . . " Joan looked at her husband, as if unable to believe that someone had actually used such a word in her presence—or that it would be possible for her daughter to bear a child for a Chinese.

"We intend to commence a family just as soon as it is possible," Ksian Fu explained. "I wish a large family. So does Kate." He smiled. "Your grandchildren, Mrs. Mountjoy."

Joan burst into tears.

"I don't suppose she'll ever get used to my being a princess," Kate said, managing at last to get Constance by herself.

"But *you* have got used to the idea," Constance said. "One can tell it by looking at you."

"Oh, yes," Kate said. "Oh, *yes*. You can have no *idea*, Constance. But I suppose you have, as you are married."

"I doubt it," Constance said.

"You mean you have never . . . well . . ." Kate held her arm and almost leaned on her to whisper. "Have you never felt that the whole world was about to explode, and you with it?"

"Good heavens no," Constance said.

"Oh, my," Kate said. "But that's what it's all about. It's slow, as he plays with you . . . Henry doesn't play with you?"

Constance had no idea what she was talking about, as Kate could tell.

"You mean he never touches you with his fingers?"

"What a . . ." Constance bit her lip. "Disgusting idea" could not be the right thing to say, looking at Kate's expression. "Marvelous idea" might have been more appropriate. But *Henry?*

"Oh, it is glorious," Kate whispered. "He strokes, and you start to feel, and come wet, and then he enters . . . and how he enters. Have you never sat on Henry's lap and let him enter you like that?''

''I have never sat on Henry's lap,'' Constance said carefully and truthfully.

''He goes in and in and in,'' Kate said. ''It seems forever. You almost expect him to come out of your mouth. And then you just explode. I can't describe it. It . . . it's like nothing else in all the world. It's just . . . just . . . oh, just marvelous. You *must* have felt it, Constance. You must have.''

I, Constance thought, have never felt anything since arriving on Chu-teh. But she had felt, not *it*, certainly not as Kate was describing it, but a suggestion that it was possible, in Yorktown. A very long time ago. And all this, she thought, might have been mine.

And could still be hers, perhaps, because Kate was still whispering. ''If you never have, and you want to . . . I'm sure the empress would arrange it for you next time you visit her.''

Constance shot her a glance.

''Oh, I know it's wrong,'' Kate said. ''For a Christian. But if you could forget about being a Christian, just for an hour . . . it's fantastic. You're prepared by a eunuch, you know. Yes, you are,'' she insisted as her friend stared at her, openmouthed. ''He bathes you and . . . well, massages you, and then wraps you in a blanket and takes you to your lord. Oh, it's unbelievable, how you feel . . . and in the palace, who's to know, Constance? Who's ever to *know?*''

Constance gazed at Henry, who was gazing at her from across the room.

''The poor girl is obviously drugged with some fiendish Chinese concoction,'' Henry remarked.

Constance, bending over Charles's cot as she tucked him in for the night, raised her head in surprise. Although the celebration of the wedding had ended three hours before—and the bride and groom had long since departed in their palanquin for the more congenial atmosphere of the Forbidden City—she had left Henry sitting on the Mountjoy veranda with James, had not heard him enter the house, and certainly had not expected him in the nursery while she was there, as he had not visited Charles with her at any time since her return from Peking. ''I have no idea what you're talking about,'' she said.

''Well, to appear so . . . so normal. Even happy, in such terrible circumstances.''

''The prince happens to have made her happy. *Is* making her happy all the time." She kissed Charles, stepped past her husband into the corridor. "There is every reason for her to appear happy. Because she is happy."

She went into her bedroom; again, to her surprise, he followed her.

"Now, you know that has to be impossible," he said. "A white woman, being forced to submit to the foul embrace of an Oriental every night . . . my dear Constance, if you could only manage to understand something of what these people are really like . . ."

She sat on the bed. "You are really quite incredible, Henry," she said. "How long have you spent in Chu-teh? Ten years? And you still regard the Chinese as being of a different species? I'll bet you suppose Kate will never have children, because she hasn't actually married a human being."

"Well, I . . ." He flushed.

"As for their sexual relations—"

"Really, Constance," he said. "Please—"

"Oh, the hell with your absurd prudery," she snapped. "I said, their sexual relations. Because they do have them, you know. As often as possible. But the Chinese happen to regard sex as something to be enjoyed, to be experienced mutually. They make love, Henry; they do not perform a *duty*. They stroke each other and they kiss each other and they make it last as long as they can, until they explode together. At least that is how Kate describes it. And it is the most wonderful thing in the world, apparently. I wish to God *I* was married to a Chinese, or at least a *man*, rather than a frightened schoolboy."

She paused, partly for breath, and partly in concern, because it was not a subject she had ever meant to discuss with him in their new circumstances. And certainly she thought she might have made a mistake. His face was red, and he was breathing heavily.

"You are a diseased thing," he said. "A woman of Sodom and Gomorrah. That is what you are. A mental whore. But a physical whore as well, I suspect, since your visit to Peking. Admit it, woman. Admit the crimes you permitted there. Tell me what they did to your body."

Constance stood up. "You are being quite obscene, Henry. Now, kindly leave my room."

Henry closed the door. "So," he said. "You want to be stroked, do you? You want to be played with. You want to *sweat*, and *moan*, and deliver yourself over to *passion*."

Constance realized that she was probably in greater physical danger at this moment than ever in the Forbidden City. Therefore it was necessary to pursue the same strategy, even more forcefully. She stuck out her chin. "Yes," she said. "Yes, I do wish to feel those things. I would suppose, if I were to die without ever having experienced what love is all about, I should only ever have half lived. But I don't want to experience it with you, Henry. Never with *you!*"

He glared at her, and then, quite without warning, swung his fist at her chin. She swayed away from the blow, but lost her balance as she stumbled into the bed, saw him reaching for her, and turned, sliding down to her knees. Before she could get up again, he was kneeling against her, pressing her into the bedpost, while his body squirmed against hers and his fingers dug into her blouse, wrenching it from her shoulders to allow his hands inside.

"You want to be touched," he snarled. "You want to be stroked."

His hand was down the front of her petticoat, holding her left breast as he might have held a baseball, she thought, squeezing it and hurting her, while his mouth sucked at her neck. Desperately she thrust her fingers into his groin, and he gave a grunt and released her. She endeavored to crawl away from him, and was seized by the boot; she tried to kick him away or the boot off, but the lacing was too tight, and she fell to her face. Henry immediately crawled up her, carrying her skirts with him to expose her stockings.

"Why don't you moan?" he asked. "Why don't you scream your pleasure? Isn't this what you have always dreamed of, slut?"

Once again she tried to rise, and once again she was forced to the floor, and now she realized that he had pulled down her drawers and was massaging her bottom with hard, angry fingers, driving them between her legs to hurt her, sitting on her thighs so that she could not move. And realized too that he must have wanted to do something like this to her almost from their first meeting, two years before. If only he had, then, while it had been possible for them to love. Even if his only outlet had to be violence, it might have been possible to accept, where there was also love. But now . . .

He fell on her suddenly, crushing her to the floor. She supposed she was about to be abused, and then realized that he was still fully dressed and that he was weeping, great sobs . . . but that he wanted her could not be doubted; she could feel him right through his trousers.

But if she accepted him now, then she *would* be the whore he had described. With an immense effort she pushed down and rolled herself over. He fell away from her, lay on his back, his arm thrown across his eyes. Constance got to her knees, and then her feet, panting, pulled up her drawers and straightened her skirt, took off the torn blouse and replaced it with a shawl. She felt more bruised than even after her set-to with the eunuchs.

Henry sat up. "Constance," he begged, "forgive me. Oh, forgive me."

She gazed down at him. He was the most contemptible creature she had ever met, she thought. And the whole world considered him one of their very finest specimens. But he was her husband, and the father of her child. And however contemptible, he still spread a great deal of good around him, and would presumably continue to do so.

As must she, because there was nothing else for her to do with her life now.

"I will forgive you, Henry," she said. "If you swear to me never to come through that door again, uninvited."

"You are not happy, Constance," Tz'u-Hsi observed.

They sat together in the empress's private garden, a place of exquisite peace and beauty, its flowering shrubs separated by the most intricately carved marble statuary—strange beasts and gods— its gentle stream the home of brilliantly red and yellow goldfish, and drank tea, while the imperial dogs, specially bred and called Pekingese, all flat upturned noses and bushy tails, snarled and wrestled at their feet.

It was a haven within the haven of the Forbidden City, which Constance had never suspected to exist. Certainly, sitting here without even the ever-present eunuchs to distract her, she had no desire to be reminded of the long nightmare that was Chu-teh.

"I, Majesty? I am . . ."

"You must practice truthfulness," Tz'u-Hsi remarked gently. "You are not happy. You sit there looking sad. I do not like to see you looking sad. Tell me the cause of your unhappiness."

Constance gazed at her. I want to be loved, she thought. Oh, I want to be loved, as Kate is being loved, physically as well as mentally, with a man's whole body, his whole being.

As Frank Wynne might love her? There was a guilty thought. She was carrying a letter from him in her handbag now. In fact he wrote to her quite regularly. But his letters had always been phrased with perfect propriety; she had come to regard herself almost as a sister to him, as that was apparently how he chose to see her. But this letter had been written after he had learned of her adventure. He did not reproach her, as every other white person save Kate had done, with the moral risks she had taken. He was concerned only with the physical danger in which she had placed herself. "Because if anything were to happen to you, dear Constance," he had written, "my entire reason for living would have ended."

Just one sentence, for which he had not apologized. Instead, the letter had then returned to mundane matters. One sentence. The first love letter she had ever received. As it was the first time he had ever used her Christian name. But a sentence which made it impossible for her ever to see him again, much less speak with him. As for opening another letter from him . . .

But if she turned away from him, a man who *might* love her as she wished to be loved, because to accept such a love from a fellow American would destroy his career as well as her marriage, what was there left? Kate might be right, and were she to ask, the empress would arrange for her to be able to commit adultery and sample at least some of the physical delights which were apparently to be found in such an act, in total and perpetual secrecy. But the man would not love her, however much he might enjoy her body. And at the end of it, she *would* have committed adultery, all for the sake of a few seconds of apparently indescribable pleasure. There indeed was a slippery slope. She might as well start smoking opium.

"You are no doubt missing your friend Kate," Tz'u-Hsi said. "Would you like to go and visit her in Port Arthur? I will give you permission to do that, provided you are not away for too long."

"Go to Port Arthur?" Escape the dreadful atmosphere of Chu-teh, for at least a while? Be with laughter, and happiness . . . and the continual temptations which Kate, having apparently entirely renounced her Christian upbringing, would throw in her way? Besides, it would mean leaving Charles; Henry was just waiting for her to make a mistake like that. "No, no, Majesty," she said. "I have no desire to go to Port Arthur. I have my duties on the mission. My days here with you. I would not forgo these, even for a moment."

Tz'u-Hsi studied her. "All is well between you and your husband?" she asked with devastating insight.

Constance's head jerked, but to confess to the empress anything about what her domestic life was really like would be catastrophic—Tz'u-Hsi would insist upon doing something about it. Yet she had to say something now; the empress would not cease probing until satisfied. "Of course all is well between

Henry and me, Majesty," she lied. "I am concerned . . . well . . . my servants, the twins, Peter and Elizabeth, you may remember them . . . they do not seem to have been happy since their return to Chu-teh. And I cannot find out *why* they are not happy. They will not tell me." They will not even speak with me as they used to, she thought.

The empress nodded. "It is a sad world," she commented. "And after you risked so very much to regain them. But you see, Constance, now they are no longer sure that they *wanted* to be rescued. The girl, Elizabeth, has had a glimpse of the life that might have been hers, the fine clothes and the perfumes, as well as the physical joys which she might have experienced. She was being prepared by my nephew's eunuchs, you see, and while they might find no pleasure in their duties, they are all highly trained in the art of stimulating a woman so that her sole thought will be to please her man, and so, too, that she will wish to do that more than anything else in the world. Elizabeth will be looking back on those moments of bliss with regret, I have no doubt."

Constance clasped both hands about her throat as she gazed at her friend; that had never occurred to her. To be stimulated by a eunuch . . . But what had Kate told her of her wedding night?

"And then the boy, Peter, well, he will be suffering the same kind of remorse," Tz'u-Hsi went on. "I told you that he also was being prepared, and not by eunuchs, but by men even more experienced in the art of love. They will have taught him things about his body, about his senses, which he will have been afraid to consider, in his youthful ignorance. And now he has been returned to that state of youthful ignorance, and his place in a Christian community, where I gather such things, even such thoughts, are regarded as great crimes. And he is still whole, and therefore unable to prevent such thoughts, such desires, from besetting him. He will be unhappy about this, because how may he put such thoughts out of his mind, when they are present in all of our minds, all of the time? Added to which, for all his fear of what was going to happen to him, his unhappiness at the thought of losing his manhood, he will have been told by my people of the wealth that could have been his had you *not* rescued him. Whereas now he is doomed to spend the rest of his life as a poor servant. This too will be distressing him."

"You are telling me, Majesty," Constance said bitterly, "that I have made the most colossal mess of things." Because undoubtedly she had. Only Kate had in any way benefited from their knight-errantry—and even Kate had been virtually forced to renounce her family and her upbringing.

Tz'u-Hsi touched Constance on the hand. "You did what you thought was best, what you thought was required of you, by your religion and your ancestors, boldly and without fear of the consequences. Any man or any woman who follows that precept throughout life, although occasionally making mistakes, can never make a 'mess' of things, as you put it. Now, come, today *I* will talk to *you*, and you will listen and tell me what you think when I have finished."

In fact, over the past few weeks the empress had been using her meetings with Constance less to learn about Europe and America than to tell her young friend about China, always eagerly awaiting Constance's comments. Her own unhappiness aside, Constance had thus found these weeks among the most interesting of her life, as she began to gain some insight, not only into the convoluted structure of the Manchu dynasty and into the very real problems which were besetting the country, but also into the unsuspected insecurity which Tz'u-Hsi herself experienced, the daily mental sleight of hand she had to practice to remain at the pinnacle of power she had chosen for herself, and dared not now renounce.

For she had risen from almost the bottom of Manchu society to rule China. When the men from the north had first swept over the Great Wall, led by the famous Nurhachi, at the beginning of the seventeenth Christian century, the Yehe Nara, Tz'u-Hsi's clansmen, had been one of the least important of the eight banners, or tribes, into which the great warrior had organized his Mongol people. It was Nurhachi who had adopted the title Ch'ing Khan and announced that he and his tribes were the heirs to the original Chin, who had ruled China several hundred years before, as distinct from the Mings then in power, and it had been under his successors that the last Ming emperor had been defeated, to hang himself in his garden, as his palace had burned about him, in 1644. Thus had the Ta Ch'ing dynasty been established, to reach its zenith in the K'ang Hsi reign of Sheng Tsu Chang Huang Ti, the Prince Hsuan Yeh, between 1662 and 1722.

Not least of the problems which Constance had to solve in understanding what her strange new friend was talking about was this remarkable system of nomenclature practiced by the Chinese emperors. Every prince was of course given a name at birth, as Hsuan Yeh had been. But on succeeding to the throne, he was obliged to renounce that name and take an imperial title—in the case of Hsuan Yeh, K'ang Hsi, after which his own name could never be used again, not even by himself. But to further complicate matters, once he died, the years of his reign became an era, and he was thus given yet another, posthumous name—Hsuan Yeh thus became Sheng Tsu Chang Huang Ti, the last two words, "Huang Ti," simply meaning "emperor." Thus Tz'u-Hsi's own son, named Tsai Shun at birth, had ascended the throne as T'ung Chih, and since his death in 1874 had been known as My Tsung I Huang Ti, while the present emperor, Kuang Hsu, had been born Tsai T'ien, and would in turn be given a dynastic title when he finally died.

But the reign of the great K'ang Hsi was now a long time in the past, and since then the Manchu had been in decline; the hundred and fifty years since the greatest of the Ch'ing had gone to his ancestors had been filled with revolts, of which the Taiping had been only the latest and most serious, as the last half-century had become further embittered by the avaricious ambitions of the Western powers. The fact was that the Ch'ing were no longer the men they had once been, after a century and a half of harem and eunuch rule had taken its toll. Thus when the young girl Lan Kuei, which means Little Orchid, daughter of the minor southern Manchu official Hui-cheng, had been summoned from Canton to Peking so that her suitability as a possible royal concubine could be assessed—"Even Peking had heard tales of my beauty and my learning," Tz'u-Hsi told her proudly—the man to whose bed she had eventually been sent, renamed and virtually regenerated, had been a far cry from the boldly brilliant horsemen who had dominated the steppes of Mongolia. I Chu, the Emperor Hsien Feng, had been an effeminate youth who was actually the least able of all the seven half-brothers—sons of the Tao Kuang emperor, Hsuan Tsung Ch'eng Huang Ti—who had grown to manhood. Of these, the five younger, including the redoubtable I Hsin, titled Prince Kung, had still been very much alive when Tz'u-Hsi had first sampled the royal lovemaking. And he and I Huan, Prince Ch'un, were still around.

In the beginning, Tz'u-Hsi had been very much a junior concubine, but she had had the good fortune to bear her lord and master a son, and in the chaos which had followed the first wars with the British and the French, and the revolt of the Taiping, she had set herself resolutely and boldly to carve herself a future. She had, to Constance's delight, been born on November 29, 1835, which was only two days after Constance's own birthday—albeit at a gap of thirty-six years—and thus made her a Sagittarian, and certainly she possessed all of the romantic, wayward, gambler's instincts that characterized the American girl. Yet the going had been hard, and when, indeed, with the death of Hsien Feng in 1861—from sheer horrified anger, Tz'u-Hsi would say, after the British had marched on Peking and burned the Summer Palace to the east of the city—his brothers had sought to seize control from their infant nephew and his southern-born mother, she had come near to catastrophe. But by then she had already surrounded herself with able and brilliant young men, of whom Yuan Shih-k'ai was only the latest and greatest, and with an impenetrable army of eunuchs, who had kept her informed of every whisper uttered in even the remotest part of the palace, and she had in addition had the foresight to make a friend of Prince Kung. Thus she had triumphed, and prepared an even more remarkable triumph, when her own son had died after a reign of only twelve years. Then by all precedent she should have stepped gracefully aside. But she had not. The mother of the present Kuang Hsu emperor had been mysteriously taken ill and died the evening after sharing tea with her rival, and Tz'u-Hsi had continued serenely on her way.

Had she really poisoned Kuang Hsu's mother, as was freely rumored? Circumstances suggested it, although the emperor himself appeared to accept his situation, and the domination of his step-aunt, without question. It was not a point Constance cared to consider too deeply as she herself sat and took tea with the empress, eating the same little cakes which were reputed to have been fatal to the young princess. That Tz'u-Hsi loved power could not be argued. And that she was far more capable of ruling the disintegrating empire than the effete young man who actually performed the sacrifices to heaven also could not be doubted. Whether she was the *best* person to cope with the problems which beset the dynasty remained an arguable point. She boasted of her mental powers and her education, but she remained bigoted and ignorant of anything outside of China, despite Constance's efforts to convince her that the Dragon Empire was no longer the greatest in the world, even in point of size. Even more, she remained entirely at the mercy of her moods and her favorites, of whom Constance currently happened to be one of the most important, just as she remained very aware that she was surrounded entirely by conspiracy, by those who hated her and those who feared her, all of whom waited patiently for her powers to begin to decline.

But Tz'u-Hsi was clearly at the very height of her physical and mental strength, prepared even to cope with the sinister and constantly growing ambitions of the reborn Japanese Empire, which, instead of regarding the Westerners as "foreign devils," drilled its army to the orders of Prussian colonels, and sent its navy to sea with British commanders on its bridges, and clearly dreamed of establishing its hegemony over at least Korea, a traditionally Chinese satellite—thus the dispatch of Yuan, the ablest of her generals, to be commissioner in Seoul, the Korean capital.

Emotionally, however, Constance could not be so sure of her friend's resilience. It was impossible to suppose that a woman disposing of such enormous power, and surrounded by men, women and half-men all dedicated to the carrying out of her slightest wish—and left a widow at a very early age—did not also indulge her sensual desires. In the beginning, indeed, Constance even suffered a nagging concern that the empress's tastes might be homosexual and that she would be forced to experience yet another variation of Chinese morality, or lack of it—or forgo her place as the current favorite, and this was not a practical possibility, on grounds of survival, even had she wished to do so. But Tz'u-Hsi never treated her as anything less than a somewhat wayward daughter, and indeed Constance very rapidly came to live only for her fortnightly visits to Peking, when she could escape the sullenly disapproving glances of the Mountjoys, the bewildered half-smiles of the nuns and Father Pierre, the obvious mistrust of the converts—who apparently feared that one day she might take it into her head to *rescue* them—and the equally obvious suppressed but volcanically unstable emotions of Henry, which varied from anger through fear to lust. Peking might contain the Forbidden City, but in that city she could relax and be herself, and laugh, for the empress adored laughter, and gamble, another of Tz'u-Hsi's passions—although they never played for real stakes—and feel that she was alive, however apostate.

Winter, with its subsequent heavy snowfalls to block the trails, was an absolute purgatory, relieved only by Henry's departure on another of his January treks and by the steady progress of Charles, who was now all but walking and making frantic if unsuccessful endeavors to talk. Her period of exile from the palace was rendered the more disturbing as she could not but believe the empress would have found a new favorite by the spring, and she was beside herself with joy when, as soon as the roads were reopened, she received an imperial summons. To find Tz'u-Hsi as pleased to see her as ever, and even more anxious to resume their private conversations, and exchange information about Kate, who had not so far, to the empress's disappointment, become pregnant.

But all of Peking, the great, bustling, teeming anthill, was a joy. She felt a mood of elation she had not known for a long while as she left the Gate of the Zenith and made her way down the Grand Avenue, escorted as usual by a squad of soldiers, under the command of the chief eunuch, Chiang, now almost a friend, his presence indicating the importance which was attached to her stately passage through the streets—so unlike her first mad gallop with Kate six months ago—knowing that nothing had changed and that she would be returning fourteen days hence. Now she could study the people at her leisure, for Chiang never hurried, enjoying the enormous variety of wealth and position that was displayed before her, from the lily-footed, expensively dressed lady being carried in her litter from shop to shop, all the way down the scale of human misery and degeneration to the criminals, either exposed in cages on the street corners, their heads protruding through small holes in the tops of the bars, the cages themselves made so that the inmates had to stand on tiptoe all the time to prevent strangling themselves, or, in less desperate cases, stumbling along the roadside on their way either to prison or to sentencing, wearing the cangue, a circular slab of thick wood, as much as three feet wide, with a hole in the center which was placed over their heads, leaving the frame resting on their shoulders; their wrists were shackled to the underside of the wood, to leave them entirely helpless and hopelessly encumbered by the weight. These were horrifying examples of Chinese justice, but they were things which she now knew she must ignore as far as she could, and thus a quick glance was usually sufficient to send her interest desperately seeking a diversion. Until she walked her horse through a group of these unfortunates and discovered that she was staring at Lin-tu.

Constance drew rein instinctively, her guards immediately copying her example, as did Chiang. Who promptly followed the direction of her gaze. Lin-tu had certainly seen her as well. He did not speak, but his grimy, sweating features conveyed a prayer for her silence.

"You know one of those men?" Chiang inquired.

Constance forced herself to think. Lin-tu was under arrest, but clearly for some petty crime rather than subversion, or he would probably have been already executed or at least exposed in a cage. Therefore no one had identified him as the man wanted for treason two years ago, and he might hope to escape with at worst a few strokes of the cane on his bare feet. Whereas were she to attempt to intervene . . . "No," she said. "How could I possibly know one of *them?* I was just struck by their number."

"There was some kind of a riot last night," Chiang told her. "These men were involved. It is unlikely all of them are guilty. But the magistrates will discover the truth of it."

"I am sure they will," Constance agreed, and rode on, fighting the temptation to look back and see if he was still watching her. Lin-tu! The sight of him brought back the memory of that terrible day as if it had been yesterday. But even more it brought back the memory of the following night, when they had sat together and talked, alone in the privacy of her home. She felt quite faint as she recalled the thoughts that had then roamed her mind. Because if she had known then what she knew now, had felt then what she so often felt now, if her relationship with Henry had already degenerated to its present level, there was no saying what might have happened. Therefore there was no saying what might happen were they ever to meet again.

Save that they had just met again, in their new and no doubt permanent situations, she the pampered favorite of the empress, he doomed to a criminal existence which must eventually, as Henry had said, take him to the headsman.

She sighed, and her head jerked as she heard her name called. "Constance! Why, Constance Baird. How marvelous to see you."

It was Harriet Bunting, out shopping with her Chinese butler . . . and walking beside her, Lieutenant Franklin Wynne.

# II

## The Sun Rises

# 6

# The Marine

Or rather, Constance realized, *Captain* Wynne, judging by his insignia. As tall and handsome as she remembered him from two years before, and more sun- and windburned, and confident, and therefore even more attractive than she recalled.

"Halt," she told Chiang again. "I wish to dismount."

"You know these people?" Chiang was doubtful, but he raised his hand and the cavalcade came to a stop. Constance dismounted, and a moment later was in Harriet Bunting's arms.

"My dear girl," Harriet said. "My dear, dear girl. How splendid to see you, and to see you looking so well. Then it is all true?"

Constance gazed at Frank Wynne, patiently waiting his turn. Gently she disengaged herself from Mrs. Bunting. "Is what all true?"

"That you are a personal friend of the empress, who goes abroad only with an escort of soldiers and eunuchs."

"Oh . . ." Constance felt her hands being taken by the tall marine. "I *am* Her Majesty's friend, to be sure." She squeezed his fingers. "It was so good of you to write," she said. "So *good.*"

"One letter?" he asked. "I don't believe I deserve any medals, Mrs. Baird. But to see you . . . I'll do better in the future, I promise."

"Oh, but . . ." She looked at Mrs. Bunting.

Who had clearly been studying the situation. "It would be simply splendid if you could come home to tea, Constance," she said. "I am sure we have so *much* to talk about, and I have so much to show you . . . of course, you *must* come home to tea, and meet William again, and . . ."

"I will go to Mrs. Bunting's residence, Chiang," Constance said.

"I am to deliver you to Chu-teh," the eunuch protested, obviously disapproving. "If we do not go now, we shall not reach there before dark."

Constance looked at Mrs. Bunting again.

"But you will spend the night with me, Constance," Mrs. Bunting declared.

"There you are, Chiang," Constance said. "You may escort me to Mrs. Bunting's house, and then return to the Forbidden City."

"And who will escort you to Chu-teh?" Chiang demanded.

"Why, I will, tomorrow," Captain Wynne said. "If you will permit me, Mrs. Baird."

"We heard all about that Mountjoy girl marrying an imperial prince," Mr. Bunting said as he carved roast pork. "She was always a very odd child, wasn't she? Did you know anything about that, Mrs. Baird?"

Mrs. Bunting coughed and went very red in the face.

"Oh, indeed, Mr. Bunting," Constance said. "I was there when the marriage was proposed. I believe they are very happy."

"Of course they are, my dear," Mrs. Bunting said. "I am sure it is entirely possible for two people, even of different races, to live together—provided, of course, certain adjustments are made. And being a good Christian, I am sure young Catherine will cope with the situation very well. After all, Constance, when in Rome . . ."

"I must say, I did not wish to cause offense," William Bunting protested, and changed his approach. "I mean, I think that if we are going to trade with these people, and . . . and . . . ah . . . convert them and that sort of thing, we simply have to treat them as equals. Oh, indeed."

"I am sure you're right, Mr. Bunting," Constance said politely, beginning to wish that she had taken Chiang's advice after all, and gone directly back to Chu-teh. But there remained Frank Wynne, immaculate in his white uniform, taking little part in the conversation, but studying her with considerable interest as he ate his dinner.

Would they be allowed any time alone afterward? And did she want that to happen? It was impossible to know, impossible even to risk attempting to analyze her motives in accepting Mrs. Bunting's invitation to spend the night. Would she have done so if the sight of Lin-tu had not started all manner of dangerously absurd thoughts coursing through her mind? Or were the thoughts, the reflections on what might have been, on what lay so tantalizingly just beyond her consciousness, ever present? Lin-tu was thus merely a catalyst, because were she ever to succumb to Kate's insidious suggestions, only Lin-tu out of all the Chinese men she had met—saving the prince himself, of course—in any way measured up to the dream she had cultivated over the past few months. And even Lin-tu was an utterly impossible concept, first because she had supposed she would never see him again, and second, now that she *had* seen him again, because of the sharp and increasing differences in their relative positions. *Were* she ever going to consider such an impossible liaison, it *could* just happen between the wife of a Methodist missionary, aghast at the social ills she saw around her, and a fervent young revolutionary who had been educated in America. But it could not even be *considered*, under the protective unreality of a dream, between the favorite of a despotic empress and a man whose entire life was dedicated to the overthrow of that empress.

But if she was in the mood to commit adultery, here was a man of her own race and her own nationality, a man who had admired her from the moment they had met, a man she had always liked and now was sure she could admire in return, a man who, because of his calling as much as his personality, could suffer none of the crippling mental anguishes of Henry Baird.

If she was in the mood to commit adultery, she thought. My God, Constance Baird, that you can sit here at a dinner table and actually permit such thoughts to roam your mind! Because she *was* in such a mood. Oh, indeed she was in such a mood, to snatch at any suggestion of happiness, even purely physical happiness, before the dull weight of the unloving responsibility she had so carelessly accumulated weighed her down forever. Soon she would be twenty-one years old, and the future stretched in front of her, bleak and empty, because in the presence of the Buntings' domestic bliss, however sterile it probably was by Chinese standards, and with Frank Wynne smiling at her from the other side of the table, she understood that even tea with the empress had to be a totally unrewarding and pointless pastime.

"I'm sure," Mrs. Bunting said, as William Bunting produced a box of cigars, "that dear Franklin would like to take Constance for a stroll in the garden. It is so pleasant in the garden on a nice night, after dinner. And tonight I think is the best we've had this year. So far.''

"Dear Harriet," Frank Wynne remarked. "She is absolutely ruthless."

Constance turned her head sharply, inhaling the night-blooming jasmine which filled the little garden with its glorious fragrance, listening to the sounds of Peking at night, sounds she had never heard before, as they never penetrated the Forbidden City, the bursts of high-pitched conversation and of even higher-pitched laughter, the strangely discordant notes of Chinese music—the whole overlaid by the distant very European rhythm of the band in the British legation, only a block away, where the minister and his lady were having a dinner party to the strains of Offenbach.

It was a magnificent night, she supposed, clear and still, with as yet no hint of summer rain. And she was walking in a private garden with a handsome young man who had just suggested . . .

"She feels, you see," Frank explained, "that you have a great deal to tell her, but somehow that you are more likely to confide in me than in her. I can't imagine why."

"And I have no idea what you are talking about," Constance said, realizing that she had, as usual, been overly optimistic—it would never be part of Harriet Bunting's scheme to encourage adultery.

There was a wooden bench at the end of the garden, as far removed as possible—some fifty feet—from the house itself, and facing one of the little ornamental ponds, with its attendant stream, which were so popular in Peking. Here Frank Wynne sat down, stretching out his long legs. "I quite agree," he said. "I think it is insufferable, the way people like to pry. But . . ." He shrugged. "I figure women like Harriet Bunting don't have a lot else to do. And of course, my dear Constance, you are all the rage."

"Me?" She sat beside him, although at the far end of the bench.

"Oh, indeed. Why, I'll bet they're talking about you now, down at the legation. Can you imagine? Any one of those stuffed shirts would give his eyeteeth for an audience with the empress. And you take tea with her twice a month."

"I'm sure they have but to ask," Constance said. "And I would see if it could be arranged."

"Ah, but there's the rub," he said. "They'd have to ask *you*."

"And I'm some kind of a pariah, is that it?"

"I sure didn't bring you out here to fight, Constance."

"I didn't come out here to fight, either, Frank. It is *so* good to see you again. So . . ." She bit her lip, grateful to the gloom which mostly hid her face. "But I *would* like to know what people think of me, honestly." Because she had to find out what *he* thought of her, before she could decide if it was worthwhile even continuing this conversation.

Another shrug. "The legation johnnies? Why, they're jealous, as I said. And as regards approaching you, it would mean some kind of recognition of the missionaries, as you happen to be the wife of one of them—quite apart from anything else. I guess they just can't bring themselves to do that, after all the dispatches they keep sending to their various foreign offices saying what problems the missionaries are causing."

"It's the 'apart from anything else' I'm interested in, Frank."

"Oh, well . . . like I said, women in these parts just have nothing else to do but gossip. As for Harriet, well, I guess you don't know that Joan Mountjoy corresponds with her."

"No," Constance said. "No, I didn't know that."

"And comes to see her. And talks about things. Talking about things to Harriet is rather like getting hold of a newspaper and circulating it free to everyone who can read. But the fact is, I've an idea Mrs. Mountjoy blames you for Kate going off and marrying that Chinese fellow."

"Well . . . I suppose I am partly responsible." Although I thought he was going to propose to me, she thought, still with regret. "Do *you* blame me for it, Frank?"

"I don't know anything about it. Hell . . ." He flushed. "I beg your pardon, it just slipped out."

"So don't bother about it. It's a word I use myself. I'd like you to be absolutely frank with me . . ," Her turn to check, with an embarrassed smile.

"And that happens all the time," he assured her. "So like I said, I don't know enough about it. But if you really want me to be Frank, as well as frank, if you follow me, well . . . I guess it goes a little against the grain to think of a white girl with a . . . well, an Oriental."

"A Manchu prince with a pedigree longer than any European royalty."

"Don't you figure we all have the same length pedigrees, Constance?" he asked. "What with Adam and all?"

There really wasn't any answer to that. And her dreams, as usual, were crumbling away before the harshness of reality. And were being replaced, again as usual, principally with anger. "I don't suppose I could ever convince you that Prince Ksian Fu is a very fine gentleman," she said. "Or that Kate is now happier than she has ever been in her life. Or could be . . ." She had to bite her lip again. She had been going to say "married to an Englishman." But there wasn't too much difference, at least in manners and morals, between an Englishman and an American. "But I suppose," she went on, "that Joan Mountjoy, and Harriet Bunting, and all your legation johnnies, as you call them, think that I have also . . . well . . . I *do* spend a night every fortnight inside the Forbidden City."

"Yes," he agreed. "Well . . ."

"You mean they *do*?" she cried. But what was she so aghast about? she asked herself. Or so angry? Would she not have proved them right, if she had only possessed the courage?

"They've got nothing else to do," he said for a third time, and lamely.

She had been staring at the pond. Now she turned to face him. "Do *you* think that of me, Frank? Do you?"

He gazed at her. "I would like to think about you, Connie Baird, just what you tell me to think, now and always. Just tell me."

They swayed toward each other, and their lips almost touched— then she swayed away again. Because if she allowed herself to make love to him now, would that not confirm everything that was said about her?

He held her hand. "Joan Mountjoy also tells Harriet how you and Mr. Baird don't get on so well nowadays," he said. "I gather *he* tells *her*."

"And that means I'm ready to fall into the arms of the first man who asks me," she said. "Is that what you think?"

He hesitated. "No," he said at last. "No, I'd hate to think that, Mrs. Baird." He released her, stood up. "I suppose we should turn in. It's a long ride out to Chu-teh."

You fool, Constance Baird, she thought. Oh, you fool.

"Because," Frank went on, "I guess I am going to go on putting my foot in my mouth if we stay here. It's just that if you were ever going to call it a day with Baird . . . I have an idea that I'm in love with you, Constance."

She stood up, almost against him. "Are you, Frank? Could you?"

She was in his arms, held tight, and he was kissing her mouth. And his mouth was open, as was hers. She was shocked at herself; Henry had never allowed his tongue to touch hers. But what a satisfying feeling spread downward from her throat. Could this be the first of those emotions Kate had tried so inarticulately to describe?

She felt Frank's fingers on her back, moving from her shoulders down her spine, reaching her bustle and all but sliding past, and then moving back up again.

His lips slid around her cheek to her ear. "Like I said, it's a long ride to Chu-teh," he reminded her.

"Frank . . ." She tried to hold him close again.

"I imagine you'd like to sleep on it, Connie," he said. "Alone. And so would I."

"Mind you go straight home," Mrs. Bunting said with an arch smile, and reached up to adjust the picnic hamper she had prepared for them, which had been strapped behind Constance's saddle. "It's a long way to Chu-teh."

As if it mattered for more than gossip, Constance thought somewhat bitterly—Harriet would never have let her ride off into the country by herself with a man were she not in any event convinced she was already a fallen woman.

But Constance was feeling out of sorts this morning, quite apart from Harriet's machinations. Frank had had to stop her making a fool of herself last night, and in the hard light of day, with the Forbidden City and Lin-tu both fading into memory—what was he suffering now? or had he managed to talk himself free?—she could understand that but for his polite caution she *would* have made a fool of herself. A criminal fool. And worse. For would she not have accepted his love with Lin-tu's image in her mind?

And now they were to be alone together for several hours.

"We'll be there by nightfall," Frank said. He had changed from his uniform into civilian clothes, as he was going riding in the Chinese countryside, wore a wide-brimmed slouch hat and an open-necked shirt beneath his riding jacket, brown breeches and army boots. Constance thought they made a splendid pair—she was in her new sky-blue riding habit, made for her by the empress's own seamstresses, to replace the one ruined by the eunuchs last summer.

"Do you suppose . . . well . . . that Harriet knows what is going on?" Frank asked as they walked their horses through the gate, nodding to the guards—who knew better now than even to ask for a pass from the famous Mrs. Baird—and beneath the pine trees.

"I have no idea," Constance said. "What *is* going on?"

He glanced at her, gave a half-smile, and then looked away again. While her heart pounded with a curious mixture of anticipation and uncertainty all over again. Because she did have no idea at all what was going on. She had just been . . . "Propositioned," she supposed, would be the word. Certainly she had not expected to sleep a wink last night—and had actually slept very soundly indeed. Quite apart from being foolish, the very idea was somehow dirty, or at best dishonest. And not just because of Henry. Strangely, she thought, she would not have been aware of the dishonesty had it been Lin-tu riding beside her—which made her very little better in her regard for the Chinese than Henry, she knew. But it would have been different, because she would have been stepping into a different world, populated by different manners and different morals, and a world, too, from which she could escape merely by stepping onto a ship bound for San Francisco.

Frank was one of her own. Last night, before bed, that had been a comfort. Now it was the biggest obstacle of all.

He had suggested that he loved her. He had not said so, only suggested it. And had then suggested that they might sleep together. The very words, when framed in her mind, gave her goose pimples. But would a gentleman who genuinely loved her ever suggest such a course? She just did not know. She was realizing that was her biggest problem of all. She just did not know enough about life and humanity.

But even if he was behaving like any other man, could she allow herself to accept his love without *knowing* her own feelings? Again, she thought, to have had a liaison with Lin-tu would not have required love at all. It could almost be regarded with clinical detachment—if I am going to understand these people, I must know all about them. But to allow Frank to love her, to make love to her, unless she loved him—that would be the most dishonest thing of all.

They were out in the country, and trotting down that so-well-remembered track. Well-remembered, at least to her. It was still very early in the morning, as they had left at dawn, and thus still cool, while the track was deserted. "The best time of the day, early morning," Frank remarked.

"Oh, it is," she agreed.

"You go into Peking every two weeks." It was not a question.

"That's right."

"To visit the empress. That's a remarkable friendship, if I may say so."

"Not so remarkable," she pointed out, "if you knew the empress. She is desperate to learn about the outside world and to have outside opinions on her own problems. I don't pretend to know much, but she feels that what I tell her is true and unvarnished. You have no idea what it's like, to be completely shut away behind a wall of eunuchs and advisers, each giving her *his* version of what is happening outside."

He glanced at her. "You're genuinely fond of the old dragoness."

"Why, I suppose I am," she agreed.

"And is she . . . well . . . ?" He gazed in front of them, a faint flush darkening the tan of his cheeks. "The fact is, Connie, I can get leave to come to Peking fairly regularly. My being able to speak Chinese is regarded as important by the bigwigs down at Tientsin. They think I may learn things that could be useful. So seeing you from time to time is no problem. But finding somewhere . . . well, I usually stay with Harriet, you see. I don't have to, of course. It's just that she's always inviting me, and, well, I haven't had any reason to refuse, until now. On the other hand, I'd hate to take you to one of those Chinese joss houses. *And* I imagine the whole city would know of it five minutes later. So if the empress would allow me into the Forbidden City, maybe give you somewhere you could entertain, somewhere private . . ."

He was taking her utterly for granted, laying his plans as if they had decided their future weeks ago, and had only the details left to solve. Because she had let him kiss her? But he had warned her, after that. Then it had to be because, having been warned, she was still allowing him to escort her back to Chu-teh, with a lonely thirty miles in between. And to top it all, he was suggesting that she approach Tz'u-Hsi for the use of a room . . . She dared not trust herself to speak, kicked her horse into a gallop, soared over the gently undulating plain. It took him some minutes to catch up with her.

"I didn't mean to offend you, Connie," he shouted. "Honestly I didn't."

She made no reply, and they rode in silence for some time. She *could* say nothing, until he had spoken first. She *had* been offended. But she couldn't repel the excitement which kept surging into her chest, making her feel almost sick.

"I guess that's me, all over," he said at last. "Always putting my foot in my mouth." He squinted at the sun, which was now quite high. "How far do you think we've come?"

"About twelve miles."

He pulled out his watch. "And it's eleven. If we called a halt and had an early lunch, we'd still be at Chu-teh by dark. What do you think?"

He looked from left to right.

Well, she thought, this is it. But they did have to stop sometime. They couldn't possibly ride all day, and through the midday heat.

"What we really need," he said, "is a stream or something. So the horses could have a drink," he added hastily. "But I guess we could do with one too."

"Mrs. Bunting made us some lemonade," she told him. "But I am sure the horses *could* do with a drink." She pointed. "There's a place over there about a mile. It has water."

They cantered over the slight rise she had indicated, drew rein to look at the ruined pagoda, glowing crimson in the sunlight, the bubbling stream hurrying past it. "Why," Frank said, "that's quite beautiful. But do you know, I thought the Chinese never abandoned things like pagodas."

"Oh, they do if they think it's become unlucky," Constance said. She touched her horse with her heels, and it walked forward. What am I doing? she asked herself. What am I *doing?* But they did have to stop to eat. "This one was inundated by the last floods, and some people who had taken refuge here were drowned. So they think it's unlucky."

"Those floods were quite something. Tientsin was nearly washed away. And the debris, bodies and animals too, which came out into the gulf had to be seen to be believed." He dismounted, held up his hands for her. "Were you involved?"

She slipped from the saddle, felt his fingers close on her ribs as he gently set her on the ground. He did not let her go, and she remained standing against him, looking up at his face. "Indeed I was," she said. "I met the empress only because of those floods. And if that hadn't happened, I wouldn't be here now."

"Thank God for the empress," he said, and kissed her mouth. This was a more positive, demanding kiss than last night, and his hands were more confident too, slipping from her shoulders, down her back, to hold her buttocks and press her against him. No man had ever touched her there—she could hardly count the eunuchs who had manhandled her—but she had known he would wish to. She shivered against him, and felt his hands move up again, to her back and shoulders. Her hat had fallen off, and now he drove his fingers into her hair, which had been loosely tied on the nape of her neck with a ribbon. His lips left hers, to kiss her forehead and then her ear. "Oh, Connie," he said. "My darling, darling Connie. I dream of you every night. Every single night."

She didn't know what to do, as waves of desire spread up from her belly and encountered waves of cold guilt, and therefore cold fear, drifting down from her brain. Her heart was in the middle, and had the deciding vote. But her heart seemed paralyzed, unable to make a decision—or afraid to.

She turned away from him, but he stayed with her, and as she turned, his hands came around her front to close on her breasts—and now she could feel him against her thigh. But here again he was doing to her what had been done by Henry in only a most perfunctory manner. She allowed her knees to give way, and sank to the grass, gazing at the pagoda, feeling him kneeling with her, his fingers gently plucking at the buttons of her blouse.

"We should water the horses," she said.

He hesitated, then released her and moved away. She got up again, not turning her head, went to the steps and up them, sat on the sagging, rotting planking at the top, only then turning to look at him. He had taken the horses to the stream, and they were drinking. Now he glanced at her, and she realized that he had supposed she would undress while he was busy. Undress? Here? And before him? There could be no comparison between bathing naked before a eunuch, and even before Prince Ksian Fu, and undressing here in the bright, hot sunlight before Frank Wynne.

He unstrapped the picnic hamper, brought it across, came up the steps, and sat beside her. "Problems," he remarked, and handed her a glass of lemonade. He attempted a smile. "Apart from the risk of going through the floor."

She drank. "I . . . Oh, God, Frank. Oh, God!"

"I have a feeling he'd rather be left out of this one, Connie." He gave her a cold chicken leg, took one himself. "Is it Henry? Or the boy?"

Easy solutions. And she had not given Charles a thought. "It's me, Frank."

He frowned at her. "I'm not sure I understand that. Or do you really mean *me?*"

She shrugged. "You're part of it. I don't love Henry. You know that. I guess the entire world knows that. But I am his wife. And Charles is my son. Those are things I have to decide about. Because, don't you see . . . if I decide, I can't go back."

"You don't have to. I'm going to marry you," he told her. "I don't know about Charles. Maybe we could work something out.'' He was completely misunderstanding her, supposing the decision was whether or not she would return to Chu-teh.

Nor would he ever be able to understand, she realized. The concept that he might only be a *part* of everything she wanted—that if he did not supply what her overheated imagination thought might be possible, if, for instance, he could not equal the prince as Kate had described him, she would again dream, and want . . . and having stepped beyond the bounds of civilized Christian behavior once, would feel less frightened about doing so again—would not only be foreign to him, he would regard it as insulting. The decision had to be hers alone. Either remain what she had been born and educated to be, a Virginia gentlewoman and a missionary's wife—in which case their being here at all was sinful and should be ended as rapidly as possible—or let go, with results even she was afraid to consider.

Gently he was again unbuttoning her blouse. As she had not restored the earlier damage, he was finished in seconds and was lowering his head to move the bodice of her petticoat and kiss her breasts. ''Frank,'' she said absurdly and ineffectually as he used his hand to cup the flesh and take the nipple between his lips, again with the utmost gentle care. Now she was feeling sensations she had hardly supposed possible, sensations which were spreading through her entire body, made her welcome the slipping away of his hand, to her knee and then down to her boot, sliding over the leather, underneath the skirt to find her stockinged calf, beginning to rise again, carrying the material with it. She lowered her head to rest it on his, knowing that within seconds . . . and listened to noise approaching them from just beyond the rise.

''Frank!'' she gasped.

He raised his head so rapidly they nearly bumped, and then leaped away from her, running down the steps to gain the horses, dragging them toward the pagoda by their bridles while at the same time fumbling inside his saddlebag to bring out a heavy military-issue revolver.

''Maybe you'd better do yourself up,'' he suggested quietly.

She looked down at her blouse, hastily scrabbled at the buttons, and stood up to smooth her skirt, while watching the men coming over the rise. They were unlike any other men she had ever seen, because while they were definitely Chinese, in place of the large hats worn by most of their countrymen, they had tied red handkerchiefs around their heads, into which their pigtails had apparently been folded—supposing they had not been cut off—and in addition they had taken off their heavy jackets and wore only shirts, also red, opened to bare their throats and necks. But the most unusual thing about them was their movements, for they did not walk or trot like so many Chinese, but instead took enormous strides, and not always directly ahead, but varying from side to side, giving the impression that they were almost dancing their way forward, and at the same time were making the most remarkable gestures, thrusting their clenched fists to and fro, arcing their arms above their heads, pushing out their chests, shooting their fists straight from the shoulder and then down at their sides, as if they were performing some weird form of calisthenics. Constance stared at them with her mouth open, while Frank retrieved her hat and then came back to stand with the horses at the foot of the steps.

"Prepare to mount and ride like hell," he told her, still speaking with quiet authority. Whatever his clumsiness at the art of seduction, here was the sort of situation he had been trained to deal with.

"What about the hamper?" she asked, pleased with the calmness of her own voice.

"We may have to abandon it," he said. "Just keep watching them."

She realized that the young men—not one of them was over thirty, she estimated—had seen them. The movements stopped, and they gathered closer together, forming a compact group, about fifty yards distant. She counted eleven of them.

And every one of them carried a long knife in his belt. "Frank!" she said, her voice at last beginning to tremble as she recalled that he would have only six bullets in his gun.

"I think you're right," Frank said. "Mount!"

He held her stirrup, and she settled herself into the sidesaddle, right knee clenched on its horn. Frank mounted beside her.

"Foreign devils," one of the young men said loudly.

"You have defiled the temple," said another.

Frank placed his horse between Constance and the Chinese and raised his right hand to let them see the revolver. "Walk your horse, Connie," he commanded. "Nice and slow."

She touched Rufus with her heels, and he moved forward, hooves silent on the springy turf.

"Now canter," Frank commanded from immediately behind her. Another touch with her heels and Rufus quickened his speed.

"Foreign devils," came the shouts from behind them.

Constance refused to turn her head, kept staring at the ground in front of her horse, rising and falling to his movement.

"You can relax," Frank said, moving up beside her and tucking the revolver out of sight again.

"Thank God you were with me," she said. "And with that thing. Frank . . . would they have harmed us?"

"Could be. That bunch, in particular."

"You knew them?" .

"I never saw them before in my life. But I've heard about them. And read reports. They're members of a new secret society. They call themselves the Righteous Harmony Fists, hence all the arm waving. And like most secret societies out here, they don't go for foreigners. The skipper will be interested to learn I came across them this far north. So will your friend the empress, I'd bet." The sexually animated young man was suddenly and completely absorbed into the serious Marine officer, in a way she would not have thought possible. Now he recollected himself and grinned at her. "The best-laid schemes of mice and men, eh? I know I should take you straight home, right this minute. Anyway, we've no lunch left. But, Connie . . ." He leaned across to squeeze her hand. "I do love you. I do want you, so very badly. I do dream about you every night. Connie . . . could we talk about that?"

"Ah, yes," Henry Baird said. "The Boxers."

"The what?" Frank asked.

"That's the name we have given them," Henry told him. As always when he had guests to whom he presumed himself superior, he was at his most insufferably dogmatic—a quality which she had once admired, Constance remembered. "You've seen the way they move. Do they not remind you of pugilists in training? We've seen quite a few of them around Chu-teh recently. I do assure you that they are quite harmless. Of course I'm very grateful that you were with Constance and brought her home safe and sound, but I doubt they would have troubled her, even had she been alone. As I say, they are quite harmless."

Frank gazed at him, and then glanced at Constance. Like her, he was undoubtedly remembering those long sharp knives in their belts, and also their obvious hostility. "Well, I'm sure glad to hear you say that, Reverend," he said. "As I have to go back that way tomorrow."

"Oh, but . . ." Constance bit her lip as the men looked at her. "I really don't think you should make that journey again tomorrow, Captain Wynne," she said. "You'll be absolutely exhausted. Stay a day or two, and then we'll probably be able to find some company for your return journey."

What am I doing? she asked herself yet again. She sat next to Charles's high chair and fed him his supper, while trying not to listen to him; his vocabulary had reached the "Ma" and "Da" and "Ba" stage, and he talked incessantly. But he was her son, and the dearest possession she would ever have. To put him at risk for the sake of physical gratification . . . But there was more than that. Frank *did* love her. She was sure of it. And she wanted to *be* loved, even more, she thought, than she wanted to *make* love. She wanted affection, and caring, and a feeling of pleasure at seeing someone, and a feeling of knowing, too, that she was giving pleasure in return. Her life was completely empty, save for her dreams and this little boy.

But the dreams and the boy could not be shared; that was the problem. It would have to be one thing or the other. The amazing thing was that Henry did not seem to have the slightest suspicion that she and Frank might be anything more than good friends. No doubt Henry did not suppose people ever had immoral thoughts and did not, like him, immediately suppress them. But that he loathed her, and loathed the position of strength she had assumed through her friendship with Tz'u-Hsi, could not be doubted either. He could do nothing as long as that friendship endured . . . but were he to suspect her of adultery, Charles would most certainly be lost to her, and forever.

She felt herself go quite cold with fright as she realized how close she had come to disaster yesterday. Because had it happened, Henry would have had to know. He would have seen it in her eyes.

And the danger still existed.

"I don't suppose I'll get another furlough for six weeks or so," Frank said.

They sat together on the front veranda, Henry having left them to attend some church meeting to which she had pointedly not been invited; he had even taken away her Sunday-school lessons, had left her with almost nothing to do, no doubt in the hopes that sheer boredom would bring her back to him.

"But I'll be counting the days," Frank went on. "Do you suppose you could write to me, say, in a month's time, giving me the exact days you'll be . . . in Peking?"

He had all but said "available," she thought. He did love her. She was sure of that, and she wanted to believe it. But being a man, he could not imagine that she would sit and discuss it with him, and still have any doubts. "If you handed the letter in at the American legation, it would get to me within a week. Then you could tell me if you'd managed to arrange something with the empress. Don't worry about it too much," he added, as she did not reply. "I've an idea . . . well, I've a friend who's in the legation. Actually, he's an acquaintance more than a friend, but he's the brother of a chap I was at the Academy with. I know he'd be more than happy to help us. We could use his rooms. I know we could."

Constance got up and walked to the rail to look out at the village, basking in the rays of the setting sun. She wondered if any Chinese lover, out to seduce his lady, would dare indulge in so ham-handed an arrangement.

"I know," Frank said. "It would mean letting him know the score, but hell, Connie, I'm sure he can be trusted. And, well . . . you *do* want to get together, don't you? When I think of yesterday . . . I almost wish I'd had two guns with me. Then I could've cleaned up those bastards and we'd have been alone again."

She turned, and he gave a guilty grin.

"Just joking. But, Connie . . . to sit here and see you, and not to be able to touch you . . ." He gazed at her. "You do *want* to get together, Connie?"

"Yes," she said. "Yes, Frank. I do *want* to get together with you. I want that more than anything else in the world." But I'm not going to, she thought. I just haven't got the guts, either to risk Henry finding out or to risk being disappointed. Because that was the greatest risk of all.

He got up, touched her hand lightly as they watched Henry coming toward them. "Then just tell me when, and leave the arrangements to me."

"Port Arthur?" Henry cried. "And taking Charlie? That is quite absurd, Constance. Quite absurd. I absolutely forbid it."

"It is not at all absurd, Henry," Constance replied quietly. "I have discussed it with Her Majesty, and she thinks it would be a good idea. She also thinks I should take Charles. He is far too young to be separated from his mother for any length of time. You need not worry, I shall have Miriam, as well as Elizabeth and Peter. Charles will be well looked after."

"Not worry?" he shouted. "Not worry? Taking a small child into the depths of Mongolia . . ."

"Oh, really, Henry," she said. "Port Arthur is not a hundred miles from Tientsin. And it is an international city. Now *you* are being absurd."

As if it mattered what he was, or felt, or said. She *had* discussed the idea with the empress, and Tz'u-Hsi had given her full approval. She had in fact almost broached the matter herself, Chiang no doubt having given her a full account of why he had been unable to escort her protégée out to Chu-teh. Tz'u-Hsi had made no actual comment, not even when Constance had told her about the Boxers, as Henry so quaintly called them—although she had listened very carefully, and asked Constance to repeat her description of them—but then she had immediately returned to the theme of a visit to Port Arthur, which had in fact suddenly appeared as the only possible solution to Constance's problems.

"I wonder if I should come with you," Joan Mountjoy mused.

"That would be splendid," Constance said. She was telling the truth. She was fleeing, in the wildest disarray, from a situation she could no longer cope with. But she was fleeing to Kate, who was also sufficiently difficult to cope with. The more encumbrances she could hang around her neck, the better. And the safer.

"Yes," Joan said. "But I do not suppose I can leave James . . . there is so much to be done here."

Clearly she had no desire to travel as companion to the empress's favorite, especially when that favorite was the woman she most heartily disliked in all the world—even had she any desire to see her daughter in total domesticity with a Chinese husband.

On reflection, Constance decided, she was better off without her. Because, if she *was* being a coward—and she had no doubt of that—she was at least an optimistic coward. She was shutting the door on Frank Wynne because she just could not face the problems an affair with him would necessarily entail, the decisions it would require, the disasters it might well involve. But she had not renounced her dreams altogether. She was going to Kate, and however much she feared the possible results of that, Kate could well provide what she so desperately needed. And in total confidence. She could reason that if it were possible to have one *fling*, without any fear of the consequences, then she could make herself spend the rest of her life contentedly as Mrs. Henry Baird, even if it involved readmitting Henry to her room from time to time.

She could think that, and reason that, in the privacy of her own mind, knowing full well that she would never *do* it, and that if Kate even suggested it, she would be on the next ship back to Tientsin. Was that not why she was taking Charles? She was going to be away for only a few weeks. But with Charles along the chances of her behaving stupidly were that much more reduced.

She supposed she must be the most miserably confused woman in all China, if not the world.

But ending Frank had to come first. Should she write to him? The visit to Port Arthur had been timed to overlap his next furlough, and now was when he had asked her to write. But what could she say? Again the coward. Because she knew that if she once put pen to paper, she would have to give him some hope, some dream of his own, and therefore the affair would not be over. It would be waiting, *he* would be waiting, for the next time they met. But even Frank, determined and optimistic as he was, would have to accept the fact that when she should have been writing to him to establish a liaison, and then anticipating the liaison itself, and then enjoying it in his arms, she had taken herself off to Port Arthur. Even Frank would have to be angry at that. And in making Frank angry was the only safety she could be sure of.

The trouble was that to reach Port Arthur she had to pass through Tientsin, and then out into the Gulf of Chihli, where the warships lay at anchor. Tientsin did not appear to have changed at all, and when she checked into the hotel, with Elizabeth and Peter—both pleasantly excited by the coming journey—and Miriam, less so, as she was no traveler, Tao-li was there with the rest of the staff to cluster around Charles and admire him. "You fine lady now," Tao-li remarked, suggesting, Constance supposed, that she had been far from that on her arrival. But Tao-li, like everyone else in China, would know that the celestial-haired young woman was the empress's favorite.

Next day they took the sampan out across the bar, to where the SS *Kowshin* waited. The freighter surprisingly flew the British flag as well as the Chinese, as she was apparently a Hong Kong vessel chartered by the Chinese government as their link with Port Arthur—it was far quicker to steam the hundred miles across the Gulf of Chihli than to make the very long and arduous journey around by land, through the mountains of Jehol—and in fact she possessed an English captain, as well as an English engineer, both of whom were delighted to welcome their famous passenger.

"Which one is the *Alabama?*" she asked, gazing at the half-dozen American warships which were moored perhaps a mile distant.

"She'll be that one," said Captain Cuthbertson, pointing. "The cruiser. Would you like to use the glass?"

Constance leveled the offered telescope, could make out the guns, the sailors on deck, even the odd marine—but no Frank

Wynne. And why should she wish to see him? she wondered. That was futile. She had made her decision. She would discover what Port Arthur and Kate had to offer, and then she would mend her fences with Henry and settle back into domesticity and be the perfect missionary's wife. She dined with Captain Cuthbertson, tucked Charles in, and went to her own bunk in a happier and more contented frame of mind than for a very long time—since that tumultuous ride to Peking had first launched her into this world which was so strange, so abhorrent in many ways . . . and so sinisterly attractive.

Franklin Wynne walked up the steps of the American consulate in Tientsin, winked at the marine guard. He supposed it was outrageous of him to be so happy. So excited. He felt like a small boy again.

Because he was in love. He knew this now. And because it was going to happen. In just seven days Constance would be in his arms. He found it difficult to believe.

He supposed what he was setting out to do, seduce another man's wife, was incredibly caddish. He would never have dreamed of it, he knew, but for the reputation she had accumulated; however much she had attracted him on the voyage out from San Francisco, however much he had enjoyed thinking of her, and even, guiltily, of *them*, he had determined to put her from his mind the moment they arrived in China. And had done so successfully—for a while. He had thought her quite exorcised from his mind after he had written that letter, to which he had never had a reply, and certainly when the news had come down the coast that she was pregnant.

And then, last year, the rumors had started. Begun by Harriet Bunting, certainly; she really was a poisonous woman. But in a country where white people had nothing to do *but* gossip, the tales of Constance's carryings-on had spread like the plague. She spent whole nights in the Forbidden City—the very title conveyed every possible suggestion of orgiastic sin. And if anyone doubted, there was the marriage of Kate Mountjoy to a *Chinese*. That he was a prince had really not been very relevant. So, by association, Constance had to be . . . what? No one had actually dared put the suspicions into words.

And so she had once again forced her way into his life. In the most masculine of fashions. She was a beautiful woman to whom he had always been extremely attracted . . . and she was *available*. It had been in that totally selfish mood that he had approached her, in the Buntings' garden, and immediately realized how wrong he was. Constance Baird *might* be available, but on her terms; she was no whore. Yet, the thought, the idea, already in his mind, he had blundered on . . . and she had not refused him. In fact, had those Chinese louts not turned up at the crimson pagoda, anything might have happened.

In the heat of those moments he had said a lot of things, partly to excuse his conduct and partly to persuade her to do as he wished. He had wanted *her*, physically, because she had a greater physical attraction for him than any other woman he had ever met. He had not been prepared to consider what might come after. But now he had done nothing but think about it for six weeks. And he knew he had not, after all, been stringing a line. Of course he still wanted her, with an utterly consuming passion, increased because he had not yet succeeded. But there was more than that now. Her image filled his every thought, and not just physically. Having spoken with her again, gotten to know her, to understand her, he now knew that she was everything he had ever wanted in a woman. So perhaps she remained unsure whether or not she loved him. That was understandable. She was in a very difficult and confused position. But she *would* love him, as he already loved her. Thus the coming visit to Peking was far more than an affair, if it was an affair at all. He no longer cared about that. It was to be a proposal, and a discussion, and a time for plans and decisions. Therefore he was not being a cad, after all. He was attempting to correct a mistake which was threatening to blight all of their lives—the fact of her marriage to the wrong man.

It wasn't going to be easy. He accepted that. The Navy frowned on their junior officers—or their senior ones, for that matter—making off with other men's wives. But the problems would be overcome, because he was determined to secure her divorce and to marry her. Nothing was going to stand in the way of that. Nothing in all the world. He loved her.

"Well, Milner," he shouted at the mail clerk. "You've a letter for me, I think."

"I'm afraid not, Captain," the little man said, riffling through the envelopes.

"Oh, damnation. You mean the mail hasn't come down from Peking yet?"

"Oh, yes, Mr. Wynne. The mail is in."

Frank frowned at him. "And there's nothing for me?"

"No, sir." Milner looked suitably depressed, his mustache drooping almost like a mandarin's. Then he smiled brightly as a thought came to him. "Did you see Mrs. Baird yesterday?"

Frank, turning for the door, turned back. It was difficult to estimate how much people like Milner actually *knew*. But that was no longer relevant. "Yesterday?"

"She was in Tientsin yesterday afternoon."

"Here? Constance?" Frank's heart gave a great bound. Why write a letter when she could come herself. "She's at the hotel, you mean? Why didn't you say so before, you scoundrel?" He ran for the door.

"But she's not at the hotel, Mr. Wynne," Milner said.

Frank checked in the doorway. "Not at the hotel? Then . . . where is she?"

"She boarded the *Kowshin*, for Port Arthur. I understood that she was going for a holiday." He pointed. "I think you can still see her smoke on the horizon."

Constance slept soundly, and was on deck at dawn to watch the approaching land, the two clawlike arms which extended from the very end of the Liaotung peninsula to hold within their embrace the huge landlocked harbor that was Port Arthur. She exclaimed over the beauty of the scenery, the craggy mountains so different from the flat plain of North China. The town's busy docks and teeming streets contrasted with the utter peace of the houses climbing up the hillsides behind it, the whole softened by the gentle breeze from the sea, seemingly propelled by the huge sun rising out of the Sea of Japan to the east.

"Port Arthur is just about the finest natural harbor in all Asia," said Captain Cuthbertson. "You'll like it here, Mrs. Baird. Oh, you'll like it here."

"I am sure I shall," Constance agreed as she looked at the dock where they would berth, and made out the tall figure of Prince Ksian Fu, himself come to meet her.

# 7

# The Prince

"Constance!" Ksian Fu spoke English, and held out both his arms, as any Westerner might have done. Constance entered them cautiously. He was exactly as she remembered him from the last time they had met, on Chu-teh the day he had been properly married, tall and handsome and utterly confident. His embrace was gentle, and he brushed her cheek with his lips. "And you have brought Charlie," he said with evident pleasure. "How splendid. Kate will be so pleased. Do you know"—he tucked Constance's arm under his as he escorted her to the waiting palanquin, while his escort stood to attention and the dock officials bowed obsequiously—"it may even help her to conceive, to have a child about the place. We try, you know, but . . ." He shrugged. "Man proposes, and God disposes, eh?"

Constance realized she had not actually spoken since landing. But she had nothing to say. She had jumped with both feet from the frying pan into the fire. But this man, for all the way in which he looked at her, as if stripping her naked with his eyes—or perhaps he was merely remembering, as that was all he *had* to do—had chosen Kate in front of her, and seemed happy enough with that choice. So it was once again only her overheated imagination tormenting her, the idea that she should be alone in a palanquin with such a man, reclining on soft cushions and yet being moved continuously by the jolting walk of the bearers—the maids and Charles had been placed in another litter behind them.

"She *is* well?" she asked. "Kate, I mean."

"Of course. But I wanted to meet you by myself."

Constance's head turned sharply.

He smiled at her. "I wanted to be sure that you were as beautiful as I remembered."

She opened her mouth, and closed it again, took a long breath instead. "Is it possible," she asked, "to open the curtains? I would so like to look at the town."

"It is certainly possible," he agreed. "But I do not really recommend it. If you can look at the town, you see, Constance, the town will be able to look at you."

"I don't mind being stared at, really I don't," she said. After all, she was stared at whenever she rode through the streets of Peking. But he would not know that.

The prince regarded her for a moment, then shrugged and reached up to pull the curtains back on both sides, revealing that they were making their way through a narrow and very crowded street, and making Constance realize that she had never traveled in a litter through the streets of Peking. They were accompanied by the prince's guard, who marched on either side of the palanquin, swords resting on their shoulders, and yet the crowds pressed close, real Chinese as well as obvious Mongols, men and women, with their children and their dogs, hawking and spitting, all craning their necks to stare at the white lady with the yellow hair, and at their governor, whom presumably they had never seen so close before. Constance could smell them, and despite the guards, she instinctively shrank away from them into the center of the litter at the thought that they might be able to reach inside and touch her.

"You see?" Ksian Fu drew the curtains again. "I shall arrange for you to be taken on a tour of the city, by my people. It *is* a city. It is booming and expanding all the time. All we have to do is keep the Japanese from making nuisances of themselves, and Port Arthur may well become the greatest seaport in Asia, greater even than Shanghai."

"And is there really a chance the Japanese may become 'nuisances'?" she asked.

He shrugged. "They are nuisances already. The Japanese have always been nuisances. They are hereditary enemies of China, because they can only expand onto Chinese territory. And every time they are ruled by an ambitious general, they dream of acquiring Korea, which has been our client since time began. Now they are ruled, in the name of this reinstated emperor of theirs, by a whole clutch of ambitious generals. And ambitious admirals, too. Oh, we shall have to teach them a lesson sometime soon, you may be sure of that." He sank onto his elbow beside her, touched her hand. "But you did not come all the way to Port Arthur to worry about the Japanese, Constance. Now, tell me all about Peking and about the empress. Is the old Dragon Lady still as formidable as ever? And are you still her favorite confidante?"

The Governor's Palace was set high on the hills behind the town. From the front patio, where they left the palanquin and its panting bearers, Constance could look down at the teeming city beneath her, then at the docks, equally busy, and then at the harbor, and understand that it was even larger than she had supposed, with little coves and inlets stretching in every direction.

"The entire British Navy could ride at anchor in here," Ksian Fu remarked with some pride. "In perfect safety."

To the north, she again looked at hills, several of them higher than even the one on which she stood, guarding the approaches to the port.

"Those are our inner defenses," Ksian Fu explained. "Each one contains a fort, and we are actually adding to the fortifications all the time. But they are unlikely ever to have to fire a shot in anger. Beyond them, you see, the peninsula narrows to a neck of land hardly fifty feet across. There we have built more forts, and there is where we would stop any assailant. No army in the world could batter its way across that isthmus, were it adequately defended, and I promise you it always will be adequately defended. And here in Port Arthur we have sufficient food and water to withstand a siege of years, even if we did not also have the sea as a lifeline."

"You are speaking as if there is no question you will have to fight," Constance said.

"There *is* no question that we shall have to fight," Ksian Fu said gravely. "And when we do, Port Arthur will certainly be the prize the Japanese will wish to gain above all others."

"But . . . Kate?"

He took her arm to escort her up the broad stone steps to the three-story, veranda-fronted, pagoda-roofed palace, a glow of red lacquer and copper sheeting in the morning sunlight. "Kate will be perfectly safe. As I have just explained, Port Arthur is impregnable."

Constance felt somewhat breathless; she had had no idea relations between China and Japan had so deteriorated—there was no suggestion of it in Peking. But presumably Ksian Fu had every reason for his confidence; there was no way a tiny group of offshore islands like the Japanese Empire could take on the mighty power of the Dragon—even the Dragon in decay—with any hope of success.

Certainly Kate did not seem the slightest uneasy. "Constance!" she squealed, almost tumbling down the inner staircase, quite literally, as she wore a loose Chinese robe and seemed to get her feet all mixed up. Her husband fielded her at the bottom, while her servants waited gravely above her. "Oh, Constance." They hugged each other. "It is so good to see you. And you've brought little Charlie. Oh, isn't he a darling. And Lizzie and Peter? How good to see you. Let me see, you're Miriam, aren't you? Oh, welcome, welcome. It's so nice to see familiar faces."

"I've brought letters, as well," Constance told her. "From your mother and father."

"Oh, yes?" Kate asked without great interest, tucking Constance's arm beneath her own to escort her into the house. Constance glanced at Ksian Fu. He smiled, but there was little amusement in his eyes. Oh, Lord, Constance thought. They are not happy, after all.

He was not happy, at any rate. There was no suggestion of unhappiness on Kate's part, and certainly no suggestion that she might be aware that her constant prattle or her lack of dignity might be annoying to her husband. And she had a great deal to be happy about, Constance thought as she was escorted through the various open galleries and into reception rooms filled with priceless furniture of oak and ebony, and even more priceless ornaments in jade and ivory, with every table a mass of exquisite chinaware. "Quite a lot of the furniture was here already, of course," Kate explained. "But we had to do some shopping to make it just right. We even have our own chapel." She giggled. "And a Chinese priest. But he says all the right things. He was properly ordained."

Again Constance turned her head to look for the prince, but he had abandoned them. And now she was being shown into her bedroom, a splendidly light and airy apartment which looked out over the harbor, and contained a European four-poster. But no cot. "Where will Charles sleep?" she asked.

"I have arranged separate rooms for the servants. Charles will sleep with them. But you can have him in here whenever you wish."

"Oh," Constance said. She had never actually slept with Charles more than a few feet away, except when she had been absent from Chu-teh. But, she thought, when in Rome . . . and wondered what Harriet Bunting would make of all this. And then had to shake her head to get rid of the reflection, because thinking about Harriet would lead to thinking about Frank.

"Now," Kate said, "I know you'll wish to get changed, and put on something comfortable, and then have a bath."

"That would be very nice," Constance agreed, looking around her for either tub or servants, and finding none.

"I will send Hyacinth to you," Kate said. "That is what I call her, Hyacinth, because she is as pretty as a flower. But we have our own bathhouse here. No tubs. Hyacinth will bring you down as soon as you are ready."

"Oh," Constance said again, less because she did not really wish to be bathed than because Kate had suddenly become all pink-cheeked and breathless. "All right."

"Quick as you can," Kate gasped, and hurried from the room. Constance scratched her head—an automatic gesture, as she had taken great care to have Lizzie check her scalp before landing—and then looked at the Chinese girl who had entered the room and was now bowing. And she *was* as pretty as a picture; she made Constance think of a female version of Lin-tu—which again made her want to stamp her foot with annoyance. She had not come here to think about Lin-tu any more than Frank Wynne. Rather she had come to forget them both.

"You wear pretty robe," Hyacinth said, holding it out. It was silk, in green and silver, and had matching slippers.

"Thank you very much," Constance said, and undressed herself. The girl waited, obviously trained by Kate, not attempting to help but gathering up the sweat-sodden garments as they were discarded and throwing them into a wicker basket. Then she again held up the robe for Constance to wrap herself in.

"You come," she said. "For bath."

Constance nodded, and pinned her hair up on the top of her head before following the girl down the corridor, and then down a flight of steps, across an inner patio, open to the sky—rather a long walk for a tub, she thought—and then down another flight of steps before Hyacinth opened a door to admit her into a room very like the bathhouse in Peking, although somewhat smaller. Kate was already in the pool in the center, soaking. With her was Ksian Fu.

Constance stood absolutely still. For although she had never doubted that in coming to Port Arthur she would be entering a world more intimate than any she had previously experienced, it had not really occurred to her that she would be expected to take part in that intimacy. To share a bath with Kate would have been unusual, and somewhat disconcerting—but they had shared a bath before, and more besides, and they were close friends. To be asked to share a bath with Kate *and* her husband, especially when that husband was Ksian Fu . . .

Who was now standing up; the water came only to his thighs. "Assist Mrs. Baird, Hyacinth," he said.

Constance's head jerked. She had been so preoccupied with his presence she had not realized there were yet other people in the room. But now that she had desperately to try *not* to look at him, she discovered that there were two other maidservants as well as two eunuchs waiting at the far side of the bath, with cakes of soap. Two eunuchs? They were at least fully dressed, like the maids. But that was still too much, she told herself. Far, far too much.

But Hyacinth had already removed the robe from her shoulders, and she was standing, totally exposed, at the top of the marble steps leading into the water, while Ksian Fu had advanced to the foot of the steps and was holding out his hand for her. "You are even more beautiful than I remember," he said.

She looked at him without meaning to. But he kept himself under perfect control. And why should he not find it easy to do so, she wondered, if he enjoyed so sybaritic a life-style all the time? His fingers closed on hers, and she descended into the warm water, no longer looking at him, afraid to look at Kate. . . .

"You have embarrassed her," Kate said. "Constance! My dear Constance. This is what life is all *about*."

What, exactly? Constance asked herself, and sank beneath the water; not that it offered a great deal of concealment, being quite translucent. Where was the prince? Her head turned anxiously, but he had retreated to the far side of the bath, although he continued to smile at her. Hastily she looked away again. "We are having a small supper party for you this evening," he said. "Just to introduce you to Port Arthur society."

"It's so nice here," Kate told her. "We meet so many interesting people. Ksian has to do a great deal of entertaining. I do love entertaining. When I think of those dreary days on Chu-teh, never seeing a soul, ugh." She clapped her hands, and her voice changed, sharpening like a whip crack. "Chou! Soap!"

One of the eunuchs immediately knelt on the side of the bath and began lathering her neck and shoulders, slowly moving down her body, careless of his sleeves dipping into the water. Constance gazed at the prince in consternation, but he did not seem to mind. "Are you ready now?" he asked. "To be soaped?"

To be . . . She turned her head wildly from left to right and saw the other eunuch approaching her.

Constance sat on Ksian Fu's right, a French lady, Madame Ligonier, wife of the French consul, opposite her. On her right was a Japanese naval lieutenant, Shige Yamamoto, and next to him was the wife of the German consul, Frau von Werner. Next to the Frenchwoman was an English naval officer, and next to him the wife of the Russian consul. As there were sixteen to dinner, the far end of the huge table was lost in a fog of conversation, the only certain factor being the presence of Kate, auburn hair upswept, pink shoulders glowing—she wore European evening dress, with a deep décolletage.

So did the other ladies. And so did Constance. Her hair was also up, and she wore her best cream satin gown, with its deep crimson sleeves and bodice, to set off at once the paleness of her flesh and the luster of her golden hair, while at Kate's suggestion she also wore her emerald—Tz'u-Hsi had had it set in a ring for her, and it was by some distance the largest stone in the room: Constance had never dared wear it in public before. But the emerald, glowing and winking in the candlelight, was only one aspect of the total unreality of her surroundings, of her very being. She hardly heard what was being said around her, as she had hardly caught any of the guests' names. But then, she could hardly bring herself to look at them. Because if they *knew* . . . But didn't they have to know? And if they did not, did she not have the wildest urge to tell them? Do you know, she wanted to say, I bathed this afternoon, naked, with the prince only inches away. And I was lathered by a eunuch. A *eunuch*, soft hands slipping across her breasts and under her arms, and then sliding beneath the water to soap the rest of her. She had been touched, caressed, by a half-man, where no *man* had ever touched her before. She had supposed she would explode, or at least faint . . . certainly she had supposed she would leap out of the bath and run from the room screaming. Yet she had done nothing save stand there and submit, staring at Ksian Fu, because he had been watching her, while her knees had turned to water.

While Kate had bubbled with happy embarrassment. Because Kate had planned it all. No doubt about that. Kate had planned to shock her and embarrass her, make her understand what she was missing—and had been embarrassed herself. And a little put out, Constance thought with some satisfaction, that she had not visibly turned a hair.

That all of that could have happened only a few hours ago,

and that she should now be sitting next to him at dinner, that he should be wearing a Western-style evening suit, and gravely engaging in conversation, when every time he looked at her he would be remembering . . . But then she had a sudden terrible thought—that if this was his normal way of living, perhaps he would not be remembering at all. Perhaps it was just no longer interesting or exciting to him. And perhaps every woman in this room had at some time or other shared his bath.

As if it mattered. Because she could remember *him*. All about him.

"The key to Port Arthur is the sea," Lieutenant Yamamoto was saying in perfect English.

More unreality. Ksian Fu had told her he was sure China would have to go to war with Japan, and soon. Yet here was a Japanese naval officer sitting at the prince's own dining table and calmly discussing the strengths and weaknesses of the port, in *English*.

"For while I entirely agree with you, Highness," the lieutenant continued, "that the isthmus can hardly be rushed in the face of a determined defender, it can be flanked by a naval force. Would you not agree?"

"I doubt even that would succeed, my dear lieutenant," Ksian Fu said. "But as you say, in any war fought on the eastern seaboard of China, and in the Japanese Sea or off Korea, command of the ocean will be a very important factor. Do you suppose we are boring the ladies?"

"I think it is terrifying, all this talk of war," remarked Madame Ligonier. "Why should men fight? Why should your two countries wish to fight? You do not wish to fight with Lieutenant Yamamoto, Prince Ksian Fu? Surely. And I am equally sure that Lieutenant Yamamoto has no wish to fight with you."

"A terrible thought, madame," the Japanese officer agreed. "But we are both the servants of our governments, are we not, Highness? We merely take orders."

Ksian Fu looked as if he might have liked to argue that point as well, but decided against it. "As you say, Yamamoto, we must go where our duty takes us."

"And be sure that at least, should it ever come to a conflict between our two great nations," Yamamoto went on, "it shall be fought in the most civilized of spirits." He smiled at Constance. "In that direction, perhaps, we might be able to teach *your* people something, Mrs. Baird."

"I hope so," she said. "I do hope so. But I entirely agree with Madame Ligonier. I can see no reason for it."

"Perhaps one day," Yamamoto said, "the world will be ruled by women, and wars will become obsolete. Although . . ." His eyes twinkled. "History does not suggest that would be the case. Even Queen Victoria may have kept Great Britain out of any European involvement since the Crimea, but British soldiers are fighting a hundred and one little wars all over the world, all the time. Other female monarchs have been even more warlike. But in Japan we have not had a female ruler for over a thousand years. Have you ever been to Japan, Mrs. Baird?"

"Why, no," she said. "No, I haven't."

"Then I invite you to visit us whenever it becomes possible. I promise you, it is the loveliest place on earth. I think perhaps even His Highness might agree to that."

"I have never been to Japan," Ksian Fu said a trifle coldly. But Constance gained the impression he was less displeased with what his guest was saying than with the way the young lieutenant was monopolizing her conversation.

Kate had noticed it as well. "He is quite a charmer, isn't he?" she said when the ladies had withdrawn to permit the men to smoke their cigars in masculine peace. "But, well . . . he *is* Japanese."

"Is that so very bad?" Constance asked.

Kate rolled her eyes.

"Japanese are not to be trusted," said Frau von Werner. "Especially Japanese men. I have never met a Japanese woman," she added, as if this proved her point.

"My dear, the things one hears said of the men," said Madame Ligonier.

And what do they say of Chinese men? Constance wondered. But it was not a question she felt she could ask in her present company.

Constance lay awake and listened to the soft rasp of the cicadas in the bushes beyond her window. This far north, the gardens were less formal than the superb but rather monotonous paradises created by the wealthy Chinese south of the Great Wall. Or perhaps Kate's influence had already been at work, and a certain element of waywardness allowed to creep in, occasional differences in size between the various flowerbeds, an irregularity in the width of the paths. It was still a magnificent garden, a teeming wonderland of miniature waterfalls and rushing streams, quiet pools where the inevitable goldfish gathered, and damply blooming hydrangeas dominating the walks.

She rolled on her side, gazed out of the window, waiting for a breeze. Although it was late autumn, it remained very close and warm; her cotton nightgown was soaked with sweat. The nights were invariably still, relieved only toward dawn by the land breeze which would spring up and sough through the house with surprising strength, cooling and even chilling the air. But this was the first night the heat had made her quite so wide-awake.

She sat up, and then swung her legs out of bed and stood up, crossing the floor to the window. It was difficult to convince herself that she had been here a week. It had been the pleasantest seven days of her life, as well as the most exciting. More exciting even than stepping ashore at Tientsin two years ago, because then apprehension had so rapidly been overtaken by disappointment at not seeing Henry, and the disappointments, as well as the apprehensions, had only grown. Here in Port Arthur there were no apprehensions, but instead a continuous awareness of being alive, of herself as a human being, which she had never felt before on this constant level. It was entirely controlled by her hosts, of course, but she could no longer feel that their behavior was intended to project a new way of life at her. It happened to be *their* way of life, and she had been invited to join it.

She could not help but wonder what would happen when Joan Mountjoy *did* come to visit her daughter. But she could not see Ksian Fu allowing any compromises, so Joan would no doubt stagger back to Chu-teh in a state of total shock. Which was an absorbing thought, because the prince and his wife bathed every day, and their guest was expected to join them. It was no longer even the slightest bit embarrassing, but rather an event to be keenly anticipated, just as she spent a good deal of each twenty-four hours awaiting the ministrations of the eunuch D'ao, who was her personal assistant on these occasions. If it was amusing to consider what Joan Mountjoy's reactions might be to such a way of life, it was impossible to imagine what Henry's or, for that matter, Frank's reactions would be to know that she was bathed by a eunuch every day, and enjoyed it. It would be quite impossible to convince them that there was nothing obscene in it. Erotic, certainly, at least for her. It left her for the rest of the evening in a glow of self-awareness, a glow in which Kate seemed to exist all the time, but which undoubtedly gave her a tremendous vivacity, an outpouring which could not help but be attractive, just as it left her all the next morning waiting only for

the bath time to arrive again. But D'ao never put a finger wrong,
never gave any one part of her body more attention than any
other, never suggested, by either look or action, that he was
achieving any satisfaction from his work, just as he had nothing
to do with any other of her domestic offices, which were left
entirely in the hands of Hyacinth and Lizzie and Miriam.

Yet there *was* obscenity in the atmosphere. At least there was
what Henry, and again, probably Frank, would certainly consider
obscenity. She took part in Ksian Fu's and Kate's life, bathed
with them, ate with them wearing the thinnest of Chinese robes,
and also laughed with them and walked with them, and rode with
them, and played cards with them, for Ksian Fu, like the empress,
was a passionate card player. But Constance did not *share* their
life. Because, with Kate and Ksian Fu, the sexuality which
pervaded their household was clearly a means to an end. There
could be no doubt about that. And that end, by means of the
prince's bed, made Kate sparkle far more than any of her guests
could do. So undoubtedly she would provide a substitute for any
of those guests who required it. Constance indeed often got the
impression that Kate was deliberately steering their conversation
in that direction, certainly whenever they were alone together,
and she always just as hastily steered it away again. Because
having come here and sampled what she had always dreamed of,
she *had* no desire to carry it to the ultimate. It was not just an
awareness of the criminality of it, in Christian eyes. It was not
even a reluctance to physically submit as completely as she knew
would be required by a Chinese man, even one hired for the
occasion. And it was not even a fear that the anticipation would
have to be better than the event.

Rather was it a certainty that to surrender to that basest and
most basic of instincts would leave her no longer Constance Baird,
and even less Constance Drummond—which was nowadays far
more important to her—just as Kate was no longer Catherine Mountjoy. Kate was no longer even the Princess Ksian Fu. She was Prince
Ksian Fu's wife, which was something very different. She was
his woman. His chief concubine, no more than that—Constance
could see little evidence that the prince paid anything more than
lip service to the Christianity he professed, and she could not
doubt that he sought his pleasures wherever his fancy took him.
Certainly there was an inordinately large number of females
about the Governor's Palace, and not all of them appeared to have
any work to do. A situation Kate either was not aware of, or,
more likely, had to accept, because she had no voice in her
husband's affairs. Her domain was the house and the garden;

Ksian Fu never discussed politics with her, and when he took Constance to see the defenses at the isthmus, Kate was rather pointedly left behind. Thus she had failed to secure the position gained for her by her beauty and her nationality—and she was continuing to fail by her inability to produce a son. But Constance doubted that even to become pregnant would really rescue Kate now. For all his Western ideas and professions, Ksian Fu was yet a Ch'ing prince, and regarded women as naturally inferior beings. Kate's only chance had been to prove her equality by means of her conversation and her learning and her intelligence—as Constance had proved her equality to Tz'u-Hsi—and she was quite incapable of doing that.

So all was not perfect in paradise, she thought sadly. Perhaps it never was, and never could be. She turned from the window toward her bed, illuminated by the moonlight streaming across the floor, and stopped in surprise. Because a man stood just inside the door.

A man? Surprisingly, she was not the least afraid, because she knew at once that it was not a man, after all. "D'ao?" she asked. "What are you doing here?"

"You are to come with me, lady," D'ao said.

"With you? It is the middle of the night."

"You must come," D'ao said. "As you are awake." He held out a robe. "You will wear this."

Slowly Constance extended her hand, touched the robe. It was silk. And now her heartbeat was increasing even as her stomach seemed gripped in a vise. And her brain, too. She took the robe, made to pull it over her nightgown, and was stopped by an impatient shake of D'ao's head. "Not over the other," he said. "Remove the other first."

"D'ao," she said, "I have no intention of changing my nightgown. I don't know what you are doing in here, but I think you had better be off."

Words. She didn't believe one of them. He had come for her, and she would go with him. As she had known would happen from the moment she had seen the prince waiting for her on the dock, without ever being able to admit her knowledge even to herself.

D'ao didn't believe her either. "You come," he said. "Or I carry. Carrying is proper," he explained.

But it would certainly be uncomfortable, and difficult; she was taller than he. She turned her back on him to drop her nightgown on the floor and put on the silk one sent by the prince. This formality was absurd, of course. But it was happening, and it was what she wanted to happen. What she had wanted to happen, she knew, almost from the day she had landed in China, and certainly since the day she and Kate had blundered into the Forbidden City.

And the fact of it, of her adultery? Or Kate? She knew these things were there and would have to be faced eventually. She knew that had the prince acted like Frank Wynne, or any Westerner, she supposed, and made a formal proposition, she would have refused him as angrily as she would have refused him had he attempted to touch her in the bath, or made some other physical advance. Instead he had merely summoned her, not doubting that she would come, because he had looked on her and found her desirable, as she had looked on him and found him the most desirable man in the world. That was probably more insulting than any other approach he could have made—but it was different, non-European. It was *Chinese*.

She followed D'ao along corridors and down staircases, and then up again, until a door was opened for her, and she stepped into the prince's bedroom. She had not been here before, although she spent much time in Kate's bedroom—the fact that Kate and her husband maintained separate rooms, and in widely different parts of the palace, had been one of the earliest confirmations of her deduction that theirs was not a conventional marriage, by Western standards.

The room was lit by two candles set on tables in opposite corners, so that although there was light it was a vague, flickering glow. The prince sat in the center of his bed, which was hardly more than a couch—although as broad as it was long—cross-legged, and naked. Constance stopped just within the doorway, aware that the door itself had closed against her back. She drew a long breath, but waited for him to speak first.

He said nothing. She took a step into the center of the room, and checked again. If you go through with this, Constance Drummond, she told herself—it was quite impossible at this moment to think of herself as Constance Baird—then you will never be able to look yourself in the eye again. But if she did not go through with it, she would hate herself for the rest of her life.

She took another step forward, checked, and shrugged the robe from her shoulders, felt it slide down her arms and past her thighs to the floor. And now her eyes were sufficiently attuned to the gloom for her to see properly. She had never looked at a man so totally aroused before, and sitting, he seemed even larger than she had supposed possible. She took another long breath, and reached the bed. But she couldn't just go and sit on his lap.

"How . . . how did you know I was awake?" she asked.

"D'ao has watched you every night since you came," he replied. "We knew you would be awake, one night. Awake, and wanting."

"And you were prepared to wait?"

"All things are improved by waiting," Ksian Fu said. "Even death. Love is doubled, trebled, quadrupled, by waiting."

Her knees touched the mattress. She would have to crawl toward him. As no doubt he wished. Constance Drummond, crawling naked toward a man. As if it mattered anymore. She thought she would lie on her belly and *squirm* toward him if he demanded it. She crawled up the bed, gazing at him, only stopping when he could reach her. But unlike Frank, or any Western man, she supposed, he made no attempt to touch her breasts, instead cupped her buttocks, and sent his fingers sliding between her legs. She wanted to scream, but it was at least part ecstasy. Then she wanted to close her thighs on him, but she remained kneeling, panting now, fallen back onto her haunches as he stroked and played, while kaleidoscopic thoughts tumbled through her mind, and her heartbeat rose to a crescendo, and she was on his lap, with him inside her, but he had lain down, so that she was astride his thighs, while he moved his own body, to and fro, as well as up and down, seeming to be scouring her, sending sensation shooting away from her vagina to the tips of her toes and then it seemed the very ends of each hair on her head. And now he did touch her breasts, stroking and caressing the nipples, and bringing them hard, while the explosion Kate had promised her, and of which she had dreamed for so long, ignited within her.

As Kate had promised her. She had betrayed her friend as she had betrayed herself. She was damned. How could she ever face herself again? Or Henry? Or even the empress?

But facing Kate came first. They walked together in the garden, as they did most mornings, Ksian Fu gone from the palace to attend to affairs of state. They followed Charles, being pushed in his pram by Miriam, Lizzie at her side, but at a distance, so that they were out of earshot. It was a morning like any other. But it was unlike any morning Constance had ever known before.

Her confusion was increased by her physical feelings. For she *could* still feel, and still remember. She had spent two hours with the prince, and he had sent her soaring into that wonderworld she still could not believe possible, on three more occasions, the last with his fingers alone, as he had himself been exhausted. She felt as if she were floating along the garden path on a cloud of physical ecstasy. She did not wish the feeling ever to fade. And should it do so, she wanted it renewed, again and again and again. As it would be, because when he had finished, and before he had summoned D'ao to take her back to her bedchamber, he had stroked her chin lightly with one finger and said, "You are even *more* beautiful than I suspected. You might have been a virgin."

Because she *had* been a virgin, mentally. But what was she now? She was an American gentlewoman, the wife of a missionary, who had just surrendered herself in the most abject and obscene fashion to the ministrations of a man. In the space of two hours she had thrown away everything she had ever treasured about herself, her privacy and her dignity, her moral sense and her upbringing. She was utterly ruined. And she was utterly guilty. And yet she was also utterly happy, more happy than she had ever been in her life before, or would be ever again, she suspected.

But Kate, walking at her side . . .

"Was it as good as I promised you?" Kate asked.

Constance stopped walking. Her knees seemed to have solidified.

Kate did not even look wistful, much less angry. But as Constance did not reply, she *did* look a little apprehensive. "You did let him?" she asked.

They were close to a stone bench. Constance sat down, before she fell down. "I . . ." I have no idea what you are talking about, was what she had to say, if she could get the words out. Only complete denial could possibly save the situation now.

Kate sat beside her. "I can see that you did," she said. "Was it the Fish Interlocking Their Scales? That's what they call it, you know, when the woman is on top. That's Ksian's favorite position. But he also likes the Fish Eye to Eye. That's lying alongside each other. And he likes the White Tiger Leaps, that's the woman taken from behind. Which one was it?"

It was all three, Constance thought in stupefied horror. It was all *three*.

"Well, it doesn't really matter," Kate said. "I know that he will have made you happy. Then you may be sure that you have made him happy too. And that must make me happy." Now there was at last a touch of sadness in her voice.

"You . . . Oh, Kate." Constance took her hands. "Oh, Kate. How you must *hate* me."

"Hate you? Good heavens. That would be silly. I invited you here, didn't I?"

Constance stared at her, the enormity of what her friend had just said only slowly penetrating her numbed brain.

"Oh, Constance," Kate said. "You *are* innocent. You must be the most innocent girl I have ever met. Ksian Fu has wanted to take you to bed since the day he saw us in the bath in Peking."

"But . . . he chose you."

"Because he is somewhat more intelligent than the empress, believe it or not. He knew that to ask for you would have been to receive you, but he also knew that that would have caused endless repercussions, quarrels with the American legation, perhaps even war. He knows that you cannot just take another man's wife, in our Western society. Besides"—she gave a half-smile—"he wanted *me* as well."

"You *know* all this?" Constance cried.

"Of course. Ksian Fu himself has told me these things. But as soon as we arrived here, he also told me that I must invite you to stay."

Constance scratched her head in sheer bewilderment. "And you *did*?"

"Ksian Fu is my husband," Kate said gravely. "I must do as he wishes."

"Yes, but surely not to the extent of . . . well, procuring for him."

"Now you are speaking like any American," Kate said. "Or any Englishwoman, for that matter. Every Chinese wife looks after her husband's requirements, just as every Chinese mother sees to her son's needs. What, would you have Ksian pick up some girl off the streets? I have personally selected every girl in the palace."

"You . . . Every girl? You mean they *are* concubines?"

"Of course. A Chinese prince must have concubines. He cannot be expected to sleep with the same woman every night of the week."

"And you . . . you just accept the situation?"

Kate sighed. "I was a little put out at first. I had thought, as he was a Christian . . . But when he explained that he had no intention of ever allowing his religion to interfere with the way of life to which he has been born and educated . . . He is a genuine Christian, Constance. He does believe in Jesus, and God, and the Resurrection, and things like that. But he cannot bring himself to accept our moral values. He is sure they are wrong."

"My God," Constance said. "But . . . what are we to do?"
Last year, she remembered, it had been Kate asking *her* that.

"I think everything is going to work out very well," Kate
said. "I think it would be best if you came here twice a year
from now on, for about six weeks each time. That way no one
will ever ask any questions, and Ksian Fu will be happy. And
there is no need for you to fear pregnancy. Should it happen, you
will just decide to stay here awhile longer, until you have given
birth."

"Pregnancy?" Constance gasped. She had not even considered the possibility.

"I will adopt the child," Kate assured her. "The way things
are going, it may be the only one I will ever have. And Ksian
will be delighted. I think it is going to work out *very* well. And
with you here, and then away again . . . He really does prefer
white women to yellow. I think he will come to my bed more
often."

Constance stared at her. "You mean you *want* this to go on?"

"It must, don't you see? We must keep the prince happy."

"We? My God, Kate, I . . ." She was outraged, she told
herself. And wondered why. Had Kate not said anything, she
would have continued to deceive her, and probably returned to
the prince's bed the next time he summoned her. Oh, no
"probably" about it. With her conscience battering at her enjoyment every second. All Kate was offering her was the delight of
sharing Ksian Fu's bed, with no conscience at all involved.
Except now the sudden fear of pregnancy.

"I couldn't bear him to take someone else, Constance," Kate
said. "You and I are friends, and I can trust you. But without
you . . . He has spoken of it. Of seeking a Western secretary or
something like that." Another twisted smile. "He understands,
you see, that he cannot just behave like a Manchu and go to a
European home and say, 'I will have two of your daughters for
my household.' But he will have the same result. You must
understand that he is a prince. He does not know what it is like
to be told no, even to be frustrated at anything he wishes. Life
for him is simply a matter of deciding what he wants, and telling
the appropriate person, and it is delivered to him. Women fall
into the general category of things he wants. But, Connie, you
must admit that he is very good."

I am a thing, Constance thought. I have *been* a thing. An *objet
d'art*, picked up and delivered to the prince for his gratification.
And Kate would now have me become one of his personal
possessions. She was aware of anger, where before she had

known only guilt. But she wasn't sure whom to be angry with: Kate, for having so meekly accepted her situation? Ksian Fu, for living his birthright to the full? or herself, for having been so easily sucked into his net? She only knew for sure that she had to break through the meshes, and quickly, or she *would* become a thing.

"I know it's strange," Kate said. "To think about, and realize it is happening to *you*. You know, one reads about situations like these in books, but you never suppose it can ever happen to *you*. And yet, Connie, life here is a delight. In every way. If you just lie back and let it happen. So many people spend so much time fighting and struggling to better themselves, to gain moral or physical positions, to *do* things and *make* things . . . so let them. Here there is nothing to do but lie back and be loved. And loved and loved and *loved*."

Constance shook her head. "No."

Kate's eyes had been half-shut. Now she opened them wide in alarm. "What do you mean?"

"I mean that it is quite impossible. The whole concept is quite impossible. My God, to think of it . . . to think what I have *done* . . ."

"Connie, you haven't done anything wrong. You have only done something that people have *told* you is wrong all of your life. But here it is *not* wrong. And you are here."

Constance shook her head again and stood up. "I must have been mad ever to *come* here. I would like to leave on the first available sailing."

"You . . ." Kate's eyes filled with tears. "Constance, you can't. I told you, if it's not you, it'll be someone else."

"Yes," Constance said. "Am I that much of a lifeless lump of flesh? If I even could believe that he loved me, not as much as he loves you, of course, but just a little . . ."

"He does," Kate cried. "I know he does."

"He wants the use of my body, and my hair," Constance said bitterly. "I could be a statue that happens to move. He has made me into . . . into a criminal. Against you, against Henry, against everyone. I'm sorry, Kate. I must go. I simply must go." Because if I stay here, she thought, I *shall* surrender. Whether he loves me or whether he never thinks of me at all except when I am in his arms, last night was the most beautiful experience of my life, and I will wish it to happen again. And again and again and again, until I am a nothing. A concubine, like you, Kate. "I must go," she said again.

\* \* \*

Ksian Fu himself accompanied her to the dock; Kate had taken to her bed with a headache.

"I have used the telegraph to inform Peking that you are returning," he said. "And you will be met and escorted to the Forbidden City. No doubt Her Majesty will wish to talk with you, after your separation."

"I . . . That is very kind of you." As usual, she was quite confused. She had expected him to be angry, or at least piqued. But he was as blandly smiling as ever.

"I understand that you have been . . . shall I say, disturbed by our way of life here, Constance. Kate has told me this, but I have observed it for myself as well. Believe me, I would not have had it so."

A flash of spirit whipped through her uncertainty. "But it no longer really matters, because . . ." She gazed at him, feeling herself flush.

"Because I have had my evil way with you, as your American novelists would put it? Believe me, Constance, I shall miss you far more than you will ever miss me. But I do not think our separation is forever. Or even for very long."

She raised her head.

Ksian Fu smiled. "I think it is good for you to go, now, back to your home and your husband. I think it is right for you to have the time to think, and remember, and decide how you wish the rest of your life to be. I think you will make the right decision. So I would hope to see you again soon. You will be invited."

She gazed into his eyes. "I shall not be coming back, Prince Ksian Fu. The night before last was the most beautiful I have ever known. I wish you to understand that, and to understand too my gratitude to you, even if . . ." She bit her lip. There was no point in angering him by telling him that *she* understood it had meant nothing to him at all, for all his flowery words. "Even if I now know it was a mistake. Unlike Kate, I cannot be a part of your world, Highness. I belong in another."

"My dear Constance," he said. "*You* do not decide the world you will belong to. You may as well decide that you will not eat, ever again, and yet still survive. It is Fate decides your world, your future, your happiness or your misery. It is our fate, yours and mine, to meet again. And love again. I am content to wait for that day."

Never, she thought as she stood at the rail of the *Kowshin* and watched the hills of the Liaotung peninsula dropping beneath the horizon. Never, never, never. She had had the adventure she had craved. She had had the experience she had craved. She had sinned. Perhaps she had even craved that, too. But she had survived. Her own strength of character had come to her rescue, and brought her out unscathed. Well, not unscathed, she supposed. Were she pregnant, she could still be very scathed indeed. But that apart, the only damage had been done to her memory, and that could well prove to be an asset. In fact she felt reborn, a complete woman, for the first time in her life, and not only because she had been made to *feel* a complete woman for the first time in her life, but because she had had the courage and determination to walk away from paradise, to be her *own* woman, to rise above her circumstances.

Life had suddenly become a very simple business. A matter of making decisions and knowing that she would abide by those decisions. A matter therefore of deciding what was best, what needed to be done, and doing it, without a single sidelong glance. Thus, if she *was* pregnant, she would abort. The empress would help her to accomplish that. And if the empress would not help her, then she would do it by herself. This resolve was necessary because she was concerned to discover, on her arrival in Peking, with Charles and Peter and Lizzie and Miriam, that Tz'u-Hsi had neither commanded her presence nor arranged an escort to accompany her to Chu-teh. She refused to be frightened, however, herself hired the necessary carts and animals, and relied upon the fact that there were four of them, including a man, for safety.

She had a goal, which was achieved; they rode into Chu-teh on the morning of her twenty-first birthday. No celebration had been planned, of course—she was not even expected, although she doubted there would have been a celebration even had they known she was coming—so she herself organized a dinner party, and invited the Mountjoys and Father Pierre, as well as Sister Ambrosia, the senior of the nuns, a fat and jolly fifty-year-old Provençal woman. It was the first positive act she had performed on Chu-teh in eighteen months, and Henry was obviously pleased.

"I must say," Joan Mountjoy remarked, "your visit to Port Arthur seems to have done you the world of good. Perhaps I *should* visit Kate, after all."

"I am sure she would love to see you," Constance agreed wickedly.

"Joan is quite right," Henry said after the guests had departed, entering her bedroom for the first time since Kate's wedding night. "You should have gone sooner. I would say that the sight of true domestic bliss may have suggested to you how empty you have made our lives."

She gazed at him. But suddenly even Henry was acceptable. He was not someone she could respect, but he was not anyone she could fear, either, anymore. He was a man, with certain weaknesses, which she could understand, and with certain wants, wants she could now cater to, perhaps without his even knowing it. There was also the faint possibility that if she *was* pregnant . . . As if she could possibly hope to pretend Ksian Fu's child was Henry's. But he *was* her husband, and all the physical pleasure she was ever going to receive, for the rest of her life, would have to be provided by him.

Her gaze as usual disconcerted him. He went to the door. "I am sorry," he said. "I but wished you to know that I am pleased to have you home. I had forgotten our bargain."

"Perhaps I would forget it too, tonight," she said. "As I remember, I am entitled to invite you to stay."

Once again, a happy Christmas, reminiscent of her first on Chu-teh. It was in fact happier than she had dared hope, because by a month after her birthday she was quite reassured that she was *not* pregnant, and because her newfound independence of spirit had been achieved in the nick of time. The one thing she had feared over the past year had come to pass: she had clearly been supplanted as the empress's favorite. This much became very evident as week succeeded week and she received no invitation to the Forbidden City, not even an acknowledgement of her polite letter informing Her Majesty that she had returned from Port Arthur, and thanking her for the arrangements she had made. She had either been replaced, or Ksian Fu had told the empress what had happened, or both.

It should have been the moment that Henry had been waiting for, to assert himself, to renew his threats to send her home—perhaps even to carry out the threat. But Henry was too pleased at having regained her, too pleased with what she had become. *He* could not change. She did not expect him to. Anything but the Dragon Turns, as the Chinese interpreted the missionary position, would have been utterly abhorrent to him, as any suggestion of loveplay either before or after would have been opening the gates of hell to loose every available demon. But he clearly enjoyed it when she moved her body against his, and he clearly wanted her more desperately than ever. They developed a little charade, never mentioning the subject, but she would leave her door slightly ajar whenever she wished his company—she rationed herself to three times a week. When her door was closed, he continued to sleep in the spare room.

Their situation had entirely reversed itself, without his being able to understand how it had happened. Nor would she explain it to him, even if she dared. Her personality had swelled where his had diminished. And undoubtedly she had Prince Ksian Fu to thank for that.

This made the prince's memory the more positive, the more demanding, but in a curious way the clarity of the memory made it easier to refuse Kate's repeated invitations to return. Constance's powers of determination were aided by the very fact of having lost her former intimacy with the empress, for the two things, Tz'u-Hsi's fondness for her and Ksian Fu's infatuation with her, were closely linked in her mind. But that was over and done with. She had come to China, been fascinated and perhaps even a little hypnotized, by the strangeness of a civilization she had never suspected to exist, had thrown herself into it, sampled it, and rejected it—and was really very lucky to have emerged almost totally unchanged.

But she had undoubtedly gained a great victory, even over that Fate which Ksian Fu regarded as the ultimate arbiter. Fate could only dictate to those who allowed its dictation. So, to overcome it, it was no doubt necessary to withdraw from the hurly-burly of life, but she was content to do this. She felt that, having experienced so much, life really had little more to offer her in the way of excitement or increased knowledge, and was perfectly content to sink into total domesticity, watching Charles grow, playing the organ on Sundays, and taking her Sunday-school class after service. And cutting herself off entirely from Chinese politics and Chinese problems. These did not in any event reach out as far as Chu-teh, although occasionally they did see groups of Boxers on the road, performing their peculiar gyrations as they marched, and shouting curses at the mission.

"Poor devils," Henry would say. "I should go among them and preach, really I should."

But he didn't. He did not lack physical courage, Constance knew, but his concern was entirely with the well-being of the mission, and that meant not opposing the government in any way—it was difficult to decide whether the Boxers were for or against the Manchus, and no one could be sure whether or not the Manchus intended to suppress them. Until this was certain, they were best avoided.

There was, of course, a continual awareness of the emptiness of her life, punctuated by moments of real distress, such as the day she went shopping in Peking and came face to face with Frank Wynne outside the American legation. They gazed at each other for several seconds, then he flushed and turned to walk away. She had nearly called after him, and then thought better of it. That would have been foolish. And would he not have walked away even more decisively had he known the man to whom she had gone, when she should have been with him?

There was a moment of sadness, too, when she realized that the invitations from Kate had definitely stopped coming, although this was not certain for a year after her return to Chu-teh. And it was in any event alleviated by the entrancing spectacle of Joan Mountjoy at last setting off to visit her daughter, and returning in great haste only a week later, quite distraught—she took to her bed for several days. Constance realized that the visit might actually prove a possible danger to herself, and certainly Joan stared at her as if seeing her for the first time—but then she obviously decided that as Constance had also returned very abruptly, and had immediately sought to regain normal domestic relations with her husband, she must have been equally shocked by what she had found in Port Arthur.

"Of course Kate is rapturously happy," Joan lied to everyone who would listen. "She has a superb house, and gardens, and so many servants . . . but I am afraid the climate did not agree with me."

She also let drop the information that Prince Ksian Fu had now not one, but two European secretaries, one Russian and one French, both female, and both young—and attractive. "He has to work so hard," she explained. "Sometimes Kate does not see him for days on end, although they are living in the same palace." An example, Constance thought, of either total innocence or very deep understanding. Having known Joan for several years, she opted for innocence.

But it was in any event all behind *her*. Let the prince practice his Tiger Leaps on the French girl. She was no doubt far more emotionally equipped to enjoy it. The dull monotony of life became almost pleasant, the adventures she had enjoyed once upon a time almost surrealistic, as if they were no more than half-remembered stories she had read in a book. She even began to *wish* for a second pregnancy, for Henry, as she passed her twenty-second birthday, but it did not happen. Yet it would, she was sure—there was time.

It was almost like receiving a slap in the face or a sudden douche of ice-cold water when she heard her name being called on an early July day in 1894, and hurried onto her front veranda, to discover Chiang, the eunuch, waiting for her. "The empress commands your presence," he said. "You will come with me now."

# 8

# The Japanese

"I don't want to go," Constance said. "I don't want to *go*."

"I think you must," Henry insisted. "We simply cannot afford to antagonize the empress. And what harm can come of it? You used to enjoy your visits to Peking and your chats with the old girl."

Yes, she thought. I used to enjoy my visits to Peking. As I have no doubt I shall enjoy this one. But to return to the Forbidden City would be again to enter that forbidden world which she had so successfully rejected for eighteen months. Yet there was nothing for it. All Chu-teh apparently wanted her to return to the fold, sure that through her they would continue to bask in the imperial favor.

How memory came back to her as she rode beside Chiang, surrounded by her escort of soldiers. It might have been yesterday that she had last passed through the Gate of the Zenith. The city had not changed in the slightest. And yet . . . the people had, she thought. At least toward her. They stared more boldly, and one or two shouted curses after her. No doubt they had forgotten who she was, she supposed. Or they remembered too well, and felt that *she* had been cold-shouldering the empress. As if it mattered. With Chiang and his soldiers around her, she had nothing to fear even from the Peking mob.

The empress waited for her in her favorite flower garden. She too had hardly changed, although she was in her fifty-ninth year. "Constance," she said. "It is so good to see you again. You should not have abandoned me for so long."

Constance kissed the offered knuckles. "I have never abandoned you, Majesty," she said. "But I will never intrude where I am not wanted."

The empress gazed at her for several seconds. "Things change," she said at last, with disturbing enigmatism. "No one knows what the future will bring, and I am not always permitted, by my responsibilities as regent, to follow my own inclinations as I might wish. Although I would hope and pray that changing circumstances never bring *you* any harm, Constance."

Which Constance found even more disturbing.

"But as usual you are not being truthful with me," Tz'u-Hsi continued.

Constance raised her head.

"Because you will not even go where you *are* wanted," the empress said. "Where, indeed, you are most ardently desired."

So that's it, Constance thought. She had suspected that it might be the reason for her summons. And of course it was flattering to think that Ksian Fu wanted her so badly, despite his "secretaries," that he had at last enlisted the aid of the empress herself. It was the temptation she had most feared about returning to the Forbidden City. Well, it would just have to be rejected as firmly as before.

"I am a married woman, your Majesty," she said. "In my culture, my religion, that is a woman's duty. If I once strayed from that duty, it is to my eternal shame and disgrace. I would not do so again."

Once again the appraising stare. Then Tz'u-Hsi said, "The Princess Ksian Fu is with child."

"Kate?" Constance cried. "Oh, how splendid for her."

"Yes," Tz'u-Hsi agreed. "I too think it is very good news. Thus I wish you to go to Port Arthur and escort your friend back here to have her baby with me, in Peking."

Constance frowned. "I cannot do that, Majesty."

"Cannot?"

"Majesty, I beg of you. If you know anything at all—"

"I know everything, devil woman," Tz'u-Hsi snapped. "Everything, do you understand? I doubt the prince still wishes to enjoy your body. But if he does, then you will submit, if it is necessary. Your duty is to bring the princess to Peking."

"Majesty," Constance said desperately, "if you would but hear me—"

"It is your business to hear *me*," Tz'u-Hsi reminded her. "And obey me too, you naughty child. You have been away from Peking for too long. You are not aware of what is happening in the world."

That decision was yours, Constance thought. But she decided against saying it.

"Within another two months, at the very outside," Tz'u-Hsi went on, "China and Japan will be at war."

"Majesty?" As nothing had happened since her return from Port Arthur, she had supposed Ksian Fu's apprehensions to have been only apprehensions.

"The Japanese behavior is increasingly intolerable," Tz'u-Hsi said. "They act as if Korea belonged to them, and as if we have no say in the matter. They have been landing soldiers, entirely without consulting us, to 'protect' the people, they say. Protect them against whom, I should like to know. And this while we maintain a garrison in Seoul. Now I am told that they have suborned the queen, and she has issued an edict saying that the Chinese must be expelled from her country. As if we could accept that. There are Chinese who have lived in Korea for hundreds of years, as we have protected the Koreans against the Japanese for hundreds of years. The Koreans are fools. They have listened to Japanese agitators, and now only think of being rid of our suzerainty, not realizing that they can only exchange us for the Japanese, and they will discover that the Japanese are far worse. They are being led astray. Their queen is a criminal. We shall chastise her and her advisers. Soon. That is why there is no time to be lost. After all this time, the Princess Ksian Fu is pregnant at last. She carries in her belly an imperial prince, possibly a future emperor. But even more important, he will be a half-English imperial prince. This may be of enormous value in the future, the immediate future, when it may be necessary to select certain Western powers as our friends, while recognizing that the others are our enemies."

She paused, as if awaiting a reply. Constance could only think in basics. "You cannot be sure it will be a prince and not a princess, Majesty."

"Bah," Tz'u-Hsi said. "Of course it will be a prince. If it is not, then the princess will have failed in her duty again. But we must assume that she has *not* failed. Thus she must be brought home, and the child delivered in the safety of Peking, before we go to war with Japan. But the silly girl refuses to leave Port Arthur. Thus I must send you to fetch her. You are her friend, her closest friend, as I understand it. She will listen to you, whereas she is suspicious of those *I* send. She is even more suspicious of her husband, and says he but seeks an excuse to send her away. Absurd child. If Prince Ksian Fu wished to send her away, he would send her away, not seek some excuse to do so. You will sail on the *Kowshin* on Monday, and return with the princess by the end of the week. Those are my instructions.''

''Monday?'' Constance cried. ''But . . .'' This was already Thursday.

''You will return to Chu-teh now,'' Tz'u-Hsi told her, ''and pack some clothes. You will travel with a single servant. Chiang will come for you the day after tomorrow and escort you down to Tientsin. There is nothing for you to concern yourself with but the safe delivery of the princess here in Peking.''

Nothing to concern myself with? Constance wondered. Because it had to be a trap, some scheme of Kate's to regain the affection of Ksian Fu, by supplying him with the one thing he had ever wanted and not been able to have simply by snapping his fingers.

But oh, how she wanted to go.

And could not. Dared not.

''Majesty,'' she said, ''may I ask how long the princess has been pregnant?''

''Four months,'' the empress said. ''We are approaching the most delicate period.''

Four months, Constance thought. Kate would hardly be showing. There could only be her word for it that she *was* pregnant. But that would be dangerous to suggest to the empress. She chose the other alternative. ''That is true, Majesty,'' she agreed. ''Four months pregnant is not the time to undertake a long and arduous journey. She could lose the child.''

''Oh, nonsense,'' the empress said. ''What is long and arduous about traveling from Port Arthur to Tientsin? It is an overnight voyage which she will spend in her bunk, and the weather is settled. The seas will be calm. Once she reaches Tientsin, she will travel either by train or by imperial litter. I have told you, it is all arranged. You have but to see that she embarks.''

''But it would still be better to wait,'' Constance said desperately, ''until she is more advanced. Six months, or seven.'' She did not know what she was hoping for, for a miracle, perhaps.

She was not going to have even a small one. ''That is quite impossible,'' the empress declared. ''By then we shall be at war.''

''Prince Ksian Fu has assured me that Port Arthur is impregnable.''

''And so it is. But wars are incalculable things. I wish the princess here before hostilities start, and I wish you to see that that happens, because there is nobody else. Do not attempt to argue with me, Constance. If you are afraid of the prince, I will give you a letter forbidding him to touch you. In any event, you will be in Port Arthur only a few hours, long enough for the princess to pack.''

Constance drew a long breath. ''Then I would like such a letter, Majesty.'' *Did* she wish such a letter? Would she use it? She had to. She had to make herself. Were she to backslide now, she would be lost forever.

''Very well,'' Tz'u-Hsi said. ''I do not understand your point of view. Any woman in the land should be happy to go to a prince, especially when he is as healthy and handsome as Ksian Fu. But if that is what you wish, you shall have my letter. Now, be off with you and prepare. You have ten days to return here with the Princess Ksian Fu.''

Constance took a bewildered Lizzie with her, said good-bye to an equally bewildered but utterly grateful Joan Mountjoy. ''Pregnant,'' Joan kept saying, perhaps to accustom herself to the word. ''She has not told me.'' But there was less pique in her tone than confusion. ''You *will* fetch her back safe and sound, Constance? You will?''

''I do wish you'd come with me, Joan,'' Constance said.

Joan hesitated and then shook her head. ''I couldn't,'' she said. ''I couldn't. I . . .'' She peered into Constance's eyes. ''You are young, and able to accept things, perhaps. I . . . I couldn't.''

I suspect I am a great deal older than you, mentally, Constance thought. But it was clear that Joan was not going to come, however much she wanted to see her daughter brought to safety. And it was time to leave.

Henry was delighted with her mission. ''The empress trusts you,'' he said with great satisfaction. ''She relies upon you. And after Catherine has had a son, an imperial prince . . . I see great possibilities for the future.''

Constance had the wildest vision, that if she had returned from Port Arthur and announced that she was pregnant by Prince Ksian Fu, Henry might have been more pleased than horrified.

It could still happen.

But it was not going to happen, she told herself with grim determination as she and Lizzie were whisked down the Han-ho to Tientsin, their journey superintended and made easy by the presence of Chiang and an imperial escort. ''We shall be waiting here for your return, Mrs. Baird,'' the eunuch told her.

''Four days,'' Constance reminded him, and stood on the dock to watch in consternation the sampans laden with Chinese soldiers, their modern magazine rifles and bayonets and cartridge belts sitting quaintly against their age-old garb, waiting to be ferried out to the *Kowshin*.

"Orders." Captain Cuthbertson was himself ashore to greet her. "It seems that General Yuan Shih-k'ai has sent an urgent request for more troops to reinforce the garrison in Seoul."

"Seoul?" Constance was aghast. "But I am going to Port Arthur. And in great haste. I must be back in Peking in six days."

"And so you shall be, Mrs. Baird," Cuthbertson reassured her. "But we must go to Seoul first, to unload these men. Believe me, it is only a few hours further on than Port Arthur. We shall return the moment they are disembarked. You shall not be more than twelve hours late."

Even twelve hours seemed like an extra eternity; she was filled with an inexplicable sense of foreboding. "Does the empress know of this change of plan?"

Cuthbertson shrugged. "It is impossible to say who knows what, and who orders what, in this country, Mrs. Baird. The empress says one thing, the imperial princes say another, the generals say something else, and the local viceroy says something else again. I've learned that it pays to obey the man on the spot, provided he will put his instructions in writing. I have a written order from the viceroy of Chihli province, old Li Hung-chang himself, to transport one thousand men and their equipment to Seoul just as fast as I can. And that is what I intend to do. There is really no need to be alarmed, Mrs. Baird. They are the most docile of fellows." He winked. "And they'll probably all be seasick."

She did not doubt for a moment they were docile. It was the thought of that not very large vessel, crowded to the gunwales with soldiers . . . On the other hand, Cuthbertson was an entirely competent seaman, who must know what he was about. And the weather was, as the empress had promised, utterly calm. She was worrying needlessly—there would be no soldiers on board for the return voyage, the important one, with Kate and her babe.

"Good morning to you, Mrs. Baird."

She turned sharply, unable to believe her ears.

Franklin Wynne saluted. "Returning to Port Arthur, I see."

He was as handsomely bronzed as ever, his face expressionless, but his eyes, on this occasion, surprisingly warm. He had decided to forgive her. The idea that the decision was his made her angry, the more so because she was so very aware of how shabbily she had treated him—and of the ambivalent mood in which she was returning to the prince.

"Why, yes, Captain," she said. "I am going to visit Kate."

"You must give her my regards." He flushed. "I guess I owe you an apology."

"Indeed? Whatever for?"

"Well, I was a little rude when last we met. I guess I was piqued. Constance . . ."

Almost he reached for her hand. She closed her parasol preparatory to entering the waiting sampan. "I imagine you were entirely justified, Captain Wynne," she said. "I am sure you have no wish to discuss the matter further. I know I have not."

He gazed at her as if unable to believe her coldness, then looked past her at the laden sampans going out to the bar. "I see you have company. I imagine you know things have reached a critical stage in Korea?"

"So I believe," she said. "But I am not going to Korea. I am going to Port Arthur."

His flush deepened, but now it had a touch of annoyance about it, as she had intended. "I apologize again, Mrs. Baird. I just happen to feel that anywhere up there is not the right place for a white lady at this time. But I guess you would say I'm being officious."

She met his eyes. "Yes, Captain," she said. "I would say you are being officious. Now, if you'll excuse me, it is time to embark."

There was nothing else she could have done, she told herself. No other attitude she could have taken. Her life, which she had sought to reduce to the simplest possible terms, was suddenly threatening to explode about her all over again. Was it possible that Ksian Fu had been right after all, and no human being could ever hope to dictate to Fate? She was determined that should not be so. But she went to her cabin in a thoroughly bad humor, having been very poor company for Cuthbertson and his English officers, and, despite herself, being terribly aware of how overcrowded the steamer was. There were Chinese soldiers everywhere, sleeping shoulder to shoulder on all the decks, chattering and laughing, smoking cigarettes—she wondered if they were opium—and doing their own cooking on little pots, which she regarded as dangerous, since the decking and much of the superstructure of the *Kowshin* were made of wood. Cuthbertson continued to appear entirely unconcerned, however, and the Chinese colonel, who with his two senior captains dined with them in the little saloon, did not seem to have anything on his mind at all, but spent the meal staring at the yellow-haired devil woman or celestial being—it all depended, apparently, on the current feeling toward white people—of whom he had obviously heard a great deal.

She had insisted that Lizzie be put in the small cabin with her, as she had no desire to leave *her* on deck with a thousand men, but soon regretted it, as Lizzie snored. It was well past midnight before she fell into an uneasy and sweat-drenched sleep, and she awoke at dawn a clammy mess. She was out of her bunk and dressed in seconds, splashed some water from the basin onto her face, and hurried on deck . . . only remembering as she gained the rail that of course this morning she would not see Port Arthur opening before her.

In fact, the mountains of the Laiotung *were* just visible on the northern horizon, beginning to drift to the west as the ship steamed northeast. And in front of her there were more distant shadows just starting to come into view. "The Korean Archipelago," Captain Cuthbertson said, leaving the wheelhouse to stand with her. "We'll be altering course in a little while, for Asan."

"Asan?" she asked. "I thought we were going to Seoul?"

"One speaks of going to Seoul, but of course the city itself is inland. Asan is where we'll disembark these fellows. As a matter of fact it's a good twenty plus miles south, so it's that much closer. They'll have to walk the last bit."

"And when will we be there?"

"By this afternoon, I would say. We'll have these fellows off by tonight, and sail again at dawn tomorrow. You'll be in Port Arthur for lunch."

Constance looked down at the well deck, with its carpet of men, just beginning to stir, giving off a vast effluvia, for like Chinese coolies in general they were not concerned with where or in front of whom they performed their necessaries.

"Believe me," Cuthbertson said, "I'll be happy to see the back of them."

"I beg your pardon, Captain," said Mr. Smallpiece, the first officer, who was also English. "But that fellow is signaling."

Constance followed the direction of his pointing finger, to the southeast, where a ship could just be made out against the glow of the rising sun. There was a light winking on her foredeck.

"He's been with us all night," Cuthbertson observed. "What is the message, Mr. Smallpiece?"

"He wishes our name, our port of departure, our destination, and our cargo, sir."

"Hm."

"It looks like a warship," Constance said as the shape of the strange vessel became more visible.

"It is a warship," Cuthbertson said. "Japanese, I would think. They've been showing a great deal of interest in shipping movements in these seas the last month or so. It's none of his business, of course, what we are about. These are international waters. On the other hand, I suppose we'd better humor him, if he *is* a man-of-war. Make to him, Mr. Smallpiece, requesting *his* name and business, and when you have received that information, tell him that we are the British vessel *Kowshin*, on passage from Tientsin to Asan with a general cargo." He winked at Constance as the mate hurried off. "Never does any harm to wave the flag at times like this, Mrs. Baird."

"You don't really think he'll try to interfere with us?" she asked.

Cuthbertson shrugged. "He might. He may want to have a look *at* this cargo of ours. There's nothing to worry about, Mrs. Baird. All he can do is tell us to go home again, and he doesn't even have the right to do that."

"But . . . suppose he does tell you to go home? What will you do?"

Another shrug. "If a warship tells me to do something, Mrs. Baird, I do it. Mind you, if he says I can't proceed to Asan, I'll just down helm and head for Port Arthur. He can't stop me going there. These fellows can be disembarked, and then General Yuan and your friend the empress and the British legation and the Japanese government can all argue the rights and wrongs of the situation."

Constance gazed at the warship—she could see the two big guns mounted on the foredeck now. She hoped the Japanese *would* stop them. She'd be in Port Arthur that much quicker. Certainly the approaching ship was closing all the time; she clearly had at least twice the speed of the *Kowshin*.

Smallpiece was back, looking anxious. "She declares herself as the imperial Japanese cruiser *Naniwa*, Captain, Captain Heihachiro Togo in command. She says we must heave to and accept a search party."

"He does, does he?" Cuthbertson remarked. "Well, you can just signal back that this is a British vessel and that we are not in the habit of stopping in international waters at anybody's command save that of a British warship."

"You said—" Constance protested.

"And I meant what I said, Mrs. Baird. But I have to make a strong protest before obeying him, or any protests I may make later will be called second thoughts."

They had been joined by Colonel Wu, fully dressed and wearing sword and revolver. "That is Japanese warship," he announced.

"Right the first time, Colonel," Cuthbertson agreed. "It looks as if our voyage may be coming to a stop. At least as far as Korea is concerned."

"Eh?"

"He intends to send a search party over. I have an idea that when he learns that my cargo is reinforcements for the Chinese garrison in Seoul, he is going to say no dice."

"He has no right," Colonel Wu declared.

"I couldn't agree with you more. But if she's the cruiser *Naniwa*, she has four six-inch guns. It's my opinion we should argue about the rights and wrongs of the matter whenever we can find a Chinese cruiser to hitch up alongside. Yes, Mr. Smallpiece?"

"Reply from Captain Togo, sir." He looked down at the notepad in his hand. "It says: 'Humble apologies for interfering with English vessel if proceeding lawfully, but duty requires search is made. Stop engines immediately or I will fire into you.' "

"That's it," Cuthbertson said. "Ring down to stop engines, Mr. Smallpiece, and tell Mr. MacAndrew to blow off steam so the Japanese are in no doubt that we are obeying. Colonel Wu, the best thing you can do is draw up your men in some sort of order, so we can at least impress those fellows when they come aboard."

"No," Wu said. "You will not stop, Captain."

"You heard the man, Colonel. I have an idea he means what he says. And don't suppose we can beat him for speed, either."

"Bah," Wu said. "He will not dare to fire into us. That would be an act of war. Against Great Britain."

"That's a technical point," Cuthbertson argued. "Now he knows our name, he will also know we are on charter to your government."

"Then it would be act of war against Chinese government," Wu insisted. "He will not dare."

"Yeah? Well . . ."

There came a rumble from over the water, and their heads all turned together. Exactly two hundred yards in front of the *Kowshin* a plume of water rose into the morning air.

"He can shoot, too," Cuthbertson said, and ran for the bridge. "Smallpiece . . ."

"You stop," Wu snapped, and drew his revolver.

Cuthbertson hesitated in the bridge doorway. Smallpiece looked past him with an amazed expression.

"We do not surrender to Japanese ship," Colonel Wu said. "Captain Tang!"

The two captains had also come on deck. Now one stood to attention. "Sir!"

"Go down the stairs and tell the men to load their rifles and prepare their machine guns," Wu ordered.

"Sir!" Tang hurried for the companionway. And certainly some kind of commands were necessary for the soldiers, who were setting up a tremendous hubbub and also crowding the starboard rail to stare at the Japanese cruiser—at the same time inducing a severe list.

"Are you mad?" Cuthbertson shouted. "You think you can fight six-inch cannon with machine guns?"

"We will defend this ship to the last man," said Colonel Wu.

"You don't understand. This isn't a fort. One shell from that warship . . ." Cuthbertson looked at Constance in despair. "For God's sake, Mrs. Baird, pull rank. Reason with him. Or we are all going to drown."

Constance had been almost hypnotized by the argument. Now she gathered her thoughts. "The captain is right, Colonel Wu," she said. "We must surrender."

"I shoot the next person who says surrender," Colonel Wu warned, pointing his revolver at each of them in turn. "You too, devil woman."

"But . . ." Constance heard a vague noise, and then seemed to be lifted up by giant hands and hurled forward. She saw Wu's face changing expression, and expected him to shoot her, thought indeed that she *had* been shot as she struck the bridge rail with a force which drove all the breath from her body and might well have broken several ribs. Then she found herself on the deck, gasping, staring above herself at the funnels, the black smoke belching at the sky, listened to screams and shrieks, the explosions of rifles and machine guns being fired at random, and realized too that she was slowly sliding away from the rail as the *Kowshin*'s list increased. The ship was sinking.

Constance's first concern was for Lizzie. She pushed herself up, ignoring the waves of nausea spreading upward from her stomach, and ignoring too the chaos around her, as the crescendo

of noise grew, now increased by the roar of the *Kowshin*'s
boilers blowing off steam. Standing was very difficult on the
deck, and she had to crawl to the companionway leading down
to the cabins. She caught hold of the rail, got one foot onto the
ladder itself, and had her shoulder seized by Captain Cuthbertson.

"Not down there," he shouted. "She's going over. Take
this."

A life belt was thrust into her arms.

"I must get down there," Constance shouted. "My maid—"

"You stay," bawled Colonel Wu, waving his now empty
revolver—he had fired all six chambers at the Japanese cruiser in
a gesture of despair. "You stay."

"She's going," Mr. Smallpiece yelled, tumbling out of the
wheelhouse doorway. Constance supposed that everything was
actually happening very quickly, but time had suddenly taken on
a curiously static quality. She looked down, almost without
interest, across the width of the steeply sloping deck, and saw
that the starboard gunwale of this, the top deck, was in the
water, and that water was only about twenty feet away from her.
She listened to screams and shrieks coming from the well deck,
which had to be already submerged. She watched Colonel Wu
lose his footing and slide downward, still holding his revolver,
an almost comical expression of outrage on his face. Then she
was sliding behind him, skirts ballooning, bustle catching on
some obstruction and ripping away. She entered the water feetfirst,
still clutching the lifebelt. She had learned how to swim as a girl
in the rivers of Virginia, but it was a long time since she had
actually been out of her depth. Out of her depth, she thought:
several thousand fathoms!

Desperately she kicked with her feet, feeling her clothes beginning to soak and become heavy, being weighed down by her
boots and the skirts clinging to her legs, refusing to let go of the
life belt clutched in her arms. She listened to a roar and was
rolled over and over and submerged by a gigantic wave which
came up behind her, a warm wave, she thought to her surprise,
when the sea had previously felt cold. She felt herself sinking,
but still clung to the life belt, and then shot upward, just as her
lungs seemed to be bursting. She saw light diffusing through the
water and had to breathe, inhaling the sea as well as blessed
fresh air, lay on the calm surface, gasping and spitting and
vomiting.

And listening to a gigantic wailing noise. Several hundred
throats uttering a combined paean of despair and fear. She
looked left and right, and saw Colonel Wu. But he lay facedown

.in the water and did not move; she wondered if he still held his revolver. Desperately she turned her head away from him, saw several Chinese soldiers trying to climb onto a floating piece of debris, crawling over each other like beetles; even as she watched, one drowned with a ghastly spluttering noise. She looked behind her and realized that the *Kowshin* had entirely disappeared, carrying how many souls with her?

And saw Captain Cuthbertson swimming toward her. He had no life belt, and his face was gray with exhaustion.

"Over here," she gasped, and reached out to catch his hand and place it on her life belt. "Oh, Captain . . ."

He gasped, and spat water, rested his head on his arm as he could at last stop swimming. "He was mad," he muttered. "Mad. He has sunk my ship."

She understood he was referring to Colonel Wu. But the colonel had expiated his madness. At what cost? "My maid," she said. "Did you see my maid?"

Cuthbertson shook his head wearily.

"Lizzie!" Constance shouted. "Lizzie! Are you there, Lizzie?"

She heard the rumble of engines, looked up, saw the Japanese cruiser surprisingly close at hand, and even closer, a steam pinnace nosing its way through the wreckage toward her. She waved her hand, but they had already seen her, and a moment later she was being dragged alongside by a boat hook attached to the life belt, and lifted over the side. Captain Cuthbertson followed, to lie beside her on the deck and pant for breath while water drained from their clothes. Constance blinked at Lieutenant Yamamoto.

"Lieutenant?" she asked. "Oh, Lieutenant!"

"Mrs. Baird," he said. "Thank God we found you. We had no idea you were on board." He waved a sailor forward with a glass of brandy, and poured one for Cuthbertson as well. "Now we must get you back to the ship," Yamamoto said. "And get you out of those wet things."

Constance shook her head. "My maid, Elizabeth . . ."

"If she is in the water, we shall find her," Yamamoto promised. "I would be obliged, Captain, if you could tell me how many Europeans were in your crew or on board as passengers."

Cuthbertson sighed. "Five in all, including Mrs. Baird and myself," he said. "Only five."

"We'll find the others," Yamamoto said confidently.

Constance gazed as the pinnace came close to a group of swimming Chinese soldiers, waving and shouting for help. But the pinnace did not stop for these, and those men who tried to clamber on board were thrown back by the Japanese soldiers.

"They'll drown," she shouted at the lieutenant. "They'll drown."

"It is our intention that they should, Mrs. Baird," Yamamoto told her. "My orders are to rescue the Europeans. Not the soldiers."

"You, sir, are guilty of piracy," Captain Cuthbertson declared.

Captain Togo bowed. Like most Japanese, he was a small man by European or American standards, but size apart, he was remarkably Western in appearance, with aquiline features and both a beard and a mustache, very unusual in his nonhirsute people. "I would rather say an unfortunate act of necessity, Captain Cuthbertson," he said, speaking English with the invariable ease of a Japanese naval officer—their fleet had been largely created by British advisers. "My orders were to stop *any* reinforcements from reaching General Yuan in Seoul. We could see your decks were crowded with soldiers. If you had stopped your ship when commanded to do so . . ."

"You did not give us very much time, sir, if I may say so," Mr. Smallpiece said. "At the very least, what you have done today is an act of war."

"That, sir, is very probably regrettably true," Togo agreed. "But I cannot say for certain. An officer in the Imperial Navy but does his duty, carries out his orders. He leaves it to His Majesty the Emperor and his advisers to consider where those orders may carry the nation."

"All those men," Constance said. "All of those men." She could still hear their screams, still see the hundreds of floating bodies through which the *Naniwa* had cut her way once the last English officer had been rescued. She could still hear the curses shouted at them by the few Chinese who had still survived as they had steamed away, but who were now certainly dead. She did not suppose she would ever forget a moment of that morning, as long as she lived.

And among the men there had been one woman, she thought, even if she had not seen her. She had really been poor Lizzie's evil genius. She shivered despite the warmth of the wardroom in which they sat, the brandy in her system, the voluminous kimono which she had been lent to replace her sodden clothing.

"It is a soldier's duty to die for his country, Mrs. Baird," Lieutenant Yamamoto reminded her. "And a sailor's also."

"Words," Captain Cuthbertson said bitterly. "And high-flown

sentiments. I am only certain of one thing, gentlemen. My ship was sunk while proceeding about her lawful business in international waters. Be sure that my government will know of this.''

"And do you expect that they will send a British fleet to bombard our ports, as they have done so often in the past?'' Togo's smile was sadly contemptuous. "I doubt your government will do that this time, Captain. You were on charter to the Chinese government, and thus are their responsibility. And you were carrying their soldiers. And even the British fleet, dare I say it, would find us less simple to overcome nowadays. In any event, the war will no doubt be fought and over long before the British government even learns of this incident officially.''

Cuthbertson glared at him. "You intend to make us your prisoners?''

"I intend to take you back to Japan as my guests, Captain Cuthbertson. As soon as I have disposed of Mrs. Baird.''

Constance's head came up. "Disposed of me?'' she asked in alarm.

Togo smiled at her. "You have said you were bound for Port Arthur. It is no part of my country's intention to make prisoners of white ladies, Mrs. Baird. We are now approaching the Liaotung peninsula, and will be there just after dark. You will be set ashore. I regret that I cannot actually land you on the dock in Port Arthur, but I am sure you will agree that in all the circumstances that would be unwise. You are not afraid to walk into Port Arthur alone at night? I understand you are well known to the Chinese.''

She glared at him in turn. "Of course I am not afraid of the dark, Captain. But do you not suppose *I* will tell the world what happened today?''

The captain bowed. "That is your right and your privilege, Mrs. Baird. I would only say this to you: do not delay in Port Arthur. Complete your business there and leave as quickly as you can.''

"Because you intend to capture it?''

"It will be one of our early objectives, once hostilities commence,'' the captain said.

"Port Arthur is impregnable. Prince Ksian Fu has told me this himself.'' She looked at Yamamoto.

Who smiled at her. "And I have argued that point, Mrs. Baird. Now it seems the matter will shortly be put to the test.''

He himself commanded the pinnace which nosed into a cove on the outer shore of the port to set her ashore. "If you walk up that path,'' he said, "you will find a road into the town.''

Another of his smiles. "I reconnoitered it when I was here with my ship two years ago. I am deeply sorry that we can offer you no escort. You are sure you will be all right?"

Her clothes had been dried and pressed, and she was again properly dressed, except that her skirt was torn. She had also been fed, and her physical shivering had stopped. But she did not suppose her mind would ever stop shivering again. And now she was aware of anger, bitter hostility toward these men who had so abruptly taken her life and torn it apart. "Yes, I will be all right," she said. "Do not expect me to thank you for saving my life, Lieutenant Yamamoto. I do not care about great affairs of state, about men's duty. I am only aware that you have this day murdered my maidservant, and a great many other people besides. And I shall so testify to the world. And once you spoke to me of conducting war in a civilized fashion."

"By that, Mrs. Baird, I meant that we would hope neither to involve civilians nor to mistreat our prisoners. We will continue that policy, from which you have benefited." The lieutenant bowed. "I pray for you, Mrs. Baird, that you will never have to experience a war as a participant and not an innocent bystander. That is a very different matter from what you have suffered this morning. Now, please, take my captain's advice and leave Port Arthur. Quickly. Before it is too late."

# 9

# The Sack of Port Arthur

Constance had the strangest feeling that she had come home. Port Arthur was where she had been happier, for a single glorious week, than at any other time in her life. And here in this bath was where it had begun. The warmth of the water at last seemed to restore some peace to her tortured mind, even as it alleviated the aching of her feet and her back—it had been a walk of several miles over the hills from the beach to the town—and her ribs, still bruised from being hurled against the rail of the *Kowshin*; it really was a miracle that she had not broken anything.

She lay, half-floating, and allowed D'ao to massage her neck and shoulders, her breasts and her stomach. This was where she wanted to be for the rest of her life. Here in this bath, only the present was important. The horrors of the past could be forgotten; a consideration of the likely horrors of the future could be rejected.

Even the agitation about her no longer disturbed her tranquillity. Kate had not entered the pool. She still wore her nightclothes—it was not yet dawn—sat on one of the marble seats, hunched and aghast at what she had just heard, saying over and over again, "But, Constance, how terrible for you. How terrible for you."

What had happened to a thousand men and one woman did not seem relevant to an imperial princess.

Ksian Fu had also not entered the pool to be with her, but preferred to pace up and down above her. If he *had* laid this plan to bring her back to him, he had been completely astonished when he had been awakened to find her in the palace, escorted by his soldiers, exhausted and dusty, parched with thirst and still shivering with terrifying memory. "War," he said. "An act of piracy. With no declaration, no ultimatum, even. Is that the behavior of civilized people? Oh, we shall destroy them. We shall shatter them into the littlest pieces. Constance . . . Constance, open your eyes and listen to me."

Constance opened her eyes; he was kneeling at the edge of the bath, looking down at her. Are you going to send D'ao for me tonight? she wondered. Because right this minute she wanted that. She wanted the physical reassurance of knowing a man, of knowing that she was alive, alive, alive, when so many others were dead. She had never actually seen anyone die before. The man who had been castrated by the soldiers outside of Chu-teh had still been alive when he had been dragged away, however soon afterward he might have perished. But yesterday morning she had been floating in the midst of a thousand dead men. And one dead woman.

She could understand that she was suffering from a minor nervous collapse, that she would eventually recover her strength and her determination, that anything she did now, as a result of her distress, she would probably bitterly regret—yet that knowledge had no effect at all on what she *wanted*.

"You must tell me everything again," Ksian Fu was saying. "I must use the telegraph, you understand. Both to General Yuan, in Seoul, and to Peking, to tell them what has happened. But what I say must be absolutely true. You must tell me again."

Never had she seen him so agitated. Her memory of him was as an utterly imperturbable man who proceeded serenely through life knowing what he wanted and seeing that his will was done. Now he suddenly looked far younger than his years, and his hands were shaking—with honest outrage, no doubt. He was a man with a duty to perform.

The thought recalled to her that she was a woman with a duty to perform. That whatever she might want, she could not have it now. And in any event, *he* could not give it to her. "You must also arrange transport for Kate and me," she reminded him. "Back to Peking."

Exhausted as she was, Constance could not sleep. She had spent most of the day in her bedroom—the same room she had occupied two years before—resting, and occasionally dozing, visited from time to time by Kate as well as Hyacinth, to find out if there was anything she needed, and in Kate's case, to ask continuous and repetitive questions about what had happened. Kate's taste for the macabre had been whetted by such an example of human destruction.

Now Constance felt more tired than ever, but real sleep would not come. There were too many things rushing to and fro across her mind, too many memories, too many uncertainties, too many apprehensions. It was also very hot and still. But above all, she was waiting. And that was the greatest uncertainty of all.

Kate had lent her a nightgown, but although it fitted her shoulders well enough, it came only to her knees; Constance had discarded it almost as soon as Hyacinth had left her for the night—one of the attractions of Port Arthur lay in being able to sleep naked. For the rest, she would be wearing borrowed clothes tomorrow as well—hers were at the bottom of the Yellow Sea. Thank heaven she had not on this occasion brought her emerald ring. As if that mattered, when she thought of the other things which were also lying at the bottom of the Yellow Sea.

She got out of bed, walked to the window, watched the moonlight streaming across the lawn and the flowerbeds. Here in Port Arthur it was almost impossible to accept what had happened. Here all was peace and quiet, whatever excitement might be rippling through the garrison. Because of course now there would *have* to be a war. A chastising of the Japanese, as everyone put it. She had never been in a country at war before. She could only remember her father's drunken stories of Sherman's bluebellies sweeping through Georgia and the Carolinas, burning and destroying. Lieutenant Yamamoto had no doubt been thinking of episodes like that when he had suggested that wars could be fought without involving civilians to that extent. But Lizzie had been a civilian.

She listened to her door open. Now was the time for decision. And it had to be her decision alone—the letter from Tz'u-Hsi forbidding the prince to touch her was also at the bottom of the sea. But such a decision would not be difficult tonight; she had too many aches and pains—the euphoric mood of the bathhouse was long past.

"No, D'ao," she said. "I am not going anywhere tonight. And if you try to carry me, I shall box your ears."

"When the mountain would not go to Muhammad," the prince said, "Muhammed went to the mountain."

She turned, gazed at him standing by her bed, took a step forward, checked herself, and was in his arms.

His fingers traced designs on her bare flesh, slid down to play with her buttocks, came up again to thrust into her hair as he kissed her mouth with fervor. She was responding, her bruises forgotten in the sudden rush of passion. For the first time she understood how much the pale shadow of lovemaking with Henry had cost her these last two years.

But she could not surrender. She got her hands between them and onto his chest. "Ksian," she said. "No. I did not come back to you. I came because the empress sent me to fetch Kate." She pulled her head back. "She *is* pregnant?"

To her combined relief and disappointment he released her and sat on the bed. "Yes," he said. "She is pregnant. I am delighted." His tone was dull, and Constance realized that his embrace had lacked the assurance she remembered, and had dreamed of, as well. Once again he seemed younger than she remembered. A terrible thought began to enter her mind.

She picked up her nightdress, but did not put it on, left it draped across her lap as she sat beside him. "Everyone is delighted. And the empress wishes her returned to Peking to have the child, just as quickly as possible. Did you manage to make contact with the Tsung-li-yamen? The Foreign Office?"

He sighed and shook his head. "No. I have exchanged telegrams with Li Hung-chang in Tientsin, and acquainted him with the situation. I have also communicated with Yuan Shih-k'ai in Seoul. Do you know what his reply was? That the Queen of Korea has declared war on China and has ordered him to evacuate his men into Mongolia."

"Well, we knew that was going to happen," Constance told him. "Have the Japanese declared war yet?"

"Not yet. It is expected momentarily. We will then declare war on them."

"I would have supposed you would have already done so, after the way they sank the *Kowshin*," she said.

"That incident still has to be authenticated," he said. "You are the only witness, at the moment. Li Hung-chang did not know what to do. He did say, however, that it would be best for you to remain here until he has spoken with Peking."

"Are you trying to tell me he does not believe me?" Constance demanded. "How does he suppose I got here, as I sailed from Tientsin on the *Kowshin*. And to wait while he contacts Peking . . . that could take weeks."

"We must do as he says," Ksian Fu insisted.

"He is a Chinese viceroy," she reminded him. "You are a Manchu prince."

"But he *knows*," Ksian Fu said despondently. "He knows all

things. He may be only a Han, but he has been in the forefront
of Chinese affairs for many years. Since before I was born. Do
you know what he has told me? He has said that we may not be
able to defeat the Japanese so quickly. He thinks they may be
stronger than they appear." His voice rose an octave. "He
thinks they will force us out of Korea and then attack Port
Arthur."

"Which is impregnable," Constance reminded him.

"Impregnable." Ksian Fu got up, walked to the window, and
stared out. "Impregnable."

"As for the rest," Constance said, "they may be able to gain
a temporary advantage in Korea by treachery, as they did with
the *Kowshin*. But they can never defeat China. Does the empress
not have ten million men under arms? Is not the Chinese fleet
twice as strong as the Japanese?"

"Yes," Ksian Fu said. "Yes, of course you are right. We
have battleships. They have no battleships. We have ten million
men. But war . . . fighting . . ." The enthusiasm faded from his
voice. "The Japanese are so *ruthless*, Constance. I have heard
tales of it. You have *seen* it. And now they will attack Port
Arthur. . . ." He came back to the bed, threw his arm around her
shoulders, and pulled her down to the mattress beside him.

It was impossible to reject so distraught a man. But suddenly
she felt like a mother with a small child, and realized that her
unimaginable suspicion was absolutely true: Prince Ksian Fu,
debonair, serene, arrogant, was afraid.

The ladies played at croquet, a game the prince had learned
during his stay in England and of which he was very fond; the
hoops and sticks and balls had been shipped to him from London.
But he did not play himself, today. Constance partnered Aimée
Pinay, the French girl, against Kate and Alexandra Repnin, the
Russian girl, and won very easily.

Not that anyone took the game or the result very seriously.
The prince's harem at play, Constance thought. His principal
harem, because his Chinese concubines were not allowed into
this part of the garden, and so far as she could gather, were
hardly concubines at all anymore. But then, were any of the
other three? Kate certainly not; in the six weeks that they had
waited in Port Arthur, her belly had definitely begun to swell—
she seldom even saw her husband nowadays. The other two had
definitely been displaced by the new arrival. In the strangest
way. She had not come here to return to the prince's bed, and
indeed she had not done so. He came to hers, whenever he was

not exhausted by his efforts to convince the people of Port
Arthur, and more especially the garrison, that there *was* a war
on—and by his own fear, as well. And in the context of their
new relationship, he came as suppliant, so disturbed and confused by the circumstances in which he found himself that more
often than not he was incapable.

She knew that she should reject him. She knew that she was
betraying all the ideals and the determination she had prided
herself on possessing—and she was risking the disaster of pregnancy every time he *was* able to enter her. Nor could she still take
refuge in pretending she remained shocked by the sinking of the
*Kowshin*; her natural resilience of spirit had soon come to her
rescue, however much she looked forward to the eventual defeat
of the Japanese, to avenge Lizzie and all those helpless men.
What she would give to see the USS *Alabama* steaming into the
harbor below her, and even more, to see Captain Wynne marching to their help at the head of a company of U.S. Marines.

She continued to accept Ksian's love, as she was forced to
wait in his home. He could still make her feel more of a woman
than any other man she had ever known. And he needed her so
very badly. This was not only gratifying; she could persuade
herself that without her he would collapse entirely, and with
him, no doubt, all of Port Arthur. Besides, circumstances were
entirely different from those she had envisaged. She was staying
here much longer than she had anticipated, and there was a war
on. The whole world had gone mad. Time enough for *her* to
regain her sanity when she regained Tientsin.

If sanity was ever to be regained. Because the most disturbing
thing of all was that the war was really as nonexistent as her
dream knight. It was now the middle of September, and the
summer heat was beginning to cool into autumn. She had been
here six weeks, and it was six weeks since China and Japan had
formally declared war on each other. Six weeks in which, so far
as she could gather, the only casualties remained those soldiers
drowned in the sinking of the *Kowshin*—and Lizzie. General
Yuan, realizing that he was not going to receive sufficient reinforcements to hold Seoul against the considerable Japanese army
being established in Korea, had evacuated the capital and withdrawn toward the Yalu River. But he had not abandoned Korea
altogether, held the fortified city of Ping-Yang on the northwest
coast, and there awaited the coming of the mighty Chinese
armies which were surely being raised for his relief.

The odd thing was that the Japanese were apparently waiting
too, slowly building up their strength. While the Western powers

surrender; a shot across the bows; and then a shot into the waterline. No hesitation, no temporizing, and some remarkably accurate shooting. And then, with equal determination, total extermination of the enemy force. She could think of no Chinese, she could not even envisage Frank Wynne, acting with such single-minded callousness. For which she supposed she should be truly grateful.

But how incredible that four young ladies, three European and one American, should be sitting in the cool of the morning, drinking tea, bending over their needlework, listening to the sounds of war and destruction—and all of them sharing a single immense knowledge, that of the same man, able to look at each other and know what she, and she, and she, had experienced, because *she* had experienced the same. She could not suppose there were four other Western women with such a common factor dominating their lives in all the world, for they had each, by allowing themselves to be here at all, turned their backs on their cultures and their religions, their very morality. Even she, who could tell herself over and over again that she was only playing at this, dabbling in crime, in sexual depravity, because of her circumstances.

She raised her head to smile at Kate, who smiled back. They had not actually discussed their domestic arrangements since her return; Kate had been too distraught at what was happening. But that she was glad to have her friend back again could not be doubted, although she seemed to get on perfectly well with her husband's secretaries. But of course like any woman she had to be feeling at her most vulnerable right this minute, and even more so with a war going on, even if it might never directly enter her life.

Was Kate aware of Ksian Fu's fear, which sometimes was so intense as to amount to terror? Constance thought not; he very seldom spent much time with his wife apart from a routine daily visit to discover if her health remained good. And his fear was not easy to discern; Constance did not think either of the other two women knew of it. She sometimes wondered if *she* were not misreading some of his moods. Certainly they were difficult to explain. There was no *reason* for fear, she kept telling herself. Port Arthur *was* impregnable. No one argued about that. And the Japanese were in any event miles away, their fleet presently being destroyed, their armies held in check before Ping-Yang. Peace would be made long before they could possibly launch an attack, even if they dared attempt to force so strong a position. There was no possible *reason* for the prince to be in such a state of total apprehension. Thus it had to be purely a character weakness; having been born into the most omnipotent family in the world, he could not bring himself to accept that some outside force might actually be challenging that omnipotence. She supposed she should be sorry for him. Well, she *was* sorry for him. But she felt contempt for him as well.

And yet, in the strangest fashion, that contempt made her accept his embrace with less guilty turmoil. He needed her even more than she craved him. Once again she was dominating a man.

She had the oddest thought, that were she ever to meet a man who would totally dominate her, as the prince had sought to do two years ago—then she would fall in love.

But never with the prince, now. They watched him approach, instinctively rising to their feet together at the sheer ashen catastrophe written all over his face. But out at sea the guns continued to roar.

"Ksian," Kate shouted, forgetting to say "Highness," obligatory at least in public. "What has happened?"

He stared at her. "I have received a telegram from Mukden," he said. "Ping-Yang has fallen. The Japanese have stormed it. Our armies, what is left of them, are falling back to the Yalu River."

"Oh, my God!" Kate sat down again.

"They will hold them at the Yalu," asserted Alexandra Repnin.

Ksian Fu stared at her in turn, and then sat down himself, head hanging.

"If they do not," said Aimée Pinay, "the way to Port Arthur is open."

Ksian Fu looked at her, and then at Constance. To her horror she saw that his eyes were filled with tears.

They hurried down to the docks to greet the fleet. All Port Arthur was there, crowding the streets and the waterfront, waving dragon flags, shouting and cheering, as the two great battleships slowly steamed into the harbor, followed by one or two light craft. They gazed at the shot holes, at the dead men lying in neat rows on the decks, and realized that there was no joy on the faces of those who still lived.

The cheering and the shouting slowly died. Prince Ksian Fu stood at the foot of the gangplank as it was run out from the *Tsi-Yuen*, Admiral Ting's flagship. Sailors came to attention on the deck, but there was no music. The women, peering from behind the curtains of their palanquin, watched the prince slowly climb the gangway and go on board, where Admiral Ting and his officers awaited him. They had no means of seeing the admiral's expression, of knowing what he was saying, other than Ksian Fu's reaction to it. The prince stared at the admiral, then looked up at the shot-torn superstructure of the battleship, then down at the deck, and then, without a word himself, turned and went back down the gangplank. His horse waited for him at the foot, and he mounted and rode away from the dock, looking neither left nor right, his shoulders bowed.

"Oh, my God," Kate said. "Oh, my *God*!"

"The fleet had several cruisers, as well as the battleships," Alexandra Repnin said knowledgeably.

*Had* several cruisers, Constance thought. Now there were only two.

They climbed out of the palanquin on the palace patio, looked up at the verandas and at the prince . . . and Yuan Shih-k'ai. Constance felt a great glow spread through her body. Yuan! Come to help them. She gathered her skirts and ran upstairs, pushing aside Chou, the head eunuch, who would have stopped her. "General Yuan," she shouted, bursting onto the veranda.

The two men gazed at her. Yuan looked tired, and she realized that he had not changed his clothes or washed his face for several days; his boots were thick with mud. But he smiled. "Mrs. Baird. I am pleased to see you. Perhaps I may enlist your help."

"My help?" Constance looked at the prince.

"He wants men," Ksian Fu said bitterly. "Men! How many men did you have at Ping-Yang, General? Fourteen thousand? And you were beaten."

"My estimate is that General Nozu had twenty thousand," Yuan said without anger. "If I am to hold the line of the Yalu, I must match him for strength."

Ksian Fu flung out his arm. "I have ten thousand men," he shouted. "Ten thousand, to hold Port Arthur. That is not enough. I need twenty, thirty thousand. But I have ten, and I can receive no more. Our fleet has been shattered. Defeated, shot to ribbons, by an inferior Japanese force. I must hold Port Arthur with what I have. And you would take some more away from me?"

Yuan sighed. "The best, the only defense for Port Arthur is the Yalu River, Highness," he said. "If I am forced to withdraw, there will be no Chinese soldier between you and the whole Japanese Army. It will not matter if you did have thirty thousand men here. Now that they command the sea, the Japanese will be able to bring fifty, a hundred thousand men against you, if they wish. But they cannot do so while we hold the Yalu and lie across their flank.''

"No," Ksian Fu declared. "You are seeking to save your own worthless skin from the consequences of your defeat at Ping-Yang. Well, I will not help you. My business is to hold Port Arthur. If it can be done." He sat down, stared out at the harbor, the Yellow Sea beyond. "If it can be done." His voice trembled.

Yuan gazed at him for several seconds and then turned away. "I will bid you good-bye, Mrs. Baird," he said. "And wish you good fortune."

"But . . ." The thought of him leaving, having once been here, was too painful to bear. With Yuan here, Port Arthur *could* be held, she was sure—however inadequate its "impregnable" defenses. "You will come back?" she begged.

Yuan shook his head. "I must go and fight with my army, what is left of it. On the Yalu." He half-smiled. "And I must die with them, if I have to. Port Arthur is the prince's responsibility." Once again he glanced at the sitting figure, and this time there could be no doubting his contempt. "I will pray for you, Mrs. Baird," he said, and left the veranda.

It rained, a slow and steady November drizzle, a certain portent of the winter gales to come. Today there was no croquet; there had been no croquet for several weeks. Today there was only Admiral Ting, bowing to the prince, glancing curiously at the white women with whom the viceroy had surrounded himself. "We will sail at dusk," he said. "With fortune, we will gain Wei-hai-wei under cover of darkness. And of the weather."

Constance opened her mouth, and closed it again. She should not have been present at all. And it was not her business to suggest alternatives. Especially was it not her business to suggest that she at the least might be allowed to flee with the fleet. The remnants of the fleet.

"Then go, Admiral," Ksian Fu said. "As it is so ordered, go."

Ting looked as if he would have said something more; then he saluted and left the veranda. Constance had no doubt that he was a brave man, if not perhaps a born fighting sailor. Like everyone else touched by this war, at least on the Chinese side, he was bewildered. He had been bewildered the day he had led his powerful battle squadron into action two months ago against a numerically inferior Japanese force, and been shot to ribbons. He could not account for that. He had remained bewildered at the orders he had received not to leave Port Arthur to avenge himself. And he was more bewildered than ever, now, when the Japanese were at last apparently poised for their assault, that he had been instructed by the telegraph from Peking to leave the port, which he could at the least have helped defend with his sailors and his powerful guns, and go scuttling back across the Yellow Sea to Wei-hai-wei. And no doubt, more than anything else, and like everyone else, he was utterly confused by the fact that the Dragon Empire, which boasted of having ten million soldiers under arms, could have allowed itself to be swept away from the Yalu River by the bustling but tiny Japanese armies, and now, apparently, could be preparing to abandon the "impregnable" fortress of Port Arthur with its scanty ten thousand defenders—and its fifty thousand noncombatants—to the worst the Japanese could do.

Constance could not imagine any future historian ever understanding that. Just as she could not understand why *she* had been so utterly abandoned. She had made Ksian Fu telegraph asking for instructions regarding her, and when the orders for the fleet to leave had arrived two days before, he had telegraphed again, asking if Mrs. Baird should be placed on board a warship. The reply on each occasion had been the same: Mrs. Baird will remain with the Princess Ksian Fu. So now, she thought bitterly, I am to become a midwife; Kate was past eight months pregnant.

And *she* had spent four months in Port Arthur. Four of the most miserable months of her life, as she now recognized. No doubt, for her to be here, in a paradise which was turning into a hell before her very eyes, was the punishment which had been her due for two years. She had thought to laugh at Fate, to dictate to it, to take from it what she would, and then reject the rest. Fate's answer had been to bury her alive, with a moldering corpse.

It was not that the corpse had suffered any loss of bodily functions, as yet. Port Arthur might largely be cut off from the outside world, and the international community might therefore be suffering a diminution of income and freedom of movement, but as yet there was no food shortage, in a real sense—the sea was still full of fish, and there were still cattle and pigs in the fields, and barley and oats in the storehouses, and the freshwater lake behind the town was ample for the needs of even sixty thousand people. The deaths had taken place in the minds of the defenders. Port Arthur waited, collectively, like a criminal already bound and delivered to the executioner, lying on his board, awaiting only the fall of the ax.

It was a despair which found its truest expression in the city's governor. Ksian Fu gazed at her now, his eyes as usual filled with tears. "You heard?" he asked. "You will bear witness as to how I have been abandoned?"

She sighed. "I am sure there must be some strategic reason for the fleet's withdrawal," she said.

"Bah," he said. "They have forgotten about me. About us. About you."

Which seemed true enough. In four months there had not been one message from Chu-teh. Not one that she had received, anyway. They had indeed abandoned her. She did not even know if they had been informed that she had survived the sinking of the *Kowshin*.

But then, she did not even know if they were aware that the *Kowshin* had been sunk. Or if there was a war on at all. Certainly nobody else in China seemed aware, or to care.

"I must ride out to the Neck," the prince said. "You will accompany me, Constance."

He did this almost every day, rode out to the narrow strip of land which connected Port Arthur with the bulk of the Liaotung, and stared up at the mountains. Again, he made her think of a man going to the cemetery every day, to stare into his waiting grave. And every day he took her with him. Perhaps he felt that with her at his side he would reveal the proper courage, the dignity and, more important, the aplomb expected of him when he faced his equally frightened soldiers. Or perhaps he felt she was his lucky charm. Or, more likely than either, perhaps he knew that with her he could weep, if he chose, and bewail his fate, and even reveal his fear, and not be disgraced. It was the greatest intimacy she had ever shared with anyone, and the most unwanted. But it was the *only* intimacy they had shared for over a month, for all that he came to her room almost every night. He *wanted* only to weep, in her arms, with the petulant misery of a frustrated schoolboy. If he was a typical representative of the remaining male members of the Ch'ing dynasty, Constance thought, then she could understand the chaos that China was in—and she could understand too why Tz'u-Hsi desperately clung to power, and why she found it simple to do so.

They walked their horses down the sloping drive from the palace, met an army colonel coming up. He saluted as he drew rein beside the prince; he carried a satchel slung from his saddle. "You must see these, Highness." He offered Ksian Fu a sheet of paper.

The prince scanned it and then handed it to Constance. "They are fiends," he complained. "Is this any way to wage war?"

The sheet contained a proclamation, in Mandarin, from Field Marshal Oyama, supreme commander of the Japanese Army, calling upon the people and the garrison of Port Arthur to lay down their arms and surrender when summoned to do so by the approaching Japanese Army. It promised that no man or woman would be harmed, no property sequestrated, if the city was surrendered peacefully.

"How many of these are there?" Ksian Fu demanded.

"A great number, Highness. My men have collected what they could . . ."

"But how did they *get* here?" Constance asked.

The men stared at her; the question had not occurred to them.

"They must have been smuggled ashore during the night," she told them.

"And then distributed by Japanese agents within our walls," Ksian Fu said. "You must find these people, Colonel Choong. You must find them, and deal with them."

Choong saluted, wheeled his horse, and rode back into the town. The prince and Constance turned to the right, riding across the parade ground, which was situated immediately north of the town and separated from it by a small rushing stream which fed the freshwater reservoir. The stream was spanned by a narrow bridge on which their hooves clattered as they crossed. Beyond the parade ground, forming a natural amphitheater around the city, were the inner hills, each hill a fortress. Here, as they rode through the defiles, they could see the soldiers of the various garrisons looking down on them from behind their rifles and machine guns, and from behind, too, the sinister barrels of their cannon. Certainly they looked determined enough. And equally certainly, their positions were immensely strong.

North of the hills the country flattened out into a series of undulations, gradually descending again toward the Neck, and the subsidiary port of Dairen situated on the east coast, a few miles away from Port Arthur itself. Over these low hills they could allow their horses to canter, and enjoy the morning breeze; the drizzle had temporarily stopped, although the clouds remained low and threatening. Here there were no defenses, save that the open country was a defense in itself; no force sufficient to assault Port Arthur could hope to advance on the forts without being watched, and fired upon, every inch of the way. Supposing they could ever reach here, for now she and the prince had reached the Neck itself, hardly wide enough for a dozen men to cross at the same time, and here there was another fort, situated on a low hillock dominating the isthmus.

Ksian Fu drew rein. "What am I to do, Constance?" he asked. "What am I to *do*?"

"What you are doing," she told him. "Hold the peninsula."

He stared at the huge mountains which rose to the north. "Listen."

Because there was sound out there. Distant as yet, but distinct, carried through the mountain passes by the gentle breeze, the creaking of wheels, and the clip-clop of horses' hooves, and above all else the immense stealthy thud of thousands of booted feet. The Japanese Army! Constance found it uncanny that they should be sitting their horses in this spot, as they had done so often before, and this morning hear their doom approaching, while nothing that they could actually see had changed.

"They are coming," Ksian Fu wailed. "They are coming. And my people will surrender."

"They will not surrender," Constance snapped. "Not as long as they are *led*."

But what am I saying? she asked herself. Do I not want them to surrender, just as quickly and as peacefully as possible, so that there will be no more bloodshed, and this war will be over, at least for us? And I will be able to go home. Because how desirable did Chu-teh suddenly seem. Nothing ever happened on Chu-teh, no blood was ever spilled, and if no one ever achieved any spectacular heights of ecstasy, no one ever knew the absolute depths of misery, either.

Ksian Fu had been staring at her. Now he looked at the mountains again. "Yes," he breathed. "Yes. I must lead them. I must die at their head." His fear was really pitiful to see, almost as pitiful as the efforts he was making to overcome it. "I must . . ." His mouth sagged open, and Constance turned her head to see where he was looking, and gazed at a patrol of cavalry, very smartly dressed in blue jackets and white breeches, with blue peaked caps and black belts, carrying lances as well as saddle-holstered rifles, walking their horses down to the sea, not a hundred yards from the Neck. At their head was an officer, who was calmly leveling his binoculars to study the fort and its defenders, who were staring back at him as rabbits might stare at a huge snake; he was so close Constance could make out his neat little mustache.

"They're here," Ksian Fu muttered, his brief surge of courage visibly dissipating. "They're here." His voice broke, and tears dribbled down his face.

"A patrol?" Constance cried. "Just a patrol? They are treating you with contempt, Ksian Fu. You must show them that you mean to fight. You must prove to your own men that you mean to fight." You fool, Constance Baird, she thought. Why do you not just keep your mouth shut? But the Chinese were *her* people. She had adopted them, as she had adopted their ways. And whatever the cost, to lose Port Arthur would be an unimaginable catastrophe, because it would mean losing the war—her instincts told her that even Chu-teh would have to suffer from such a disaster; China might have lost several wars in the past fifty years, but they had always been to European powers. To lose to another Asian country, with a population hardly a tenth of her own . . . Thus logic and sound common sense. But she knew in her heart that she hated those blue-clad horsemen because it had been men like them who had drowned Lizzie. "You must kill those men," she said.

"Kill them," Ksian Fu breathed. "Kill them," he muttered. "Kill them!" he shouted, kicking his horse to gallop down to the fort. "Kill them!" he shrieked. "Shoot them down."

The sudden movement alerted the Japanese patrol, even if they had not actually heard what the prince was shouting. But they had come too close, and the garrison of the fort had obviously been already debating whether or not to open fire. Now they did so with alacrity, using their machine guns as well as their rifles. The deadly sounds filled the morning, smoke eddied into the air, and Constance watched the Japanese falling about the place as if they had been puppets suddenly released from their strings. It was all so absurdly easy. But those men were dying.

The firing ceased. It had lasted for only a few seconds. Constance counted seven men lying on the ground; the rest of the patrol had ridden for the trees, but as she watched, another of the horses stumbled and fell, throwing its rider before galloping on. Instantly one of the troopers drew rein beside his comrade, waving the remainder on to safety.

"That is their captain," Ksian Fu shouted from immediately beneath her; he was using his binoculars. "We must capture that fellow. Hurry."

A squad of Chinese infantry ran from the fort and across the neck of land. Ksian Fu rode back up to Constance, his chest swelling, his whole demeanor a glow of pride. "We have taught them a lesson," he said. "Now let us see what manner of men they are. Come."

"Over there?" She hesitated. It was more than a distaste for looking at dead men; it was a feeling that to cross the isthmus was to risk instant destruction. But not all of the men were dead; one or two were still writhing in agony, and one at least was trying to sit up. They would need help. Her hatred for them had disappeared in the instant she had seen them fall.

She walked her horse forward, beside Ksian Fu, across the Neck and onto the mainland, drew rein at the sound of shouts, clasping both hands around her throat as she watched the tragedy in front of her. For the Chinese soldiers had run past the scattered patrol to close on the Japanese captain. He had sat up to look at them, realized that he could not escape them, and had given his aide a quick command. Now, as Constance watched, the trooper's sword flashed in the morning sunlight. Blood spurted, and the captain's head, slowly it seemed, slid from his shoulders and hit the ground. It might have been several seconds later that the sitting figure also fell over.

"Oh, my God," she whispered.

"It is the Japanese way," Ksian Fu said contemptuously. "They regard it as a dishonor to be captured. There goes the other one."

For the trooper had now reversed the sword and fallen forward on to its point, sinking down with such force the steel protruded from his back. Constance felt sick, and her feeling grew as the Chinese sergeant who had led the rush across the isthmus came back toward them, carrying the Japanese officer's head by the hair; the mouth sagged open and the eyes stared at her, while blood dripped from the skull cavity.

"Ha-ha," Ksian Fu shouted. "A first trophy. But we shall have others. Bring me those others."

Constance's head jerked with horror as the Chinese gave shrill cries and ran at the dead and wounded Japanese. "Some of those men can be helped," she shouted.

"Bah," Ksian Fu said. "They are our enemies. They will die. Cut off their heads."

The Japanese soldiers did not appear to anticipate any better fate; they surrendered their necks without the slightest attempt to escape. As she and Kate should have done three years ago on the lawn outside the throne hall, she thought. Her sickness was compounded by anger. But her mouth was too filled with saliva to speak. Slowly she wheeled her horse.

"Bring them here," Ksian Fu was shouting. "Oh, yes, bring them here. Stake them out along the road. Stake them out, that their comrades may know the fate that awaits them should they dare to attack Port Arthur." He gave a great shout of glee, kicked his horse to ride beside her. "That was sport," he shouted. "Oh, that was sport, eh, Constance?"

She stared at him, and swallowed. "You are not a *man*, Ksian Fu," she whispered. "You are a filthy crawling thing from the deepest cesspool." She galloped away from him.

Constance lay on her bed, chin on her hands. She had lain here most of the day, having refused to join the others for any meal. Now it was again night. And now she waited. For him to come to her? He invariably did. But now she had nothing to offer him, not even the pity of contempt. In his fear he had reached back into his savage past, and she had encouraged him, not realizing the *beast* she would reveal. He was no different, in his essential being, from the officer who had chased Lin-tu to the mission gate.

And she had lain naked in his arms. And been happy to do so. Once again she felt sick.

She listened to a hand on her door, and raised her head. No doubt, she thought, when she rejected him he would fly into a rage. He might even strike her. Well, she would hit him back. She knew the measure of his courage now.

"Constance?" the voice whispered through the darkness. "Are you awake, Constance?"

Constance rose to her knees. "Kate? Whatever is the matter?"

"Constance! Put something on, and come. Oh, come and look, Constance."

Kate's voice was trembling. Constance dragged on one of the Chinese robes with which she had been supplied to replace her own lost clothing—and in which she now felt even more comfortable than in European dress—and hurried to the door. The candles burned in the hallway outside her room, guttered on the rear verandas in the breeze which still came in from the sea; it was only just after midnight. Alexandra and Aimée were already on the upper veranda, with several Chinese women, both concubines and servants; Hyacinth was there as well. All stared over the fortified hilltops to the north, pointing and whispering. Constance followed the direction of their gaze, and caught her breath. No one had told her that the Japanese Army had crossed the Neck. The impregnable, unstormable Neck, abandoned by the Chinese at the approach of their enemies. But out there, in the open country beyond the forts, was either the Japanese Army or every firefly in the world, gathering in the night. Wherever she looked, the pinpoints of light danced and moved, but not at random, she realized in a moment. Where the main body of lights was accumulated, directly in front of her, at a distance of perhaps ten miles, she estimated, and was moving only slowly forward, there were two bodies, or rather columns, she supposed, moving much faster to either side, like gigantic pincers, seeping toward the forts.

She listened, but could hear nothing. No guns were being fired at the approaching columns, no bugles called the various garrisons to arms. Port Arthur seemed to sleep. But that had to be impossible. "Where is Ksian Fu?" she asked.

"I do not know," Kate said. "Out there. Somewhere."

Preparing to fight? Constance wondered. Or shivering in a corner? But to let the Japanese cross the Neck without a major battle, and now the open country as well . . .

"Constance," Kate gasped. "Oh, Constance . . ." Her face was twisted, and she was holding her swollen abdomen.

Oh, my God, Constance thought. What a time. But hadn't this been certain to happen? "Quick," she snapped. "Alexandra, Aimée, help the princess to her bed. Hyacinth, we shall need . . ." She paused, because she didn't really know *what* they needed. When she had given birth to Charles, Joan Mountjoy had made all the preparations. And Joan should be here now, she thought angrily, whatever her moral objections, to care for her daughter.

"I fetch water," Hyacinth volunteered.

Constance nodded, hurried behind Alexandra and Aimée, who were escorting Kate to bed. She chewed her lip. Should Ksian Fu be found and told? But he had enough on his plate. More than *he* could cope with, certainly, apart from the trauma of becoming a father.

"Constance!" Kate lay in her bed, propped up with pillows, staring at her, sweat dripping down her face. "What am I to *do*, Constance?"

"Have your baby," Constance recommended. "Just lie there. Everything is going to be all right. Nothing matters, Kate. Nothing at all matters except the baby now. Remember that. Nothing matters."

Kate shuddered as another series of cramps rippled through her system, and she squeezed Constance's hand. Hyacinth arrived with several other maids carrying buckets of water, hot and cold. Constance set them to bathing Kate's face while she tried to think. There were things which had to be done, when the time came, like perhaps assisting the child out, and cutting the cord . . . but maybe some of the Chinese women would know all about that. She could not stop herself listening to the uncanny silence beyond the whispers in the room, waiting for the shooting to start.

In time the whispers died, as even the maids grew tired. Kate still held her hand, but her fingers had relaxed, and Constance supposed they had all dozed, to awaken with a start and a scream as the morning exploded. Because it was morning, pale fingers of light streaming from the window across the floor, and bringing with them the most terrible noise Constance had ever heard, like the most severe of electrical storms taking place immediately above Port Arthur, with not a second's respite between thunderclaps.

She pulled her hand free and ran to the window, where the rest of the women had already gathered. Kate's room faced the sea, looking over the town. The town was awake by now, people running about the streets; some of the hubbub drifted up to them on the breeze. Out at sea, they could make out the cruisers of Admiral Ito's victorious fleet, ranging up and down in line, and as they watched, the distant ships flickered with light which was immediately obliterated by white smoke, and the women instinctively shrank together as they heard the whistle of the shells. But the Japanese, with their usual accuracy, were taking care not to shell the town itself. Part of their much-vaunted civilized conduct toward noncombatants? Constance wondered. Or more likely a desire to seize the port installations intact? In any event, their shells screamed overhead to burst on the hill forts behind the city.

The reply from the Tiger's Tail was desultory, and the Chinese shooting, as usual, was wild. Constance ran for the back veranda, and was checked by a wail from Kate. The women tumbled into the bedroom, gasping and chattering, crowding around their mistress. Kate moaned and attempted to rise. Constance had to signal Alexandra and Aimée to hold her down, had herself to draw the baby girl from her friend's body, and hold it, uncertain what to do next, until one of the Chinese maids reached across and gave the infant a smart slap across the rump, which brought a weak cry of protest, but an immediately resultant gasping for air from the tiny lungs.

Thus inspired, the Chinese women took over and did everything. Constance could only watch them in relieved admiration as they washed and cut and cooed. She held Kate's hand.

"Is it a boy?" Kate whispered. "Oh, say it's a boy, Constance."

"It's a girl," Constance said. "But the sweetest little girl in all the world."

"A girl," Kate moaned, and began to weep. Constance placed the babe in her friend's arms, but Kate would not look at it.

While outside the noise grew to a crescendo so that she could hardly hear the chattering of the women, many of whom had already left the room for the verandas.

"You'll stay with the princess," Constance told Hyacinth. She was afraid that Kate, in her disappointment, might hurt the child. Hyacinth nodded and took her place by the bed, although she kept looking at the door. Constance ran onto the veranda, stood with Alexandra and Aimée, gazed at the forts, almost obliterated by the smoke and the flying dust as the shells exploded. "What's happening?" she shouted.

"I think the Japanese are attacking the forts," Alexandra shouted back.

"But the forts are holding," Aimée said with her invariable confidence.

For the moment, Constance thought, gazing down at the parade ground and the narrow bridge, over which a thin stream of Chinese soldiers was hurrying back for the town. Presumably those men were wounded, she thought. But they did not look wounded to her.

The women continued to watch, as the sun rose higher, and the noise grew louder, and the smoke clouds all but darkened the sky. They stood there for several hours, without being aware of the passage of time, without feeling any desire to eat or even to make tea. Constance recollected herself sufficiently to return to the bedroom, where Kate was sitting up, still holding the baby. "What's going on, Constance?" she begged. "Tell me what's going on?"

"They are fighting," Constance told her. "But we are holding the forts. The Japanese have been attacking since dawn. They will soon run out of impetus. Or men. They will have to stop soon."

"She *is* a pretty child," Kate said, looking down at the babe. "Don't you think so, Constance?"

"I think she is beautiful," Constance said with careful exaggeration.

"Do you think Ksian will like her? He so wanted a boy."

"Ksian will adore her." She was lying with increasing skill. "Now, Kate . . ." She was alerted by an immense wail from the back veranda, ran out to the women, and stared at the Rising Sun flag of Japan flying above one of the hill forts, and looking down, realized that the stream of men beneath her, running from the battle to the imagined safety of the houses, had become a flood. It was quite incredible, but Port Arthur, regarded as the most impregnable fortress in Asia, was going to fall in a single morning, to a single assault. Because even as she watched, Japanese flags appeared above two more of the fortresses, fluttering in the midday breeze.

She turned away from the women, stood at the top of the stairs. She wanted to think about everything that needed doing, and could not. She simply had to pull herself together. Soon the Japanese soldiers would be in the city. Soon . . . She looked down the stairs and saw Prince Ksian Fu.

It was the first time she had actually laid eyes on the prince since she had left him at the Neck. That was twenty-four hours ago. But it might have been ten years.

He climbed the stairs slowly. His hat had fallen off, and his robes were stained with dust. "They just kept on coming," he said. "We killed them, but they never stopped. They just kept on coming."

Constance was in no mood for sympathy. "You abandoned the Neck," she told him. "In the name of God, why?"

"There were so many. . . ."

"But they could only get to you a few at a time. And now you have left your men?" she demanded. "You should be there rallying them. You can still hold them, at the stream."

"Nothing will stop them," he said. "Nothing. I always knew that. I told Li Hung-chang so. I told Yuan Shih-k'ai. I told the empress. Nothing will stop them."

He had reached the top of the stairs; clearly he had no intention of returning to the battle. Constance caught his arm. "At least go to Kate," she said. "She has given birth, prematurely."

His eyes were dull. "A boy?"

She shook her head. "A girl. But there will be boys. Now that she has had one, she will have many."

Ksian Fu glanced at her, and then pulled his arm free and went along the gallery in the opposite direction from Kate's room. His shoulders were bowed, but he moved quickly and with some purpose. Like all Chinese princes, she thought, having been defeated, he had returned to his home, to his women and his eunuchs, to . . . My God, she thought, and hurried behind him. Chou, the eunuch, emerged from a side passage and stepped in front of her, hand extended. "His Highness will wish to be alone."

"Step aside, Chou," she said. "Or I will break your arm."

He looked at her in amazement, and stepped backward. In the distance she heard the bang of a door closing. Now she ran, scooping the skirt of her voluminous Chinese robe almost to her thighs to free her legs, arrived before the door, pulled at the handle. It had not been locked, swung open at her tug. She stopped, panting, gazed at the prince, who had seated himself behind his desk.

He almost smiled. "You are so beautiful, Constance," he said. "So animated. And with such hair, such legs . . ."

She realized she was still holding the skirt, dropped it into place. "You must command your people," she said. "At the least you must surrender formally. It is your duty."

"I have failed in my duty," he said. "My duty was to hold Port Arthur. I have failed." His eyes filled with tears. "How could I succeed, Constance, with what they gave me? How could I succeed? You will tell them that I could not succeed with what they gave me. You will tell them that, Constance." He opened his drawer, took out his revolver.

Constance hurled herself forward, reached the desk, leaned across it. "You cannot," she shouted. "You were contemptuous of the Japanese for doing that very thing. You cannot run away from your men. From Kate and the baby. From your other women. You cannot run away from *me*."

"I have failed," he said again. "I do not fear capture, Constance. But they will send me back to the empress. She will have me publicly beheaded."

"Oh, don't be absurd," she cried.

"You do not know her very well," he said, and raised the weapon.

Constance grasped his wrist, and he pushed back his chair, dragging her across the desk. Dimly she heard shouts and screams and explosions from close at hand, from the patio outside, and the floor beneath. But she refused to release his wrist.

"Devil woman," he shouted, attempting to throw her off. "They are here. Let me go, devil woman."

"Ksian," she begged. "Ksian . . ."

He swung his left hand, caught her a blow across the side of the head which tumbled her from the desk to the floor, her fingers at last relaxing their grip. She sat up, and was blinded by the flash of the exploding revolver.

Constance slowly pulled herself to her feet, gazed at the dead man. He had placed the muzzle of the revolver inside his mouth and blown the top of his head away. And she had seen so much death these last twenty-four hours that she did not even feel sick anymore. She felt only angry that he had betrayed them all, for the last time, left them to face the Japanese by themselves.

Left Kate and her infant alone.

She stumbled out of the room, along the corridor, reached the first flight of stairs, and looked down, at a Japanese soldier. He shouted something, but she did not understand what he said, was aware only that he carried a rifle with a fixed bayonet, and that the bayonet was stained brown. She stepped back, ran along the gallery, listened to the explosion; he had fired at her. At the next flight of stairs, Chou waited. "What must we do, lady?" he asked. He did not have to inquire after the prince.

She opened her mouth, looked down the steps, and drew a long breath as she saw more men coming up. These were not dressed as soldiers, but rather as laborers. Yet each carried a fearsome two-handed sword, which he waved from side to side, hissing as he advanced. "Run," she shouted. It was all the advice she could give.

She ran herself, for the next staircase, listened to a ghastly sound from behind her, looked over her shoulder and saw that Chou, hesitating, had been hit on the shoulder with a downward blow which had all but split him in two as far as his navel, slicing through bones and muscles and arteries as if they had been butter. Now her stomach did threaten to revolt, and she fell to her knees, but instantly regained her feet and kept on going up, gained the upper gallery, and the women. They had huddled against the door to Kate's room, clinging to each other. When they saw Constance they cried out to her in terror, seeking instructions. She stopped running, and panted. She had no advice for them, either. There was nowhere for them *to* go, or for her as well, now; this was the top of the house.

She leaned over the veranda, looked down at the servants, some fleeing and being cut down or bayoneted from behind, others kneeling in supplication and being cut down or bayoneted from in front. Blood splashed everywhere, coated the murderers' hands and faces, splattered over walls, dribbled on the mud like rivulets; she had not supposed there was so much blood in the world. Nor were the Japanese concerned merely with destroying human beings; she watched the gates to the piggery swinging open, heard the terrified squeals and grunts as the coolies, wielding their fearsome weapons, cut and slashed at the unfortunate beasts.

Someone screamed, and she turned back, to gaze at the soldiers coming down the gallery. She actually felt relief that they were soldiers, and not the coolies. But there could be no doubting the blood lust in their eyes. It occurred to her that the

Japanese must have received orders to kill every living thing in the city.

"In there," she shouted, and pushed the women at Kate's door. It swung in, and they tumbled through. Constance heard Kate's voice, calling out in fear, but she was the last of the women, and as she reached it the door swung shut in her face and the key turned, leaving her to face the soldiers. She turned, her back pressed against the paneling, and a bayonet thrust at her, actually passed through her robe. She caught her breath, expecting to feel the rush of pain, and realized that the steel had missed her flesh and embedded itself in the door. Yet she was caught there, pinned by the material of the gown, and there were other bayonets, while she could feel their breaths, stare into their lust-crazed eyes, look at their faces and know that these were young men, younger even than herself, who were probably obedient sons and loving husbands, turned into raving maniacs by the passion of their victory, checked for these few moments only by the realization that she was not Chinese.

A shot rang out, and then another. The men stepped away from her, while the morning seemed to spin around her head. An officer came up to her, waving the still-smoking revolver he had just fired twice at the roof, shouting at her in Japanese, seizing her arm to jerk her away from the door, to the sound of ripping material. She could stand no longer, fell across his arm, while he gave another order and the men charged the wood, hurling it in, to a chorus of wailing screams from beyond.

The soldiers stopped, gazing at the women, waiting for the officer to push through their ranks into the room, still half-carrying Constance. She gazed at Kate, sitting up in bed, her child clutched in her arms, her red hair loose and scattered, at Aimée and Alexandra, also on the bed, crouching, at the Chinese women gathered around them, insensibly aware that the white women were their only hope of survival. The officer pushed Constance toward the bed, and she staggered, half-falling into Alexandra's arms. "Oh, Constance," Kate shrieked. "Oh, Constance!"

The officer gave another order, and the men surged forward. In total disbelief Constance realized that he had just told his men they could have the Chinese women. She wanted to leap from the bed, to throw herself in front of them, but she could not make herself move. Hands scrabbled at the bedclothes, at the white women's hands and legs, and were torn or cut away, leaving dripping blood; bayonets flashed and gun butts swung as the women were herded outside, several being pierced in the doorway itself by the thrusting steel, others being shot at point-blank range if they struggled too hard. The bedroom became utterly bestial, a place of vicious death and utter animality. Robes were ripped and pale limbs gleamed, obscene laughter rose above the screams of the women, the stamping and the panting of the men.

Hyacinth called out to Constance for help as she was dragged across the floor by the ankles, gown falling back above her knees, long black hair trailing in the blood which swamped the floor. The sight of her at last galvanized Constance into action, and she scrambled from the bed, only to be sent reeling backward by a blow on the chest.

"You stay *here*," said the officer.

Constance fought for breath. Hyacinth had disappeared onto the veranda, and the last of the dead women was being thrown out behind her, allowing the door to be closed. Kate retched and began to vomit; she was holding the babe so tight Constance feared she might smother it, and pulled the child away. Aimée had burst into tears and buried her face in the bedclothes. Alexandra just stared in front of herself with wide eyes.

The officer smiled at them. "You be safe," he said. "You white ladies be safe. You have word of Japanese officer."

"Japanese officer?" Constance screamed at him. "Japanese butcher!"

He looked hurt. "Men are angry," he explained.

"Angry?" Constance gasped. She could not find any words to say.

"You did not see Japanese heads staked on road," the officer said. "Men are angry. They will kill all Chinese." Again he grinned at her. "White ladies will not be harmed."

The four women remained in Kate's bedroom for three days. Food and water were brought to them, as well as water to scrub the floor clean of blood, a task they were happy to undertake. They didn't want to have to think. They understood there was an armed guard on the door, as much, Constance decided, to prevent them from leaving as to stop anyone molesting them. But they had no desire to leave, either. As unwholesomely fetid as the atmosphere within the room soon became, as they had no means of changing their clothes or washing themselves, and could only empty the single slop bucket out of the window onto the patio beneath, it was yet preferable to the atmosphere outside, even when the screaming and the shrieking and the pleas for mercy ceased—and that was not for at least twenty-four hours after the Japanese had entered the city. Because then there came the smell.

Amazingly, Port Arthur did not burn. It had not, so far as Constance could gather from looking out of the window, even been sacked, in the historical sense of a city being handed over to a victorious army for looting. It had merely been turned into a charnel house. But after forty-eight hours, when the killing had stopped, it appeared to the casual glance as if it had not fallen at all, as they watched the warships steaming into the harbor to lie alongside the docks, watched smartly uniformed soldiers parading the streets beneath the palace— only the ships and the soldiers were Japanese rather than Chinese.

Yet there remained always the smell.

They feared for the babe more than for themselves. But the little girl thrived, for Kate's milk came in that first afternoon, and she had more than sufficient. But for the babe, Constance thought, she might have gone mad; the child had given her a retreat into which she had crawled and barred the entrance. *She* never looked out of the window, and she asked no questions. She did not even ask about Ksian Fu. And Constance was certainly not going to tell her. She had problems with her own sanity, she sometimes thought.

The other two girls did not speak much either. They just sat and waited, or stared out of the window. But that was all Constance wanted to do, as well.

On the third morning, the door swung in before a brief rap, to admit a man. They raised their heads without great interest, presuming him to be one of their jailers, and hastily straightened their robes and pulled stranded hair from their eyes as they took in the pressed white suit, the panama hat, the waxed mustache, and the indefinable aplomb of an English gentleman.

He raised his hat. "Forgive my intrusion, ladies," he said. "I but wished to make sure for myself that you are indeed alive and well, as General Nozu claims."

They stared at him.

He gave a little cough. "My name is Frederick Villiers. I am correspondent of *The Times* of London, with the Japanese Army." He looked at Constance. "Princess Ksian Fu?"

Constance shook her head and pointed at Kate.

"Ah," Villiers said. "Princess? My deepest sympathy. Then you, madam, must be Mrs. Henry Baird."

"Yes," Constance said.

"I am delighted to meet you," Villiers said. "Having heard so much about you. I wish the circumstances could be happier. But you will be pleased to know—"

"You say you came here with the Japanese Army?" Constance asked. "Then you saw what happened when they took the city?"

Villiers nodded gravely.

"And you will report it?"

"I will, madam. General Nozu knows that. I will have to report *all* the circumstances, of course. As you may know, certain Japanese prisoners of war were executed in the most barbarous fashion, by order, I have been given to understand, of . . ." He glanced at Kate, and changed what he was going to say. "Of the Chinese commanders. I will also have to report that the Japanese officers were unable to control their men when they entered the city. I am afraid this does sometimes happen when towns are taken by assault. There have been unfortunate incidents even in British history, following *coups de main* like this."

"The Japanese officers made no *attempt* to control their men," Constance cried. "They were encouraging them."

"Yes, Mrs. Baird," he said. "I have formed that impression myself, in certain cases. I was going to say that I shall also have to report that nothing which happened prior to the assault, no Chinese crime against Japanese soldiers, can possibly justify such a massacre as this. I have been a war correspondent for twenty-five years, and I have never seen such mass destruction of life. Do you know that it is estimated there are but twenty-four Chinese left alive in Port Arthur? Twenty-four!"

"But you will tell the world of it," Constance insisted.

"You may be sure of that," he promised. "I can only say, in some slight mitigation of the Japanese, that the worst outrages were committed by the army laborers rather than the soldiers themselves. The coolies are all former samurai, you see, who were refused recruitment into the army just because of fears for their lack of discipline on occasions like this . . . so they joined as bearers."

"What happened is still the responsibility of General Nozu and his officers," Constance said. "Will they be adequately punished?"

Villiers sighed. "They will not be punished at all."

"Not punished?" Constance shouted.

"The emperor and his advisers have been placed in a very difficult position, you see, Mrs. Baird. If I may explain, by Japanese custom—and in Japan, custom has the force of law—any officer in the army, from General Nozu downward, who is publicly criticized by the emperor, is obliged immediately to commit hara-kiri, that is, ritual suicide."

"My God," Constance said.

"Quite. Here you have an army which has really performed prodigies of valor, has fought its way from Ping-Yang, across the Yalu, and down the Liaotung to take the greatest prize of all. Would you really expect the Emperor of Japan now to call for the suicide of all that army's officers? Even if he might wish to, the people of Japan would never stand for it."

Constance made no reply. She had nothing to say. Her shoulders merely slumped, as she thought of Hyacinth, as pretty as a flower, and as delicate, too, being dragged across the floor to be butchered.

"The way of the world," Villiers said sadly, as if he could read her mind. Then he forced a smile. "But I really have come to tell you some excellent news. General Nozu has authorized a British man-of-war to enter Port Arthur for the purpose of removing all European noncombatants. She is on her way from Tientsin now, and will be here tomorrow morning."

"Thank God." Constance sat down. "Oh, thank God!"

"In the meantime, if there is anything I can do for you ladies . . ."

She raised her head. "A bath? A change of clothing?"

"I will see to it immediately. Ladies . . ." He paused, and a faint flush crossed the lean cheeks. "It is so good to see you alive and well. So very good."

"Twenty-four hours," Constance said. "Twenty-four hours, and we will be out of here. Did you hear that, Kate? Twenty-four hours."

Kate raised her head to look at her, then looked down at the babe again. But she would be better when they finally left Port Arthur. Twenty-four hours, Constance thought. She wanted to count the seconds, but in fact there was more than enough to occupy their time, as Villiers was as good as his word, and they were provided with a change of clothing and two bathtubs, carried into the room by several of the coolies, perhaps the very men who had charged up and down the corridors with their swords. But they no longer mattered, for the women could see from the window the British warship entering the harbor, and only an hour later the door swung in again, to admit the British Captain Jellicoe, and with him, Franklin Wynne of the United States Marines.

# III

Twilight of the Dragon

# 10

# The Outcast

The train chugged slowly across the North China plain, stared at by crowds of curious Chinese peasants lining the tracks. It was slowly penetrating through even to the villages that there had been a great catastrophe. But no one was sure what had actually happened. So they watched the trains from Tientsin, hoping to see or hear something definite.

A great catastrophe, Constance thought, gazing back at the patient yet curious faces. What would the history books say? That Port Arthur had fallen in a single morning? That the city had afterward been handed over to the maddened soldiery and their samurai servants? But as the histories would be written by English or American professors, they would also say that the lives of all Europeans in Port Arthur had been strictly protected, and end their chapter on that reassuring note—if their readers happened also to be Europeans.

Kate sat opposite her, the baby in her arms. Kate did not speak much nowadays. She had in fact never mentioned Ksian Fu at all. Constance was not even sure she knew he had committed suicide. But that was hardly relevant. She knew he was dead, and that was all that mattered.

Chiang, Tz'u-Hsi's head eunuch, who had met them in Tientsin, sat beside Kate; the armed escort waited in the corridor outside. The other two women had left them. Aimée was already on her way back to France, on a French ship, together with Madame Ligonier and all the other French residents of the city. Alexandra Repnin was presumably already on her way back to Moscow or

St. Petersburg, by means of the railway the Russians were building right across Siberia. They had been tearfully sad to leave, uncertain that they wanted to face their friends and relations so soon. But the empress had given orders only that Mrs. Baird and the Princess Ksian Fu be brought to her in Peking.

Frank Wynne sat beside Constance. He also said very little, for which she was grateful. But then, there was very little for him to say. He had been able to tell from the expression on her face how pleased she had been to see him entering the bedroom. She had gone to his arms then, and clung to him, seeking all the strength that she knew was there. But he could also tell, from an inspection of the city, as well as from talking with people like Frederick Villiers, that she had looked down into the pit of hell and that it would be necessary for her to wait until those images she had seen lost their sharp outlines before she could even think of living again, much less loving.

All the officers, British and American, had been as kind as possible, had attempted to cheer up the women without ever appearing to be treating their experience lightly. Constance and Frank had walked the quarterdeck of the cruiser together as it had steamed back across the Gulf of Chihli. She had needed to ask so many questions about Chu-teh, which was apparently continuing as always, about Charles, who was well, so far as Frank knew—there seemed little point in asking about Henry, as Henry had not apparently asked about her, had not even journeyed to Tientsin to be with her.

"Well," Frank had said when she had mentioned it, "it's difficult moving about the country right now. And the fact is, he didn't even know you were coming. Or *if* you were coming."

"How did *you* know?" she had asked.

He had shrugged. "I didn't. But I sure as hell wanted to find out. So the moment I heard the British were being allowed in, I applied for a couple of days' furlough and hurried over to volunteer."

As Henry could have done, she thought. As he would have been in Tientsin, waiting and worrying, had he cared about her at all. But she could not take the thought any further at this moment, any more than Frank could. Any more than he dared ask any of the thousand and one questions which were clearly screaming at *his* mind. But he had stayed at her side, pretending at the least that she needed his strength to face up to the ordeal of appearing in public, when everyone knew who she was and where she had been.

The train slowed to enter Hachiapo; the walls of Peking were immediately in front of them. And Chiang was calling the escort to order, to take them into the Forbidden City.

Frank squeezed her hand. "Stop by the legation on your way out," he said. "I know Mr. and Mrs. Conger would like to meet you. And . . . I'll be there."

"Come," Tz'u-Hsi said. "Come closer, Princess. Show me the child."

Kate crossed the floor slowly, walking on the celestial yellow carpet. Constance remained by the door, as she had not yet been summoned. But she was concerned to see that the empress was not alone, or surrounded only by her ladies and her eunuchs, as was usual. The women and the eunuchs were there, but there were also several men, and among them she could recognize the heavy, arrogant features of Prince Kung, Tz'u-Hsi's brother-in-law, a man the empress alternately accepted into her councils and then disgraced, as he angered her. Now he was obviously back in favor, and his reputation was that of an antiforeigner. But Constance supposed some such sentiments were inevitable, following such a defeat.

"What do you wish his name to be?" Tz'u-Hsi asked, carefully taking the child from Kate's arms.

"She is a girl, Majesty," Kate said. "I wish to call her Adela."

"A girl?" Tz'u-Hsi cried. She handed Adela back as if she had been a bundle of dirty clothing, and glanced at Prince Kung, who gave a contemptuous shrug and a smile. "Do you suppose we need princesses at a time like this?"

"I . . ." Kate flushed, and Constance knew she was near to tears. Yet was she far more courageous than she often seemed. "I would have had boys, Majesty, given the time."

"I doubt that," Tz'u-Hsi declared. "You married a weakling. A failure. As you are a failure, yourself. Do you know *why* Ksian Fu was a failure? Why you are a failure? It is because you are Christians. Because he allowed this pernicious doctrine perpetrated by you long-nosed barbarians to eat away his manhood. A suicide, capable only of siring *girls*."

"Majesty," Kate said, her voice stronger, "Prince Ksian Fu did the best he could with the forces at his disposal. You have no right to denigrate his memory. Had you provided him with more soldiers, with better defenses, then he would have held Port Arthur for you."

Tz'u-Hsi stared at the English girl in stupefaction for several seconds. Then her arm came up, forefinger pointing. "You dare to question my words, my dispositions? You, the wife of a suicide. Of a failure. Who is a failure herself. You, a *Christian*? Leave my presence. Leave it now, before I send for the executioner. Leave me. And take that puling infant with you.''

Kate hesitated. ''Where would you have me go, Majesty?''

''Go?'' Tz'u-Hsi demanded. ''Go to the devil. Yes, that is it. Go back to the foreign devils. Leave my sight. I do not wish to lay eyes on you ever again.''

Kate turned and walked from the room, without even a curtsy. She did not look at Constance as she passed, but Constance could see the tears falling down her cheeks. She hesitated herself, uncertain whether or not she had also been dismissed.

''Come here, devil woman,'' Tz'u-Hsi said. Certainly she appeared to be more angry than Constance had ever seen her. She advanced, curtsied before the throne. ''Down with you,'' Tz'u-Hsi said. ''Down with you, devil woman. Show a proper respect.''

''Down with you,'' said Prince Kung.

Constance bit her lip. But discretion had to be the better part of valor at this moment. She sank to her knees, placed her hands on the floor, and lowered her forehead to the carpet.

''You have failed me,'' Tz'u-Hsi said. ''Like all Christians, you have failed me.''

Constance raised her head. ''I could not dictate the sex of an unborn child, Majesty,'' she said. ''Or the course of history. No one can do that.''

''Excuses,'' Tz'u-Hsi shouted. ''Arguments. I do not care for your arguments. You have failed me. I sent you to Port Arthur to put some backbone into that spineless nephew of mine. And he commits suicide and surrenders the harbor.''

''The Princess Ksian Fu was right, Majesty,'' Constance said. ''The prince did not have sufficient men, and perhaps he did not have the experience to hold Port Arthur. Had you sent him General Yuan—''

''General Yuan.'' Tz'u-Hsi sneered. ''He is at least a *man*. He fights. He does not commit suicide. But you and your Christian prince . . . it is all your fault. Everything is your fault. In the last fifty years, China has known nothing but catastrophe. And it is fifty years since your Christian missionaries forced themselves upon us. Now we have been defeated by the *Japanese*. Prince Ksian Fu has been defeated, and has committed suicide. Admiral Ting has been defeated twice—''

Constance's head jerked up in dismay.

''Oh, yes,'' Tz'u-Hsi said. ''The second time *inside* his base at Wei-hai-wei. The Japanese sailed in and destroyed his ships in his own harbor. So *he* has committed suicide as well. Only Yuan still fights, and he can do nothing by himself. I am told I must make peace. I must surrender. The Dragon Throne has never surrendered, but I must now do so in the name of my nephew. How can I face my ancestors? But do you know what else my advisers tell me? That the Middle Kingdom can only regain its greatness by the immediate execution of every missionary. Every white person. Every *Christian*." Once again she pointed. "What would you say to *that*, devil woman?"

Constance knew that her only mistake would be to cower, to reveal how afraid she was. "I would say that would be a grave mistake, Majesty," she said. "And it would bring upon the Middle Kingdom the most dire consequences."

"You dare to threaten me?" Tz'u-Hsi demanded, but her voice was more controlled.

"I dare to advise you, Majesty, because I have your welfare ever at heart."

Tz'u-Hsi stared at her, and Constance felt the faintest thrill of victory. But she had forgotten Prince Kung.

"Devil woman," he said. "She seeks to suborn Your Majesty."

"Devil woman," Tz'u-Hsi said. "Leave my presence. Leave it, and do not return. You have failed me. Leave me, and pray that I choose to be merciful. Leave."

Constance stood up. "May I ask a question, Majesty?"

"Well, what is it?"

"Had Prince Ksian Fu returned here with us, would you have had him executed?"

Tz'u-Hsi's eyes were opaque. "That is the usual punishment for failures," she said.

"I think I would like a large brandy and soda," Constance said.

Mr. Conger, the American minister, signaled his butler. "I think I'll join you, Mrs. Baird," he said. "Frank?"

"Thank you, Mr. Conger," Frank said.

"Just tea for me," said Mrs. Conger. "You must have had quite an ordeal, my dear."

"Yes," Constance said.

"And seeing the empress was the worst of it, eh?" Conger was determined to be jovial. But then, Constance thought, he was a jovial man, at least in appearance, with his red cheeks and his walrus mustache.

"Yes," she said again. She could not possibly convey to these people, at ease in the civilized drawing room of the American legation, what conditions had been like in Port Arthur, so it would be a waste of time to try. And remarkably, the minister was not as wide of the mark as might have been supposed. Her interview with Tz'u-Hsi had supplied a crushing climax to the whole dismal episode. She had not expected such ill temper, such a dismissal. She had not expected the empress to be so unreasonable, when she had to know the fiasco of Port Arthur, the entire war, was the fault of herself and her ministers. As Ksian Fu had said, Constance did not know the old lady very well.

And she could no longer doubt that the prince had been right about his likely fate, as well. She shivered.

"Have a drink of this," Conger recommended, pressing the glass into her hands.

She drank, and felt the warmth of the liquid tracing its way down her chest and sending some welcome relief up to her brain.

"How seriously do you take what she said?" Conger asked, proving that he was not just a pleasant smile and a welcoming manner; she had reported the gist of her conversation in the Forbidden City. "I mean, do you suppose there is any risk people like this fellow Kung might actually encourage her to attack the whites?"

Constance winced at his choice of words. "I doubt it," she said. "She goes through moods like this from time to time, and we'll all be 'foreign devils' for a while, but she knows how strong we are, and how weak China is. Especially right now. She'll not try anything which might face her with another punitive expedition—she remembers the last one too well, even if it was thirty years ago. Could anyone tell me where Kate is?"

"She went home with Mrs. Bunting," Frank said.

"We'll get you both out to Chu-teh tomorrow," Conger said. "With an adequate escort."

"Do we need an escort to reach Chu-teh?"

"Indeed you do, Mrs. Baird. There seems to have been a general breakdown in law and order these past few weeks, since the war with Japan started. All manner of brigands are roaming the countryside. That's why I was wondering if the empress could be behind it. But as you say, she's probably just incapable of controlling events right now; these people seem to be causing as much trouble to the Chinese themselves as to the Europeans and the Americans. You must have an escort, though; I'll put Frank here in command."

"I'm afraid I won't be able to accept that, sir," Frank said.

"Much as I would like to. I'm due back on my ship. I should be there now."

"Oh, Frank," Constance said. "You'll be in trouble."

"I doubt it. Not if I go back tomorrow with a note from Mr. Conger saying I was unavoidably detained. The fact is, I . . ." He drank some brandy, and flushed.

The Congers exchanged glances. Clearly they were in a dilemma. They could see, if they did not in any event already know, how much Frank worshiped the ground she walked on. He had made it plain enough, anyway, by the manner in which he had dashed to Port Arthur to rescue her. But she was a married woman, and more, the wife of the leading American missionary in China.

Constance decided to take care of the matter herself. The moral requirements of being an American lady seemed rather irrelevant right this minute. Because for all her efforts, Frank's love had not been killed. But now it had to be. Frank had to be told exactly what she was and how she was, what she had experienced and what would haunt her for the rest of her days. Or he would be throwing his life away behind hers. She finished her drink and got up; the brandy provided her with an ample supply of Dutch courage. "I wonder if you'd excuse Frank and me," she said. "Just for a little while. There are some matters we have to discuss."

Mr. Conger opened his mouth and then closed it again. Mrs. Conger also stood up. "Of course, my dear," she said. "Would you like us to leave you here?"

"That would be awfully kind of you," Constance said. The late-November afternoon was a little chilly for walking in the garden.

"Yes," Mrs. Conger said, having apparently made the offer out of politeness rather than in any belief it would actually be accepted. "How odd it is that I should have lived here for two years now, and we are meeting for the first time. I really think we should have a nice long chat, whenever you can spare the time. Well, come along, Edward."

Mr. Conger hastily went to the door. "You'll help yourself to brandy, Frank," he said. "And, Mrs. Baird, of course."

"Thank you, sir." Frank also stood up and smiled as the door closed. "More reason for gossip."

"I'm sorry," she said. "I did wish to speak with you."

"Oh, Connie," he said, and sat beside her.

She got up in turn. "Frank," she said, "you have just got to listen to me, very carefully."

"Connie, I know what you've been through. I know . . . Hell, you didn't think I was going to make advances to you right now?"

"Of course I didn't think that, Frank."

"But I *would* like to talk with you," he said. "I've been doing a hell of a lot of thinking. Sure, I was mad when you stood me up that time. I told myself you were just a tease, who only wanted to flirt, but was quite happy in her marriage. But the more I thought about it, the more I realized I was wrong. I was going to try to see you sometime, maybe get Harriet to arrange it, and make a fresh start, with a different approach. Of course you must have thought all I wanted was to . . . well . . ." He flushed. "Make love to you. Of course I *do* want to do that, Connie, but I want more. I want—"

"Frank," she said. "Don't say it."

He frowned at her. "But . . ."

"*I* was going to talk to *you*, remember," she said. "I stood you up, remember. Can you also remember what I did when I stood you up?"

"You went to Port Arthur, to visit with Kate."

"I went to Port Arthur to be with Prince Ksian Fu."

He stared at her.

"Well, maybe I didn't quite plan it that way," Constance said. "But that's the way it happened."

"You?" he asked. "And Ksian Fu?"

He looked so stricken that she had to defend herself; she hadn't intended to.

"It had been planned," she said. "By Kate, and by Ksian, too. He had to make the choice between us, you see, and he didn't want to. He chose Kate, but he wanted me too. So he got Kate to arrange it." She shrugged. "Kate is all but Chinese now. And in China, especially if you happen to be married to a royal prince, you do what he tells you to, even to the extent of getting his outside women for him."

"You . . . you let him . . ."

"I let him make love to me, Frank," Constance said. "I enjoyed it. Then I was shocked by what I had done. So I ran away and came back to Chu-teh. I mended my fences with Henry, and I settled down to being a good wife. I was determined to do that, Frank, even if it meant never seeing you again. Or the prince."

"Sure," he said. "Of course you did that. Connie, to have a single slip isn't anything to be ashamed of. Even when it was with a Chinaman. Hell . . ."

She realized he was trying to convince himself. "Then last summer the empress sent me back to Port Arthur again, to fetch Kate back to have her baby here. I got stuck there for four months. With Ksian Fu."

"Oh, Christ," he said. "Oh, *Jesus*."

"I'm afraid he rather let me down at the end," Constance said. "Just as he let Kate down . . . and all the others. He turned out to be a coward, and eventually a suicide. But that doesn't alter the fact that I was his mistress for four months. I would say you want to think about that, Frank, and then I would say you want to tiptoe through that door and just let me get on with my own stupid life now."

He gazed at her. "Does . . . does Henry know about this?"

"No. Not yet."

His gaze became a frown. "You mean you are going to tell him?"

"Yes," she said.

"But . . ."

"I don't want to have secrets anymore," Constance said. "I want to be able to look myself in the mirror and not wince. It's pretty difficult to do anyway. When I look at myself in the mirror, I see that I am alive. Why am I alive, Frank? What reason have *I* got to be alive, when so many people are dead? When I watched women, better women than I, more moral and more good and with more guts than I, being dragged across a floor and cut to pieces, simply because their skins were yellow. But I survived, simply because my skin was white."

"Connie . . ."

"And don't come over with any superior-and-inferior bit. These people have forgotten more about civilization than we will ever know, in my opinion. So they've retained a bit of savagery, but haven't we, Frank? Only we spend so much time trying to suppress our savagery, and our instincts, our *sexual* instincts, Frank, that half the time we don't even know we're alive. We live a sham life most of the time. Well, I'm done with that."

She paused, and he finished his brandy. "What do you suppose Henry is going to say?" he asked.

"I guess he'll put me on the next boat back to San Francisco. He can do that now, I guess. I was hoping, with the empress behind me, that I might be able to stay. But that's all done."

"You mean you don't *want* to go back to San Francisco? You want to stay here? After everything that's happened, everything you've *seen*?"

"Yes, Frank," she said. "I would like to stay here. I . . .

well, I'm like Kate, I guess. I'm more Chinese than American now. I don't think I could go back to being a proper American housewife anymore.''

"What about Charlie?''

She sighed, and sat down. "Maybe I'm not the right mother for Charlie. Maybe I'm not the right mother for anyone.''

Frank came across the room to sit beside her. "After you've told Henry," he said, "Constance, will you marry me?''

Did he mean it? She didn't know. Once again she was in the position of just not knowing enough about people. She knew how people died, with what terror and horror in their faces and in their screams, and she knew how they killed, with what lust and vicious anger in their souls. She did not know how they loved. Because, she was realizing more and more with every day, she had never *been* loved. She doubted she had even been loved by her parents; she had merely been an extra mouth to feed. Certainly she had never been loved by Henry. And of course she had never been loved by Ksian Fu. To each of them she had been an object; to the one, an object to be feared, because of the obscene desires she had aroused in him, to the other, an object to be used, because he found her body desirable.

She had used the word "had" in her thoughts with regard to Henry. Without intending to. Now Frank offered her . . . love? Or pity? Or something even worse, a stiff-necked concept of male chivalry which was more absurd even than the Japanese code of honor, which demanded that he take her and protect her for the rest of his life, even if his stomach revolted every time he held her in his arms, at the thought that he was treading where a "Chinaman" had gone before; she could not forget his reference to Kate after her marriage.

Dared she find out his true feelings for her? But then, dared she turn away from those feelings? Because after she had told Henry—and she was determined to do so—there would be nothing. Nothing, nothing, nothing. Not even her child. She had no money, and she knew no trade—and she would certainly not be welcome back in Richmond as the divorced wife of the Reverend Henry Baird, even if she wanted to go. But for all her fine words, she could not stay in China by herself. So there was only Frank Wynne.

The most damnable aspect of the entire situation was that she thought she *could* love Frank. Certainly, out of all the men she had ever met, he was the only one never to slip from her ideal of manhood. Which was not to say he never would. And if he did, she would hate him. But she would hate him too if he did marry her out of pride or pity. And she would hate them both if he could not do for her what Ksian Fu had done, because then she would again want.

She had allowed her life to be ruined. She had been mesmerized, been drawn to the sexual license of the Orient like a moth to a flame, and she had been burned. She had supposed that she could sample forbidden fruits and withdraw from them as she chose. And she had been wrong.

They were seated next to each other at dinner. She had made no definite reply, but already there was a certain proprietary air about him, which did not escape the Congers. Fresh source of gossip. But now he no longer seemed to mind.

No one appeared surprised when he walked with her to her room after the meal. "I know you want to come to me, Constance," he said. "But I think I also know all the memories, all the horrors, that are holding you back. I can be patient. I can wait forever for you. But will you write to me this time and tell me when next you'll be in Peking or Tientsin?" He smiled, and laid his finger on her lips. "No borrowed apartment, Connie. No clandestine rendezvous. I just want to see you and talk with you. And hear your plans."

She hesitated, feeling absolutely helpless. The bedroom door was swinging open behind her. And she had deliberately drunk too much wine with her dinner. "You can come in, Frank," she said. "I guess everybody knows you're here, anyway."

He shook his head. "I said, no more secrecy. When you come to me, Connie, I want you to *want* it. As I said, I'll wait forever."

"Kate?" Joan Mountjoy stared at her daughter in total disbelief. "Kate? Can it really be you?" She gazed at the Chinese robe, the upswept red hair, the rings, and more than anything, the poise.

"Of course it is I, Mother," Kate said. "And this is Adela."

Joan peered at the baby girl as if expecting to see a hairy ape.

"But . . . where did you come from?" James Mountjoy asked.

"We heard that Port Arthur had fallen," explained Father Pierre. "But we did not know . . ."

Constance looked at Henry; he had made no move to kiss her.

"Of course we knew that white people would be all right," he said.

"I suppose she is a pretty little thing," Joan was remarking, still peering at the baby.

Kate did not take offense. "She's beautiful," she said.

"But . . . how long are you going to stay?" Joan asked.

"Forever," Kate told her.

"For . . ." Joan gazed at her husband.

"The prince . . . ?" he asked hesitantly.

"My husband is dead," Kate said quietly. "He died commanding his soldiers against the Japanese, as was his duty. As an imperial princess, I am of course entitled to a home in the Forbidden City, but I have decided against that. I will live here with you and bring Adela up as a good Christian."

Constance turned away. She wished she could create such a world of make-believe and live in it with such determination that everyone would have to believe her. She faced Peter.

"Is there news of Lizzie, Mistress Constance?" he asked.

She sighed. "Lizzie is dead. She was drowned when the *Kowshin* was sunk, last July. Had you not been told?"

He shook his head, his eyes filled with tears. Clearly he could not speak.

"She . . ." Constance changed her mind. She could not possibly tell him that his sister had been fortunate, that if she had survived to reach Port Arthur she would then have been butchered by the Japanese samurai.

She stepped past him, went to the bungalow, where Miriam waited, holding Charles by the hand. "See?" Miriam told the little boy. "I told you your mummy would come home. He did fret for you, Mistress Constance."

"Mama," Charles shouted, tumbling down the stairs and into her arms.

She picked him from the ground, held him close. "Oh, Charlie," she said. "Oh, Charlie."

She carried him up the stairs, aware that Henry had followed her and that Miriam had left the veranda. She went inside, looked at all the old familiar tables and chairs, the ornaments and the pictures, things she had put in place, and realized that she had not expected ever to see them again. Or her son.

"I understand that your paramour is dead," Henry said.

Constance turned sharply.

"Joan has told me of the goings-on in Port Arthur," he said. It was always difficult to gauge his true expression because of the thick beard which covered his mouth and chin, but his eyes were hard. Harder than she had ever seen them.

"And you think that I . . ." She was preparing to lie, instinctively, when she had come here determined to tell him the truth. But in her own time. First she had wanted to rest, and think, and know where she was and where she was going . . . but she was not going to be given that time.

"You stayed there, didn't you?" he asked. "When any decent woman would have come home immediately. As you did two years ago. But this time you stayed, and you revealed your body to him every day. Joan has told me of it."

Constance set Charles on the floor. "I did not come home, Henry," she said, "because I could not. Had you taken the slightest interest in the matter, in my whereabouts, in whether I was alive or dead, you would have discovered that for yourself. But since you wish to know the truth, yes, I revealed my body to Prince Ksian Fu. But I didn't just do that, Henry. I let him touch me. I slept with him, naked. I was his mistress, Henry. I was his mistress the first time I went to Port Arthur, two years ago. And as you say, now he is dead."

He stared at her, unable to believe that she would actually admit it.

"So under the circumstances," she said, "I think it would be best if you arranged to divorce me. I shall admit adultery with the prince."

His eyes narrowed. "Divorce you?"

"Henry, I have committed adultery."

"And you think that entitles you to run off and leave me? Run off where?"

Constance drew a long breath. "Frank Wynne has asked me to marry him. There is nothing for you to be afraid of, Henry. I appear to be out of favor with the empress at the moment, so there are not likely to be any repercussions there." She thought it best not to tell him they were *all* out of favor with the empress at the moment. "I would hope and pray that you would allow me to take Charles, as I cannot believe you really care for the boy. But if you will not, then I must ask that you allow him to visit me from time to time, as I love him very dearly."

"Divorce you?" he asked again. "Why should I divorce you?"

"Henry . . ."

"You are my wife. So you were always a wanton. I suspected that from your first night here, when you came to my bed naked and unashamed. But I even suspected it on our honeymoon, I think. I thought then, my God, Henry Baird, what have you done, to take such a scarlet woman to your bed. But then I realized that God had sent you to me, both that I might attempt to lead you into the paths of righteousness, and as a reward for my years of service to his cause."

"You . . . you are unutterable," she shouted. Charles looked from one to the other of his parents, his eyes filling with bewildered tears.

"And you are vicious," Henry retorted. "But I shall not fail in my task."

"To enjoy me?" she demanded.

"To do my duty by you as a woman and as a Christian. I am glad to have you back, Constance. I have missed the comfort of you."

She glared at him, unable to believe what he was saying, unable to believe that his mind was so perverted he wanted her more than ever now *because* she had been to Ksian Fu's bed. "And if I just leave you? Leave Chu-teh?"

"To go where?" he asked. "As you have told me, you are out of favor with the empress. So that avenue is closed to you. Ah, Frank Wynne, of course. I suppose you have been sleeping with him as well. Whore! But I do not think Captain Wynne will welcome you as an adulteress on the run from her husband. The Navy would not welcome you, Constance. They might just welcome a divorced woman marrying one of their officers. They would not welcome one of their officers setting up house with a woman who is another man's wife. I think your Captain Wynne, much as he desires you, is very well aware of that fact. Or he soon will be made aware of it. I think you should forget your mistakes and endeavor to behave yourself. At least in public. I do not mind your misbehaving yourself when we are alone together and when we can correct your errors together."

"You call yourself a man of God? You are a creature from the pit."

"I am your husband, Constance. As I say, I have missed you. Why do you not put Charles to bed, as it is getting late, and then come and tell me about this prince of yours. And about Franklin Wynne, if you like."

# 11

# The Affair

Constance dismounted, gave her reins to a groom at the foot of the legation steps. One of the secretaries had seen her approach and now came to greet her. "Mrs. Baird," he said, "I'm afraid Mrs. Conger is out shopping, but she won't be long. She did ask to be informed next time you were in Peking."

"I'm sure she does not wish to be disturbed," Constance said. "Actually . . ." She changed her mind. Why she was here would no doubt be obvious soon enough; there was no need to overpublicize it. "I'll just sit on the veranda and wait, shall I?"

"Of course," the young man said. "I shall have some tea prepared. Oh, and . . . ah . . . Happy New Year, Mrs. Baird."

"Why, thank you, Mr. Lowry," she said, sinking into the cane chair he had offered her and pulling her riding coat closer about her; if the snow had not yet begun in earnest, the air was growing increasingly chill. She did not suppose she would be able to return to Peking for at least three months after this visit. So if he could not make it . . . would she be sorry, or glad?

"What are you going to do?" Kate had asked. Having Kate as a confidante was a boon she had never properly evaluated. *This* Kate, who had charged into life with such élan, and charged into a brick wall, as well, but who had refused to accept the knockdown blow the wall had given her. Because out of the impact she had gained Adela, and to the little girl she was obviously preparing to devote the rest of her life. As *she* should be doing, to Charles. As she had intended to do, down to last July.

And as she was secretly so happy at being forced to do. But not *all* of her life. That would be to make a mockery of being alive at all.

"What are you going to do?" Why, whatever she liked, she supposed. Incredibly, she was suddenly as free as air, in real terms. Henry certainly knew where she was, and although she had not told him, he would also know whom she was going to meet. Yet he had raised no objection. He had in fact been quite pleased when she had announced she was going into Peking. He *wanted* her to go to another man, knowing that she had to come back to him, to submit to whatever he chose to do to her. As she was in any event a wanton, he could do what he liked to her. Without love, without even affection, without even gentleness. She should thank God, she supposed, that his upbringing was so narrow, his whole outlook was so limited, that he could think of nothing *to* do to her, save the orthodox, in his eyes. If he had also taken to massaging her with heavy hands, well, she had been bruised often enough before. Besides, it was only temporary. Perhaps. Because what she was going to do about it depended upon Frank.

She knew it was strange, and felt it was also somehow sinful, to be contemplating her future in the hands of a man she did not even know if she loved. But then, she was terribly aware of no longer knowing what love was. She had come to China determined to love Henry, as if one could love by determination. In any event, that had soon been turned into loathing. She had returned to Port Arthur determined *not* to love Ksian Fu. As if one could not love by determination. But in any case her attraction to the prince was primarily physical and had died when she witnessed his weakness of character.

Frank did not appear to lack either certainty or courage. Or gentleness. The boy she had liked without admiration had entirely disappeared in a man she could admire enormously. A man she could love, if she dared let herself. But there was the point. She could no longer risk either rejection or disillusion. Frank had to be *everything* she dreamed of, before she would dare be able to pull away the drapes shrouding her mind, her heart, and her emotions. And she did not yet *know*.

She stood up as he came onto the veranda, took her hands, and kissed them; there were servants as well as secretaries about.

"Connie," he said, "it's been so *long*. But getting leave right now is a problem. All these rumors . . . You've had no trouble?"

She shook her head. "The trouble is in the south. As usual. Anyway, it's directed against the empress, mainly. Those concessions she has had to make to the Japanese . . ."

He sat beside her, still holding her hands. "She's going to get away with that."

Constance frowned at him. "What do you mean?"

"Simply that the European powers are refusing to let the Japs have all they're demanding. Between you and me, our experts think that the Europeans mean to take a bite at the cake themselves. There's no doubt that the Russians have always wanted Port Arthur, for instance. But the Japs are going to have to accept an indemnity." He grinned. "The Chinese are used to finding indemnities."

She remembered that he had always been a marine first and a lover second. And determined to match his mood. "Well, maybe it'll put the empress in a better humor."

"I doubt that," he said seriously. "What's bothering every-one is how the Chinese are going to respond to having more large chunks of their country carved up by the Russians and the British and the French. And the Germans are in on the act now. They're telling the Japs, hands off, settle for cash. But there's a rumor they're demanding Wei-hai-wei as the price of their help, from the empress. I think there's going to be some trouble ahead. I know you love the country, Connie, and want to stay here. But I think the sooner we get you somewhere safe the better."

"We, Frank?"

"Well . . ." He flushed. "As you're here . . . how did he take it? You didn't tell me in your letter. I didn't really expect you to. But it's been quite a job, waiting to see you."

Constance got her breathing under very careful control, made herself sit still when she wanted to get up, so that she would not have to look at him. "Henry refuses to give me a divorce, Frank."

"Refuses . . . But . . . You did tell him about . . . well . . ."

"I told him about Ksian Fu. It didn't matter, because he had already guessed."

"And you mean . . . he still loves you?"

"No," she said. "He doesn't still love me. I don't think he ever loved me, Frank. Now I think he hates me. But he isn't going to let me go."

"For Heaven's sake . . ."

"He knows, you see," Constance went on, "that I have nowhere to go, as his wife. I could leave him, but I couldn't stay here. And I'd be nothing in the States save the woman who ran away from Henry Baird. He's quite a hero back home for his work out here. So he knows I'm helpless. And, shall I say, he retains the use of me?''

''By God,'' Frank said. ''The scoundrel. The utter scoundrel.''

''I told him that you had asked me to marry you,'' Constance went on, watching him very closely. ''And he just laughed. I told him you would take me in if I left him, and he laughed even more. He said you couldn't. He said the Navy wouldn't let you.''

Frank slowly closed his mouth.

''And I guess he was right,'' Constance said. ''But if you want me, Frank, on a catch-as-catch-can basis, well, I'm yours. What have I got to lose, that I haven't lost already?''

It occurred to her that she might have phrased it better; certainly Frank seemed taken aback. But then, she was still not sure she wanted to go through with it. Until she was, he remained a dream, a mental refuge, such as Kate seemed to have discovered, to her great advantage. Once it happened . . .

''On the other hand,'' she said, ''I can have a cup of tea and a nice long chat with Mrs. Conger, call on Harriet Bunting, do a little shopping, and go home again. I should tell you that I doubt I'll make it back to Peking before next spring, at the earliest.''

''Connie!'' He held her hand. ''I . . . I was just taken by surprise, I guess. After . . .''

''After I stood you up the last time? That was before . . .'' But it would hardly encourage him to remind him too definitely of Ksian Fu. ''Before everything,'' she said.

''Yes,'' he said. ''Yes. Connie, I am so *sorry*. About everything. But most of all about us. You don't think there's a chance Henry might change his mind?''

''No,'' she said, carefully keeping her feelings in abeyance.

''But . . . won't he ill-treat you?''

She shrugged. ''I don't think so, any more than the next man. Henry has a very complex character. You know, he is basically a very good man, even a great man, in what he is doing and what he wants to do. Yet at the same time, like all men, he has a bad side. The difference between Henry and most men is that he genuinely wants the bad side to come out from time to time. Maybe he thinks that it will make his good side better. Or maybe it just allows him to wallow in self-disgrace and thus somehow cleanse his soul. His tragedy is that he just cannot do it. He says I must have been sent to him by God for his use. That's not very flattering to me, but that's what he apparently feels. So he looks at me, and he says to himself—sometimes he says it to me as well—here is an absolutely wanton woman who deserves the worst I can do to her, and to whom I will therefore do the worst things I can think of . . . and then he can't think of anything really bad to do to me. Even when he wants to hit me—and I can see that he often feels like doing that—he can't bring himself actually to swing his hand.'' She gave a guilty smile. ''I'm sorry. I didn't mean to go on about Henry. I certainly didn't mean to defend him. But I have a lot of time to think.''

''It must be pretty soul-destroying,'' Frank said. ''Having to live like that.''

Not half so soul-destroying as sitting here with you, she thought. She got up. ''I'd better go see if I can find Mrs. Conger.''

''Connie!'' He caught her hand again. ''You said . . .''

''And you didn't exactly jump over the moon with joy.''

''I . . .'' He stood up as well. ''I guess I'm a little out of my depth. All I want to do is love you, despite . . .'' He bit his lip.

''Despite all,'' she said. ''Well, if you want to do that, Franklin Wynne, you'd better go see if your friend Wilberson is about and if his apartment can still be borrowed.''

Because now it had to be done. She had fought and struggled, against her own desires as much as against his. In her determination not to succumb to the temptation of him, she had turned herself into the most scarlet of women, as Henry would have it. Now she *wanted,* as he wanted her to want. *Her* tragedy was that now it was less desire for Frank Wynne than anger against Henry and her captivity that was driving her onward.

Waiting to see Mrs. Conger was obviously out of the question. She went shopping instead. She had brought only an overnight valise with her, and this Frank took with him. If the plan fell through—did she still wish it would?—he would merely return the valise to the legation, and it would be waiting for her when she went back there; the Congers were prepared to give her a room for the night, as usual. If the plan *did* work, then they would no doubt scratch their heads and wonder where she had gone. But she did not suppose they would scratch their heads very long.

She realized that so much had things changed, the risk was now entirely Frank's. Which did not seem to bother him. Or had it not yet occurred to him? But how she hoped he had considered it, and discarded the idea with contempt. How she hoped he would prove as masterful in bed as he had been that day when they had been surprised by the Boxers.

She reached the corner one block down from the legations, by the Roman Catholic cathedral, and stood there, sheltering from the afternoon sun beneath her parasol, watching Peking whirling past her, eyed by the crowds, certainly, but in no way molested—most of the passersby knew who she was—and realized that someone had used red paint to scrawl on the church walls "Foreign Devils Go Home." She turned her head impatiently; she certainly didn't want politics to intrude upon this evening—and gazed at him.

His cheeks were pink. "It's just along here."

She gave him her shopping bag. "Mr. Wilberson won't be there, will he?"

Frank shook his head. "But . . . it's above a Chinese restaurant. You won't mind that?"

"It'll mean I won't have to cook," she said.

He smiled, and squeezed her hand. "Connie, it's so . . . I just don't know what to say. I think I've waited all of my life for this minute."

She couldn't make up her mind what to reply. She didn't want to lie to him. But in the strangest fashion she did feel she was on her second honeymoon.

They went in a side door to the restaurant, passed by the kitchen, were stared at by the girls working there, encountered a blandly smiling gentleman, folded arms lost in the sleeves of his blue silk jacket. "Ah, Mr. Wynne," he said in English. "How good to see you, sir. Madame. A secluded table for two?"

"We're not eating, Chin-lo," Frank said. "We're going up to Mr. Wilberson."

"But Mr. Wilberson has gone . . ." Chin-lo checked himself and bowed. "You are welcome, sir. Welcome. And the beautiful lady. May I send up some of our humble food, in due course?"

"I think right away," Constance said. "I'm starving. And perhaps some sake?"

Chin-lo bowed again. "Sake, of course, Madame Baird. Right away."

Frank led her up the narrow, dark steps. "I'm sorry about that," he said.

"I had no idea you were known here," she said.

"I should have told you. I eat here quite often. But I didn't know you had."

"I haven't," she said. "But just about everyone in Peking knows Madame Baird." She shrugged. "And everyone in Peking will know about this by tomorrow morning."

He checked on the landing outside the apartment. "Does that bother you?"

"No," she said. "Or I wouldn't be here. Does it bother you?"

"The hell it does," he said, and grinned at her. "Or I wouldn't be here either."

"Frank," she said, and was in his arms. It was the first time she had really been in his arms for four years, since that night in Harriet Bunting's garden. For all of that time they had looked at each other, and wanted, and dreamed, and turned away, she because of her uncertainty, he because he was a Boston gentleman who knew no other way to behave. But now . . . Their tongues locked against each other, their bodies pressed against each other. She could feel him right through her heavy skirt. It was going to be all right, she suddenly knew. It was going to be magnificent. It was—

"Excuse, please," said the girl. There were four of them, in fact, each bearing a laden tray.

"Oh, damnation," Frank said. "I haven't even unlocked the door."

Constance smiled at the girls as they waited for the key to scrape in the lock. Surprisingly, she was not the least bothered by the interruption. So everyone knew what they were about. She *wanted* everyone to know. She wanted to shout it from the rooftops. This was what she should have done four years ago— and perhaps saved herself an awful lot of grief and misery. And pain.

The door swung in. She had anticipated the worst in the apartment, a place of shabby filth. She was delighted. Frank's friend Wilberson was obviously a man of considerable taste, if that taste lay rather toward the dramatic; heavy red-and-gold curtains shrouded the windows and also formed the partition between living and sleeping areas—presently drawn—for the apartment was really just one vast room. But the bed was a European four-poster, with a red-and-gold coverlet, needless to say. Even more important, everything was spotlessly clean, and although there was clearly no plumbing, the air was sweet with the gentlest of fragrances.

The girls busied themselves setting the places on the low table; there were no chairs to match the height, but red-and-gold cushions were arranged on the floor. The jug of sake was placed in a bowl of boiling water. "You drink while hot, eh?" the senior girl recommended, and giggled. Then they scuttled from the room; Frank locked the door behind them.

"This looks delicious," Constance said. "But somehow . . ." She hesitated, uncertain how much of a lead she needed to take. "Not to be eaten in European clothing."

And realized with a start of delight that she need not take the lead at all. His earlier uncertainty had quite disappeared. "I think you're absolutely right. Would you like me to close that curtain?" He looked at the bedroom.

"No," she said. "If we're going to be Chinese, let's be Chinese." She caught the quick flit of an expression across his face, and held his arm. "I shouldn't have said that."

"I'm glad you did," he said, and kissed her again, then stooped to fill two of the little cups with sake. "Chinese." He held his to her lips, and she held hers to his.

But he was a red-blooded and totally American male, and this was what she wanted, because she had never known one before—she could scarcely consider Henry in that light. Here she could love, and be loved, without uncertainty or embarrassment. And here too she could look for something more than the physical act. She could dream.

But the physical act came first. She undressed, facing him, laid her clothes on the settee by the bed. She had brought one of her Chinese robes, and this she put on, feeling his gaze on her all the time.

And also feeling remorse—an awareness that she was sinning? No matter what excuses she could make to herself, she was Mrs. Henry Baird. To the outside world she was married to a good and dedicated man, even a great man, as she had described him to Frank, without consciously selecting that word. What had happened with Ksian Fu had been sprung on her, unplanned. She had been helpless to resist, even if she had not really tried very hard.

But this was a deliberate act of betrayal. No one would ever believe that she could possibly have cause, that quite apart from her feelings for this man, she desperately needed to be *loved* instead of merely owned, if she was going to keep her sanity. No one in all the world could ever know the horror of submitting to Henry, night after night after night—most of the time she refused to admit it even to herself. So everyone would condemn her.

Well, she thought, let them. I *will* love, and I will *be* loved. She squared her shoulders and smiled at him.

"Connie," he said. "You are the most beautiful thing I have ever seen."

She waited, gazing at him, and he seemed to recollect himself.

Perhaps he had not expected her to wish to watch *him* undress in turn. But suddenly he was eager to do so.

Here was the height of Ksian Fu, but none of the paunchy softness. Here was rippling muscle and latent power, in every movement. Here was manhood personified. And here too was tremendous desire.

They sat opposite each other to eat; she had not fastened her robe, he had not put one on. They chewed slowly and sipped sake, feeling the heated rice wine penetrating their veins, seeping up to their minds, and they gazed at each other. Now the time for conversation was past, but she was glad of that. She wanted only to feel.

His way. Because it was a way she had never known. Henry's uncertain fumblings had frightened her; Ksian Fu had shown her a world of sensation rather than love. Now she was held tight while he entered her, could feel his weight and his love at the same moment, could reach for heights greater than even Ksian Fu had given her. Together they could reach for it a third time, before lying exhausted in each other's arms, her hair flopping about her in sweating profusion, their breaths mingling, their very souls seeming to lie dormant together. And that, too, had never been possible with Ksian Fu. I am twenty-five years old, Constance thought. And I have found my man. She could even tell herself convincingly that this could not have happened four years ago, that had she gone to Frank without first being taught how to feel by Ksian Fu, they would neither of them have known what they wanted, what they could achieve, and they would have been mutually disappointed, mutually prepared to settle for only the pale shadow of love that, she supposed, so many people had to put up with.

"Do you mind if I smoke?" he asked.

"Be my guest. Maybe you'd let me try one too."

He lit a cigarette, gave it to her. She inhaled, and promptly choked. Hastily he poured her a cup of cold sake.

"Is that supposed to be enjoyable?" she asked.

"It's supposed to calm the nerves." He took the cigarette back, sat beside her.

"What have you got to be nervous about?" she asked.

"Letting you go. Connie, I *can't* let you go. I don't know . . . I haven't dared think about it, but I know we can work something out. I can only get to Peking every three months or so, so that's out. But if you came down to Tientsin . . . I'm sure I could find you an apartment there, and I should be able to get ashore every weekend . . . I've enough money to support you in sufficient style, Connie. You wouldn't want for anything. And—''

She laid her finger on his lips. ''What do you suppose your captain would say?''

''Well . . . old Farley isn't actually a bad chap. He'd snort a bit, and probably lecture me like a Dutch uncle, but after that . . .''

''He'd tell you to forget it. He's the captain of a United States warship. He has things like discipline to keep, and morals to uphold . . .''

''I'm not suggesting you come to live on board.''

''It wouldn't work, Frank,'' she said. ''Listen, we've known each other five years, and we've suddenly found each other. We've still got a lot of time in front of us. Let me work on Henry. He'll get tired of having me around soon enough. And we'll be able to see each other every three months. How many day's furlough will you be able to get at Easter?''

''The whole weekend, I suppose. Three days.''

''Then I'll come to you for three days, here, Frank. Three whole days. And it's only three months away. I couldn't come again before then anyway; the roads are certain to be blocked most of the time.''

''And for all of those three months you'll be sleeping with him,'' he said.

''Frank, we're going to be Chinese about this, remember?''

''Sure.'' He stubbed out his cigarette. ''And you can't bring yourself to abandon Charlie.''

''Yes,'' she said. ''I can't just run away from him. Not now. Not until he's older. If Henry would have agreed to a formal and civilized separation, allowing me to see Charlie from time to time . . . But he won't, so that's it. I can't run away from him, Frank. You must be able to see that. He's my child.''

''Oh, my darling.'' He held her close. ''Forgive me. I don't want anything to spoil tonight. It has been the most wonderful night of my whole life. It's just the thought of you going back to him . . .''

''He can't give me anything you can, Frank. Every night, between now and Easter, I'll be dreaming of you. And I'll be back in Peking at Easter. For three whole days. With you.''

She would dream of him every night between now and Easter. Every day, as well, as she sat on her veranda and watched the snow clouding down, and thought of the ships riding out the winter gales at their anchorages outside Taku. But one man on board those ships would be as warm as she was. However unsatisfactory their arrangement, it was still *there*, something to look forward to. And once again she was happy, because she was ordering her own life, deciding what *she* wanted to do, instead of allowing herself to be buffeted to and fro by Fate. Besides, she felt she had the measure of Fate now. It had caught her with her defenses down last summer. But she had survived. Fate *could* be combated. And it could even be overcome.

"Oh, *Constance*," Kate said. "I am so happy for you." Her eyes filled with tears.

"Darling Kate," Constance said. "Don't you think I am the most profligate of women?"

"I think you have more guts than any woman I've ever known. Or even read about. I wish I had some."

"But you'll find another man, Kate."

Kate smiled sadly. "Not here."

"Well, of course not here. I suppose you'd find it tricky anywhere in China. Princes' widows cannot remarry, can they? But you could go home to England now. I bet you'd be the rage. I bet Queen Victoria would have you to tea."

"Do you know," Kate said seriously, "I have thought about that. But . . ." She flushed. "I don't want to."

"Why ever not?"

"Because . . . there could never be another Ksian Fu. I'm not just talking about bed. I'm talking about everything. I can never live again as I lived for those three years in Port Arthur. Do you know, I never had to do *anything* I didn't want to? No other man could give me anything like that. So I'd have to be disappointed, and we'd be unhappy."

"But, Kate . . ." Constance looked from the veranda at the compound, quiet in winter, but still filled with tasks which needed to be done. "You can't spend the rest of your life *here*."

"I don't think I'll have to," Kate said. "When the empress gets over her mood, she'll send for me. You'll see. I'm the mother of an imperial princess. She'll send for me when she's ready. And for Adela. And we'll go. So I won't ever marry again. I'll live like a princess."

Constance wished she could be so confident about the empress's mood. By all reports, this one was lasting a long time. But it was not something she was prepared to let impinge on her happiness. It was a frame of mind which could not escape Henry's notice. He had said nothing upon her return from Peking, but he raised the matter a few weeks later. "I am delighted to see you looking so well and so happy, Constance," he said one evening after Charles had been put to bed.

She was immediately watchful. "Thank you, Henry," she said. She did not really want a crisis tonight; she had just missed a period, and it was something she wanted to think about. Of course, she had missed periods before, owing to one thing or another . . .

"It seems," he went on, "that I am the only man *unable* to make you happy."

Constance sighed. "I am sorry, Henry. You know as well as I that our marriage has been a total disaster. You had no idea what you were getting. Well, I had no idea what you were getting either. I do apologize."

"You mean you had no idea you had the lusts of a Cleopatra," he said.

There was no point in becoming angry. "As you say, Henry. You must have awakened something in me. But when you could not satisfy what you had aroused—"

"My God, the words you use," he cried. "Even your mouth is tainted. Your very saliva."

"Then let me go," she shouted back. "For God's sake, let me go." She had lost her temper after all.

He stared at her, and for a moment she thought she *was* going to tell her to leave. Then he got up and went to the door. "No," he said. "Never. You are mine. Mine, do you hear? Mine!" He slammed the door behind him.

He had never before made such a definite refusal even to release her, and for the next few weeks his lovemaking was more desperately unsuccessful than ever. But by the end of March she was no longer in any doubt; she was pregnant. And it had to be Frank's. She was certain of it.

So what was to be done about it? Henry would of course claim the child as his own. And it would therefore be one more link in the chain binding her to him. Because she continued to make plans. It was a part of her essential being, considering possibilities, weighing alternatives—and one of the plans was the one she had outlined to Frank, that of leaving Henry in due course, as soon as she felt that Charlie was old enough, not only to do without her but also to understand. She would explain it to him, and he *would* understand, she was sure, and then not even Henry would be able to stop them from seeing each other as often as possible. She thought Charles might be old enough to face that situation when he was twelve. Certainly by the time he was fifteen, if she prepared him for it. Even then, she would be only thirty-five. But she would be twenty-six before this child was *born*.

Then there were the possible ramifications of telling Frank. But she had to tell Frank. Because she was so happy that she should be bearing a child for him. She had to tell Frank, and between them they could decide what was best to do. As if there was anything they could do, save continue as they had planned. But Frank would *know* that they shared something no one could ever really take away from them.

Now she could hardly wait for the snows to melt, was in a terror that they would not before Easter—although they always had in the past. And now, too, sleeping with Henry was an added purgatory. She could have ended it immediately, of course, by telling him her condition. He held it the ultimate in indecency to sleep with a pregnant woman, as he would never dream of touching her while she was menstruating, for which she was heartily thankful. But she did not want to tell him of the child until after she had told Frank. It was only for a few more days, anyway; the snow was beginning to melt.

"Mrs. Conger has invited me to visit with her over Easter," she lied. Three whole days, she thought. Three whole days.

"That was awfully kind of her," Henry said. "Do you suppose I should come too?" He gazed at her. "But you would not wish that, would you? Your marine captain might be there."

"Yes," she said. "I would not wish that, Henry."

To her surprise, he made no further comment, merely turned and left the room. Nor did he come to her again before she left. But she had no time to think of him as she walked her horse down the trail, accompanied and guarded by the marketing party from the mission, into Feng-tai and thence on to Peking itself. She was going to Frank. For three whole days. Three whole days of Chinese food and sake and delicious intimacy. She had no intention of leaving the apartment for a second for those three days. And on the first night, she would tell Frank, and make him the happiest man in the world.

But first of all, appearances had to be kept up. She went to the legation, as all Europeans and Americans from the outlying districts went to their respective legations immediately upon entering Peking, at once to inform their ministers that all was well and to collect any mail which might be waiting for them. In any event, Frank was not due in until the train arrived late that afternoon.

"Mrs. Baird." Mr. Lowry looked somewhat embarrassed to see her, but she supposed that everyone in the legation knew why she was there. "How very good to see you. All well at Chu-teh?"

"All well, Mr. Lowry. We haven't seen hide nor hair of a single malcontent for six months."

"Yes," he said. "They lie low during the cold months. Mrs. Baird . . . Mrs. Conger asked to be told when you came in. She would like you to have a cup of coffee with her."

Constance sighed. Elaine Conger was so keen on this *tête-à-tête* she kept proposing and Constance kept putting off. But she supposed there was no possible reason for putting it off now. "Why," she said, "I'd like that very much."

Mr. Lowry looked relieved; Constance wondered if he'd been told to insist upon it. "She's waiting for you now," he said, and himself escorted her upstairs and into the minister's private apartments. "Excuse me, Mrs. Conger, but Mrs. Baird is here."

"Mrs. Baird." Elaine Conger came across the drawing room to greet her. "How splendid you look. I hadn't realized the roads were clear."

She was lying, of course; she had obviously been expecting her. "Quite clear," Constance said.

"I'm so glad," Mrs. Conger said. "Thank you, Tom, that will be all."

Lowry nodded and withdrew.

"We shall have coffee directly," Mrs. Conger said. "But I so wanted to have a little chat with you. Shall we sit over here by the window?" She led the way to the window seat; a Chinese servant peered through the curtain at the rear of the room, received a quick nod from his mistress, and disappeared again. Constance decided she could only wait; Mrs. Conger obviously had something on her mind, and she had a pretty good idea what it was. Well, she thought, she would just have to grit her teeth and endure it.

"Do you suppose," Mrs. Conger said, "that I could call you Constance? And you must call me Elaine, of course," she added brightly.

"That will be very nice," Constance said.

"As I probably told you before now," Elaine went on, "it seems so odd that we should not have met sooner than last autumn. Why, do you know, almost the first name I heard when we arrived was yours. Constance Baird. Everyone was talking about Constance Baird. Because of your intimacy with the dowager empress, of course."

"She liked to listen to me talk about the outside world," Constance explained. "She's not quite the dragon lady she's portrayed. Not when she's in a good mood, anyway."

"Yes." Elaine gave the impression that she had not actually

been listening to the reply. "Still, it is very important for us white people, and especially us Americans, to be on good terms with the Chinese, don't you think? To be *respected* by them," she hurried on.

"I think they respect us in accordance with how we behave," Constance said, deciding to preempt the lecture which was obviously on its way.

"I am sure you are right," Elaine cried. "That is exactly what I wished to speak with you about."

"I meant," Constance said, "it depends on whether or not we meet them man to man, or in the case of Tz'u-Hsi and myself, woman to woman, with no suggestion of superiority, and equally, no suggestion of servility. I can tell you, Elaine, that the Chinese, and especially the empress and her advisers, are not the slightest interested in our ideas on morality or in our ideas of religion, except where they might consider that these ideas lead to a weakening of the characters of the Chinese themselves. Because, you see, if they think about our absurdities at all, it is with total contempt."

Elaine Conger's face stiffened. "I'm afraid that is not how Mr. Conger views the situation, Constance. Nor how I see it, either. Every American national in China has a duty to uphold the dignity and the moral stature of our great country, and to act, always, in accordance with the ethics and principles of Christianity. Not turn herself into a source of street-corner gossip."

Constance gazed at her, and Elaine flushed.

"I am sure everyone in the community is trying their very best to understand you," she continued in a softer voice. "And your problems. It is very easy for a young girl like yourself to have become, perhaps, swayed by the Chinese way of life, fascinated by the way they seem able to do things, to live in a fashion which is quite foreign to our way of doing things. Which is abhorrent to us, in fact. Unfortunately, Constance, you are no longer a young girl. You are a mother, and the wife of a very fine man. And do not pretend that your husband is unaware of your carrying on. What tortures he must be suffering—"

"You have absolutely no right to pass judgment upon my marriage, Mrs. Conger," Constance said. "Until you have experienced it. And as you say, I am not a young girl, to be lectured upon her private life."

"Not even when that private life has become a very public one, to the disgrace of the entire white community?"

They glared at each other. "You are asking me to give Frank up," Constance said. "It may interest you to know that we love each other, that Frank wishes to marry me, and that I have repeatedly asked Henry for a divorce, but that he has refused to give me one. Under the circumstances, I am determined to live my own life. I am well aware that it may be an embarrassment to you and to Mr. Conger, and for that I apologize. If you prefer it, I shall cease calling at the legation or in any way intruding upon you. I only came here today to meet Frank.'' She looked at her lapel watch. ''He is due in any moment now. If you wish, I will wait on the street outside.''

''Constance,'' Elaine Conger said, ''Frank is not coming in. Now or at any other time.''

Constance stared at her. ''I'm afraid I don't believe you,'' she said.

Mrs. Conger sighed. ''And I'm afraid it is true, Constance. The *Alabama* has been ordered to Samoa.''

''The *Alabama* goes to Pago Pago every year for a refit,'' Constance said. ''I know that. I also know that she is not due to go this time until the autumn.''

''She has already left,'' Mrs. Conger said. ''And she has not been sent merely for a refit. She has gone for good. She will not be coming back, Constance.''

''Because of *me*?''

Mrs. Conger shrugged. ''Let us say the circumstances, as Mr. Conger felt bound to represent them to Washington, encouraged a move which was already under consideration.''

''You . . . Mr. Conger . . .''

''Did what he considered to be his duty by the entire American community here in China,'' Elaine Conger said quietly. ''In case you feel that you have been betrayed, I may say that Captain Wynne at first refused to leave, and actually tendered his resignation. This, Captain Farley naturally refused to accept. The matter has been referred to Commodore Dewey at Pago Pago. I am afraid Frank has done himself no good.''

Constance drew a long breath. Once again Fate had slapped her in the face for overboldness; she could feel her cheeks burning with a mixture of anger and embarrassment—and despair.

''He has sent you a letter,'' Elaine said. ''Would you like it?''

Constance looked up, thankful that her eyes had remained dry. ''Thank you.''

Elaine fetched the envelope from the sideboard. ''But I would beg you not to reply to it, Constance. It can only make matters worse. He is well on the way to ruining his career. And it was a career full of promise. I imagine he will survive this setback, although the fact of his having resigned must be entered on his record. But were he to do anything else, anything foolish . . ."

"As he might do when he discovers that I bear his child," Constance said.

Elaine Conger frowned at her. "Are you sure?"

Constance hesitated, then squared her shoulders. "Yes. I am sure."

"That you are pregnant," Elaine said. "But you still have . . . relations with your husband, is that it? You amaze me, my dear girl. But in those circumstances you cannot be sure, except that you must *make* yourself sure, that the child is your husband's. Constance . . ." She picked up Constance's hand. "I believe I can understand how you feel, how desperately unhappy you must be. I *know* how desperately unhappy Frank is. But if you love him, you will abandon this course, will not make his decision yet more difficult by telling him you think this child is his. He is a marine. His entire life is dedicated to that cause. The only way he can ever share *your* life is to leave the service, and that would be the ruination of him, believe me. You would be sharing your life with a nothing, with a man who would *know* that he had ruined himself. You and he have snatched at a happiness not given to most of us to enjoy. But it was an illicit happiness and could not endure, Constance. If you honestly feel you bear his child, then perhaps you have taken more from that illicit happiness than you deserve. To tell him, to make him give up his chosen career, to ruin him, would make you unworthy to be a mother."

Constance gazed at her. Then she handed the letter back. "You had best burn it," she said.

"Constance . . ."

"If I am going to forget him, and have him forget me," she said, "it must start right now. Surely you can see that?"

Elaine sighed. "Yes, yes, I can see that. Now, would you like a cup of coffee?"

Constance stood up. "I shall go back to Chu-teh. There is really no point in staying here."

"Back to Chu-teh? But, my dear girl, you won't get there before dark."

"I have arrived at Chu-teh after dark before, Mrs. Conger."

"Well, at least wait until I arrange you an escort."

Constance shook her head. "I would rather be alone, thank you. As you have reminded me, I am very well known. As is Henry. No one is going to molest me, Mrs. Conger. I promise you that."

She left before she could be persuaded otherwise, called for her horse, rode out of the legation compound and through the crowded streets of Peking. She dared not stop to think. To consider. To understand. That would have to come later. She had supposed all such decisions were hers. To see Frank or not to see Frank. How she hated them all. How she despised them all. How she knew they were entirely guided by envy that she should have so come to terms with life in China, while they had always to sit on the sidelines, strangers.

Yet she knew they were right, in the consequences, if she defied them. She had observed too often that Frank was a marine first and a lover second. She thought she might have reversed those orders last January. But not sufficiently. He *would* be a ruined man, while the ambition of soldiering still coursed through his veins. And then he would hate her for having done that to him.

And she bore his child. Another concomitant of her sins. She did not know whether she wanted it or not. She did not know anything at this moment.

Outside the city gates she kicked her unfortunate horse into a gallop, charging along that so-well-remembered road where she and Frank had ridden that day in 1892, and where she had trotted only this morning, her whole being charged with glorious anticipation. People stared at her as she galloped by, hat slipped from her head and held only by the ribbon around her neck, golden hair streaming in the breeze, Rufus panting and gasping, until in his exhaustion he missed his footing and stumbled and sent her flying over his head into the road.

# 12

# The Boxers

Constance was aware of great pain, of people, of faces, of hands lifting her from the ground. But she could not identify anyone, could not be sure of where she was and what was happening; the pain masked her mind in searing red. Next to the pain she was aware of movement, continuous, agonizing movement. She screamed at the people who were torturing her, begged them to stop, and they ignored her as if they could not hear her, although she could hear their voices quite distinctly, without being able to understand what they were saying.

She knew she was going to die, and wished it to happen as quickly as possible, to offer relief from the pain. And when the jolting movement finally stopped and she felt herself sinking, sinking into softness, she was sure that she had at last escaped the torture of being alive. But strangely, the pain accompanied her into the softness, and she became aware of new faces and new voices, and realized that she was dying on Chu-teh, with Henry and Kate and Joan Mountjoy in the room, and Charlie crying in the background. She had not wanted to die on Chu-teh.

In time the pain lost some of its agonizing sharpness, but she did not seem to be able to rise through the clouds of uncertainty, of half-heard voices, of half-seen lights, of half-recognized sounds which surrounded her. It was as if she had been wrapped in a cocoon of some thick material, so that she was not really part of the world about her. Until the day when she found that her eyes were open, and she could see, and hear . . . and that her brain was as sharply clear as it had ever been in the past. And that

Kate was sitting by her bed. Her own bed, in her own bedroom, on Chu-teh.

"Kate?" she asked. "I am so thirsty, Kate."

"Constance!" Kate screamed. "Oh, Constance." She leaped to her feet and ran to the door. "She's awake," she shouted. "Constance is awake. Listen to me, everybody, Constance is awake."

People flooded the room. Miriam and Charles, Peter, the Mountjoys, Father Pierre and Sister Ambrosia, and Henry, standing at the back and peering at her over the heads of the other people.

"I'm so thirsty," she said.

Kate held a cup of water to her lips. "Oh, Constance," she said. "We thought you were going to die. Oh, Constance, why didn't you tell us you were pregnant?"

"My baby," Constance said, grasping her hand. "Where is my baby?" She looked from face to face. "Where is my baby?"

Joan Mountjoy sighed. "Your baby is dead, Constance," she said. "No fetus could have survived such a fall as you had. It is a miracle that you are alive yourself."

She wanted to scream, but it was too painful to fill her lungs with air. So she closed her eyes instead, and prayed for them to go away. And for her to die. Because she had to die now. She had nothing left to live for.

"You really have been very fortunate," Kate said.

They were again alone together, and she had not died.

"You broke seven ribs," Kate told her. "*Seven*. And one of them was quite splintered. Father says it is a miracle it did not puncture your lung. Then you would have died. It was sticking out, you know, right through your skin." She smiled. "Father bound you up. He did medical training before entering the Church. And he says you are going to be all right. But you must be very careful. The bones are knitting, but the slightest accident could make them snap again."

She was going to live, despite herself. "But . . . is Rufus all right?"

"Oh, yes. The trouble is, he kicked you with one of his hind legs. You went over his head, you see, and he kicked you. Father thinks he was actually trying to avoid you. He's a good old horse, Rufus is."

"And how did I get here?"

"Some Chinese found you, and recognized you, and brought you in. You were bleeding terribly, mainly from the miscarriage, of course, but they thought you were all cut up inside. Which you were, actually. Father was quite horrified when he examined you. But things turned out much better than any of us dared hope."

Father, Constance thought. Always Father. "Was Henry here?" she asked.

A shadow passed over Kate's face. "Yes. Yes, Henry was here. Connie . . . you should have told us you were pregnant."

Constance shut her eyes again. Once again Fate had stepped in and crushed her as she might have crushed a scorpion or a flea. Crushed her utterly, and almost killed her into the bargain. And killed Frank's child.

"You have committed murder," Henry said.

She opened her eyes. It was evening, because the oil lamps had been lit, and Kate was no longer present.

"You have murdered our child," he said, his eyes glooming at her.

Oh, God, she thought. Oh, God, why can't he go away?

"Have you nothing to say?" he demanded.

"I am very tired, Henry. And I am in pain—"

"You should be dead," he spat at her. "Murderess."

Wasn't he right? She wished she could be sure. She had wanted to gallop, in an attempt to exorcise the sheer frustrated anger that had been bubbling through her system. No more than that, she was certain. But she had been aware, deep down in her mind, that she had been risking a fall. Again, no more than that. Yet she had to have known that a fall would dislodge the fetus, even had Rufus not kicked her in the ribs. She was haunted by her earlier thoughts, that the child would be another link in the chain binding her to Henry. She had dismissed that idea, until after she had shared the news with Frank, but she had not been allowed to share the news with Frank, and so . . . Could she possibly have *wanted* the baby dead, without ever knowing it?

She felt a tear trickling down her cheek.

"Ha," Henry said. "You confess your guilt."

"It wasn't your child, Henry," she said.

He frowned at her. "You can't possibly know that."

"I know it," she said, and closed her eyes again. A moment later she heard the door close behind him. But had he not been right?

He certainly believed so. Or believed that the child *had* been Frank's. Either way, he hardly spoke to her from that day. He could not in any event have acted the husband for several months, as her ribs slowly knitted back together, as the pain, every time she breathed, slowly dwindled, as her strength slowly returned. But he left her sitting alone on the veranda save for the company of Charlie and Kate. Even the Mountjoys and Father Pierre largely ignored her. They had rallied round, with every possible effort, when she had been brought in, a shattered wreck. But that had been because they were Christians, not because she was Constance Baird. They knew where she had been and what she had gone to do. And no doubt, like Henry, they felt that she had committed murder.

"What nonsense," Kate said. "They just don't understand. Because they don't *want* to understand, Connie. I've tried to explain it to Mother and Father, and do you know, even as I'm speaking, I can see a sort of curtain dropping over their eyes. And over their minds, as well." She smiled, and sighed. "Isn't it strange, how you and I seem to be yoked together? In everything. But, Connie, when Her Majesty sends for me to go and live in the Forbidden City, I'll insist that you come too. We'll go together. It'll be better than staying here. We'll live together, you and I, and we'll grow old together." She giggled. "Retired concubines, you and me."

Without Kate, as she had thought so often before, she would have gone mad. But as usual she was not sure that Kate had the answer. The long months of pain, and of mental pain as well, as she faced her own guilt, as much as the memory of that happiness which had been wrenched from her grasp, left Constance very aware of how crushed she was. She had sought to assert herself, always against Fate, always afraid to admit to herself that in so doing she was actually asserting herself, or attempting to do so, against God himself.

Despite having spent so many years listening to Henry preach, she had never been sure of the truth of it. Was everything predestined, as Henry believed, and thus to attempt to change the circumstances in which one found oneself futile? Or did one have entirely free will? But she had always supposed, if the latter, that one's sins were not totted up, and one's punishments did not begin until after death. Yet every time she had sought to practice her free will, retribution had been swift and terrible.

She had always supposed that God had been on her side, had understood her point of view. It would not have been possible to exist without believing that. But now she was left with no alternative but to believe the opposite. She had sinned, again and again and again, in pursuance of the desires of her own tumultuous nature. And she had been punished for it. That she had been left her life, having ruined so many other lives, was simply a part of the punishment. And it would continue, she understood, as, in the depths of her misery and contrition, she even attempted to make it up with Henry.

"I know how wicked I have been," she said. "I know what a trial I have been to you. I would like to say how sorry I am."

"Make your peace with God," he replied. "If you can. But do not suppose I will let you go. As you are a millstone which he has chosen to hang about my neck, so will we suffer together."

Fortunately, he did not seem to understand that the thing she was more afraid of than any other right now was that he *would* decide to let her go. Because once again she *had* nowhere to go, and as the months stretched into years without the looked-for summons from the Forbidden City, it became obvious that both Kate's and her fates were to live out the rest of their lives in the restricted atmosphere of Chu-teh, regarded as dangerous women by their relatives, and by the converts as well, forbidden to take any proper part in the running of the mission, left with only their children to care for and educate. So thank God for their children, and for Charlie in particular, as he grew into a bright and intelligent and inquisitive little boy.

She no longer even went into Peking. She had no reason to. Nor, she thought, would she have gone even if she did have a reason. The thought of having to face Elaine Conger, or Harriet Bunting, or any other of the women whose gossip had left her groveling in the dust, or even Tom Lowry, made her physically sick, just as she knew that the sight of Chin-lo's Chinese restaurant or of Mr. Wilberson would reduce her to tears. Frank was gone, and he had taken all the joy of Peking with him.

And he had gone, eventually, to war. When the news reached them, in the spring of 1898, that the United States had declared war on Spain and was fighting in both Cuba and the Philippines, she and Henry were both aghast. It had not occurred to either of them that their country could ever become involved in a conflict with a European power. The Mountjoys were pleased. "America's place is upon the world stage," James Mountjoy declared. "Whether she likes it or not. I think this is a very important step in world history."

"Hardly a point of view worthy of a man of God," Henry remarked coolly. It was the first time Constance had ever heard the pair of them disagree about anything. As if it mattered. The country was at war. And where the United States armies went, there went the Marines first. She did not even know where Frank was, but she knew he would be either in Cuba or the Philippines, being shot at.

And did *that* matter? It was over, over, over. They had had one magnificent, unforgettable night together. But it was over. It was three years in the past. And for him, almost certainly, it had been surpassed far too often during that time.

Yet the war was a momentous event. It overshadowed even the rumors that came seeping out of Peking concerning the reforms being promulgated by the emperor. He was apparently attempting to copy the Japanese and make up for his armies' defeat by that nation by himself adopting Western methods and armaments. This was in total opposition to the view of Tz'u-Hsi and her clique, and their anger was increased by the growing number of concessions Kuang Hsu found it necessary to grant to the Europeans in return for their advice, and more important, for their financial aid. Yet there was nothing even the dowager empress could do about it. If the emperor chose to rule, he was the supreme power in the land.

Until the day news arrived that Kuang Hsu had abdicated! This was not really credible. There was no *reason* for him to abdicate three years after the defeat of his country by the Japanese, when he was at last stemming China's decline, and while he was still a young and vigorous man. If there were the usual rumors of rebellions and uprisings in various parts of the great empire, if the Europeans seemed to be constantly demanding more and more treaty ports and railroad rights, if even the Boxers were constantly reported to be a growing movement, commanding more and more support among dissatisfied young men, all of this was as unchanging in China as the night and the day, the summer and the winter—and as usual, very little of it was evident in the neighborhood of Chu-teh.

Besides, in whose favor could the young emperor possibly abdicate? *His* nephews were all still in their uttermost infancy.

"The dowager empress has taken all power into her own hands," the converts returning from the Feng-tai market told them.

"But she has always had all the power in her own hands," Constance said.

"In the name of the emperor. This time she acts in her own name, as empress."

That also seemed incredible, as it was against all Chinese tradition and all Manchu law, and Tz'u-Hsi had always in the past been careful to observe both those pillars of Chinese society. Yet Constance knew how bitterly the old dragon lady could set herself against anything of which she disapproved. Not that, in the unchanging monster that was China, even a palace revolution could really change things, she supposed, any more than Kuang Hsu's "hundred days of reform" had been able to change things. She remained more interested in the course of the Spanish-American War, breathed a great sigh of relief when in the late summer the Spanish admitted defeat and sued for peace. She had no idea whether or not Frank had survived, and no means of finding out, save by inquiring at the embassy, and she was not going to do that. But the mere fact that the shooting had stopped made her feel happier. While the Mountjoys were in turn dismayed the following year when the British in South Africa found it necessary to go to war with the Boer republics of the Transvaal and the Orange Free State. Unlike the Americans against the Spanish, early news from South Africa suggested that the British were being resoundingly defeated.

But South Africa was a very long way away from Chu-teh, and by now Constance had come to terms with her new life, that of being a mother and nothing else, her spare time spent sitting with Kate on the veranda and watching the seasons drifting by, reminiscing, which was no longer painful to do, as their joint memories concerned only Ksian Fu and Port Arthur. It was as if they were both, for all their twenty-nine years, old women, remembering the events of their youth, so far away. Retired concubines, even if not in the Forbidden City. Even that was all but forgotten. Thus they were both aware of an almost frightening surprise when at the beginning of April 1900, as soon as the snows had melted to make the trail passable, the eunuch Chiang appeared at the Chu-teh gate with an escort of soldiers.

Kate stood up, face flushed. "You must give me an hour to prepare myself, Chiang, and the Princess Adela."

"I have come for the devil woman," Chiang said.

Kate's mouth opened and then shut again.

"For me?" Constance was also on her feet, her heart pounding. She had thought the Forbidden City behind her forever.

"Her Majesty would speak with you, devil woman," Chiang said. And added, as usual, "Now. You must make haste."

Constance gazed at Henry, hurrying across from the schoolroom to find out what was happening. But as soon as he saw Chiang and the soldiers, he knew what was happening, knew that his control of their lives was again slipping from his grasp. He turned and went back to the schoolroom without a word.

"It is obviously to prepare your return to the Forbidden City,"

Constance told Kate reassuringly. But Kate went back to her parents' house, also without a word.

Constance did not take her friend's pique too seriously. She would get over it, and *she* was being recalled to Peking, to that world within a world, or outside a world, that world in which she had first started to live, where all things were possible. . . . She realized that once again, without even intending to, she was preparing herself to challenge Fate. And that she had resolved never to do again. Besides, had it not been Fate summoning her from Chu-teh?

"Her Majesty is well?" she asked Chiang as they rode down the trail, the escort jingling behind her.

"Her Majesty is always well," Chiang reminded her. But apparently he did not wish her to be recognized, insisted she wear a voluminous black veil, which concealed not only the yellow hair which was her trademark but also even the fact that she was a Westerner at all.

Soon she thought she understood why the precaution was necessary; as they approached the ruined pagoda that lay just north of the trail, they saw a large number of people apparently encamped around the old building, and from the weird calisthenics many of them were performing, Constance knew at once they were Boxers. But Boxers had not been seen in any numbers in the North China plain for several years.

"Times change," Chiang said when she asked him.

Several of the Boxers approached the little cavalcade, but retired again on recognizing the dragon flags, for which Constance was grateful. But now she was aware of a sense of urgency, an impatience to reach the empress and find out what was happening—and then get back to the security of Chu-teh again.

Tz'u-Hsi was not actually in the Forbidden City. For the first time, Constance was taken beyond the purple walls, out to the I Ho Yuan, the Summer Palace. This had been burned by the British as an act of reprisal for Chinese mistreatment of their envoys in 1861, and had lain derelict for many years. It had eventually been rebuilt by Tz'u-Hsi herself, using funds, it was rumored, appropriated for the improvement and modernization of the Chinese Navy. Constance could not help but wonder if Admiral Ting, as he had pulled the fatal trigger against himself, had reflected on that betrayal which must have been part of the cause of his two defeats by the Japanese.

At least the embezzled funds had been spent with the utmost artistic taste. Amid a succession of lakes, known as "seas," there arose a profusion of palaces surrounded by weeping willows and tall bamboos, feathery cassias and clustering rhododendrons, all transplanted—save for the rhododendrons—from the southern provinces where Tz'u-Hsi had been born and spent her childhood, the memories of which she was now trying to recreate in her declining years. Here there were gazebos, and deep patioed dwelling houses, lotus-filled canals, and, amazingly, a vast stone replica of a Mississippi paddle steamer, all dominated by the famous White Dagoba which was visible even from the crowded streets of Peking itself.

And here the empress sat and painted. Chiang and Constance halted some distance off, standing beside the group of ladies and eunuchs and snapping Pekingese dogs who also watched, and who glanced at Constance with curious indifference; on Chiang's instructions, she had not yet removed the heavy veil.

Tz'u-Hsi did not appear to have turned her head, but she knew they had arrived. "Come closer, devil woman," she said.

Now the heads did turn to stare at her. Constance could see no further point in being incognito, so she shrugged the veil from her head as she went forward.

Now Tz'u-Hsi did look at her. "As beautiful and as willful as ever," she remarked. "Do you like my painting?"

It was of one of the palaces, and was really very good, with accurate brushwork and a splendid sense of color.

"Your Majesty has great skill," Constance said.

"Yes," Tz'u-Hsi agreed. It was difficult to say whether or not she had aged much in the five years since Constance had last seen her, although she was in her sixty-fourth year. Certainly her complexion was well concealed beneath a liberal layer of pinkish face powder—which she had always worn, to alleviate her somewhat dark complexion—and heavily rouged cheeks and bottom lip. "I do not know why I care for you, Constance," she remarked. "You have all of the typical white woman's vices, and few of her virtues. But you have courage. Perhaps that is what I like about you."

Constance decided not to be put out by the criticism; she was the only white woman the empress had ever known personally—apart from Kate. "The Princess Ksian Fu sends her felicitations, Majesty," she said. "The baby princess is a lovely little girl."

"Little *girl*," Tz'u-Hsi said scornfully. "Baby Princess. My family has been a sore disappointment to me, Constance. All of it. But I wish the princess and her child no harm. Just as I wish you no harm. Which is why I have summoned you here today. Constance, I wish you to leave China. Immediately."

Constance frowned at her in total bewilderment. "You are expelling me, Majesty?"

"I am not expelling you," Tz'u-Hsi said carefully. "I am suggesting to you that it is time for you to go home to your own people. I wish you no harm. There was a time I enjoyed your company. Now I wish you to leave. Take your husband and your child. Take the Princess Ksian Fu and her child; there is no place for them here. Take her parents as well. But go back to your own countries."

Constance felt as if she had been kicked in the stomach. She could see no reason for what she had just been told, unless . . . "May I ask if your decision has anything to do with the presence of a large number of members of the Society of Righteous Harmony Fists north of the river, Majesty?" she asked.

"You may ask me nothing. I am telling you to leave China. Now. Certainly by the end of the month. Do not think to disobey me, Constance. Do it now."

"Your Majesty," Constance said, "I very much doubt that my husband will ever leave China. His entire life is here, and his work. He can never leave all the converts who so depend on him. Besides—" She had been going to say: There is nowhere else he can possibly live now. Just as there was nowhere else she could possibly live. Life as Henry's wife anywhere else in the world apart from Chu-teh would be even more unbearable than life as Henry's wife on Chu-teh.

But Tz'u-Hsi cut her short. "Do it now," she said again. "I will not look upon your face again. Do it now."

She turned back to her painting.

The command was as disturbing as it was unequivocal. It left Constance curiously breathless. But despite her isolation from the social world of Peking's Western society, she had no doubts at all what she had to do. "I will go to the American legation to spend the night," she told Chiang.

"You return to Chu-teh," he said. "Now. With escort."

"I am going to the legation, Chiang," she said. "You can go where you like."

"You are stupid woman," he said. "You want to be chopped up?"

"No one is going to chop me up, Chiang," she said. "I am the devil woman, remember?" And smiled at his discomfiture. But she was remembering more that dreadful evening five years ago, when Rufus had thrown her and left her bleeding and possibly even dying by the roadside. Then she had been found by Chinese, and not even robbed of her watch. Rather had she been tenderly carried back to Chu-teh to regain her health.

Nor did she believe even the Boxers would do more than shout curses at a group of Europeans, and Conger would have to provide her with an escort—especially after what she had to tell him. Besides, the empress had promised her she had until the end of the month. She had no real idea what she was going to do as regards the mission—that depended to a large extent upon the Congers' reaction to her news—but she was aware of an almost peaceful feeling in that her life once more had some purpose to it, however momentarily.

She patted the eunuch on the shoulder. "Believe me, Chiang, I will be all right. I will obtain an escort from the legation."

Elaine Conger was obviously amazed to discover the identity of her caller. "Why, Mrs. Baird," she cried, and then recollected herself. "Constance! How good to see you. And to see you looking so well. We were all so worried after your accident."

"Thank you," Constance said, recalling that she had never bothered to reply to Mrs. Conger's get-well card. "I have something I would like to discuss with the minister. Urgently."

Elaine frowned for a moment, obviously wondering what new scandal was about to be launched at their heads, and then nodded. "You had better come with me."

Edward Conger seemed equally taken aback to see her, but gave her a chair beside his desk, at the same time motioning his wife to stay in the office. Constance repeated her conversation with the empress. Conger stroked his chin and looked at Elaine. "You think this is significant information, Mrs. Baird? I mean, for all Westerners in China?"

"Yes, Mr. Conger, I do." Or I wouldn't have come, she thought. How these people always managed to annoy her, with their careful manners and their cautious approach to everything.

"You don't suppose the empress, in referring specifically to you and to the Princess Ksian Fu, was in fact expelling you, although she would not pronounce the exact words?"

"She was referring specifically to the princess and me, yes, Mr. Conger. But her implication was that all Christians in China are in some danger."

"Yes. Hm. You understand, of course, that I could not possibly suggest such a course as wholesale evacuation to any of my colleagues. Nor could I consider it myself. Western finance has too great a stake in this country now, ever to abandon it. And the Chinese, by treaty, are bound to allow open travel around their country to any European or American national. I really do not see what the empress can be about, if she *was* speaking in general terms. Of course, she is a very old woman . . .''

She is more in possession of her faculties than you, Constance thought, but she kept her temper. She merely leaned forward. ''Mr. Conger, Tz'u-Hsi last year carried out a coup d'etat, deposed the emperor, and assumed complete control of the state herself, openly, in her own name. That is an unheard-of thing for a woman to do in China. It means that a revolution of enormous proportions has taken place within the palace. And that means a similar revolution is about to take place outside of the palace as well. The mere fact that she has brought the Boxers north of the river in such numbers proves that surely. Such a revolution can have only one direction. The emperor was deposed, and Tz'u-Hsi has seized power because she and her advisers are determined that this growing acceptance of Western ways and Western advice, and this growing Western immigration into China, must cease.''

''And you think she means to turn loose the Boxers on us?'' Mr. Conger smiled. ''It may interest you to know, Mrs. Baird, that the empress did not *bring* the Boxers north of the river. They came. And the empress is very angry about it, and intends to send them packing back again. In fact, she means to crush the entire movement. I have this on the authority of Jung-lo himself, and you must know that since Prince Kung's death, Jung-lo is Her Majesty's principal adviser.''

''I did not know that,'' Constance said, feeling that she was banging her head against a stone wall. ''And *you* must know, Mr. Conger, that what a Chinese official tells a Westerner, and what his government is planning, as well as the plain truth, often bear no relation whatsoever to each other. Mr. Conger, I am *sure* the empress is planning the expulsion of all foreigners in China, and she knows what a painful process it is going to be. So she has suggested Kate and I leave before it happens.''

Conger studied her, stroking his chin. ''You know the empress very well, obviously, Mrs. Baird. Tell me, is she an intelligent woman?''

''She is a very intelligent woman.''

''Then do you honestly suppose she imagines for one moment that she can get away with that? Do you really think she feels she can take on all the European powers, as well as us? My dear Mrs. Baird, that is an absurdity.''

''Mr. Conger, the empress is a very intelligent woman, as I have said. But she also refuses to believe that the European powers command quite the strength they do. That together they might be too strong for China, she knows. But she studies the international situation more than you may suppose. She is well aware that the British have their hands full in South Africa at this moment, and more important, that the French and the Germans support the Boers. She may well feel that she will never have such an opportunity for reestablishing the integrity of China than while the Western powers are in disarray.''

Mr. Conger smiled. ''Then she is making a grave mistake. Mrs. Baird, I can tell you that there are enough Western soldiers and marines right there in Tientsin or on the ships in the gulf to shatter the whole Chinese Army. You saw how these Chinks fought against the Japanese. Why, one Yankee marine would lick a hundred of these pigtailed fellows. And the empress knows that. As for the Boxers, they are a bunch of religious fanatics, and it is up to the Chinese government to control them. Like I said, they know that, and are taking steps to deal with the situation. I think you're just frightening yourself, Mrs. Baird. I know what worries you missionaries—you're always worrying about the Tientsin massacre. My dear girl, that was thirty years ago. Thirty years ago Custer didn't know where the Little Big Horn was. And now you can ride from New York to San Francisco without even seeing a hostile Indian. Times change, Mrs. Baird. For the better. Now, I tell you what you do. Come along and have dinner with Mrs. Conger and myself. We have guests visiting, you know. My niece and some other ladies from the States. They'll just adore meeting the famous Constance Baird.'' He leaned across the desk to pat her hand. ''And tomorrow I'll send you back to Chu-teh with a nice strong escort. And you can leave the worrying about what the empress may be planning, or may not be planning, to me. That's what I'm paid for, remember?''

The ladies from America were indeed delighted to meet the famous Mrs. Baird. Nor could Constance doubt for a moment that Elaine Conger had told them everything she knew of her, which was really very little, but it certainly included the night she had spent with Frank Wynne, and, she suspected, at least rumor of the goings-on—as she would consider them—in Port Arthur. She bitterly regretted having come. If Conger intended to treat her like a silly little woman, when her every instinct told her that the empress had been trying to warn her—and very probably without the knowledge or the consent of her advisers, hence the necessity to wear a veil—that something was about to happen, then the minister would have to take a large share of the blame for any disaster that might occur. She had even toyed with the idea of going down the road to the British legation to tell her story to Sir Claude Macdonald—but from all accounts, Sir Claude was even more inclined to treat the Chinese with contempt than Mr. Conger, and was a soldier into the bargain.

And if no one here was going to listen to her, then it was her duty to get back out to Chu-teh as rapidly as possible, and alert the mission, at least to prepare themselves to be cut from the coast for some time.

Instead of which she must sit at table and make polite conversation with a collection of silly women who obviously viewed China with the disgusted wonder she had first experienced, ten years ago, and who kept making vaguely risqué remarks, no doubt in the hopes she would take them up on one of them, not to mention the detestable Lowry, and several other gentlemen she was prepared to put in the same class—and worst of all, the Buntings, who treated her with cool disdain. The only guest she felt had the slightest real feeling of warmth toward her was her dinner partner, the Baron von Kettler, from the German legation. With his close-cropped hair and his coldly handsome features and his monocle, he also seemed to find the rest of the company uninteresting. While it was a relief to discover that his interest in her very definitely had nothing to do with her femininity or her reputation—even if the reason was perhaps even more disturbing.

"You are returning to Chu-teh in the morning," he said. "Good. I will accompany you. Mr. Conger," he called across the table, "there is no need for you to arrange an escort for Mrs. Baird. I will see to it."

Which certainly stopped conversation for a few minutes. But the baron ignored the sudden silence.

"I wish to look at the country," he said to Constance, and began arranging saltcellars and mustard pots. "The Russians, you know, have obtained a concession to build a railway to Port Arthur. Can you believe that the Chinese have actually allowed them to do that, *and* have leased them Port Arthur itself for twenty-five years? Do they seriously suppose they will ever get it back? It is that fellow Li Hung-chang. He is in his dotage. I wonder the empress does not decapitate him, as she seems so fond of doing to her degenerate statesmen. However, Mrs. Baird, I digress. The Belgians are building a railroad here." He placed a fork leading south from the mustard jar that represented Peking. "The French have one there . . ." Another fork went into place. "And the British, needless to say, have one here." This time he used a knife. "Everyone has a railroad in China, except the Reich. And of course, you Americans. I must confess I cannot understand that. You are the greatest railroaders in the world, are you not? Yet you are not interested in building one in China."

Another cause for despair, she thought. Would these people never learn that the Chinese were at last becoming fed up with being exploited? But his offer to escort her had given her an idea. The trouble with all the legation officials was that they sat in their offices in Peking and listened to what the Chinese told them was happening in the rest of the country, or was about to happen—and believed what they were told. If the baron was coming with her, and they actually saw the Boxers on the march . . . She smiled at him. "Perhaps we have sufficient railroads already."

"But think of the profits. And are not you Americans the greatest bankers in the world, as well? But . . . I do not complain. One man's meat is another man's poison, eh? I think there is room for my country to build a railroad *here*." His dessert knife descended in a direction northwest from Peking. "And there"—he used the saltcellar—"is Chu-teh, eh? Will it not be a great benefit for you to have a railroad from Chu-teh to Hachiapo, Mrs. Baird? Instead of all this tedious horseback riding, which I am told all but cost you your life a few years go, you will ride to and fro in your very own railroad car, made in Berlin, and free of charge. You, free of charge," he repeated carefully. "There, you have my word. The only cost will be a capital investment, the pleasure of your delightful company tomorrow, and your advice on the best areas in which to lay the lines. And perhaps . . ." He winked at her. "Your husband's agreement to allow a German mission to join him on Chu-teh. Because you see, Mrs. Baird, the object of the railroad will be to develop Chu-teh into *the* Christian center for North China. We shall make it into a city. A Christian city, fed by our railroad. Do you think Mr. Baird will agree to that?"

"I am sure he will be delighted," Constance said. "But do you suppose the dowager empress will be so delighted?" She looked across the table at Edward Conger, who was obviously listening to them very carefully.

"Bah," Baron von Kettler said. "The dowager empress is an old woman, and from all accounts, a decrepit one, entirely at the mercy of her advisers. A few thousand marks, deposited in the right hands, will accomplish wonders. But I forgot, you know the old lady well." He squeezed her hand. "You may tell me all about her on our ride tomorrow."

                          \*     \*     \*

Although the baron was clearly a somewhat detestable man, he also suggested that he would prove entertaining company, and Constance was rather pleased to have so quickly accumulated another admirer, to the obvious discomfort of Elaine Conger. Besides, she was very interested to discover what *would* be Henry's attitude toward the baron's plan, or, for that matter, toward the baron himself.

When she went downstairs the following morning, with true German efficiency he was waiting for her, and with an escort of two male secretaries. She would have preferred a larger number, but all the three men were armed with revolvers, and certainly they looked confident enough. Besides, she reminded herself, she was only taking them to *look* at the Boxers. Not actually to interfere with them.

The baron noticed her expression. "There is nothing for you to fear, Mrs. Baird," he told her. "I can promise you safe delivery into Chu-teh."

She waved good-bye to Mesdames Conger and Bunting, both standing on the legation steps to watch her departure, and no doubt waiting to tear her to pieces the moment she was out of earshot, and then concentrated on guiding her horse through the Peking streets, as always, crowded in the cool of the dawn.

"You understand that we are entirely in your hands, Mrs. Baird," the baron told her, smiling. "I personally have never been north of Peking in my life."

"It is a well-marked trail," she said, leading them through the An-tien-men, watched by the guards, who however made no move to stop them or even to ask for their passports. Yet it seemed to her that they *were* more than usually interested in the little party. Or was she just, as Mr. Conger had said, imagining things? She found herself hoping that when they reached the pagoda there would not be a Boxer in sight.

"Nice flat country," the baron observed after they had ridden for a couple of hours. "Do you mind if we halt and take a couple of photographs?"

One of his aides had a very elaborate camera, which he now dismounted to set up and use.

"Photographs will convince our principals that here is ideal country for a railroad," the baron explained. "Not an obstacle for as far as the eye can see."

"When the rivers are in flood," Constance said, "the whole plain turns into a vast lake."

"Ah, but we shall put our tracks on the top of an embankment several feet above the level of the plain itself,'' he explained. ''Believe me, Mrs. Baird, we have studied the problem of flooding.''

She decided that a man like the baron would have studied the problems of everything to do with his projected railroad, and that therefore she had very little to offer him on that subject. She rode in silence, deliberately keeping Rufus to hardly more than a walk, and not merely because he was now a very old horse indeed. Her memory, and his as well, presumably, went back to that day in 1895 . . . and even further, to that day in 1892, when they had ridden beside Frank Wynne along this same trail, and eventually come to this same ruined pagoda.

And it *did* seem to be deserted. At least from a distance. Disappointment at not being able to convince the baron that there was some substance to her fears mingled with relief.

''How interesting,'' von Kettler observed. ''That building will make a good photograph, eh, Eisner? And it is somewhere to stop for lunch, would you not agree, Mrs. Baird?''

''It's rotten,'' she told him. ''And about to fall down.''

''We shall picnic in its shade,'' he promised her. ''Not in the building itself.''

''There are people over there, Baron,'' the man called Eisner said.

''So there are,'' the baron agreed. ''Some fellows performing exercises, it seems.'' He put away his glasses. ''Well, we shall tell them to move on and exercise somewhere else.'' He wheeled his horse.

''Baron,'' Constance said urgently. ''I do not think we should stop here.''

''Not stop because of a few Chinks?''

''Those men are Boxers,'' Constance said. She did not have binoculars, but she could make out the waving fists and the grotesque movements. There were only about thirty of them, she estimated, suggesting that the rest of the group had continued their march, but these were sufficient to prove her point.

''Boxers? You mean this secret society everyone is speaking of?'' inquired the baron.

''The same,'' Constance said.

''Then I must have a closer look at them. Do not be afraid, Mrs. Baird. Mr. Conger says they are quite harmless. Come along.''

Constance obediently turned her horse, and then drew rein. She had the strangest feeling that this had all happened before. Because it had, with Frank. But Frank had known how to cope with it, had had the sense to ride away from them as quickly as possible. Her stomach seemed to be filled with lead. While her heart suddenly started to pound violently. "Look," she said. For there were more people in the distance, several hundred of them. They had not continued their march, after all, had been resting in the dip beyond the pagoda, and had been alerted by the approach of the horses. They were all men. They were all armed, with at least knives. And they were all Boxers, the same as yesterday.

"Baron," she begged. "You have seen them. Please let us ride on."

"I told you, Mrs. Baird, there is nothing to be afraid of. You do not wish to lunch here? Then I defer to your wishes. But a photograph of those fellows I will certainly have. Schnappel, you will stay with Mrs. Baird. Eisner, bring your camera."

"Baron . . ." Constance tried again, but he and Eisner had already ridden toward the pagoda.

"There is nothing to be afraid of, Mrs. Baird," Schnappel told her, taking his lead from his employer. "The baron is well used to dealing with native peoples."

With native peoples, she thought. It was that that was bothering her. She watched the two Germans ride up to the pagoda, saw that they were entirely surrounded by young men now, still waving arms and fists. The baron appeared to be talking to them, and then shouting at them, and she watched Eisner lose his camera, the box ripped away from his saddle. Then she watched the baron's hand come up, holding a revolver, as Frank had done on that day eight years ago . . . but Frank had had more sense than to ride into the middle of them.

"Oh, my God," she said, and listened to the sound of the explosion. Von Kettler had fired into the air, but he might as well have fired into the mob.

A knife flashed in the sun, and blood spurted from the baron's coat.

"I must help them," Schnappel cried, and kicked his horse forward.

"Come back," Constance said, feeling sick with helpless fear. "Come back, you'll be killed."

He hesitated, drawing rein beside her, then leaned across and pressed his revolver into her hand. "I have another one, Mrs. Baird. You ride on." He kicked his horse again, galloped for the melee. "Ride on," he shouted over his shoulder.

Constance watched him plunge into the midst of the mob, firing his second revolver and using his whip as well, guiding his horse with his knees—he was a superb horseman as well as a very brave man. But neither quality was going to save his life, or any of the others' lives, either; the baron had already fallen or been dragged from the saddle, and now she watched Eisner also being pulled to the ground.

And now several of the Boxers were looking toward her. Constance thrust the revolver into her satchel, wheeled her horse, and rode for Chu-Teh.

Constance rode at full speed for perhaps a mile; then, as Rufus began to wheeze, she drew rein to look over her shoulder. There was no sign of any of the three Germans—she had to suppose they had all been murdered. And she could still see Boxers, a seething mass of excited men. They had no horses, save for the three taken from the Germans. But as she watched, those three suddenly became visible out in front of the main crowd. They were coming behind her.

She gasped in her fear, wheeled Rufus again, and again kicked him forward. Only another eighteen miles to Chu-teh. Eighteen miles!

She dared not gallop again, for fear Rufus would collapse, made herself think, and reason. Here was Fate indeed. A situation she could not alter by dreaming, or by a simple act of will—she could only attempt to escape it. Therefore, her first priority must be to keep Rufus going. He would not cover eighteen miles at anything more than a steady trot. But the horses behind him were no fresher. They were a trifle younger, no doubt. Yet they would hardly catch up to her before Chu-teh, as long as Rufus kept going.

She kicked him forward again, looked over her shoulder. The three Boxers were riding somewhat faster than a trot, and had slightly closed the distance. But they were still at least a mile away. She had merely to keep going. And of course she had the revolver, thrust into her satchel. She had never fired a revolver before in her life. But that would surely frighten them off. If they came too close.

She concentrated, watching the ground in front of her, listening to Rufus wheezing and gasping. She was killing him. But what else could she do? If she slowed to a walk, the Boxers would certainly catch up. But did they mean her any harm? She was the famous devil woman, still the favorite, so far as anyone knew, of the empress. Perhaps they simply had not recognized her, supposed she was a German.

And if they did mean her harm, she would frighten them off

with the revolver. Certainly she could not kill old Rufus, who had served her so faithfully and so well for so many years.

She pulled him back to a walk, took the revolver from her satchel and inspected it. All the chambers were loaded, and it looked simple enough to operate. She still didn't know if she would actually be able to fire at a human being, or if she did, whether she would be able to hit anyone—and reminded herself that she did not *wish* to hit anyone, only frighten them off. And certainly it was a fearsome-looking weapon.

An explosion drifted to her on the wind. She turned her head, realized that the three men were now quite close, within half a mile, she estimated—and one of them had fired at her. Because they had taken the revolvers from the dead Germans.

"Oh, my God!" she muttered. She had not considered that possibility. Of course there was no chance of them hitting her at half a mile's range. But if she let them get closer . . .

"Come on, Rufe, old boy," she said. "Let's manage a trot for a little while." The sound of her own voice, so apparently unafraid, restored a little of her confidence. Rufus gallantly responded to her urging, but immediately began to wheeze again, and to stumble as well. He was literally on his last legs. Hastily she pulled him up again, and dismounted. Her heart still pounded, and her stomach felt curiously light, but her brain was clear. She could not believe, having survived the sinking of the *Kowshin,* and then the Japanese soldiers in Port Arthur, that she could be in any danger from three Chinese peasants.

She turned to face them, standing beside Rufus, waited for them to come within a quarter of a mile, she estimated. Now she could see that two of them carried revolvers, and all three of them had the fearsome long knives thrust into their belts. "Stop there," she shouted. "I am armed, and will shoot if you come closer. Tell me what you wish."

The men stopped and muttered at each other, clearly taken aback by her fluent Chinese.

Constance decided to press home her advantage, took off her hat and shook out her hair. "You know me," she shouted. "I am the devil woman, the favorite of Her Majesty the Empress. Be sure it will go hard with you if I report what has happened here today. Ride off. Go back to your people before the vengeance of the empress falls on you."

She realized she might have made a mistake. The three men had a brief discussion, and then two of them kicked their horses and rode, not away from her, but to each side. They were going to come at her from three directions at once, because, clearly, whatever they had earlier intended, they had now decided that she could *not* be allowed to carry a report to the empress of what had happened.

Her heart seemed to have slowed, her stomach had tightened into a hard ball. But she no longer felt sick, for all the dryness in her throat. Now it was no longer a matter of frightening them. She had to be prepared to fire *at* them. To hit them, if necessary.

She looked from left to right; the two horsemen were still circling. She licked her lips, held the revolver in both hands, and turned a slow circle herself, watching each man in turn, feeling sweat trickling down her back inside her blouse. Her hands, too, were clammy, and the revolver kept sliding against her palm.

"Aieeeee!" screamed the man directly in front of her, and charged. He was the one armed only with the knife, but this he had drawn.

"Aieeee!" came the shout from either side, as the other men urged their horses forward, firing their revolvers as they came, but without the slightest chance of hitting her as they bucked in the saddle.

She wanted to scream herself, but she didn't. She dropped to one knee, hesitated, and then leveled her weapon at the right-hand man, who seemed closest, and pulled the trigger.

To Constance's consternation, she hit the horse. The bullet entered the animal's neck, and apparently killed it instantly; it pitched forward onto its knees, struck the earth, and lay still. Its rider was propelled over its head, but kept on coming, running straight at her. Constance fired again before she had really made up her mind that she wanted to. This bullet took the Boxer squarely in the chest, at a distance of not more than a hundred yards, and sent him tumbling backward.

Constance swung the revolver toward the man behind her, who was now even closer, riding at full gallop, still firing at her and still missing by a considerable distance. Once again she leveled the gun, held in both hands, and fired, this time taking more careful aim. The man fell backward out of the saddle and hit the ground with a crunch she could hear even at fifty yards away.

The third man was upon her, leaning from the saddle to swing at her with his knife. Desperately she threw herself to one side, rolled over and over, skirts flying, but retaining her grip on the gun. She landed on her stomach, and thrust her hands forward again, gasping for breath, tasting dirt in her mouth, but filled with an almost exultant pleasure of combat—it was occurring to her that she had wanted to fight with *somebody* for at least five years. Once again she fired, but this time she missed. The Boxer did not give her the opportunity to try again; he was already kicking his horse back toward the main body, now two or three miles distant.

But only two or three miles. Constance felt that she just wanted to lie on the warm earth forever. She didn't want to look at the two men she had killed, or worse, only wounded. But to lie there was to die. She could no longer have any doubts about that. She forced herself to her knees and thence her feet, brushed dust from her clothes, and went toward the unharmed horse, which, having lost its rider, was standing beside him with all the patience of the well-trained hack it was. The man was dead; she had hit him in the face and he was a quite horrible sight. She grasped the horse's bridle and then swung into the saddle, riding astride, took it back to where Rufus was standing with equal patience. Then she urged both mounts forward. She didn't want to think about what had happened, either the closeness of her escape or the two men she had killed. She wanted only to regain the safety of Chu-teh. For the first time in nearly ten years, she wanted to feel the comfort of Henry's strong arms about her, to know the reassurance of his faith and his determination.

And by the time she got to Chu-teh, the Boxers would of course have given up their pursuit of her. Surely.

It was dark before she reached the first of the rising ground which led up to the mission, and she drew rein to catch her breath and allow the horses also a breather, and to look at the glowing lights which marked safety. Then she looked back at the glowing lights behind her. They covered an enormous area, and were reminiscent of the Japanese as she had seen them flooding down from the Liaotung toward Port Arthur. These were not so numerous, but they were not so distant, either—only about four or five miles away, she estimated. They were the Boxers, still coming behind her.

# 13

# The Rising

Once again Constance urged her weary animal onward, followed by Rufus; without a rider to weigh him down, he had lasted the journey quite as well as the German's horse. "Hello!" she shouted as she approached the gate. "Hello! Let me in."

There was movement from in front of her. "Who is there?" someone called.

"Constance Baird. For God's sake, let me in."

"Mrs. Baird?" It was William, opening the gate for her, assisting her as she almost fell from the saddle. "We didn't expect you back tonight."

No one ever expects me, no matter when I arrive, she thought sadly. "Close the gate, William. Close the gate and call everybody out. Quickly, now."

"Mistress?" He blinked at her.

There was no time to argue with him. She stepped past him and herself picked up the metal bar to hit the triangle which hung beside the gate, as hard as she could, several times. The noise reverberated across the evening, and across the mission compound as well. Doors and windows opened, a hubbub of voices rose into the air.

"What the devil is going on?" Henry strode from his bungalow in his shirt sleeves. And stopped to peer at her. "Constance?" He looked up and down her disheveled clothes, her wind-tangled hair. "What on earth . . ."

She had led the two horses to the trough, watched them drink. Surprisingly, she was not very thirsty herself—she was too frightened. "Boxers," she said. "Boxers, Henry. Hundreds of them, coming here."

He frowned. "Boxers? We had heard there were some in the vicinity. But . . . I don't understand. They are harmless fellows. What has happened to you? Where is your escort?"

"Dead," she shouted. "Murdered by the Boxers. Harmless? They are out to kill us all, Henry. They tried to kill me. They would have, if I hadn't shot two of them."

"You shot two Boxers?" He held her shoulders. "You have shot two *men*?"

"I killed them," she said. "Yes. It was them or me."

"Good God!" He let her go. "Good God!" He gazed at James Mountjoy, hurrying toward them, followed by his wife and daughter. "My wife . . . You *shot* them? What with?"

Constance took the revolver from her satchel; the Chinese crowding around gave a gasp of horror and backed off again. "It belonged to one of the Germans who were with me," Constance said. "Baron von Kettler's men. Now they are dead. So is the baron. The baron, Henry. He was murdered by the Boxers."

There was a moment's silence. Then Kate gave a scream and ran forward to hug her friend. "Oh, Constance! You are so *brave*. Oh, Constance."

"Brave," Henry said. "My wife, a murderess, on top of . . ." He sighed, and squared his shoulders. "I cannot believe it. I just cannot believe it."

Constance pulled herself away from Kate, ran to the wall, climbed the steps to stand on the platform by the gate. "Then believe *that*," she screamed, pointing at the flickering lights.

"There do seem to be a lot of people out there," James Mountjoy remarked. "What do you suppose they want, Henry?"

"I imagine they want Constance," Henry said. "If she did shoot two of them."

Constance's knees gave way, and she sat on the step. She just could not accept that no one would believe her. That they would, inevitably, seek to blame her. And all she had wanted was to feel Henry's arms go around her.

"But what are you going to do?" Mountjoy asked. "I mean . . . you can't let them take her. She'd be lynched."

"The matter will have to be settled by due process of law," Henry said. "I'll have to talk with them. When they get closer."

"You had better not stay here," Joan Mountjoy said to Constance. "Come along and have a glass of brandy. And then something to eat."

Constance stood up again. "You just don't understand," she said. "They attacked the baron and his secretaries. They murdered them."

"Yes, yes, my dear," Joan said, clearly remembering the last time Constance had arrived at Chu-teh at night. "Come along and change your clothes, at the least." She took Constance's arm.

Constance jerked herself free. "Do you suppose I was coming out here by myself?" she cried.

Joan gazed at her, then looked at Kate. Because the last time she *had* been coming out by herself. Constance's shoulders slumped, and she turned away, ran to the bungalow and up the steps. "Where is Master Charles?" she asked Miriam.

"He is in bed, mistress," Miriam said. "It is past nine."

Constance looked over her shoulder, gazed at the lights. And listened to the noise. The Boxers were flooding up the slopes toward the mission gate, shouting, "Death to all Christians!" and "Death to all barbarians!" and "Death to all foreign devils!"

"Oh, God!" Kate came up the steps beside her. "Oh, God, Connie, what are we to do?"

There was not a single weapon on all Chu-teh, save gardening knives and the revolver she had given to Henry. And that had but two bullets left in it.

Joan had remained at the foot of the steps. "Henry will talk with them," she said. "Henry and James will talk with them."

Someone was clanging the triangle, but the hubbub outside the gates was becoming louder.

"My good people," they heard Henry shouting as he looked down on them from the platform. "My good—" There came a crash, and Constance realized the Boxers had charged the gate. It could not hold for very long. "My good people," Henry shouted again. "You must stop this and listen to me."

The gate crashed again.

"Oh, God," Joan Mountjoy muttered.

Constance wanted to lie down. She had never been so exhausted in her life. And now it was partly the exhaustion of despair. She had watched this happen before. She had expected to die in Port Arthur, had braced herself for that inevitable event. But she had survived.

They why should she not survive again? She squared her shoulders. They were white women. By being white women, she and Kate had faced the Japanese soldiers and survived. There would surely be someone in authority among the Boxers who

would know that to kill white people would bring down upon
China the wrath of the entire West.

Crash went the gate. And once again, as with Lin-tu nine
years before, both the Mountjoy women were looking at her.
Hoping for her courage and determination to save them.

"Fetch Adela," she told Kate. "Joan, get Sister Ambrosia
and all of the nuns, bring them here. Quickly, now."

She ran into the bedroom, pulled Charles from his cot, wrapped
him in a blanket; at nine years old he was already a considerable
weight. She listened to the tremendous racket from outside, the
whoops and yelled threats of the Boxers mingling with the
crashes against the gate and the moans and yells of the converts
inside the walls. Probably there was no hope for *them*, poor
devils, she thought.

Kate stumbled into the house, carrying Adela in her arms.
Constance had already come to a decision about the two children,
pushed the half-asleep and protesting Charles in front of her to
the pantry, and opened the cool cupboard. This was still well
stocked with the winter supply. She pushed aside cured hams
and sides of beef, made a space about four feet square at the very
back of the larder; the room had wire-mesh-covered grilles at
regular intervals to ensure a continuous supply of air.

"Now, Charlie." She knelt before him. "I want you to go in
there with baby Adela, and hold her in your arms, and sit there
until I come back for you. Either me or Auntie Kate. But you
must not make a sound until one of us two comes. Promise me
that."

Charles stared at her, and then slowly nodded.

"And if Adela cries, you must rock her to sleep in your
arms," Constance said. "In you go, now."

Charles crawled into the space.

"Give him Adela," Constance told Kate.

Kate hesitated, and then handed the baby girl to Constance,
who passed her in to Charles. Adela was just waking up. "Mama,"
she said. "Mama."

"Hush," Constance said. "You stay in there with Charlie.
It's a game. You stay with Charlie." She pushed the meats in
front of them, stood back, gazed at Kate, whose eyes were full
of tears. "What else can we do?" Constance asked. "Save kill
them ourselves now. They at least have a chance."

If they did not call out, there was no way anyone could tell
they were there. She could not plan for afterward. But she knew
she could never kill her own child.

"Oh, Connie," Kate said, and burst into tears.

From outside the crashes at the gate suddenly ended in the sound of splintering wood. The gate was down.

Constance ran into the outer room, Kate at her heels, found the nuns waiting for them, together with Joan, and quite a few Chinese women as well. Now the noise from the gate had become quite bestial, the shouts and yells and wails being interspersed with screams of agony as the Boxers flooded into the compound.

"Arrange yourself," Constance shouted. "Sit down. Sister Ambrosia, you here." She pushed the senior nun to the settee, sat her in the center. "You here, Joan." She sat Joan Mountjoy beside her, put Kate on the other side. "Sisters, behind here." She made the rest of the nuns, all ashen-cheeked and shivering, form a group behind the settee. "You, sit down in front," she told the Chinese women. As if I were arranging them for a photograph, she thought. For the baron's camera.

She stood on the right of the settee herself, beside Joan, took a long breath, and faced the door. There was no sound in the room except for heavy breathing and the occasional stifled sob. "Remember," she said. "Keep still, and face them. No matter what happens, keep still, and face them."

Outside, the night grew into a cacophony of hell. The temptation to go to the window or door and look out was almost unbearable. More than once Joan made a move as if to get up, and Constance pressed her back into her seat again. If James had been at the gate with Henry, he was almost certainly dead by now. Certainly they could do nothing to help him. Their business was to survive the next half-hour.

They listened to feet on the steps outside. The wood on the veranda creaked. Then the door flew back on its hinges, and they gazed at the young men, knives and clothes already stained with blood, and faces too, eyes almost as bloodshot. But taken aback by the group of women sitting facing them in apparent confidence.

"Devil woman," one man snarled.

"Barbarians," said another.

One of the Chinese girls moved, and Constance nudged her with her boot. All they had to do was keep still, and keep their nerve, and keep their . . .

Kate stood up, as more men crowded into the room, staring at them.

"Kate," Constance whispered urgently. "Sit down, for God's sake."

But Kate had stepped forward in front of the Chinese women.

She had stopped crying. "I am the Princess Ksian Fu," she announced. "Beloved cousin of the dowager empress. In the name of Her Majesty, I command you: Leave!"

The men gazed at her, taking in the deep blue gown, the red hair curling past her shoulders, the pale face, the imperious tilt of her chin. Probably, Constance thought, not one of them had even seen a princess before, even a princess by marriage.

Kate obviously supposed she was gaining control of the situation. Her arm came up, its rings and bangles glinting in the lamplight. "Leave," she said again, pointing at the door. "Leave."

There was another moment's hesitation, the longest moment of her entire life, Constance supposed; then one of the Boxers reached forward, seized Kate's wrist, and jerked her into their midst. The other men scattered away from her as she fell to her knees, obviously taken completely by surprise. "You wretch," she shouted, and swung her hand to strike at the man holding her. The man let her go to escape the blow, but instead seized her hair, jerking her from her knees to the floor, and then ran the length of the room, fingers still twined in her hair, dragging Kate behind him, body bumping and thumping on the floor, bare feet kicking as her slippers flew off, gasping for breath and whimpering with pain.

Still the others watched, the women paralyzed with looming horror, as the man reached the far wall, turned, and then dragged Kate back again, laughing and shouting to his friends to join in. Now one of them did, leaning forward as the woman was pulled in front of him, to seize her skirt. Kate gave a despairing wail as the material ripped and the man's hands dug into her petticoats as well. Then with a whoop the rest of the Boxers overcame their fear and surged forward.

The bungalow living room became a bestial chaos. The Chinese women sitting on the floor leaped to their feet and ran this way and that, pursued by the Boxers, and now the knives were out. Constance stood up, Joan Mountjoy beside her, watched the older woman plucked forward by hands seizing the bodice of her gown, to go sprawling on the floor. She herself took a step backward as a man, several inches shorter than herself, reached for her. Her knees struck the settee and she sat down, beside Sister Ambrosia—but Sister Ambrosia was being dragged away by the ankles, her head striking the cushions as she was sucked into the melee in the center of the room.

Now there were three men reaching for Constance, their faces seeming all teeth and eyes, their hands nothing better than talons. She pushed herself up, feet on the couch now, sitting on the backrest, found herself against one of the nuns, who was pressing herself against the wall, mouth open in a silent scream. For a dreadful, unforgettable moment, Constance took in the room from her vantage point, gazed at scattered clothing and naked limbs, at white bodies stretched on the floor, being crawled over by the cackling, screaming men, most of them now trouserless, raping even as they cut and thrust with their knives. Blood splashed on the floor, and as her own ankles were seized to drag her down she saw a knife severing Joan Mountjoy's throat, neatly bisecting the pulsing white for a quick second before the red came.

Her head struck the wood, sending sick pain reeling through her system. She heard the sound of ripping material, and felt searing pain, supposed she had been cut, and then realized it had only been a fingernail tearing her flesh. She was on her back, arms held above her head by two of the Boxers, while another tore away her skirts and petticoats and drawers. She shouted, but had no idea what she was saying—it was a mixture of begging and cursing. She got a foot free and kicked, as she still wore her boots, struck him in the groin. He turned away, his breeches down around his knees, clutching his genitals and moaning with pain, was immediately thrust out of the way by one of his fellows eager to take his place. Now her legs were also seized and pinned to the floor, and she discovered that the men kneeling by her head were ripping open her blouse, reaching inside to expose her breasts, one with a knife between his teeth. She screamed, a howl of mingled terror and anguish at the thought of what was about to happen to her, threw her body this way and that, gasped and spat, snapped her teeth at them, was pinned to the floor by the man who was now lying on her and who was at least protecting her from the knives, even as he sucked at her neck and she felt him driving into her—and listened to someone shouting, "The devil woman! Bring the devil woman."

The man lying on her was pulled away, unfulfilled and angry, and she was jerked to her knees by several pairs of hands grasping her arms, fell forward, and was dragged across the floor, knees and boots thumping, other bodies being thrust out of the way. She had no idea what new horror was in store for her, still screamed and fought, her voice inaudible among all the screams that were echoing about her, discovered herself on the veranda and facing a man somewhat older than the rest of the Boxers, with long mustaches and a scowling face, and the invariable blood dripping from his hands and staining his shirt.

"Devil woman!" he bawled, reaching for her, seizing her hair to bring her face closer. "Devil woman! Where is the gold?"

Constance stared at him in utter incomprehension and he shook her head from side to side, sending darts of pain racing through her scalp.

"The gold," he shouted again. "Where is the gold?"

"Gold?" she gasped. "There is no gold."

"You lie," he screamed. "Everyone knows there is gold in the mission. In all the missions. You say, or you suffer."

Suffer, she thought. Oh, God, suffer. She had been forced to her knees now, fingers biting into her arms and shoulders. "There is no gold. Please. I swear it. There is no gold."

The man stared at her for several seconds, then released her hair. She gasped in relief. But it was not to last. "Beat her," he said. "Beat her until she tells us where the gold is buried. *Beat* her."

Constance was dragged to her feet again. "There is no gold," she screamed as she was dragged across the veranda. Her feet struck something soft, and she tripped, looked down, and gagged in horror. She had trodden on the naked body of one of the nuns, who had been decapitated; her head had rolled against the veranda rail. That was how she would look soon, she realized, whenever they were convinced there *was* no gold. But before then . . . She bumped on her knees down the steps, and was flung to the earth. It felt so good, and she no longer had to look at her captors or their victims. She wanted to cling to the ground even as she felt her legs and arms being extended, stretched wide, and held by a man at each wrist and each ankle. She raised her head to look at the older man standing in front of her.

"Speak," he commanded.

"There is no gold," she gasped. "No gold," she shrieked, as a pain as sharp as a knife cut slashed across her buttocks, driving the breath from her lungs. Before she could draw another, she was hit again, so quickly she understood that there had to be two men wielding the bamboo canes, and hitting her in immediate succession. "No gold," she moaned, her face grinding into the dust, her body attempting to move but held rigid by the four men, as the blows crashed into her buttocks and thighs. The pain drove thought from her mind, all feeling from the rest of her body, all control from her muscles. Her entire existence became an enormous river of agony; she no longer could even moan, much less scream. She knew she was about to die. Cutting off her head would merely be the coup de grace. She was being beaten to death, stretched naked on the dusty compound of her own mission. She was . . .

It began to rain, a tremendous downpour screaming out of the night. The blows stopped, the men released her as they ran for shelter, although it was several seconds before she realized that she was in fact no longer being hit. The raindrops pounded on her flesh like the bamboo itself, while the fiery agony still seeped away from her seat, ate through her stomach and down to her knees, left her constantly moving as she was unable to lie still, but yet left her also unable to summon the strength to raise herself from the ground. Still it rained, cascading now from the roofs of the bungalows, forming little rivulets across the sloping earth. One rivulet splashed against her face, and she opened her mouth to suck in the precious liquid. She hoped the rain would never stop, until it drowned all who remained hideously alive, and washed away all who had already died hideously.

It rained for several hours, and then it stopped. Constance realized that at some stage she had sunk into an exhausted and pain-filled coma, but she opened her eyes as the rain slackened to a drizzle. She was lying on her side, half-sunk into the sodden earth, and there was again a man standing beside her head. Oh, God, she thought. They are going to beat me again.

"There is no gold," she muttered, as the man stooped beside her, stroked hair and mud from her face. She opened her eyes again, and gazed at Lin-tu.

Constance could not speak. She could only stare at him, as he held her shoulders and lifted her from the ground. Without thinking, she sat, and moaned with pain and fell forward; he caught her and this time pulled her to her feet, but her knees would not support her, and he had to hold her against him.

Lin-tu, she thought. It was very dark, and now suddenly chill, a combination of the rain and the invariable drop in temperature just before dawn. And she was in Lin-tu's arms, her ribs paining where they rested against the haft of his long knife on one side, against the butt of a revolver thrust into his belt on the other. But this fresh discomfort was but an aspect of the survival she suddenly knew was hers.

Tears trickled down her cheeks; she was sobbing like a baby— she had not cried when they had actually been flogging her. Then her head jerked as she heard the voice of the Boxer commander. "She will not tell us where the gold is buried."

She clung to Lin-tu with utter desperation, and he squeezed

her shoulder. "There is no gold here, stupid fellow," he said.

"We know there is gold. All missions have gold." He peered at them from beneath an absurd blue parasol, suddenly clearly visible in the first light.

"You have been told wrong," Lin-tu said. "You have finished your work here. Now you must march on, to Feng-tai. That is your objective. Destroy the railroad at Feng-tai. That will stop the foreign devils from coming to avenge their dead."

"Let them come," the Boxer growled. "We shall kill them all."

"No doubt," Lin-tu said dryly. "But you must still destroy the railhead. It were better you had done that before coming here at all. Now you must make haste."

"After we have cut off her head," the Boxer said, seizing Constance's hair.

Her head was pulled backward, and she wanted to scream with despair and terror, but could not utter a sound from the pressure on her throat.

"Be off with you," Lin-tu said. "We will keep her alive until there are orders about her from Peking. She is the devil woman with the yellow hair. She is the favorite of the empress. She may be of use to us. We will keep her alive."

The fingers released her hair. She dared not open her eyes, buried her face in Lin-tu's shoulder.

"You saved my life once," he said, speaking English, and stroking her hair. "Now I have saved yours. But you have nowhere to go, devil woman. You must stay with me. You understand this?"

She raised her head to look at him. If you touch me now, she thought, I will go mad. But she could not allow herself to go mad, no matter what he did to her. She was alive, and now she must stay alive, for the sake of the children.

He misinterpreted her expression, and grinned at her. "I am not a Boxer, as you call them," he told her. "I have been sent here because I know the country, to control these people, when possible. They should be fighting the white soldiers, not destroying the missions. When the white soldiers have been defeated, then the missions will all be ours anyway."

Constance drew a long breath. "But you *want* to destroy the missions," she said. "To kill us all."

"I want the white people to go home to their own countries," he said. "All white people. And they will not go unless one or two of them are killed. But I wish *you* to stay in China, Constance." He looked into her eyes.

"I . . . There are children," she said.

He frowned. "They have been killed?"

"No," she said. "I know they have not been killed. Please . . . let me find them."

He hesitated, suspecting some subterfuge, and there came a shout from the gate and a sudden gush of smoke from the Mountjoys' bungalow; the Boxers were firing the houses. Nor would the recent rain have much effect, Constance knew; once the sun got up, the compound would very rapidly dry.

"We must hurry," she shouted, and pulled herself free, overcoming the pain in a sudden surge of frightened energy. She made to run away from him, tripped, and fell to her knees; shredded material still clung to her ankles.

Again he raised her from the ground, and for the first time she looked down at herself. Even the mud which clung to her like a second skin could not disguise the fact that she was naked.

Lin-tu took off his own blouse and handed it to her; she dropped it over her shoulders; it hung loosely, but came only just past her thighs. Still, it was better than nothing. She led him toward the bungalow, pushed and jostled by the hurrying Boxers, who were running from building to building, waving torches and screaming at each other. And in fact Constance wanted the compound to be destroyed, to be utterly obliterated, every last vestige of last night's horror erased forever—once she had regained the children.

And every last vestige of Henry's achievement? As well as Henry himself? She supposed she *should* go down to the gate and try to find his body and say at least a prayer over him. But Henry was a reminder of too many things, just as Chu-teh was a reminder of too many things. And together they were a reminder, too, that her ordeal was not yet ended. In fact, that it was just beginning.

Besides, her duty lay with the children.

She climbed the front steps, and halted, her stomach rolling. She had forgotten just what had been the horror of last night. But the dead nun still lay on the veranda floor, even if the blood had stopped seeping from her severed neck. Constance drew a long breath and stepped over her. To reach the pantry, she must pass through the living room. She wanted to run, with her eyes shut, instinctively reached for the skirts that were no longer there to gather them from her ankles—and found that she could not run. She dared not: there might still be someone alive. So she stopped, and looked. In here the early daylight only partially penetrated, and now too she could smell the smoke drifting through the windows; it had the merit of disguising the other smells. Because here was a charnel house, of naked dead bodies, some beheaded and some stabbed and cut, almost all mutilated, a ghastly kaleidoscope of trailing hair and severed breasts and naked legs and arms, and pooling, drying blood. She saw the arm she was looking for, extending from beneath another female body, its bangles and rings a dull glint, its fingers clenched into a fist. ''Kate,'' she muttered, and had to hold on to the back of the settee to remain upright.

Lin-tu stepped past her, pulled bodies to and fro, uncovered the princess. She had retained her head, at least. But she was obviously dead, eyes staring and mouth open in a last terrible scream as they had thrust their knives into her belly; one haft still protruded from the pale flesh.

''We must hurry,'' Lin-tu said.

They were all obviously dead. Constance ran into the pantry, tore open the cool-room door. ''Charlie,'' she shouted. ''Adela.''

''Mama!'' Charles crawled through the hanging joints of meat, and was in her arms. ''Oh, Mama, there was so much noise.'' He stared at her in amazement. ''And you are all dirty.''

''Yes,'' she said, hugging him close. ''I am all dirty.''

''Mama,'' Adela said, ''Mama,'' looking for her own mother.

Constance scooped her from the floor as well. ''You are safe,'' she said. ''That is all that matters. *You* are safe.''

''This house is on fire,'' Lin-tu said. He stood in front of her, and his gaze went past the children to look at her. ''You must come with me now,'' he said.

Constance remembered the two people seated in that very drawing room nine years before. Then she had been pregnant. But then, too, she had been in command of the situation, and had been able to control the thoughts which had been springing between their brains. And then, too, it had been an act of self-denial, to so control their mutual emotions.

Now the situation was reversed, and there would be no control. Not even, she feared, the control of pain and exhaustion, and revulsion. And having seen what these people were capable of, there could only ever be revulsion.

As she had suspected, her ordeal was only just beginning. Yet only this man could save her life, and those of the children.

''Yes,'' she said. ''We must come with you now.''

* * *

Franklin Wynne sighted the wooden uprights of the stockade rising amid the tree screen which seemed to encircle the patrol, and sighed with relief. Regaining the safety of the marine encampment after a mission in the Philippines bush was always a relief.

He counted himself a veteran, as the men at his back were veterans, now. Their war had not ended with the Spanish surrender nearly two years ago. In fact, their war had then only begun, as the Filipinos, grateful enough to the Americans for freeing them from the Spanish yoke, were yet unwilling to accept a Yankee yoke in its place, and had begun a dogged guerrilla war, the worst of all wars, where often enough the first intimation of the presence of an enemy was the hiss of a blowpipe, the agonizing pain of a knife thrust tearing into flesh and scraping against bone. Only inside the stockade was a man truly safe.

He did not consider himself a coward. Not physically, at any rate. His moral courage was another matter. The lack of it, his awareness of the lack of it, had in fact increased his boldness, his disregard of personal safety, his apparent contempt for death. His men followed him and his officers trusted him *because* he was a fighting soldier and because he did not seem aware of the terrors of the jungle, the scorpions and the snakes, and sudden morasses which might engulf a man to his waist and contain unimaginable horrors, and worst of all, the endless wall of trees and vines which surrounded them like a fog. They did not seek answers to any questions concerning whence his courage might arise—the men, in any event, knew nothing of his past, while his superiors obviously felt that they had rescued a good man from a dishonorable fate. In the jungles of the Philippines he had earned his spurs.

But, like the men who followed him so confidently, their dark blue tunics stained with sweat, their khaki breeches stained with mud and tree sap, he felt relief at once again being able to relax, however the relaxation might, as usual, be accompanied by torturing doubt. Because he could not stop hoping that one day, somehow, circumstances might change in his favor, might enable Constance and him to meet again, without the continual threat of censure looking over their shoulders. And perhaps, should it happen, even *with* that threat, he would have gained sufficient stature, sufficient manhood, to laugh at the little envious world of men—and women.

One day, somehow.

Except that now, surely, he was old enough to stop dreaming. That day could never happen, and he was a fool even to think it. He had betrayed her, crept away like a thief in the night, having obtained the treasure he had sought. There was no way he could ever convince her of his love now, even supposing she did not feel utter contempt for him.

Useless to say that *she* had been the one to interrupt the growing pattern of their love by rushing off to an affair with a Chinese. Deliberately. She might claim that she had encountered circumstances beyond her control, but he found it difficult to believe that Constance Baird could ever encounter circumstances beyond her control, save where the entire weight of the United States Navy had been thrown against her. The thought of what she had done, of her betrayal of him, as he had considered it, had angered him. And yet had made him want her more than ever. But it had been a twisted wanting then, his love mingled with contempt, his desire streaked with anger . . . all of which had dissipated in the magnificence of her embrace. Then he had wanted only her. Then he would have defied the world to retain her forever. Yet the doubt had remained, and when he had been faced with the simple choice, career or Constance, he had played the coward. Entirely because of that doubt, that he would ever *possess* her.

He knew now that it did not matter. He knew now that he loved, and that he would never love as truly again. He knew now that he had made the greatest mistake of his life. And now it was too late.

"Who goes there?"

"Captain Wynne and patrol."

The gate swung in, the men wearily formed ranks.

Frank saluted them. "Patrol dismissed."

The battalion adjutant stood at his shoulder. "Psiter wants a word."

Frank nodded, followed the officer to the colonel's office, stood to attention. "All quiet, Colonel. Some signs of activity by the river. Seems to me the Moros may have withdrawn."

"They'll be back," Colonel Psiter said. "At ease, Frank. I'm afraid I have some bad news for your boys. There'll be no replacements for another month, at the earliest."

Frank frowned at him. "May I ask why, sir?"

"Sure. You're entitled to ask, just as you're entitled to those furloughs. You've been up here four months. You've been in the front of every skirmish, every bit of mayhem the Moros have thrown at us. Those boys deserve a break."

He sighed. "But their replacements have gone to North China instead."

Frank's stomach seemed to do a complete roll. "North China?"

The colonel nodded. "There's trouble up there. Revolution, mayhem, murder. Those people they call the Boxers are rampaging the country, murdering missionaries, destroying the missions, and there's some evidence that they're being supported by the government. You know, that old dragon lady they call the dowager empress. So we need men on the spot to protect the legation and to protect our people. That's where the replacements are going, and there's no chance of *them* being replaced for some time."

Frank's stomach had stopped rolling, but his heart now seemed to have slowed. "Did you say the Boxers are destroying the missions, Colonel?"

Psiter nodded. "That's right." Then it was his turn to frown. He had Frank's file in his cabinet.

"Do you have any information on the names of the places attacked, sir?"

"Nope. Seems pretty general. But, Frank—"

"I would like to volunteer to accompany the contingent to Tientsin, Colonel."

Psiter leaned back in his chair. "And I'm not about to give you that permission, Frank. Your business is here, leading those boys who trust you. Not getting involved in . . . well . . . you don't want to look back, Frank. You want to look ahead."

Frank leaned forward, placed his hands on the desk. "Do you know what happened in Tientsin, Colonel, when a Chinese mob overran *that* mission? And please don't start talking about twenty-five years ago. Mobs don't change."

Psiter flushed. "I've been around, Captain Wynne. But there's nothing *you* can do about it. Not now."

"I can *be* there," Frank said. "I can avenge her, if I have to. If you won't let me volunteer, Colonel, then I quit. And don't think you'll stop me this time. I'll let you have my written resignation in half an hour."

"And you think *that* will get you on a boat for Tientsin?"

Frank straightened again. "I'll get there, Colonel. Somehow."

Psiter studied him for several seconds. Over the past six months he had grown to like his young captain as much as he respected him. The colonel was also a pragmatist. He needed men like Frank Wynne to contain the Moros. But this Frank Wynne was no longer the man he needed, or had had, up to half an hour ago. Nor would he be again, until he had been to North China, learned the truth about Chu-teh. The alternative was to lock him up, when he would be of use to no one at all.

"I guess you will get there, somehow, Frank," he said. "But you'll get there a whole hell of a lot quicker if you travel with the Marines. As a volunteer."

# 14

# The March on Peking

"Frank Wynne, by golly." Captain Brian McCalla hurried from his tent to shake hands. "What brings you here?"

"The same thing that brings you here, Brian." Frank shook hands, looked left and right at the neat rows of tents, sheltering beneath the fluttering Stars and Stripes. There were only a few American tents, but beyond, also encamped on the plain outside Tientsin, English, French, Russian, and even Japanese flags fluttered in the breeze. "Maybe you'll fill me in on what's going on."

McCalla escorted him inside the tent; an orderly poured coffee. "No one *knows* what's going on." He sat down, sipped. "We do know the countryside is alive with Boxers. There's even talk they're in force over there in the Chinese half of Tientsin. There's been the odd skirmish, nothing more. But there's been no news out of Peking for the last week, either, and the telegraph lines are down. So this British admiral who's in command here, Seymour, figures we should do something about it."

"Like what?"

McCalla shrugged. "March on the capital. With every man we can raise."

"And how many men *have* you raised?"

Another shrug. "Pretty near two thousand. Sure, there's only a hundred and twelve of us marines; one hundred and six enlisted men, and six officers, yours truly included, but we had to do what we could. There's more than eight hundred Britishers, and four-hundred-odd Germans, and a good bunch of Russians as well. And we're told marine replacements are on their way.''

"They are," Frank assured him. "But this German and Russian bunch, they'll march under a British admiral?''

"Sure," McCalla said. "This is an international show.''

Frank went outside of the tent again, carrying his coffee with him. He gazed at the Pei-ho, flowing massively down to the bar, at the ships anchored out in the bay. What memories came back to him, of crossing that bar with Constance, both agog at seeing this tremendous land for the first time, and then of traveling up this river, again with Constance. And of the enormous distance, and even more the enormous numbers of Chinese, which lay between Tientsin and the capital.

"How can this admiral mean to move out and leave Tientsin behind him?'' he asked. "If it's occupied by the Boxers?''

"We don't know for sure that it is," McCalla said. "Right now that's only a rumor. Anyway, there will be sufficient men left here to handle a few Chinks. Even a few thousand Chinks.''

"And just how does he figure on getting up to Peking?''

"Well, as you can imagine, there was quite a debate about that,'' McCalla said. "Some were for going by river . . . but the rains are only just starting, and it's a little low in places. Others were for going by road, but the road's pretty bad, as I guess you know, and we thought it would take too long. So we're going by train. To Feng-tai. That's only a few miles from Peking.''

"I know where Feng-tai is," Frank said. "And you figure the line is still intact as far as there?''

"Oh, sure. These Chinks are terrified of the railroad. They wouldn't dare interfere with it.''

"You think so?'' Frank asked skeptically. "And you also think two thousand men can march or ride through a country which can put ten million men under arms?''

"Ten million Chinks, Frank. Rabid revolutionaries, armed with knives. There's no evidence any regulars are supporting them, even supposing the regulars are worth a damn, either. We have two thousand *soldiers* here. Well, bluejackets and marines, mostly. But fighting men.'' He grinned. "There are even one or two Japs. The Chinks are terrified of anyone in a Jap uniform.''

Frank sighed. But this had always been the attitude of the American and the European soldiers to the Chinese. "Brian, I'd like to come along.''

"Well . . . I don't know about that.''

"As a volunteer," Frank said. "And under your command.

You'll find me useful. Even this British admiral will find me useful. I know the country, and I speak Mandarin like a native."

"Yeah," McCalla said. "Yeah. Sure, we'd like to have you. But, Frank, well . . ." He looked utterly miserable.

"So shoot," Frank said. "You know that's why I'm here, really."

"The word is that Chu-teh was overrun."

"Go on."

"Well . . ." McCalla grew even more distressed. "I guess that's all."

"Then you don't actually know what happened. Who might have survived."

"For God's sake, Frank," McCalla shouted. "It happened three weeks ago. Three *weeks*. If anyone had gotten out, we'd have heard. There *were* no survivors, Frank. Not one."

So, after all, it was a case of avenging her death. If he believed it. But he could not believe it, on two grounds. He could not believe that Constance, who had survived so much, experienced so much, and always come up with that determined smile of hers, could have finally succumbed, when she was not yet thirty years of age. Even more, he could not envisage Constance, all of that strength and beauty, that solemn face which could smile so entrancingly, that glorious celestial hair, stretched lifeless on the ground, having been subjected to the bestial mutilations which were a part of the Chinese celebration of victory. He dared not envisage such a catastrophe. To do so would be to go mad.

As McCalla was well aware. That afternoon Frank found himself summoned to the tent of Sir Edward Seymour, the slight, slender officer with the quiet voice who was to command the expedition, whose features were dominated by the regal goatee he wore—after the fashion of the Prince of Wales in England and Czar Nicholas II in Russia—whose manners were as precise as his uniform, but whose courage and determination no one could doubt: he held the Royal Humane Medal for lifesaving, as well as being an officer of immense experience, much of it gained in China.

"Captain Wynne," he said. "Welcome aboard. You've met my adjutant, John Jellicoe." He gave a brief smile. "I'm using military terms, you see, as we intend to put a fair distance between ourselves and the sea."

Frank shook hands with the tall, quiet-faced young man he had accompanied to Port Arthur.

"Captain McCalla reminds me that you are a Mandarin linguist who also knows the country," Seymour went on. "And that you wish to serve as a volunteer. That is very good news. But the captain has also felt it necessary to remind me that you have a personal interest in the outcome of this expedition. Is that true, Mr. Wynne?"

Frank returned his gaze. "I have friends in the mission at Chu-teh, north of the capital, sir."

"You understand that it is our intention to march on Peking itself, to reopen communications, and to discover exactly what is the intention of the Chinese government, the Tsung-li-yamen, concerning these insurgents known as Boxers. I do not intend to proceed to *any* of the outlying mission stations."

"I understand that, sir. I hope only to obtain some positive information regarding the fate of Chu-teh and my friends. And if I may say so, sir, the Tsung-li-yamen is not the government of China. It is merely what we would call the Foreign Office. The government of China is the Dowager Empress Tz'u-Hsi. No one else."

Seymour smiled; clearly he had laid the trap deliberately, to discover just *how* much the American actually knew about Chinese affairs. "Then you are doubly welcome aboard, Mr. Wynne. But . . ." His forefinger pointed. "No heroics, and no individuality in my command. Remember that. We fight as a team." Another grim smile. "We are not so strong a team, Mr. Wynne. But a team has always to be stronger than any collection of individuals. If it but remembers that. Now, let's get moving."

Clearly the admiral was under no illusions as to the difficulty of his self-appointed task, which was all to the good. But the difficulty began with his first premise. Frank doubted that any such motley force had ever been assembled to undertake a common objective, not even in the days of the Crusades. In addition to the nine hundred and fifteen British sailors and marines and their officers, with their twelve guns which could be so officially classified, although eight of them were only machine guns, there were four hundred and fifty Germans, three hundred and twelve Russians, one hundred and fifty-eight French, one hundred and twelve Americans, fifty-four Japanese, forty Italians, and even twenty-five Austrians, with another haphazard assortment of guns, of which the French and the Russians each had a genuine field piece, while the marines possessed a thirteen-pounder which was superior to any of the other major weapons. But Frank knew enough about European politics, and indeed world politics, to be aware that the French hated both the Germans and the British, that the Russians and the Japanese regarded each other with mutual distrust, that the Austrians would follow the German lead, and probably the Italians as well, and that all the nationalities, his own included, looked askance at the British because of the war in South Africa, just as they were inclined to question the efficiency and even the courage of the British arms in view of the heavy defeats inflicted on those arms by the sharpshooting Boers. Yet here they were all moving to take on the Chinese Empire, like some old-time Spanish conquistadors, because they were Caucasians, save for the Japanese—and the Japanese had firmly aligned themselves beside the Western nations in every way—and because their womenfolk were in danger, or had been violated and murdered, and there could be no more clarion call to arms than that, for a decent Christian gentleman.

It was not for him to doubt they would succeed; they had to succeed. Nor was it for him to remind anyone in this expedition that those women and children had been imposed upon the Chinese at the point of European bayonets and had no right to be in China at all, much less to be reeducating the youth of China away from their old Confucian virtues, however good their intentions. He resented such thoughts himself. He was not here to apologize for the Chinese. He was here to avenge Constance. Any other determination was surely total weakness. He wanted blood.

But he also wanted Constance, married or not, if there was the slightest chance she might have survived. So that evening he went to the shop of a dealer in novelties, from whom he had purchased, during his years anchored in the Gulf of Chihli, various aids to fancy dress he had worn at parties on board the *Alabama*. He had an idea.

The expedition departed Peking at nine-thirty on the morning of June 10, taking the train first of all to Yangtsun, and thence across the Pei-ho northward toward Feng-tai and the capital. The train, as usual, was watched by large numbers of Chinese, but these appeared peaceful enough and certainly unarmed. It was not until they were past Yangtsun that the first orders were sent down the carriages to prepare for action, and soon they saw why; encamped to the east of the line was a large force, and these were regulars—through their binoculars they could make out the magazine rifles and the field guns, all neatly parked.

"General Nieh's command," McCalla told Frank. "We knew they were out here somewhere. Everything depends on what *their* orders are."

Everything indeed, Frank thought, and wondered at the incredible foolhardiness of the admiral—and of the men who were accompanying him—at not having ascertained General Nieh's attitude, and orders, before undertaking this expedition at all. But Seymour's colossal nerve carried the day. Either General Nieh did have orders not to interfere, or, more likely, he could not believe this pitifully small band of foreign devils could be anything less that the advance guard for a much larger Western army; his men merely glowered at the train as it passed, and shouted epithets, which few of the sailors and marines on the train could understand anyway.

"Whew." McCalla replaced his revolver in its holster, somewhat shamefacedly, and removed his hat to wipe his forehead. "So far, so good."

Frank wondered if the captain recalled having dismissed the Chinese soldiers as worthless material only the previous day. He also wondered if Seymour understood that those soldiers would still be there when the expedition decided to return—and by then they would know that there *was* no supporting army.

But the early afternoon went by peacefully, as they continued to roll with exasperating slowness through such well-remembered country, past the well where Constance and he had first seen a lily-footed woman. And always there were just Chinese peasants lined up to watch them go by. But this in itself was somewhat disturbing; everyone between Tientsin and Peking obviously knew they were coming.

The squeal of brakes announced that the train was stopping. Frank got up. The sun was still high in the sky, and his watch told him it was only just after three in the afternoon. "He can't be meaning to call a halt yet," he said. "I thought we were in a hurry."

"Let's find out," McCalla agreed. The two Americans left their compartment and walked along the track, in the midst of a jabber of mixed languages as the other compartments debouched their mystified occupants, and reached the head of the train, where Seymour and Jellicoe and several other officers were gathered, watching the British sailors moving sleepers and steel lines immediately in front of them.

"There's some damage to the track," the admiral told them. "Nothing serious, But I propose to encamp here for the night, while the line is repaired, and continue in the morning."

Frank squinted into the distance, made out the roofs of a town, recognized it as the station of Lo-fa. "Admiral," he said. "We are not yet halfway to Peking."

"I know that, Captain Wynne. So there is no possible way we can get there before dusk."

"But . . . why can't we continue throughout the night?"

Seymour frowned at him. "Throughout the night? My dear captain, we can't go on through the night."

"It's the Chinese who won't be keen on fighting in the dark, sir," Frank said desperately. "Our men will be on the train. There's not even any risk of us getting lost, as we must follow the track."

"And suppose the track is up farther along as well?" Jellicoe demanded. "We'd be derailed, and that would be that."

"We can have an advance guard marching along the track," Frank said. "We'd make slow progress, but at least we'd be *moving*."

"I think you should attempt to recall our conversation before we left Tientsin, Mr. Wynne," Seymour said. "My business is to reopen communications with Peking, not endanger my command by foolhardy adventures. We will remain here the night, sir. Good afternoon to you."

It was nearly noon the next day before the expeditionary force actually entered Lo-fa, and then there was another halt to water the trains and to arrange a small garrison, both to hold the station and to stop the track being torn up again once the Westerners moved on. Frank had spent a sleepless night, and now he could not believe his eyes at the slowness of their progress, the way the admiral was attempting to anticipate every possible eventuality, when, with the tiny force at his command, his only hope lay in the bold dash on the capital which had been the original plan. Now, clearly, even if there were no more checks, they would not make Peking tonight, either. *If* there were no more checks. When finally the train moved again, after lunch, toward Lang Fang station, itself only the halfway mark between Peking and Tientsin, they had proceeded for no more than a couple of hours before once more the breaks ground to a halt. The track in front of them was again torn up, and this time a considerable portion of it.

"I'm afraid it means another delay, gentlemen," Seymour told his officers. "However, we shall overcome it, as before. We shall get to Peking, I do assure you." He gave one of his grim smiles. "I only trust that these people will actually show themselves at some time, rather than merely acting the nuisance."

"Looks like you might have your wish, Admiral," McCalla said, pointing to the north, where there was a large body of people gathering. Glasses were brought out, and it was easy to make out the red blouses and scarves and the strange movements of the approaching men, as well as to decide that this was no sightseeing party—there were no women to be seen, and a great many knives and old-fashioned muskets flashing in the afternoon sun.

"Boxers," Seymour said with quiet satisfaction. "You'll prepare to receive an assault, gentlemen. We will form and hold a perimeter around the train. I am told these people believe they are immortal. It will be our business to refute that concept, and at the same time to teach them a sharp lesson. But there will be no counterattack." He gazed at the faces in front of him. "I wish that clearly understood. Our strength lies in our concentrated firepower; to dissipate that would be pointless and dangerous."

The officers saluted and dispersed. Frank's heart pounded with pleasant anticipation. There were several thousand men out there, he estimated, but he did not doubt the outcome of this encounter in the least. Supposing everyone obeyed orders.

"Settle yourself, boys," McCalla said, walking up and down the thin line of marines. "Choose your targets. But we'll fire by volley. Your gun ready, Mr. Manly?"

The artillery lieutenant nodded, his face pale with determination, as he watched the huge mass of Chinese advancing—they were close enough now to be heard, shouting curses at the foreign devils and taunting them with being cowards and murderers. Again, few of the marines had any idea what they were being called.

Frank loosened his sword in its scabbard, checked the chambers of his revolver. He did not know if any of those men had been at Chu-teh, but he hoped they had been. Never had he so wanted to kill somebody. Several somebodies.

"Here they come," McCalla muttered. "Here . . What the hell?"

The Boxers were within half a mile now, within range of the Western rifles, in fact, although thus far no one from the train had actually fired. But now the Chinese suddenly stopped advancing, and in a single gigantic movement, all five thousand of them, as Frank estimated their numbers to be, sank to their knees and then touched the earth with their foreheads in a kowtow.

"To us?" McCalla asked in amazement.

"To their gods," Frank muttered, some of his anger and

hatred fading; those men actually *believed* in what they were doing. And in what they had recently done?

"Now," McCalla shouted as the Boxers rose again, and with a roar rushed forward, firing their rifles and waving their swords. "Now! Fire!"

The marines' rifles crashed in a single devastating volley.

"And again," McCalla shouted.

Again the deadly magazine rifles spoke, while the thirteen-pounder now also exploded. The entire train was a ripple of deadly fire. Frank watched the shells bursting amid the advancing army, watched the Boxers throwing up their arms and tumbling backward as either exploding steel or flying lead slashed into their chests. Yet they never halted, continued to advance at a run. He emptied his own revolver, thought he hit at least two of them, and then had to drop the gun and draw his sword as a mass of men reached the American line. For a few seconds it was the wildest melee he had ever experienced, cutting and thrusting, feeling a jar which ran the whole length of his body as his blade slammed into a human chest, ducking to avoid a Chinese sword sweep, realizing his entire right arm as well as his sword hilt was covered in blood, cursing and gasping, as was everyone around him, losing his hat—and then suddenly finding no one in front of him as the Boxers retreated as hastily as they had advanced.

"By Christ," McCalla said. "Good work. Really good work." He wiped his brow. "Casualty report, Mr. Rankin."

"Two men slightly wounded, sir," the lieutenant said.

Which was about average for the Western army, Frank thought, looking left and right. While the Boxers had left several score dead on the field, and even more wounded, crawling back to rejoin their compatriots.

And several prisoners. Two had fallen to the marines. "Say, what do we do with these guys, lieutenant?" asked one of the enlisted men, thrusting the Chinese in front of him so that they fell to their knees before the officers.

"I'm damned if I know," McCalla said.

"You give them to us, Mr. McCalla," said the Japanese commander, Captain Mori, coming down from his section. He smiled, a quick flash of teeth. "We know how to deal with these scum. You give them to us, and they will tell you anything you may wish to know. The admiral will be pleased."

"Well . . ." McCalla looked at Frank.

"They're Boxers," Frank said. "Murdering bastards. You don't want to feel sorry for them. And I bet the admiral *would* like to know what's between here and Peking."

"Yeah," McCalla said. "Okay, Mr. Mori, they're all yours."

"No," screamed one of the Chinese in English. "For the sake of Jesus Christ, Mr. Wynne, do not let them take me. Help me, Mr. Wynne."

Frank stared at the man in total consternation, recognized him as William, the stableboy from Chu-teh, to whom Constance had introduced him as her guide to Peking in that famous adventure in 1891.

"You," Frank said, "are going to hang. By God, I'm going to tie the knot myself."

"Save me, Mr. Wynne," William begged. "It is not as it seems. I swear it. Save me."

"You mean you know this fellow?" McCalla asked in amazement.

Frank nodded grimly. "He's from Chu-teh."

"You mean, a convert? But we heard—"

"Yes," Frank said. "Let's get him into the train. You can have the other one, Mori." He seized William's collar, thrust him up the steps and into the compartment. "Now, talk. I want to know what happened at Chu-teh, and I want to know what the hell you are doing here, fighting with the Boxers. You convince me that you shouldn't hang."

"It is not as it seems," William said again. "I had no choice. They told me, come with us, renounce Christianity, or die."

"That sounds like a choice to me," McCalla said. "One which has been made once or twice in the past."

"I could not just die," William explained. "You must see that, kind sirs."

McCalla looked at Frank, eyebrows raised.

"Tell me what happened on Chu-teh," Frank said.

"They came behind the devil . . . I beg your pardon, sir. They came behind Mrs. Baird. She had been in Peking to see the empress, I believe, and she was returning with an escort of Germans. But the Boxers set upon the escort and slew them, and Mrs. Baird had to return alone."

"You mean she escaped," Frank growled. "By God! So she rode to the mission. What then?"

"Well, sir, there was so little time. The Boxers had followed her. Thousands of them. As many as the grains of sand on a beach—"

"Quit the poetry and get on with it," Frank said.

"Well, sir, there was no stopping them. Mr. Baird went to the gate to speak with them, but they just knocked the gate down—"

"Baird is dead?" Frank snapped.

"I do not know, sir. I do not know anything. But I think he must be, as he was standing by the gate when it fell. I do not know, sir. All I know is that they came inside the compound, shouting and killing. I was in the stable, and I hid. But they found me when they were chasing out the horses before setting fire to the houses."

"They burned the mission?" McCalla asked.

"To the very ground, sir," William told him. "But by the time they found me, they had ceased to be angry. They did not kill me, instead took me before their leader. There were others of us, sir, I swear. And we were told, abjure the Christ, and march with us, or die. We had no choice, sir. No choice at all. But we, I, always meant to escape. As I have done, sir. I ran straight for the American flag this afternoon and surrendered—"

"What about the women?" Frank asked, hardly able to believe it was his voice speaking in so matter-of-fact a tone, when his mind was such a raging torment. "What happened to the women? The white women?"

"Dead, sir. Cut to pieces by the Boxers. They were assembled in Mr. Baird's house, and there they were taken, sir. All of them."

"Oh, my God," McCalla said. Frank said nothing, but he felt McCalla's hand resting on his shoulder.

"All of them," William said again. "Save for Mrs. Baird."

Frank's head came up even as his heart entirely seemed to cease beating. His hands shot out to seize William by the shirtfront. "*What* did you say?"

"They didn't kill Mrs. Baird," William gasped. "She was in the house with the other women, but they took her out. They beat her, to make her tell them where the gold was."

"Beat her?" McCalla asked.

"They made her suffer the bastinado," William explained.

"Jesus Christ," McCalla said. "A white woman?"

"And then what?" Frank asked, still speaking quietly.

"I do not know," William said. "Then they started to burn the compound. Then they took me away with them. I do not know what happened after that."

"*Was* there gold hidden on the mission?" McCalla asked.

"I do not know. I do not think so," William said. "I never heard of any gold."

"And she was given the bastinado," McCalla said again,

obviously allowing his imagination full rein. "What are you going to do, Frank? She could be . . . well, still alive."

What am I going to do? Frank thought. Punch you in the jaw, for a start, for even thinking about it. But that was being childish. He was back to basic decisions. He had come here to learn something of Constance. To know she was dead, and perhaps to say a prayer at her grave. He had not really supposed she could still be alive. Now he knew that she could very well be alive. But he had not prepared himself for the reality of that. To be alive, she would have had to survive the bastinado, and then . . . There imagination became a nightmare. She had spent three weeks in the hands of the Boxers—and once he had doubted her because of one man, and that man a prince.

"Officers call." The command was brought down the train by a marine orderly. "Officers call."

McCalla stood up. "Frank . . ."

Frank also stood up. "Do you want to live, William?" he asked.

"I had no choice, Mr. Wynne. They gave me no choice. They said, renounce Christianity and march with us, or die. I couldn't just die, Mr. Wynne."

"You can, you know," Frank said. "Very easily. And at any moment. But maybe you won't have to. Brian, do you think one of your people could keep an eye on him until I return?"

"Sure," McCalla said, and summoned his sergeant. "But, Frank . . . what do you mean to do?"

Stop being a coward, for a start, Frank thought as he made his way along the train.

Admiral Seymour's face was grim. And he lacked the services of Captain Jellicoe, who Frank learned had been seriously wounded by a sword thrust.

"I'm afraid, gentlemen," the admiral said, "that the situation is more serious than I had anticipated. Our prisoners inform me that the entire line north of Lang Fang has been destroyed, and that the junction at Feng-tai has been burned. They also tell me that a simultaneous attack has been launched on Lo-fa, behind us, with the intention both of destroying the garrison we left there and of once again disrupting the line."

"Prisoners," sneered Captain von Usedom, the German commander. "How can you believe them?"

"I agree with you, Captain," Seymour said equably. "Unfortunately, a dispatch rider has just come in from Lo-fa, a man who has risked his life, I might say, informing us that the station there *is* under attack. It is apparently still holding, but against a vastly superior force. I have already given orders for a relief contingent to return to its aid, but whether we will be able to continue to hold the station, and with it, the line, or whether they will be forced to come up here and join us, must be the decision of the commander on the spot. It is the situation in front of us that must now be considered. My information is that there are at least ten thousand Boxers concentrated between Lang Fang and Peking.''

''Boxers,'' remarked Captain de Marolles, in command of the French contingent, with a contempt to equal the German's. ''At least we must have convinced them they are not as immortal as they supposed.''

''They are a rabble,'' declared Commandant Chagkin, the Russian. ''We will sweep them aside like flies.''

''This is probably true, Commandant,'' Seymour said. ''Unfortunately, some of the matériel we have captured in the skirmish just now, magazine rifles as well as insignia, and in one case an ensign, convinces me that the Boxers are being supported by regular troops.''

''That is impossible,'' insisted Lieutenant Sirianni, the Italian. ''That would be an act of war.''

''You don't suppose the Chinese might just feel we are committing an act of war on them, by marching through their country?'' Frank inquired.

''Gentlemen,'' Seymour said. ''We are concerned with facts, not semantics. It has become apparent to me that we lack the force to mount a successful assault on Peking, if the city *is* defended by regulars, and we must now base our plans on that assumption. On the other hand, I have no intention of abandoning the legations and crawling back to Tientsin. We know that there are considerable reinforcements on their way to us. We have soldiers coming from Hong Kong, there are United States marines on their way from Manila, there are several naval units approaching the Gulf of Chihli, and I understand a large German military force has been dispatched. It is my intention, therefore, to carry the fight to the enemy, and secure the town of Lang Fang. An assault by us might well disperse these fellows once and for all. If it does not do so, then Lang Fang is the ideal place for us to base ourselves and withstand a siege if we have to. There is abundant water there, and an easily defensible perimeter, once we have driven out the Boxers. From there we will send dispatches down to Tientsin requesting the assistance of a second column with all possible haste. With such reinforcements, I have no doubt that we shall reach Peking before too much time elapses. Thank you, gentlemen. You will prepare your men to renew the action. I intend to secure Lang Fang by dusk.''

The officers saluted and left the compartment. Frank and McCalla remained. ''If I may have a word, Admiral,'' Frank said.

Seymour smiled wearily. ''I know, Captain Wynne. Progress is slow. But it will be sure, I promise you.''

''I have no doubt of that, sir,'' Frank said. ''But I wish to request permission to absent myself from the command.''

''Eh?''

''I am a volunteer, sir. I am of no importance to the functioning of the United States contingent. And I believe I have a more important mission to perform.''

''I think you had better tell me just what you have in mind, Captain.''

Frank repeated the information William had given him.

''And you now propose to embark upon some absurd adventure in the hopes of finding this woman alive?'' Seymour shook his head. ''Really, Captain, I had expected better of you. Don't you realize the Boxers would have your head the moment you left the train?''

''Only if they knew I was a white man, sir.''

Seymour frowned at him.

''I have with me, sir, a stain which I have used in the past,'' Frank said. ''It will give my skin the correct yellow tint. I also have a pair of false mustaches, and I have black hair. I can easily obtain Boxer clothing from some of our prisoners. And I speak Chinese like a native. I believe I can penetrate their lines, sir, and come back again.''

Seymour's frown deepened. ''With a woman? Have you any idea what they will do to you if they catch you, a spy in their ranks?''

''Have you any idea what they may already have done to Mrs. Baird, Admiral?''

Seymour met his gaze. ''May I point out, Captain, that you do not even know she is still alive? As for pretending to be a Boxer . . . Of course you can dress up to look like one, and of course you speak the lingo, but that really is not sufficient. There will be passwords, things said of which you will know nothing and to which you will be unable to reply, a hundred and one ways in which you will betray yourself.''

''I am aware of that, sir. But there is a prisoner who will help me. A man who used to live on Chu-teh himself. A convert, who has been coerced into fighting with the Boxers, but has the intelligence to understand that everything they have claimed is untrue."

"That fellow William?" McCalla gasped. "You'll trust *him*?"

"I think he can be trusted, yes," Frank said.

Seymour sighed. "I think you are considering a peculiarly nasty way to commit suicide, Mr. Wynne. But I also envy your courage. As you say, you are a volunteer. I have no power to stop you abandoning the expedition. I will, however, have to make a full report of your action and your intentions. You understand this?"

"I understand that, sir," Frank said.

"What your superior officers will make of it, I do not care to suppose. On the other hand, Captain Wynne, I could *send* you out, to discover just what is happening north of Lang Fang. Then I imagine the criticism would lie at *my* door, for being so free with the life of a distinguished officer. Would you be prepared to undertake such a mission for me, Captain Wynne?" His eyes twinkled. "And of course, you would return here with any European fugitive, or fugitives, for that matter, you may be able to find."

"I should be honored to do so, sir," Frank said, and saluted.

"Go back to Chu-teh?" William was aghast. "With you, Mr. Wynne? They will catch you. They will cut off your balls. They will cut off mine as well," he added in a gloomy afterthought.

"I'll cut off your balls here and now," Frank told him. "If you won't help me. For Christ's sake, William, you know these chaps are a bunch of charlatans. You know they are going to be defeated. Do you realize how many white soldiers are at this moment gathering in Tientsin? You will never have seen so many white men. And every one will be armed with a magazine rifle and a bayonet, and every ten men will be supported by a machine gun, and every hundred by a field piece which will blow those fellows out there into little pieces. Then there is going to be a reckoning, and anyone who is found to have helped the Boxers is going to be hanged. Do you *want* to be hanged?"

"No, sir. But I do not wish to have my balls cut off either," William said dolefully.

"It won't happen, if you help me," Frank promised him. "But the hanging is a certainty, if you don't."

William remained unhappy, but Frank had no doubt that he would go through with it. He spent the next hour carefully staining every inch of his body—he knew from bitter experience that the stain would not come off merely from soaking in water, but required a considerable scrubbing—and then pasting on the drooping black mustaches, which effectively hid any suggestion of the Caucasian about his mouth. His eyes were unfortunately blue, but this was difficult to discern at night, and by the next morning he hoped to be through the Boxer lines. His beard was another problem, and it was necessary to carry a razor, even after he had scraped the bristles as close to his flesh as he could. But then, he also intended to carry his revolver, as well as his bottle of stain, both of which would also betray him should he be searched. But these were amply concealed by the red blouse he donned over the blue breeches and the soft leather boots, all taken from dead or captured Chinese, while his head, bound up in a red scarf, was equally well concealed—his hair might be both black and straight, but it lacked the lankness of the true Oriental.

Then it was a matter of waiting, concealed inside the compartment, while the train rumbled forward over the repaired track and smashed into Lang Fang station, to the accompaniment of volleys of rifle fire, chattering machine guns, and the screams and yells of the scattering Boxers. By now it was growing dark, and in the confused melee which was taking place around the station itself, Frank saw their opportunity. He and William crawled out of the carriage and ran toward the houses, accompanied by a fusillade from the marines—but the Leathernecks had been warned by McCalla to shoot wide. Several other Boxers were also retreating in haste from the hitherto deadly rifle fire, tumbling amid the houses, gasping and shouting, shrieking their defiance, but concerned, for all their superstition, entirely with preserving their lives. For the moment, at least, all was total confusion, and it was a simple matter for Frank and William gradually to withdraw from the immediate vicinity of the station, ducking into doorways whenever another body of Boxers approached, gathering from snatches of overheard conversation that the Chinese were preparing an all-out assault upon the impetuous barbarians that very night. In fact, no one paid them much attention; it was obviously inconceivable to the fanatical Boxers that anyone wearing their distinctive red scarves and blouses could possibly be less eager to kill the white men than themselves. In addition, everyone was totally preoccupied with the excitement of the coming battle.

A battle which of course Frank and William intended to sidestep. To do that, and to escape the town, they required another change of clothing; Lang Fang was full of noncombatant

Chinese, men who peered from windows and doorways and hastily closed these as the two Boxers approached, women who could be heard shrieking and wailing their misery at the calamity which was overtaking their town, and children of both sexes scurrying up and down the streets, followed by packs of barking dogs, all in a state of high excitement. Frank chose one of the more quiet alleyways, and took his time, sizing up both the houses and what he could see of the occupants, remembering to swagger and shout whenever other Boxers were seen in the distance, as well as to perform the peculiar calisthenics he remembered so well, and which William had clearly learned very carefully, waiting at once for full darkness and the promised assault.

Which came the very moment twilight ended, just after eleven, he estimated. The entire town became a huge volcano of sound, rifles cracked, machine guns rattled, field pieces boomed, Boxers screamed their defiance, houses close to the railway station caught fire and sent smoke and flame leaping into the night sky, people ran to and fro screaming, dogs barked, children sobbed— and Frank put his shoulder to the door of the house he had selected and hurled it in with a single charge, William at his heels.

The people inside stared at them in horror. They possessed but a single lamp, and had been clustered by the window listening to the noise, although they could see nothing because of the close-packed buildings. Now they fell to their knees in terror at the sight of the two red-scarved soldiers in their midst. "Lie down," Frank snarled at them as viciously as he could. "Lie down, and we will leave you your lives."

The family—an old man and a younger man, an old woman and two younger women, and three small children—obeyed without question, placing their hands on their heads as if this might somehow protect them from the Boxers' swords. The dog sat in a corner, occasionally baring his teeth but not making a sound.

"You," Frank said, pointing at the two men. "Strip."

They goggled at him.

"We need your clothes. Quickly. Just the pants and blouse."

Still they hesitated, so William ran forward and began tearing off their clothing, after which they undressed with alacrity, even if their eyes rolled as they tried to decide what new terror the Boxers were about to practice on them.

Frank and William undressed in turn, and pulled on the peasant garb. William then hunted in the tiny larder and found some smoked meat and biscuits, which he placed in a bag.

"I am sorry we must take this," Frank said. "I will pay you for it, if I can. When I can. Now, do not leave this room until dawn, under any circumstances, or you will be cut down. Remember this."

He thought there was a very good chance they might do as he had commanded, such was their terror. In any event, the only alternative was to kill them all, and he was not prepared to contemplate that. So he and William closed the door behind them and sidled away into the night.

It was still necessary to proceed with the utmost caution, but within an hour they were at the last of the houses, and able to follow a muddy watercourse to the north; in the ditch they were well concealed. Behind them the cacophony continued, and looking back from a distance of a few miles it seemed as if the entire town was being consumed by the flames; Frank could not help but wonder if the Allied column *would* be able to secure sufficient of the houses, undamaged, to use as a fortress. But already the firing was dying down, although he could still hear the reassuring rat-a-tat of the machine guns to indicate that it was the Boxers who had been defeated.

All the more reason for haste, if they decided to evacuate the town and return to the countryside; it was still some seventy miles to Chu-teh. He and William took to the roadway and jogged for most of the night. Dawn came soon after four, and found them close to an unhealthy green-slimed rivulet which had once been a stream. Here Frank allowed them to halt, to slake their thirst and eat some of the food taken from the peasants' house in Lang Fang, and to sleep awhile, while he once again scraped at his chin and cheeks to make himself look suitably thin-bearded.

William lay on his back and panted, obviously still terrified.

"The worst is behind us now, you know," Frank told him. "We're in open country. It shouldn't take us more than three days to be at Chu-teh."

"Three days," William said sadly. "And there are Boxers . . . and what then, Mr. Wynne? Chu-teh is a place of the dead. Not even the Boxers go there anymore. We will find nothing at Chu-teh but bones."

Frank got up. "Let's go," he said. He did not doubt the poor fellow was right. But there was nowhere else he could begin his search. And besides, he had to see for himself. "Come along."

William got up reluctantly and then hurled himself down again. "Men come," he gasped. "Boxers."

Exactly how he had heard them so early, Frank had no idea, but in the same instant he also heard the jingle of harnesses and the stamping of feet to indicate that a large body of men *was* approaching. Hastily he joined William in the ditch, crawling with him to a reed patch in which they crouched in mutual apprehension, while Frank pulled his revolver from his belt and thumbed back the hammer; he had no intention of being taken alive.

But the Boxers were in too much of a hurry to look either left or right as they paraded along the road, a mass of red scarves and blouses, waving swords and muskets as well as fists. Several of them were even mounted, on a variety of animals, from donkeys to horses, and at their head rode a young man, very well armed with a magazine rifle as well as a revolver holstered at his belt. He looked indeed a very tough customer, for his face, quietly handsome, was rigid with determination and with the aura of command, but surprisingly, he did not wear the red adornments of his followers.

"Reinforcements," William whispered. "They are going to launch another attack on Lang Fang."

"Who is that fellow?" Frank asked. "The one out in front."

"He? His name is Lin-tu. He is a famous revolutionary. From the south."

"But not a Boxer?"

"Lin-tu is a law unto himself. I have seen him before. He came to Chu-teh once, oh, many years ago. Then he was a fugitive from justice. Now he rides with the Boxers, and they are happy to obey him. He trains them how to fight, at a camp not far from here, where there is a ruined pagoda."

"I know it," Frank said. "It lies directly on the track between Peking and Chu-teh. You say there is a Boxer encampment there? How come you didn't tell me this before?"

William goggled at him. "I had forgotten."

Frank studied him. Clearly the convert had not yet entirely made up his mind whether he was going through with this adventure or whether it would not be safest to turn his white companion in at an appropriate moment—such as when they stumbled together into the Boxer encampment.

"Then we shall have to make a detour," he said quietly.

They waited for the last of the Chinese contingent to disappear from sight toward Lang Fang, from which direction they could now again hear the dull crumps of the exploding cannon, and then went on their way, inclining to the west rather than the northwest, so as to give the ruined pagoda a wide berth, passing through ruined and abandoned hamlets, empty and unsewn wheatfields, to tell of the way this country was being turned into a desert by the human locusts who were swarming about it, resting for a while on the second day in the burned and empty railhead of Feng-tai.

Progress was disturbingly slow, especially as they considered it necessary to hide whenever they saw the slightest movement on the horizons surrounding them, even if more often than not the travelers were terrified peasants fleeing to the west, seeking some respite from the ravening Boxers. But their caution was necessary, because there *were* bands of Boxers, from time to time, scouring the countryside in search of either food or recruits or women. Food indeed soon became a problem, for there was little to be found, and no wildlife at all, while water was also scarce, as the rain continued to hold off, for all the continual lowering skies.

Thus after three days they still had not reached their goal. William wanted to call a halt for the day at dusk, as usual, but Frank allowed him only an hour's rest before driving him on again, because in the twilight he could see, silhouetted in the distance against the afterglow of the setting sun, the blackened timbers of Chu-teh mission.

Now he left William behind and hurried up that so-well-remembered slope, his exhaustion forgotten, looking left and right at the fields, untended and choked with weeds, and then up at the shattered gateway, the tumbled wooden wall. Bald-headed crows flapped their wings and rose into the air as he approached, although they must long since have finished their ghastly meals— yet he was almost afraid to breathe. But the air was also clean enough.

He climbed over the rubble at the gate, pausing as his boots crunched on human bones, looked down at the skeletons lying there beneath the wood and the dust. Heart pounding, he strode into the compound itself, seeing the collapsed houses, their timbers scorched and shattered, and beyond, Father Pierre's convent. There the walls had fallen in. Only the church still stood, roofless, but otherwise surprisingly intact, its short bell tower poking skyward.

In front of him was Henry Baird's bungalow. He stood at the foot of the steps, which had survived the blaze, and looked up. This roof had also fallen in, but here too several of the walls were standing. It was as if the Boxers had suddenly been overcome with horror at what they had done, and departed, their work of destruction only half-completed.

He had to mount those steps. However reluctant his muscles were to move, he had still to see for himself what had happened inside. He moved forward, and checked as he heard a noise. He turned, dropping to his knees as he did so, pulling the revolver from his waistband beneath the blouse and leveling. The sound, like that of a chicken rooting in the dirt, had come from beneath the shattered veranda. He moved forward, peered into the noisome gloom—and realized that he was looking at Henry Baird.

Only the beard was truly recognizable. The beard and the burning eyes. The once massive body had dwindled into a heap of bones held together by lifeless flesh, and the mouth sagged open, desperately trying to speak, even as he tried to lift his hands to protect himself.

Frank held out his water bottle, and Baird blinked at it. Frank moved closer, laying down the revolver, and Baird tried to move away from him. "I'm not a Chinese," Frank told him. "I'm Franklin Wynne, United States Marines. I don't propose to take off this disguise, so you'll have to take my word for it. But you may remember the name."

He held the bottle to Baird's lips, and the missionary drank, still staring at him.

"I heard there was a chance there might be survivors here," Frank said. "So I came looking. But . . . you?"

"You are looking for Constance," Baird whispered. He had, after all, remembered the name.

"That's right," Frank said evenly.

"She's dead," Henry said. His lips drew back in a wolfish grin. "Dead."

Frank looked up the steps. "In there?"

Henry shook his head.

"Maybe you'd better tell me what happened," Frank suggested, and sat on the ground. He was carefully keeping his mind suspended, refusing to hope or to despair, to fear or to hate, until he *knew*. "How you're alive, for instance."

"Food," Henry said, trying to crawl forward, and only succeeding in a ghastly slither. "Food."

Frank took some bread from his pocket, and Henry attempted to chew and swallow. He drank some more water. "Roots," he said. "There was nothing but roots. I shall die. We shall all die." His eyes gloomed at Frank. "But they wanted *her*. Not me. They left me for dead at the gate, beneath all those bodies." His head sagged and rested in the dust. Frank lifted it up, gave him some more water and wished he possessed some brandy.

"Tell me about Constance," he said, stopping himself from shouting with an enormous effort.

Henry sighed, his eyes drooped shut. "There were thousands of them. I spoke to them from the gate, but they wouldn't listen to me. They just knocked the gate down. I fell with it. I must have hit my head, because I remember nothing for some time. Then I realized I was lying beneath several balks of timber, and several of my people, too. They were all dead. And the Boxers were yelling and screaming around the encampment, dragging people from their hiding places and cutting off their heads."

"You were telling me about Constance," Frank said. There was no reply, so he leaned forward and shook the missionary again. "Where did she die?"

"Here," Henry said, not opening his eyes.

"Here?" Frank started to get up, and then sat down again. "Tell me."

Henry sighed, and lay still. Frank had to lift his head again and give him the last of the water. "The women were all in the house," he said. "With the children. They were killed there, and burned. But not Constance. They wanted *her*. The devil woman. That's what they called her. The devil woman. They dragged her out here, naked, and they beat her with bamboo rods. I watched them." His eyes opened. "She deserved to die that way, for being too close to them." His voice grew stronger. "She deserved to die."

"They beat her to death?" Frank's fingers were curling into fists. "You lay there and watched your wife being beaten to death?"

"I couldn't watch," Henry said, eyes drooping shut again. "I only heard her scream. And then the screams stopped, because of the rain. How it rained." His eyes opened. "It hasn't rained since, and I have prayed for rain. Water."

"There isn't any more," Frank told him "What did they do with her body?"

"Food," Henry said. "I must eat."

"There is some more coming," Frank promised him. "Tell me where Constance is. Did you bury her?"

"Me?" Henry's head flopped to and fro.

"You mean you did *nothing*? You just lay here? For two months? With all these corpses?" But not with Constance's corpse, he thought, his brain tumbling. There were no bones here.

"There was no food," Henry mumbled. "Nothing." His fingers, more like claws than anything human, seized Frank's arm. "You must have food."

"Listen," Frank said. "The Boxers weren't just beating Constance to death. They were trying to find out where your gold is buried."

"Gold?" Henry's eyes actually opened. "I have no gold."

"They thought you did. And they wanted to make her tell them. So they beat her. Then, as you say, it rained. So they went away. But Constance isn't here anymore, is she? What did they do with her?"

Henry's head raised, and Frank watched William wearily staggering through the gate, pausing to cross himself. Then the groom saw Henry—by now the moon had risen and was sending brilliant white light swathing across the compound.

"Mr. Baird?" he asked in amazement. "Can it be you?"

"William," Henry said. "But you're dead. We're all dead. Constance is dead, you know. You shan't have her, Wynne. Not you, nor anyone. But you must have food. Even in hell there is food."

William looked at Frank, who nodded. The groom gave some of the bread and dried meat to Henry; he tore at it, gasping and belching.

"What is the last thing you remember about the night Chu-teh fell, William?" Frank asked.

"Well, sir . . ." William rubbed his nose. "The last thing, Mr. Wynne, that I remember, just after the rain, is seeing that man Lin-tu giving the Boxers orders."

"I saw him too," Henry said, belching. "Lin-tu."

"You knew him?" Frank asked in surprise.

"I knew him," Henry muttered. "Constance saved his life. Nine years ago. I knew the bastard."

Frank's head turned as if someone had slapped his face. "Lin-tu was the fellow Constance rescued from the imperial soldiers?" His heart was pounding so hard he could hardly speak. But Henry's eyes were shut again, while half-chewed pieces of food trailed from his mouth. "Listen to me," Frank shouted. "Lin-tu is the man whose life Constance saved. Both you and William saw Constance being flogged. Then the rain came. Then you saw Lin-tu. But you didn't see Constance again. Is that right?"

Henry made no reply.

"So Lin-tu has Constance," Frank said. "He is a general among the Boxers, and he admired Constance, as you put it.

And we know where he is encamped. At the crimson pagoda on the way to Peking.''

Still Henry made no reply.

''So we know she's alive,'' Frank said. ''And we know where we can go to find her.''

Henry raised his head. ''She's been three weeks with the Boxers,'' he said. ''She's dead. She's dead, Wynne. You shan't have her. You'll never have her. She was mine. And now she's dead.''

He made an immense effort to get up, and then fell forward on his face.

''Mr. Baird is dead,'' William said.

# 15

# The Dragon Sleeps

A cock crowed, loud and clear, and was followed by another; Lin-tu had made the Boxers accumulate all the poultry they could find in a vast run behind the pagoda, just as he had herded all the available cattle, to provide at least some protein basis for his army. Now the cocks heralded the dawn. Soon the sun, huge and round and red, would emerge from above the North China plain, and another day would begin. A day which would be much like all the others for the past three weeks and more.

But that would not be for another half-hour. Thirty more minutes of blessed rest, with the children huddled against her beneath the coarse, evil-smelling blanket, inside the even more noisome skin tent, with the woman Lu-li snoring opposite.

Thirty precious moments of not having to think, to despair, to *feel*. This last half-hour before dawn had become the most precious part of every day since her captivity had begun.

Constance kept a very careful tally of the days, and knew that this was June 16 by her Western calendar. Thus it was the twenty-sixth day since the fall of the mission. Since her beating. Since Lin-tu.

And today *would* be different from the others, just as yesterday and the day before had been different, because he was not here. He had left three days ago, leading a freshly trained battalion of the young men down to Lang Fang, he had told her, where apparently a force of Westerners was being besieged. He had told her no more than this. She doubted he knew much more than this. Like everyone else in this crazy rebellion, he existed in the midst of a fog of rumor and uncertainty; the day before yesterday was the first time *she* had known there was fighting between Chinese and Europeans anywhere.

But at least Lin-tu knew what he was about, she thought. The Boxers themselves had no such certain aims. They were a revolutionary society, like so many other revolutionary societies in the past—the fertile Chinese soil seemed to sprout them like weeds. And like most of their kind, they were violently xenophobic. They hated all foreigners, and they hated all Christians, because Christianity was a foreign and in their opinion destructive religion. Thus they hated those of their own people who had been converted even more than those with white skins. As such they were clearly very dangerous to the well-being of China, whose recent history had proved how incapable the Dragon Empire was of taking on powers more civilized, as regards weaponry and the military arts, than herself. This had no doubt been obvious to the viceroys of the southern provinces, who had expelled this crowd of fanatics with merciless antagonism, as enemies of the dynasty as well as of the country at large.

And if the Europeans were now fighting pitched battles with the Boxers, the dangers must also by now be apparent to the dynasty itself. Yet the Boxers claimed to be fighting *for* the Ch'ing, and specifically for the dowager empress; Constance could not forget the warning Tz'u-Hsi had given her, the suggestion that the old lady had known what was about to happen. And certainly the Imperial Army here in the north did not seem to be making any effort to suppress them, or even to curb their excesses—it was impossible to suppose that the Forbidden City did not know there was a vast force of Boxers encamped only a few miles away, or that the Tsung-li-yamen was unaware of the massacre at Chu-teh.

But the Boxers accepted the leadership of a man like Lin-tu, to add to the confusion. No doubt they supposed his aims to be the same as theirs, in the short run—the expulsion of the foreigners from China. Yet he made no secret of being implacably opposed to the Ch'ing, to anything Manchu. And he was equally contemptuous of their absurd superstitions. Yet he would lead them, because they were the first true weapons which had come to his hand. And they would follow him, because for all of their fanaticism, they could recognize his ability and his courage and his determination.

She sometimes wondered if they could also recognize his deviousness. No man knew which way he would turn, supposing he *could* drive out the whites. Not even she was sure of that.

Because she was as confused as any of them. He claimed not to have led the Boxers against the mission. He claimed to have been in Peking, and to have arrived here at the ruined pagoda after the murder of the Germans. He claimed to have given orders that no one riding to or from Chu-teh was to be harmed, and he claimed that had von Kettler and his people, and herself, just ridden by on that unforgettable morning, no one would have molested them—and the assault on the mission would never have taken place.

She could almost believe him, almost believe the implication that the whole thing had been von Kettler's fault, a mistake in which she must take her share of the blame just for being there—because the Boxers had not been *ready*. Whatever devious plans had been being laid in Peking, they had not been finalized, she was sure, on the day von Kettler had precipitated the explosion. Thus if the Boxers were ever crushed, and with them, no doubt, the dynasty, von Kettler would be able to claim a considerable posthumous credit for having forced them into premature action. As no doubt could she, again by implication.

Supposing she wanted them crushed, and the dynasty destroyed. This was of course another aspect of her confusion—her feelings toward these people. She should hate them, and fear them, and loathe them, and wish only to see them hanged for what they had done at Chu-teh, for what they had done to her as well. Well, she thought, she probably did hate and fear and loathe them—or would when she could sit back and think about them, supposing that day ever came.

But she could also understand them. She could understand the distress they, and most Chinese, felt at seeing the old Confucian ethics, which had obtained in their country for more than two thousand years, and had first made China great, being undermined by the utterly different Christian concept, the way the missionaries sought to impose the idea of a greater, universal family over and above the Chinese ideal of ancestor worship and its corollary, a total respect for and obedience to living parents. Worst of all, she could understand their resentment at the way so many missionaries tried to link the claimed supremacy of their religion to the obvious supremacy of the technology and armed might of the Western nations they represented. She had watched this happening on Chu-teh, and felt it to be a mistake, even if it had never crossed her mind to suggest that Henry might not know what he was doing,

But neither Henry nor anyone else, all the way down to harmless incompetents like the Congers, had ever had any idea what they were doing in tampering with a world of which they actually knew nothing, and had never taken the trouble to investigate. They had rested confidently on the awareness of that armed might of which they boasted, and which would undoubtedly always come to their aid, however tardily and at however great a cost in human life and suffering. Thus she could even understand the fanatical frenzy into which these unsophisticated youths had to work themselves, because they were so terribly afraid of that Western strength they were daring to oppose.

So could she also understand Lin-tu's ambivalence? He had saved her life; yet, having taken possession of her and her children—for she could not help but consider Adela as hers now—he had refused to consider sending them under safeguard to the American legation, as she had begged him to do. But even more amazingly, he had never laid a finger on her. She had anticipated the worst, had steeled her tortured body and even more tortured mind for the coming ordeal—and been treated always not only with the greatest consideration but almost as a superior being. Certainly he was proud of possessing her, of being able to sit and talk with her by the hour, encouraging her to argue with him, never losing his temper at any of her replies, while he played with Charles and Adela, as if he had been their father—while he never did more than touch her hand.

She could not understand, and her uncertainty kept her in a constant state of nervous awareness. Just as she was aware that she was tolerated in this encampment only because of his presence. She could not help *feel* the vicious hatred of the Boxers for all white people, their confidence that the barbarians *would* be destroyed. Most disturbing of all, she could not help but know that Lin-tu shared his people's emotions. He made no secret of his contempt for the ethics and tenets of Christianity, which he refused to try to understand as she attempted to understand Confucianism.

But he alone stood between her and a fate too terrible to consider. And when he was away, as he had been for the past three days, she felt a growing anxiety for his return. Now it was light, and the encampment was stirring. It was necessary to go down to the stream to draw water for herself and the children, and for the woman, Lu-li, whom he had left in charge of them; the stream by the pagoda, issuing from a spring, was one of the few watercourses not to have been drunk dry by the Boxer hordes, which was the main reason Lin-tu had made his headquarters here.

But she was actually glad of the necessity to labor. It limited the amount of time she had to think, and there was too much of that anyway. For what did she have to think about? She dared not remember Chu-teh and what had happened there. She did not wish to consider the present, the day that Lin-tu might overcome his awe of her, or his respect for her. And how could she consider any future, even supposing the Boxers were eventually to be crushed and herself rescued? How could she ever face Elaine Conger again? Or Harriet Bunting? Because those tight little minds could not possibly envisage the sights and sounds and smells of an entire roomful of women being torn to pieces.

Or most of all, she thought, as she carried her pitcher down to the stream, not crowded as yet, listening to the sounds of the awakening encampment, Frank Wynne? Not, at the least, that that was ever likely to happen, even supposing she wanted it to. Save that her knees were suddenly turning to water, and she was stopping, still several feet from the stream. Because there he was.

The man appeared to be a Boxer; he wore a red blouse and his head was concealed beneath a red bandanna. His skin was yellow brown, and his mustaches were long and drooping, to either side of his mouth. Yet it was quite certainly Frank standing by the stream, his pitcher half-filled with water, gazing at her, willing her to move, to come closer, to stand beside him.

She inhaled, carefully placed one foot in front of the other, reached the stream. Even the spring was in some danger of being sucked dry now, and the water was nothing more than a muddy trickle. She knelt beside him, lowered her pitcher, managed to half-fill it.

"Are the children with you?" he asked.

"Yes," she said, amazed at the quiet evenness of her voice, and equally amazed that he did not seem able to hear the pounding of her heart. She glanced left and right. But no one seemed interested.

"Tonight," he said. "As soon as it's dark. Walk due west from the encampment. I'll find you."

"But . . ." Her brain was swimming. There was so much she had to know, so much . . . He had deserted her, left her to face the humiliation of rejection and loneliness, to be a laughingstock . . . but now he had come back, risking a quite ghastly fate. For her.

The man she wanted to love more than any other man she had ever met.

But . . . what *had* brought him back? She stared at him, but his face was carefully expressionless. "Tonight," he said, walked away from her to join a group of Boxers in their invariable morning calisthenics.

She stumbled back to the tent, washed the children, helped Lu-li light the little fire to cook the meal patties which were their basic food. It would not be dark again for fourteen hours. Fourteen hours, during which she must think, and wonder, and try to believe that it had really happened, and reveal not a trace to a soul that it *had* happened. She looked for Frank several times during the day, but did not see him. The men were always coming and going from the encampment, so his departure would certainly not be noticed any more than his arrival. Nor, she supposed, would hers and the children's, save by Lu-li. The Chinese woman would have to be dealt with. But did she not possess enough hatred for that?

It was actually a question, she slowly realized, of whether she possessed enough courage. Not to leave the camp; she was sure of that. Not even to risk torture and death. But to go to Frank . . . and now she was a widow. Did Frank know that?

But even if he did, he also knew she had been a prisoner of the Boxers, with all that that suggested, for more than three weeks.

Yet he must have known that, even before setting out on this mad adventure. And he had still come. For her.

Each minute seemed like an hour as the sun scorched the encampment, as the men did their drill, as self-appointed messengers went off to see if they could learn some news about what was happening to the south, despite Lin-tu's command that they were all to wait here for his return or his instructions. While the women did their chores, with apathetic resignation. She at least had the children. In the beginning they had been a constant source of worry. Quite apart from the plain physical danger, there was the very poor food, the utter lack of cleanliness or the least idea of sanitation among the Boxers.

Now they had become jewels of comfort and companionship, amazingly healthy, amazingly cheerful, fascinated by the bustle and excitement always surrounding them. What they actually thought of everything that had happened, Constance could not decide. Adela was of course too young properly to understand anything of what was going on. But Charles had seen the burning mission, and for all her efforts to cover his eyes as they had left, he must also have been aware of the death and destruction wreaked by the Boxers. With whom he was now living. He had asked, "Where is Father?" And she had replied, "Father has gone away to get help to rebuild the mission. He'll soon be back. But until he does return, we must live with these Chinese.''

That had seemed to satisfy him, and he found the weapons and the martial air with which he was surrounded even more fascinating than Adela.

The Chinese women lacked such support; the camp had not been in existence long enough for them to have had children of their own. None of the females was even a Boxer; the Boxers did not include women in their ranks. All had been torn from their homes to supply the creature comforts of the men. With Chinese fatalism they had set about making the best of it—as had she. She had not considered this before, had included the women in the general hate and disgust she kept telling herself she must feel for all of these people. But perhaps the women would be on her side. Perhaps Lu-li would *help* her to escape.

She knew at once that that was dangerous thinking. If she *was* going to escape, she would have to be as ruthless as the Boxers themselves. She would have to kill, if necessary, as she had killed before, on that terrible day which had begun right here.

If she was going to escape. Back to a world which seemed a different existence. A world in which she would stick out like a sore thumb, the woman who had lived with the Boxers. But a world which also contained Frank Wynne.

Back to a world of totally confused emotions, of hates and fears and desires no less fervent than those in this encampment, only more hypocritically concealed.

Yet she was going. Because at least in that world there was hope, and there was none here. And because of the children. Thank God for the children.


''It is strange,'' Lu-li remarked, ''that we have not heard from Lin-tu. He should have sent by now.''

It was just dark, and the children slept. Outside there was the occasional fire, but kindling was very scarce, and most of the Boxers, or their women, preferred to keep what fuel they possessed for cooking rather than sitting around at night. Besides, the men took so much exercise during the day that they were generally exhausted by nightfall. Which was what she was counting on.

''Yes,'' she said. ''He should have sent by now.''

''He will send tomorrow,'' Lu-li said confidently, and lay down, pulling the blanket over herself. Her eyes closed, and Constance knew that within seconds she would be fast asleep. Yet she could not be counted upon to remain fast asleep, especially if she was disturbed. There was nothing for it. But not murder. The knife lay on the ground beside Constance's hand, and she picked it up and thrust it into her boot. Not murder. Shooting down a charging Boxer bent on killing her was one thing. She could not destroy a woman who had done her best to be friendly.

Yet the act would still have to be brutal. She remained sitting cross-legged on her blanket, waiting for Lu-li to give one of her deep sighs and turn on her side away from her. Lin-tu had rescued from the wreckage of Chu-teh a heavy iron pot in which she cooked his food. It was a case of hitting hard enough so that no second blow would be required, but of not hitting so hard that the skull would be split. Oh, Constance Baird, she thought, whatever became of that little girl who had stepped onto the train in Richmond with nothing but loving excitement in her heart?

She rose to her knees and swung the pot before she could think anymore. Lu-li's entire body jerked, and then subsided, and to Constance's horror blood trickled out of the thick black hair. Hastily she probed the mess with her fingers, found the bruise, felt the bone underneath, and decided no real damage was done. Certainly Lu-li still breathed, if stertorously, and her heartbeat was regular.

And she was already in the past. Constance woke Charles, while holding her hand over his mouth. "Ssssh, my darling," she said. "We are going for a walk. But we must be very quiet." She woke Adela in turn.

"A walk, Mama? In the dark?" Charles asked. "Has Father come for us? I knew he would."

"No," she said. "Someone else." She held Adela in her arms, ready to smother the slightest cry, and left the tent, Charles holding her free hand. Poor little mite, she thought; his confusion will only grow.

"A Chinese?" he asked. "But, Mother—"

"Ssssh," she commanded. "You'll see, just now."

She led him away from the tents and away from the gaunt remains of the crimson pagoda. She wondered if she would ever see it again; it seemed to have played so important a part in her life. But it had stood for so long, neglected and rotting, it was impossible to suppose it would ever actually fall down.

No one questioned her, because no one saw her. The Boxers did not maintain guards at night; they did not consider them necessary. They could not conceive of anyone approaching the camp who did not mean to fight with them, and they were not really interested in what the women did. They did not, like

Lin-tu, count individuals as important; there were always women to be had.

Her feet crunched in the stones and uneven ground, but she had covered no more than a hundred yards when she saw, looming through the darkness, the tall figure which had approached her at the stream. She still could not entirely convince herself that she was not dreaming, as he took Adela from her arms.

"William is waiting over the next rise," he said. "You remember William?"

"Yes," she said. "I remember William." Even if she couldn't understand. "I had to hit someone to get away," she said. It was important to keep talking, and not to start thinking.

"Then we'd better put some distance between us and them," Frank said. "Let's go."

He led the way, carrying Adela. William, after an embarrassed greeting, hurried behind him. Constance followed the men, still holding Charles's hand. She realized Frank was just as embarrassed as the Chinese. Because they thought they knew what had happened to her. She could only wait for the opportunity to talk and explain.

They must have walked for several hours, and it was again becoming light when Frank at last called a halt in another of the dried-up watercourses that scarred the parched countryside. By then Constance was so exhausted she could hardly put one foot in front of the other, and sank to her knees without a word. Charles lay down.

Frank stood above them. "To get back to Admiral Seymour's command," he said, "we have to pass through the Boxer lines. So you and Charles have to disguise yourselves, Constance. I have a stain which you can apply to your skin, and to his. Go easy with it, there's just sufficient left. But it must be applied everywhere, just in case you have to undress. Everywhere, remember."

He gave her the little box, and turned away. He was treating her like a stranger. And she had to go along with him. But she also had to think, and help him, as much as she could.

"Have you hair dye, as well?" she asked.

He shook his head. "So you are going to have to crop your hair."

She put up her hand; she had never actually done more than trim the ends of her hair in her life.

"It'll grow again," he promised.

"But . . . it'll still be blond."

"No one will know. We're going to make you into a boy.
Your clothes won't need to be changed, but we'll add a red
bandanna." At last he smiled. "You'll make a handsome boy,
Constance." He paused, and they stared at each other. "I'll do it
when you've finished the staining," he said.

*Did* he still love her? Could he? It was four years since their
tumultuous romance had crumbled into dust, after but a single
night, before the weight of authority and wagging tongues.

But could he be here risking his life if he did not?

He cut her hair with his knife, as close to the scalp as he
could. It slipped through his fingers, and he had to touch both
her head and her neck when gathering the strands. Once his hand
rested on her shoulders, and then slid away again.

He had not kissed her since their reunion. But why should he
wish to kiss her?

"You know that Henry is dead," she said.

"Yes. He died in my arms, virtually."

"In your . . ." Her head turned so quickly he pulled the hair
he was holding. "He died when Chu-teh was overrun."

"No," Frank said. "He lived, until yesterday." He stood
back to survey his handiwork. "That'll do. Put this on." He
handed her a red bandanna.

"But . . ." Her brain was reeling. "Frank . . . did he say
anything?"

"That you deserved to be beaten to death," Frank said.

William had apparently also been in the Boxer encampment
with Frank, and had managed to steal some food, and this they
ate before commencing their march. Frank carried Adela, as
before, while Charles walked with grim determination. But it
was necessary to rest every hour for ten minutes. The country
remained empty, although in the distance they thought they
could see a smoke pall. "Probably Lang Fang," Frank said.

There was no conversation. There was so much to be said—so
much for her to say, anyway, Constance thought—but now was
not the time. They needed to be alone and free from lurking
danger. But would they ever be alone and free from lurking
danger again?

They halted for the night and ate the last of the food. Frank
had apparently mentally marked his stopping places on the journey north from Lang Fang, and in the dried-up watercourse
where they made their camp, he dug for a seepage of evil-
smelling liquid—but it did something to alleviate their thirst.

Adela started to cry with discomfort, and Constance rocked her to sleep in her arms, while Charles noisily sucked his thumb. Frank lay down beside William several feet away.

She realized that, having refused to consider the future for weeks, now she had to. Because Henry *was* dead. She had no reason for remaining in China a day longer than she had to. And yet, despite everything that had happened, she had no real desire to leave—except with Frank Wynne. And as that did not now appear likely to happen . . .

"Time to move on," Frank said, shaking her shoulder, and she realized that she had slept soundly with Adela in her arms. "It's going to be a long day," he said. "There's no food left. But we should be in Lang Fang by dusk."

"Frank," she said. "Why did you come?"

"I came to find you, Connie," he said. His smile was twisted. "But I found Henry first."

"Frank. . ." She held his hand. She would forgive *him*. Now was not the time for puerile angers and memories. He was here, and she was here, and only that mattered. But only to her, apparently.

He gave her fingers the briefest of squeezes. "Let's make sure we're alive to talk about it," he said. "Before we talk about it."

He had always been a marine first, she recalled, and a lover second. And a moment later he was very much the marine as William said, "People come. Boxers."

They lay on the muddy earth of the watercourse, Constance hugging the children to stop them from crying out, while Frank drew his revolver. It was a considerable body of red-scarfed young men, some thirty of them—and all wounded, with bandaged arms and legs, bandaged heads, and bandaged torsos. Constance wondered how they managed to reconcile their injuries with their belief in their invulnerability.

But they were all in the best of spirits, laughing and shouting at each other as they approached.

"I must find out what's making them so happy," Frank said. "Do you know how to handle one of these things?"

"Yes," Constance said.

"Then cover me."

She wrapped her fingers around the butt, watched Frank clamber up the side of the ditch and stand on the road. The Boxers checked at the sight of him, but came on again as they recognized the red blouse and scarf.

"Where is Lin-tu?" he demanded. "I have been sent to seek Lin-tu and receive his orders."

"Lin-tu is gone to the coast," one of the Boxers said.

"He is chasing behind the barbarians," said another with a shout of laughter.

"Behind the barbarians?" Frank asked. "I have been told the foreign devils are entrenched at Lang Fang."

"They were," said another Boxer, also laughing. "But we drove them out."

"Lin-tu drove them out," said the first man. "They are running for the coast. And Lin-tu is behind them. You go and find your people and tell them to march on Tientsin. That is where the barbarians will finally be destroyed. You tell them that."

Frank stood aside to watch them pass. As soon as they were out of sight, Constance stood up, handed him back his revolver. "Do you believe that? That Seymour has been defeated?"

"I think we have to. There's no reason for them to lie to another Boxer. God knows what went wrong. Well, we'll never make the coast on foot through the entire Boxer army. I suppose we'll just have to make for Peking."

"Peking?" Constance stared at him.

"We'll go to the U.S. legation," he explained. "Call on old Conger. I would say he'll be delighted to see us."

To reach Peking they had to walk southeast instead of south, and Frank had actually been leading them more to the southwest, so as to avoid the Boxer concentration around Feng-tai, and if possible approach Lang Fang from the direction of the river. Thus they had another full day's walk ahead of them, spurred on by their growing hunger, and this was very much through the ranks of the Boxers. Now Constance had to carry Adela, while Frank and William waved their fists and brandished their swords; but she also had to carry a long knife and play the man from time to time. At least all of them spoke Chinese, so there was no risk of betrayal, and in fact none of the many crowds they passed, whether of Boxers hurrying to join Lin-tu's army by the coast—or even more disturbingly, hurrying on Peking, describing at the tops of their voices how they would destroy all the hairy barbarians in the legations—or of ordinary Chinese trying to remove themselves as far as possible from the fighting, spared them more than a glance. To the peasants they were Boxers, and best avoided. To the Boxers they were recruits, and welcomed, although no one seemed able to work out why they should be marching to battle accompanied by two small children. But Adela needed no second glance from any Chinese, and Charles soon understood what was required, and himself started throwing his arms to and fro and thrusting his fists right and left, all the while crying, "Death to the barbarians," which made him and his escort very popular.

"Even the children," the Boxers shouted. "Even the children."

"Will they attack the legations, do you think?" Frank asked Constance as they saw the purple walls of the city rising in the distance.

"I don't know what to think," she confessed. "When last I saw her, the empress was very odd indeed. She told me to leave China. I went to see Conger and told him that, and he laughed at me. And next day Chu-teh was burned."

"Um," Frank commented. "Well, we don't have any alternative now. As we're here."

Because the Yun-ting-men was already immediately in front of them, as much a throng of people coming and going as ever Constance remembered it from the past, although today the majority were Boxers, conversing freely with the regular soldiers on the gate, who were certainly not attempting to stop them from either leaving or entering the city.

"From the command of Lin-tu," Frank said as they hurried beneath the arch and up the Grand Avenue.

"To the legations," men around them shouted. "To the legations."

It was almost dusk again by now, but to their relief there was no sound of any firing, although there was a great deal of noise, for apart from the shouting and yelling, the Boxers were also releasing great numbers of firecrackers, which went off with pops and bangs and rippling explosions which only Frank's experienced ear was able to assure them was *not* machine-gun fire.

The entire atmosphere was unreal, and Constance found herself wondering if the empress *did* know what was going on, locked away as she was within the confines of the Forbidden City. Despite her exhaustion, she had a sudden tremendous urge to attempt to end the entire crisis in a single coup—as well as inform the empress what had happened on Chu-teh and involve the imperial anger on the murderers, which would surely follow. "I think there's so much confusion," she said as they pushed their way through the crowds, all out celebrating as if it were at least the Chinese New Year, "that we could probably get into the Forbidden City. And to Tz'u-Hsi. If we could do that . . ."

"From the way the Boxers are fraternizing with the regulars, we'd probably have our heads cut off,'' Frank said. ''Our first job is to get the kids to safety, anyway.''

She supposed he *was* right, and in any event, they were through the Tsien-men now, and turning to the right to hurry along the street next to the Tartar Wall, making for the American legation. And there was the gate, with a marine sentry standing just inside it, his bayonet fixed, for opposite him was a crowd of several hundred Boxers, beating drums and cymbals and shouting abuse.

''Well, glory be,'' Frank said. ''Now all we have to do is get to him.''

''We run,'' William suggested.

Frank shook his head. ''Not dressed like this. Those chaps might just think we're charging, and follow us. We don't want to *start* a war. When I say the word, throw away your scarves and blouses. You can keep your blouse, Connie.'' He led them through the center of the crowd.

''We shall kill them all,'' a man shouted.

''They are to leave,'' shouted another.

''*Then* we shall kill them all,'' screamed a third.

''All,'' they chanted.

''We shall cut off their heads.''

''Their heads,'' chanted the mob.

''They hate us,'' Charles cried. ''They—''

Constance hastily put her hand over his mouth. ''Sssh, my darling. In a few minutes . . .''

But heads were turning; Charles had spoken in English.

''Now,'' Frank bawled, and ran for the gate, tearing off his bandanna and discarding his shirt as he did so. Constance ran behind him, panting, struggling to free her headkerchief while clutching Adela to her breast. The crowd gave a roar and surged behind them, to check as the marine sentry presented his bayonet.

''Stop there,'' he shouted. ''You, there, halt.'' He made to swing his rifle butt at Frank, and then paused in utter consternation as Constance at last got her bandanna free and it fluttered away to reveal her close-cropped head of golden hair.

''Oh, Constance,'' Harriet Bunting wept. ''Oh, Constance!''

She sat on the bed in the room they were to share—because they were such old friends, as Elaine Conger had put it. All the Europeans in Peking had apparently been summoned to their various legations several days ago, as soon as the attacks upon foreigners had reached epidemic proportions. ''You mean they *beat* you?''

"You can see the marks." Constance stood up, the better to soap and scrub herself, balancing precariously in the small tin tub, while the Chinese maids assisted her. She saw no reason not to shock Harriet. She certainly had no intention of forgiving her or Mrs. Conger for the parts they had played in destroying Frank's love for her. Besides, what had happened to her *was* shocking. And as everyone knew of it, the only way to prevent herself being pitied as well as patronized was to act as if she could take the whole catastrophe in her stride.

Harriet had been pretending not to look at her. But now she could not stop herself. "Oh, my dear," she said. "How horrible. I wonder you survived."

"So do I," Constance said. "Do you think this dye will *ever* come off?"

But she did not really care at this moment. She had been fed, and given water and brandy to drink, which had turned the night into a pleasant glow. And she was safe, after four weeks of terror. She truly understood only now how frightened she had been. But that was over. True, everyone in the legation seemed equally frightened, and the building was filled with stealthy whisperings and stealthier comings and goings, but *she* at least felt safe here.

"And then you were their prisoner," Harriet said in an arch whisper. "Oh, *Constance!*"

"Yes," Constance said, and held out her arms for the towel. She was clearly going to get no more of the stain off tonight, and now she was too tired to stand anymore. All she wanted to do was sleep, even if it meant sharing a bed with Harriet, and with Adela, who was already dead to the world. She was not even prepared to worry about Charles, who had been sent off to one of the male dormitories with Frank; she was sure Frank would look after him, anyway. William had of course been found a place with the legation servants.

"I don't suppose you want to talk about it," Harriet said sadly.

"I will talk about it, Harriet," Constance promised. "If you wish me to. But not tonight, if you don't mind. I really am very tired." She bent to kiss Adela, who snuffled into her pillow.

"Of course, my dear. Of course. Off you go," Harriet told the Chinese girls. "Chop chop."

They scurried for the door, carrying the tub between them, paused to bow to Elaine Conger as she appeared in their path, and then disappeared down the corridor.

"My dear Constance," Elaine said. "You mean they cut off your hair as well?"

Constance felt the "as well" was totally unnecessary. She sat on the bed. "No," she said. "Frank cut off my hair, to disguise me as a boy, so that we could escape."

"Of course," Mrs. Conger said. "What deeds of *heroism* are being done all about us. Franklin Wynne has certainly behaved with exemplary courage. He will surely be recommended. Now, you have a good night's sleep, my dear, and we will talk tomorrow. Mr. Conger wishes to hear about Chu-teh."

"But aren't we leaving tomorrow?" Harriet asked.

"Leaving?" Constance cried.

"We are not going anywhere," Elaine Conger declared. "We received an ultimatum yesterday morning," she explained to Constance. "All the legations did, insisting that, in view of Admiral Seymour's expedition, his violation of Chinese soil, if you please, we should immediately pack up and leave Peking. I may say that most of us regarded this as an intolerable breach of international law, although there were some"—she glanced at a flushing Harriet—"who felt that we should abjectly obey. However, our decision has been made for us, if what Captain Wynne has said is true. If Seymour *is* withdrawing to Tientsin, even temporarily, and if he has been engaged with imperial troops, then obviously we cannot leave without an adequate escort, and adequate guarantees, as well. These remain to be negotiated. So you will have at least tomorrow to rest up, my dear."

"But . . . ." Harriet protested. "The ultimatum said they would attack us unless we are gone by four o'clock tomorrow afternoon."

Elaine Conger tossed her head. "They would not dare," she said. "They would not *dare*. Good night to you." She left the room.

Constance hoped she was right. But she was too tired to care. Not even Harriet's nervous and recriminatory chattering could keep her awake. She just wanted to lie down, to experience the delicious agony of feeling the aches and pains in her muscles increase as she relaxed, and then slowly begin to fade, to close her eyes, to know that tomorrow—for the first time in years, it seemed—she did not have to get up until *she* wanted to. . . . She was aware, once or twice, of being half-awake, of hearing movement about her, even that it was daylight, but none of these things really restored her to consciousness. She did not *want* to wake up and face the problem of being the most notorious woman in the legation, until she was absolutely rested. So she kept her eyes closed, too tired even to feel hungry, and went back to sleep, again . . . and awoke with a start as the entire building shook to a huge, rumbling explosion.

Constance sat up as plaster fell on her face, listened to another howling sound, and then another boom, reverberating through the afternoon. Because, she realized, it *was* afternoon. She had slept for some eighteen hours, and now . . . She didn't really know where she was. Or what was happening.

The door burst open, and Adela scampered in, followed by an ashen-faced Harriet Bunting.

"Auntie Connie," Adela screamed. "Auntie Connie. The Chinese . . ."

"They are assaulting the legation," Harriet panted. "I knew they would. I told them so. I . . ." She stopped to gaze at Constance. "My dear girl, you simply must get up and dress."

"What in?" Constance asked.

"Oh . . . wear this." Harriet seized a Chinese robe from the closet, handed it to her. It had obviously been created *for* Harriet, would hang on Constance's shoulders and come down only to mid-calf, but it was better than nothing, and she knew that she did have to get up—she could hear the shrieks of the crowd and the rattle of rifle fire coming from the front of the building.

"There are thousands of them," Harriet moaned, sitting on the bed. "Thousands. They will kill us all."

Again, Constance thought. My God, to have survived Chu-teh, and to die in Peking. But she could not believe it was going to happen. Not to a legation. She went outside, into the corridor, carrying Adela, Harriet trailing at her heels. Here there were several women, all screaming and weeping. "Quiet," Elaine Conger was shouting. "Please be quiet."

The noise inside the building slowly died, while the noise outside grew even greater. Constance wanted to go to a window and look out, see what was happening, what the men were doing, what Frank in particular was doing, but the windows were all shuttered and barred; even at four o'clock in the afternoon the candles were burning.

"Now, ladies, please," Elaine Conger was saying. "I do not know how long this is going to continue, so I think it would be best for us all to retire to the cellar. Now, ladies . . ."

"We must evacuate," Mr. Conger said, hurrying into the corridor, tie askew and looking very hot and bothered. "We can't hold against that mob. Elaine . . ."

"Mr. Conger!" He was followed by the officer commanding the marine detachment providing the legation guard. "I must question that order, sir. We *can* hold this house, against twice that number of Boxers."

"And when they bring up more field guns?" Conger demanded.

"They haven't done so yet, sir. That piece making all the noise is really out of a museum. It's a darned sight more dangerous to them than to us. Only the regulars have any *real* cannon. And we've no evidence any regulars are out there at this moment. Now, sir, if you'll let me lead a sortie, we'll knock that gun out, and gain an emplacement on the wall as well, and then . . ."

The women looked from one to the other, anxiously, aware that their fates were probably being decided on purely military grounds.

"I cannot permit anything so foolhardy, Captain Myers," Conger said. "The regulars will be here soon enough. There can be no doubt about that now. This is war. And in addition, our position is strategically untenable. We stick out from the other legations like a sore thumb. In no time at all we'll be outflanked and surrounded. But if we withdraw now, through the gardens, toward the British legation . . . I may tell you, sir, that this contingency was discussed by Sir Claude Macdonald and myself some time ago, when these troubles first started, and we both agreed, as did Monsieur Pichon and Baron Nishi, that it would be our best plan to concentrate on the British legation in the event of real fighting. Theirs is the largest and best fortified of these buildings, and they have seven wells within their gardens, sir. Sufficient water to last us all a considerable time. Now, Captain . . ."

"Charles," Constance shouted, suddenly remembering that he was not with her. "Where is Charles?" She looked left and right, while everyone stared at her. "Look after Adela, Harriet," she shouted, and ran from the corridor, pushing people left and right as she tumbled down the stairs. On the lower hall the windows were loopholed, and here several marines knelt at their posts, under the command of . . . Frank, she saw with a surge of heartbeat. "Frank!" she shouted. "Where's Charles?"

He wore a uniform clearly borrowed from Myers; it strained somewhat over the chest. But having bathed and taken off his false mustaches, he was the same Frank she remembered from five years ago, even if his face remained blotched where the stain had proved difficult to remove. When he looked at her, she instinctively put up her hands to push her hair back, felt herself flush as she found merely badly cut stubble.

"Charlie's over there under the table." He grinned at her. He was happy. He was fighting, and killing Boxers. "He *would* come in."

"Oh, *Charlie*!" Constance swept the boy into her arms, instinctively shielding him as the house shook again, turning her head as Captain Myers hurried into the room.

"We have orders to pull out," the captain said bitterly. "Frank, you'll take six men and see the minister and the ladies through the gardens to the British legation. Seems they're expecting us. We'll maintain a rear guard until the civilians are safe."

Frank frowned at him. "But we can hold here. If we can take that wall—"

"We have orders," Myers said again. "So get to it. You too, ma'am, begging your pardon."

"Ladies," shouted Lady Macdonald. "Ladies, please!"

The Chinese houseboy standing at her elbow banged the dinner gong, for they were assembled in the huge official dining room of the British legation, where the great mahogany table had been pushed back against the inner wall beside the sideboards— the silver and crystal had prudently been removed to the cellars. It was, Constance supposed, a quite unforgettable sight, for there were at least two hundred white women and their children, of all ages, and of every conceivable nationality, chattering and muttering and weeping among themselves, all overlaid by the screaming noise from outside, punctuated by the occasional crack of a rifle or the boom of the Boxers' gun, which from its vantage point on the Tartar Wall could still lob shells in the direction of the British legation.

But only in the direction. The truly incredible aspect of the situation was that although it was now again nearly dusk, and the assault on the various legations—which had now actually come down to an assault on this legation, all the others having been abandoned—had now been going on for several hours, the only casualties so far had been a few scratches, so inaccurate had been the shooting of the Boxers. The Americans had indeed made the transfer from their own legation, the most exposed of all, with hardly a bruise. She could not help but think that if only there had been a few rifles on Chu-teh, and a few resolute men, they might be holding it yet.

But that was in the past. Now they had the present to contend with, and the present, for herself and all the other women, was at the disposal of this rather large, grand-looking lady, with a big chin and a string of pearls around her neck, wearing a Paris robe and a huge garden-party hat—unlike the foreign ladies, she had not had to abandon her wardrobe—and looking over them rather as a school headmistress might regard her pupils on the first day of term.

But the gong had had its effect, and the chatter was subsiding.

"Thank you, ladies," Lady Macdonald said. "May I first of all say welcome. I wish this could be a happier occasion. But be sure that we shall do our best to make it into a happy occasion, eventually. Now, our business, and the business of our husbands, is to maintain ourselves here until either the Chinese come to their senses or the relief column arrives from Tientsin. It is, despite Admiral Seymour's apparent setback, extremely likely that it will be the latter, which makes me very sorry for the Chinese." She paused, perhaps hoping for applause, looking from face to face, and certainly daring anyone to suggest that she might be lying, or even being optimistic.

"We all have our part to play in this task," she went on. "There is food to be prepared, and there are ration menus to be worked out, because we will have to be a *little* careful with our supplies. There are a great number of sandbags required, and I think it would be helpful if we *all* did some sewing every day. I shall arrange the names in a rota, with the times this will be required from each of you. And in addition, we must face the fact that there may be, from time to time, some of our people hurt. Thus I would be pleased if any of you with nursing or first-aid training would report to me, that I may organize a hospital rota as well. Lastly . . ." Again she paused, looking from face to face. "Sir Claude feels, and I entirely agree with him, that it would be a *very* sensible thing for every one of us to familiarize ourselves with the use of firearms, at least revolvers, and to carry them with us at all times. You never know when such a weapon may come in handy." Another pause, as she allowed a moment's murmuring. But she had no intention of letting them dwell on what might be required of their revolvers should the Boxers break in. "Our motto should be," she said, "that the only good Boxer is a dead one." She gave a bright smile. "Now, are there any questions or suggestions?"

Mrs. Woodward stood up. She was an American, a relative and guest of the Congers', who had in fact apparently been about to leave Peking with her two companions, also Conger cousins, when the railhead had been burned. She was a jolly woman, and obviously intended to enjoy every moment of this strange adventure. "Have I your permission, Lady Macdonald, to take photographs?" she asked. "I brought my camera with me, and I would like to keep a record of what's going on."

"Why, I think that is an admirable idea, Mrs. Woodward," Lady Macdonald said. "I can think of nothing more calculated to keeping up the men's spirits. Oh, indeed, please take all the photographs you can think of. And now, ladies, to work."

The women milled around aimlessly, chattering as they entered their names on the various lists. Constance slowly made her way through the throng toward Lady Macdonald, who had Mrs. Conger at her side. "May I make a suggestion?" she asked.

The two older women exchanged glances. They might as well have spoken out loud, Constance thought: Oh, Lord, here is the nuisance. But Lady Macdonald turned her bright smile onto her. "My dear Mrs. Baird," she said, taking both of Constance's hands. "I have heard *so* much about you. And about your ordeal and your terrible bereavement. May I say how *thankful* I am that you at least have come to us in safety, with your son."

Constance could not help but wonder if she had meant *anything* of what she had said this morning. But now was not the time to lose her temper. "I am thankful to be here, my lady," she said. "I think I may have something to offer."

"Of course you do, my dear girl. I shall put you on the hospital roster. Or would you rather be in the kitchens? You have only to say."

Because she had *suffered*, Constance supposed, a fate which could be any of these women's, any day now. Imagination rather boggled at the thought of either Lady Macdonald or Elaine Conger in the hands of the Boxers. But she rather thought that Lady Macdonald *was* the sort to blow out her own brains rather than be raped. "As you may know, Lady Macdonald," she said, "I have in the past been quite close to the dowager empress . . ." She hesitated, watching the Englishwoman's lips compressing. As did Mrs. Conger's. But she had to try. "I am sure that if I could get to her and talk with her and explain the terrible folly of what is happening—"

"My dear Mrs. Baird," Lady Macdonald said, "everyone knows of your . . . ah, friendship with the dowager empress. But I doubt it will do us any good now. Sir Claude doubts she is even in charge of events anymore."

"I am sure she is," Constance said. She could not imagine Tz'u-Hsi *not* being in charge of events.

Lady Macdonald gave her a frosty stare; she was apparently

not used to being contradicted. "I am sure Sir Claude has a *very* good idea of what is happening in the Forbidden City," she said. "And we must leave all negotiations to him. Why, even supposing you reached the empress, without being taken and . . . well, maltreated by these thugs all over again, would it not be considered as a sign of our weakness, that we should send a woman to beg for mercy? No, no, my dear. Your business is to remain here with the other ladies and give support to our men. And leave the heroics to them."

Sometimes it rained, a steady heavy drizzle. This occasioned a respite, for the Chinese would never fight in the rain, but took shelter beneath their brightly colored parasols and waited for the sun to shine again. The rain was a blessing in more ways even than that. It filled the legation's dwindling water supplies, seemed to cool the intense heat of the summer air, did something to alleviate the increasing squalor of the crowded compound.

On the other hand, if it was raining all over the North China plain, as seemed likely from the universal grayness of the sky, it would be turning the country between Peking and the coast into a quagmire and making it the more difficult for the relief column to progress.

Supposing there *was* a relief column and they had not been entirely abandoned. This was of course impossible. Sir Claude Macdonald said so, Mr. Conger said so, and all the other ministers and envoys also said so. It was inconceivable that their employers in Europe and in Washington would not be sending help with all possible dispatch. No doubt there had been delays . . . the trouble was that all those in the legation, being connected with the diplomatic service themselves, could envisage all too clearly what those delays might mean. Italian arguing with Frenchman, Englishman arguing with German, Russian arguing with Japanese, all meaning well, all determined to march on Peking and rescue or at least avenge the legations, and every one possessed of a quite positive but entirely different idea of how it should be done.

Or at least avenge them. This was one of the most disturbing thoughts that the besieged had to bear. No one doubted that the Western powers *would* come to Peking, breathing fire and vengeance. And would accomplish all that was expected of them. But they would also feel that they had done so if it was a case of avenging five hundred murdered white people and heaven alone knew how many murdered Chinese converts, rather than actually saving them.

Those inside the legation knew absolutely nothing of what was happening outside their own half-mile square of territory. Except for what the Chinese wished to tell them. Because an even more disturbing experience was the cat-and-mouse game to which they were continually subjected. On Monday there would be a furious onslaught, with thousands of Boxers hurling themselves against the ramparts, and every man capable of bearing arms required to repel them. Then on Tuesday there would be absolute quiet, with perhaps a messenger from the Tsung-li-yamen arriving with a case of champagne for the Austrian minister, that he might celebrate the birthday of some archduke in Vienna. On Wednesday the firing would resume again. On Thursday would come another flag of truce bearing a politely worded inquiry from the commander in chief, Jung-lo, as to when it would please the ministers and their entourages to evacuate the city and proceed to the coast under Boxer protection. And on Friday the assault would again be resumed, interspersed with messages thrown over the walls to say that the foreign devils had been defeated outside Tientsin, or their ships sunk by a storm in the Gulf of Chihli, or their forces being evacuated because of some other European-involved crisis elsewhere in the world.

"Our only safe course," Sir Claude Macdonald announced, gently stroking the ends of his waxed mustache, "is to assume that every message delivered here by the Chinese is a falsehood designed to lower our powers of resistance. Why they should imagine this is possible is a mystery to me, but I'm afraid it is impossible any longer to imagine that Chinese policy is being directed by any one body or any one person. No doubt we shall discover the truth of what is happening in the Forbidden City in due course."

Constance very much feared that Chinese policy *was* being directed by one person. One woman. She could see the evidence of the dowager empress's work in almost everything that was happening, from the stop-start attempts at destruction, to the thing which most bewildered the defenders—the failure of the Imperial Army to join in the siege. Even Sir Claude, sanguine as he was, could not deny that were a few batteries of regular artillery to be brought up to bombard the legation, its fall would be a matter of hours. But the Boxers continued to bang away, with utter inaccuracy, with their single cannon, and the legation had found an answer, in an equally old and forgotten field piece of their own, for which the Russians, miraculously, happened to possess some suitable powder and ball.

The Europeans and the Americans could not fathom the working of Tz'u-Hsi's mind. Constance could. Quite apart from her natural tendency to procrastinate, as she had done so disastrously in the war with Japan, the old dragon lady had spent all of her adult life balancing one ambitious general or prince against another, surviving entirely by her own ruthless mental powers. In this supreme crisis of her life, she was merely continuing that policy. Faced with a decision as to whether or not to crush the Boxers, the most serious upheaval in China since the Taiping, who had so powerfully affected her own youth, Tz'u-Hsi had done nothing. Because the Boxers were directed, not, like the Taiping, against the dynasty, but against the foreign devils. So, she was reasoning, Constance had no doubt, why not let them destroy the foreign devils, which is what all China wishes to happen anyway. If they can. If they cannot, why, then, my government will, however belatedly, join the Europeans and the Americans in crushing these upstart rebels, as we did the Taiping. To Constance's mind, the most sinister aspect of the siege was that the Boxers *were* continuing to wage it by themselves, without the aid of the imperial troops. Because that was conclusive proof that there *was* no allied expeditionary force from Tientsin anywhere in the vicinity of the capital.

And as a wet July drifted into a scorchingly hot August, it became apparent that time was running out. There was still sufficient food to maintain the defense for several months, despite the large numbers of Chinese converts who had flooded into the legation for shelter from the bestial tortures and murders practiced on them by the Boxers, and the wells in the gardens seemed bottomless, replenished as they had been by the heavy rains of the previous month. But ammunition was beginning to run short, and more important, so were fighting men. Every day added to the casualty list. Few were killed outright, despite the risks taken by the gallant sorties launched from time to time by the defenders to dislodge the Boxers from any particularly advantageous position. But more and more men were brought down to the improvised surgery, either hit by ricocheting bullets—for the Boxers had still not learned how to shoot straight—or by flying splinters of wood and masonry.

The doctors worked in relays, two of them always on duty, as did the nurses, eight hours on, eight hours off, around the clock. Constance was so exhausted most of the time she hardly knew what day it was, could barely summon the energy to spend a few minutes each evening with Charles and Adela, who were being looked after by one of the Chinese convert women.

Presumably, she thought, Frank, on equally continuous duty

on the perimeter, was no less weary. She saw him only occasionally, for it was Lady Macdonald's policy to keep the sexes as segregated as possible when off duty, working on the very Victorian principle that everyone had sufficient to occupy his mind without allowing *that* sort of thing to creep in.

Yet Constance could not accept that they lived, and fought, virtually shoulder to shoulder, and might very well have to die, shoulder to shoulder, without at least *knowing* their feelings for each other. Or his for her, at any rate; she no longer doubted her own. What had begun as an entirely physical attraction, compounded by the catastrophe of her life with Henry, had become . . .She couldn't really find words for it. She only knew that life without Frank was not really worth contemplating.

And at last she managed, by waiting in corridors, to encounter him as he came off duty, wearily unbuckling his revolver holster, checking at the sight of her.

"Connie!" He smiled, and held her hands. "How goes it?"

"I'm fine. And you?"

"Couldn't be better. The children?"

"Thriving."

They stared at each other. "Frank . . ." she said.

"Yes," he agreed. "We seem to have been traveling a hell of a long time, to come to this."

"I'd rather it this way than any other," she said. "At least . . ."

"We're together? Do you really want to die next to me, Connie?"

She forced a smile. "I guess I'd rather live next to you, Frank."

She was in his arms, and being kissed, as she had not been kissed since that night above the Chinese restaurant. "Oh, Frank," she whispered. "Frank, listen to me. No matter what anybody thinks, Lin-tu never laid a finger on me. I think . . . I think he *likes* me too much, to want to make love to me."

"Do you think I was worried about that?" he asked. "I must have been mad to allow *anything* to stop me loving you. Connie . . . we'll come through. I know we will. And then . . ."

"Then it's all ours, Frank," she said. "Oh, Frank, I'm so *happy.*"

An absurdity in such surroundings. But she *was*, happier than at any previous moment in her life. Because she was in love. Such a feeling had never been hers before. Henry had been something she had wanted to do, to free herself from girlhood and cloying Richmond. Frank had for so long been only a man. But now . . . the very thought of him gave her an enormous feeling of contentment, just as the awareness that he was in the firing line for several hours of each day made her tremble with fear. But they had experienced so much, together and separately, during the past ten years, it was impossible for her to even consider the possibility of his being hurt now . . . until the very next morning, when the stretcher-bearers came down the steps into the surgery and placed him on the desk which served as an operating table.

Constance supposed her heart had stopped beating. She had to close her eyes and open them again to make sure that it was really him. And then they filled with a rush of tears and she nearly choked as she looked at the jagged splinter wound which had been torn across his chest. His tortured eyes found hers for a moment, and then looked away again. But when her hand brushed his, his fingers seized hers so tightly she could not free herself until after Dr. Kenny had given the wounded man a dose of laudanum.

"Will he . . . ?" she bit her lip.

"He'll survive, unless gangrene sets in," the doctor said, stitching away. "That goes for everyone, now. We just don't have sufficient antiseptics left. Next."

Frank was carried out, and Constance had to tend to the next man, while her brain went spinning through kaleidoscopic corridors of agonizing thought. It could not be a coincidence that he had been hit, within hours of holding her in his arms. She did not suppose it had been some heavenly retribution for their sins, but she could not help but feel that his happiness had made him more careless, and he had perhaps unnecessarily exposed himself. In which case it had been her fault, as so much had been her fault.

It was even possible to suppose that the Chu-teh massacre had been her fault because she had not just lain down and let the Boxers murder her at the crimson pagoda.

She became aware that her replacement was waiting beside her, and left the surgery without a word. How she wanted to go to the male ward and see him, and touch him . . . but her mind was in too much of a turmoil. He would survive his wound. She was sure of that. But what then? To lie in his bed until he was murdered by the Boxers? Because that was what was going to happen to them all, even Charlie and herself. If any relief column had been going to reach them, it would surely have come by now. So they were merely going through the motions, waiting for the last bullet to be fired, the last man to be struck down. That was incredible. It was impossible to accept, after everything she had experienced, everything she had seen happen. Someone had to be able to do something. . . . She found herself staring at the wall opposite. Out of everyone in the legations, *she* had experienced most, had come closer to death than anyone else, knew more about the Chinese, about Tz'u-Hsi, than anyone else. No one here would accept that she could do anything. But they had supposed that equally, nine years ago. She knew she could reach Tz'u-Hsi, and she was sure the old lady would listen to her. Could the empress but be made to realize that no matter what happened here in Peking, an allied army would eventually storm the purple walls and wreak the most terrible vengeance—as the French and British had done in 1861, to avenge less than half a dozen white deaths, much less several hundred—then Tz'u-Hsi would realize the utter folly of what she was doing, and call off the Boxers, or at least throw the Imperial Army against them.

*Could* she be reached and persuaded? The legation was surrounded by Boxers. Boxers who were certainly careless in their guard-keeping habits, which was why so many Chinese converts had managed to get in to at least temporary safety. Thinking about it only increased the possible dangers. Therefore, thought was a mistake. She had not wasted time in thought in 1891, when it had been Peter's and Lizzie's lives at stake. Now it was her own, and hundreds of others', and Charles's and Adela's, and Frank's as well. Together with her future.

She went in search of William.

Constance did not expect William to help her again; she did not in any event require his physical assistance. But she did require some Chinese clothing—hers had been left behind in the American legation. He rolled his eyes and looked very unhappy, but he did as she required, scrounged around and found her a blouse and pants and boots, and a red scarf for her hair, which had been growing steadily during the several weeks she had been in Peking, and if a long way from the length it had been before Frank had cut it, came down to her ears and was a paler yellow than ever—she was not at all sure it did not have one or two silver streaks in it as well.

Because she was going out at night, she did not bother with any stain; it was in any event essential to her plan to be recognized the moment she reached the Forbidden City. She merely tucked her hair out of sight, pocketed her revolver, just in case, and crept into the garden to wait. She did not even risk saying good-bye to the children.

She moved through the bushes toward the part of the garden adjoining the canal, the moment it was fully dark. Here, as there was a water ditch on the outside of the wall, there was less risk of a Chinese assault, at least without adequate warning, and so the guards were less close together than in the more vulnerable sections; it was in fact an increasing problem for Sir Claude to find sufficient men to patrol the entire perimeter in enough strength. But as there *had* been an attack that morning, the evening was quiet—the Boxers did not seem capable of sustaining more than a few hours' fighting at one stretch. Constance lay in the shelter of some withered rosebushes, perhaps thirty feet from the wall, and watched the Russian soldiers, four of them, walking slowly up and down, obviously listening to . . . a distant rumble coming out of the south. Clearly a thunderstorm, brought on by the intense heat, she thought, and therefore promising more rain—which was all to the good, as the Chinese always took shelter. But the Russians seemed very interested in the noise, and now one of them was sent hurrying off to summon the duty officer, while the other three clustered at the far end of the wall to stare in the direction of the thunder.

Constance took advantage of their distraction to crawl up to the wall itself and get into an embrasure, arms and legs drawn up tight, collecting her breath and her determination; it was necessary to drop straight down, a matter of some eight feet. If she went outward at all, she would fall into the canal.

The officer came hurrying up, and there was much pointing and conversation. They spoke Russian, which Constance did not understand, but she suddenly realized that they were wondering if the noise could be gunfire. Gunfire! If it were gunfire, then the relief column *was* on its way, and coming close. For a moment her resolution faltered. It was so tempting to crawl back to bed and pull the sheet over her head. But it was very unlikely to *be* gunfire. And if it was, would that not spur the Boxers to launch a final, all-out assault before the Western soldiers arrived? Besides, if she could *say* that it was the gunfire of the approaching allies, she had a powerful additional weapon to use on the empress.

She sucked air into her lungs, pushed her legs through the embrasure, and dropped. The thud of her landing alerted the guards, as she could tell from the sudden concern in their raised voices. She regained her feet and raced along the wall, while above her, someone fired, but not directly at her. Yet the report of the rifle helped her, for the Chinese on the other side of the canal immediately returned fire, sending bullets whanging and ricocheting in every direction; Constance, already at the far end of the wall, dropped to her face and lay there until the shooting died down—it would be absurd to be hit by a stray shot at this moment.

Soon she felt safe enough to move again, crawling around the walls of the abandoned building beyond the legation and gaining the streets. These were not at all crowded; it was late at night, and the people of Peking had become used to the little war going on in their midst. Besides, it soon became apparent that everyone who was about was just as interested in the distant thunder as had been the Russian guards—no one paid any attention to the tall figure of indeterminate sex who hurried through their midst, and within a few minutes she was at the gate to the Forbidden City.

"Go away," said the soldier on duty. "Go away."

"I have business with the empress," Constance declared.

"You?" scoffed a second man, emerging from the gloom. "Go home, woman. Go home to your husband."

Constance drew a long breath. "The empress will wish to see me," she said. "I have vital information about the barbarians. I am the celestial-haired devil woman." She pulled the scarf from her head.

Constance's plan worked rather better than she had anticipated, to her discomfort. The guards argued no longer, but immediately seized her and bound her hands behind her back, at the same time searching her with extreme roughness, to remove her revolver. Then she was hustled up the avenue toward the palaces, and handed over to two eunuchs, who took her straight to Tz'u-Hsi's residence, marched her through the door, and hurled her to her knees before the throne. By then she was so breathless she could only raise her head with difficulty, trying desperately to keep her balance, as the loss of the use of her hands made her topheavy.

Despite the hour, Tz'u-Hsi was dressed, and was surrounded by a whole group of men, some dressed as soldiers, others as mandarins, while sitting beside the throne in a smaller chair was a pale-faced, nose-running young man, in a state of considerable nervousness from the manner in which he constantly moved his feet and plucked at his face, whom Constance realized was actually the Kuang Hsu emperor. She had never been allowed to see him before.

"So you did not take my advice, devil woman," Tz'u-Hsi said.

Constance got her breathing under control. "I was not given

the opportunity to do so, Majesty," she said. "As I was attacked the very next day."

"Insolence," Tz'u-Hsi said. "Always insolence." Her eyes gloomed at her prisoner. "And now you have come to beg for mercy? Perhaps you have been *sent* to beg for mercy."

Constance studied the old lady. Tonight she was looking her age, for all her makeup. And she was afraid, like her nephew, for all her arrogance. Certainly she was unsure of herself. So now was no time for supplication. She made herself kneel as straight as she could. "On the contrary, Majesty," she said. "I am disobeying Sir Claude Macdonald's express commands in being here. But because of our long friendship, and of the many kindnesses you have shown to me, I felt it my duty to warn you, before it is too late."

"Warn me?" Tz'u-Hsi's voice was harsh. "Warn me of what?"

"Within twenty-four hours, Majesty, an allied army will be inside Peking."

For a moment there was absolute silence, while everyone stared at her.

"Their guns have been heard," Constance said, warming to her theme. "They are coming closer momentarily. Majesty, I beg of you, should the white soldiers come here and find you even appearing to support the Boxers, they will wreak a most terrible vengeance. Your only hope is to issue orders for the suppression of the rebels now, this very minute, so that when the soldiers arrive, they will see what is being done."

Tz'u-Hsi stared at her. "My only hope?" she asked, her voice low. "*My* only hope?" It rose an octave. "You think to come here and threaten *me*, devil woman?"

"Yet does she speak the truth, Majesty," said one of the bearded mandarins standing beside her. "We have heard the guns ourselves. The foreign devils are coming."

"And will be here by dawn," said another. "If we are to act against the Boxers, it must be now."

Tz'u-Hsi stood up. Her face was quite pale beneath the rouge, and her eyes glittered with an unearthly glow. "Act against the Boxers?" she asked, her voice rising. "They are my people. Surrender to the foreign devils? Have I no armies to defeat them? Those guns you hear are Jung-lo's guns, turned on the barbarians. The Christians will be swallowed up, like the sea sand when a wave breaks upon it. They will disappear. You dare to side with the white people?" Her arm came up, pointing. "Take them out," she screamed, her voice winging around the huge room.

"Take them out and cut off their heads. Cut off their heads now. This instant."

Eunuchs immediately hurried forward to seize the two mandarins' arms. They looked at their mistress, but only with resignation, Constance realized. Even after all that she had experienced, she could hardly believe that such a thing was happening, and to two obviously senior councilors. "Majesty," she cried. "I must protest. What you are doing is not worthy of a great queen, of the ruler of an empire. You are behaving like a savage."

Tz'u-Hsi's gaze swung in her direction, and then her right arm came up again. "And she," she shrieked. "I have put up with her insolence for too long. She should have been executed nine years ago. Place her between those two traitors. Take her out. Show me her head. Show me . . ." Her voice died away, and Constance, already being dragged to her feet by the eunuchs, her breath gone, so that she thought she would choke, unable to think, to counter the frightened, insensate rage opposed to her, realized that booted feet had entered the room. "You!" Tz'u-Hsi snarled. "You are *here*, when you should be fighting the barbarians?"

"I have been sent here, Majesty, by General Jung-lo," Yuan Shih-k'ai said.

Constance's breath returned in a rush, and she felt sick. Yuan! Of all the people in the world, Yuan.

"Jung-lo has sent you?" Tz'u-Hsi's voice softened, and she sat down; Constance recalled the rumor she had heard more than once, that in her youthful years of loneliness following the death of her husband, Tz'u-Hsi had found in Jung-lo's arms the necessary solace of her womanhood.

"To save you, Majesty," Yuan said.

Tz'u-Hsi's head came up, staring at him.

"Our armies have been defeated," Yuan said. "As was inevitable. Those of Your Majesty's advisers"—he allowed his gaze to drift over the assembled mandarins and princes—"who advocated this senseless war have much to answer for. Your soldiers, brave as they may be, cannot match the steel and iron of the Western nations. General Gaselee is but a march away from the city gates, and your soldiers are running away. General Jung-lo will do what he can, but he can fight nothing more than a delaying action now. The Christians will be here by dawn, Majesty."

Tz'u-Hsi continued to stare at him, her face slowly settling into rigid lines. Constance half-expected that right arm to come up once more in the sentence of death. But this was no effete nobleman who knew nothing better than to bow his head before the sword. This was a professional soldier who knew only the *use* of the sword—and waiting in the doorway were the members of his personal guard.

Besides, he came from Jung-lo.

"What does my general recommend to me?" the empress asked, her voice now as quiet as ever.

"Jung-lo recommends flight, Majesty," Yuan said. "He recommends Jehol, or Shansi, far away from the reaches of the barbarians. He recommends that you abandon Peking and your people."

Tz'u-Hsi's head came up. "But you do not agree, General Yuan?"

"I do not agree, Majesty. Flight implies fear and guilt. Flight is ignoble."

"If Her Majesty remains in Peking, can you guarantee to hold the city?" asked one of the princes behind the throne.

"I cannot," Yuan said. "I do not think the city can be held. But if Her Majesty remains in Peking, it should at least be possible for her to negotiate a peace treaty, here and now, with the allied commanders."

"And if she cannot?" the prince asked.

"Then she can die, as we shall all die, defending the homes of our ancestors."

The prince's face stiffened, and he looked down at Tz'u-Hsi, who almost smiled. "Brave words, General Yuan," the empress said. "Were the choice mine alone, I might consider what you have said. But I have a duty to live, for China. Besides, it is Jung-lo's advice, and he knows best." She stood up. "Haste. We must make haste. We must be out of the North Gate within the hour. Haste."

Constance had not noticed the group of women who had been waiting in the shadows on the far side of the room. Now one of them left her companions and ran across the floor to drop to her knees by the side of the throne. "Majesty," she cried. "That is the coward's role you play. Stay, I beg of you, and fight or die with your people, and go to your ancestors without fear."

Tz'u-Hsi's face was again rigid. "You dare to address me?" she snapped.

The emperor slowly eased himself from his chair. Constance knew he was hardly more than thirty, but he looked twice that age. "Majesty . . ."

"Of course," Tz'u-Hsi said. "She is your favorite. But she is nothing more than a concubine. What is the punishment for a concubine who betrays her lord?"

Kuang Hsu's head jerked. "Majesty, I—"

"She has betrayed you," Tz'u-Hsi spat at him. "She has called you a coward. My actions are undertaken in your name. She has betrayed you and insulted you. Chiang," she shouted at the head eunuch. "Take her out. Throw her down the deepest well you can find." Again she pointed, "And cut off that devil woman's head."

Constance's arms were seized, and she was thrust through the door and into the night. Ahead of her the two mandarins were already being marched away, and beside her, the girl was being dragged into the darkness, fighting and screaming to her helpless lover.

"Chiang," Constance gasped, for he had himself taken one of her arms. "You cannot do it. You know she but spoke in haste and anger. We are friends, you and I, Chiang."

The eunuch smiled. "It is best to be executed by a friend, devil woman." He stroked her neck with his finger. "I have long known it would come to this one day. I have looked forward to it."

"You . . ." She could think of nothing more to say, nothing that she could do, save insist to herself that this could not be happening. But it *was* happening, she knew, as she gazed at Chiang's smiling face, as she was marched forward again, to come up against three of General Yuan's escort.

"Stand aside," Chiang snapped. "Stand aside, in the name of the empress."

"The empress is gone, Chiang," Yuan said. "And you had best scurry behind her, lest the people know of her departure and remember too well your crimes."

Chiang gazed at him. "Be sure I *will* go behind her, and inform her of *your* crimes, soldier."

"Inform her that I am doing my best to save her throne, as well as her life," Yuan said.

The hands holding Constance's arms slipped away, and a moment later her bonds had been slit. "I owe you so much, General Yuan," she said. "I do not know how I shall ever repay you."

"Fate will find a way, Mrs. Baird," he said. "Now, come."

"But you must stop those other executions," she said. "Those men—"

"Have already been beheaded."

"But . . . my God, they said no more than you yourself."

"At the wrong moment." He shrugged. "That is the way of the world. Tz'u-Hsi's world, at any rate."

"Then that girl," she begged. "Surely you can save her as well?"

"No," he said.

"But . . ." She clutched his arm.

"The empress hates the Pearl Concubine," Yuan said. "She has always hated her, because the emperor loves the girl more than his wife, who is Tz'u-Hsi's niece. She has long sought an opportunity to deal with her. She will not change her mind there. But you she has always truly loved. As you told Chiang, she acted in haste and anger, and she would have regretted it, had you been killed." He gave one of his grim smiles. "She *is* my empress, Mrs. Baird, and will continue to be so, after the foreign soldiers have left Peking."

"Do you really think so?" Constance cried. "Do you think they could possibly permit such a bloodstained monster to rule China for a day longer? And do you suppose I could ever love her again? I did once, I think. I admired her and respected her. But then I did not know her for what she really is. Now I hate her. I shall always hate her."

She paused for breath, wondering if she had said too much. But Yuan merely bowed. "Your personal feelings are your own affair, Mrs. Baird. You are one of those fortunate people who can have personal feelings. I may not, while I serve the empress. As for the future, statesmen have to learn the art of what is possible, over what is desirable. Now, come."

"You will send me back to the legation?"

Yuan shook his head. "That would be too dangerous. I think you had better remain here until your people come for you." This time his smile was sad. "It will not be a very long wait, I think."

Rippling volley fire, booming explosions, rumbling crashes, and above all, voices, voices screaming and voices yelling, voices cheering and voices shouting, all converging on the Forbidden City. And now, certainly, inside the gate.

Constance had heard it all before. But this was the first time she had heard it coming to her rescue and the rescue of all those she loved. Her heart swelled with pride. These were white men, Christian soldiers, come to strike down their enemies, and to restore that law and order, that good sense and decency which were what Western civilization, Christian civilization, stood for.

It was broad daylight, and she could contain herself no longer. "I will go outside," she decided.

The two guards who had been left in charge of her looked at each other in alarm.

"Do not worry," she said. "I will see that no harm comes to you."

She had been placed in the bathhouse, where Yuan had considered no emissary sent back by Tz'u-Hsi to make sure her last commands had been carried out would think of looking for her; he himself had felt it his duty to hurry back to Jung-lo's side and defend the city, if he could. Well, he couldn't. She opened the door.

The morning was now well advanced, and as she watched, the allied soldiers came pouring through the Gate of the Zenith; she identified Russian uniforms and French uniforms, British uniforms and German uniforms, felt a surge of relief that there were no Japanese uniforms among them. And then a pang of disappointment that there were no Americans to be seen. No doubt they were fighting in another part of the city.

The soldiers checked themselves inside the gate, gazing at the wonders of the Imperial Palace in amazement. Then one of them pointed at the houses, and Constance realized that the palace had not been evacuated; probably no one outside of the empress's immediate entourage even knew that Tz'u-Hsi had fled. Now the verandas of the houses were crowded with women, gazing at their conquerors. Who gazed back at them, and then gave a tremendous whoop, and ran at them.

The women recognized their coming fate, and screamed their terror as they scattered this way and that. "Oh, God, no," Constance shrieked, and ran down the bathhouse steps, tripping at the foot and falling to her knees, to be bowled over by a charging soldier who wore a red jacket and a kilt, and stopped to crouch above her. "Come on, me darling," he said. "Come along, get those pants off."

"Hey, she's a white woman," shouted another warrior, pointing at her hair, and they gathered around, while the first man somewhat shamefacedly helped her to her feet. "*Are* you white?" he demanded.

"I'm Constance Baird," she said. "I . . ." She listened to the screams and wails from around her. "Please . . ."

"And you've been held a prisoner by these yellow devils?" shouted the soldier. "By God, we'll sort them out, miss, that we will. There." He pointed up the steps at the open bathhouse door, where the first guard had appeared to discover what was going on. "You bastard."

"No," Constance shouted, and tried to hold his arm. But his companion pulled her away, and she watched in helpless horror as the Highlander ran up the steps, rifle thrust forward, bayonet slamming into the guard's midsection. Blood spurted, and the man seemed to explode air, his face a picture of horrified consternation as he fell backward. The soldier put his foot on the dead man's chest to pull his bayonet free, and brought the rifle up, squeezing the trigger to shoot the second guard.

"Oh, God," Constance shrieked. "Oh, *God*!" She jerked herself free, ran toward the avenue, stopped, looking left and right. There was blood and dead bodies everywhere, as the soldiers attacked the eunuchs who came running from the palaces. There were screams of agony and bestial shouts from inside the houses where the women were trapped. It was Port Arthur and Chu-teh all over again, only these were *her* people, come to rescue her.

She ran toward the throne house, and up the dragon staircase. She paused inside the great doors to watch a group of Frenchmen pulling and shoving at the huge throne, so that it at last fell over with a crash. The soldiers gave yells of joy and began prying at the jewels which decorated the chair, tearing off the strips of gold and silver, stuffing them into their pockets, trampling on the dead bodies of the three eunuchs who had been cut down before it.

Constance turned away, her stomach rolling, and smelled smoke. She looked through the door at the Imperial Library building, now entirely enveloped in flame. The most priceless collection of books in the entire history of the world, destroyed.

She fell to her knees and began to cry, huge sobs which surged up from her stomach and exploded from her mouth and eyes, and felt herself being raised by a gentle hand. "My dear Mrs. Baird," said the British officer. "This is no place for a lady."

"Another twenty-four hours," Frank said, "and I'll be out of this bed. Kenny seems quite pleased with the way things are going." He smiled. "Although it appears I'll have to avoid coughing for a while." He gazed into Constance's eyes, and then reached out to ruffle Charles's hair—the boy sat on the bed, while Adela sat on Constance's knee. "But I'm sure looking forward to it."

She found his eyes again. But she believed him now. And yet, she had to ask it. "Despite all?"

"I think you should say that to me."

She held his hand, and remembered the night above the Chinese restaurant, and then the calm, determined man who had led them to safety. Her future happiness was surely secure in such keeping. And yet the future itself was clouded, she knew, by the jumble of emotions and memories with which she viewed this land and its people. She listened to the sounds of the city drifting through the open window. A city which had almost returned to normal, with the speed with which the Chinese seemed able to adapt. The people of Peking even smiled at the Christians once again, apparently unaffected by the dangling bodies of the Boxer commanders draped along the roads like ghastly overgrown fruit, apparently able to forget that it had been their collective wish that the foreign devils be expelled.

"But I've been thinking," Frank said.

Her head raised.

"I don't want to be away from your side for a moment," he said. "Not ever."

"But, Frank . . ."

"I'm not even sure I want to be a marine again," he said. "Not after these past few days. Sure, they behaved better than anybody else, and we all want to feel it's because they're Americans. But maybe it was also just because they weren't the first into the Forbidden City; from all I've heard, they did their share of hanging and shooting on the way up here. Connie . . ." He hesitated. "Old Bunting is packing it in. Harriet refuses to remain in China a moment longer. He has a thriving agency business, and it can only grow now. I've some money put aside . . . hell, I've never had much to spend my salary on . . ." He paused again, watching her face, and sighed. "But I guess you've had China, as well."

Constance looked out of the window at the coolies working on repairing the legation walls, listened to the door opening behind her, and stood up as she realized it was Lady Macdonald. Hastily she set Adela on the bed beside Charles.

"Good morning to you, Mrs. Baird. Good morning, Captain Wynne. Hello, children." She was as brusquely cheerful as ever. "I thought you would like to know that we've finally caught up with the old dragon lady. At least we know where she can be found. Do you know, she fled Peking in disguise as a peasant? She even cut off those long nails of hers. Can you believe it?" She smiled at them, seemed disappointed that they *could* believe it. "I thought you'd be interested, as you were the last of us to see her." She allowed disapproval to creep into her voice; she had not yet forgiven Constance for being so flagrantly disobedient.

"We are," Constance said. "What will happen to her?"

"Why, she'll be brought back here as soon as is possible."

"To stand trial?"

"Good heavens, no, Mrs. Baird. To resume her throne. Supposing she can find it."

"But . . ."

"Oh, I know she's all manner of a criminal. The whole world knows that. But she holds China together. Without her, the empire would just fall apart." She gave a hearty laugh. "We'd never receive a penny of the indemnity we're demanding."

So nothing will happen at all, Constance thought. Just as the Japanese soldiers weren't punished for what happened at Port Arthur, and the allied soldiers aren't being punished for what happened here—"Victorious troops are always a problem," Sir Claude had said—so the dowager empress would not be punished for all the hundreds of people she had so carelessly sent to their deaths, or had castrated, or had dragged into the harems of her sons and nephews. Only the Boxers, who had fought for her and for China, were being hanged in their thousands. Because they had lost.

Empresses never lose.

"I knew you'd be pleased," Lady Macdonald said. "Now, I have another visitor waiting to see you." She returned to the door, opened it. "You may come in, General."

"General Yuan!" Constance took both his hands; she had not known he was still alive, had been afraid to ask.

"Mrs. Baird." He gave one of his grim smiles. "I felt I should say good-bye."

"Good-bye? Oh, my God! You're not . . . ?" She looked at Lady Macdonald.

"Good heavens, no, Mrs. Baird," the Englishwoman said. "General Yuan is not going to be punished. He always opposed the Boxers. But he has a great deal to do."

"I have been appointed viceroy of Hunan province," Yuan said. "There is still much unrest there. So I must hasten to deal with it. But I wished to say good-bye and to meet Captain Wynne." He went to the bedside, shook Frank's hand. "You are a fortunate man, Captain. Although perhaps it may be possible to hope that Mrs. Baird has done with adventuring, for both your sakes." He glanced at Charles, and then bent over Adela. "And this is the little princess?"

"Oh . . ." Constance bit her lip. "I intend to bring her up as my own daughter, General."

"Nevertheless, she *is* a princess of the House of Ch'ing," he said. "That is not something that can be forgotten. I must go. Captain. Lady Macdonald."

Constance accompanied him into the corridor. "General . . . is there news of Lin-tu?"

He frowned at her. "Are you so bent on vengeance? I had not supposed it of you."

"I had hoped to hear that he had escaped."

Yuan looked at her, and then at the door to the sickroom.

"I love Captain Wynne, General," Constance said. "And as you say, I have done with adventuing. But whatever his crimes, Lin-tu did save my life."

"He has disappeared," Yuan said. "It is possible that he was killed in the fighting and lies in an unmarked grave. On the other hand, it is equally possible that he has escaped. Lin-tu is a great survivor."

"I hope he has," she said.

"I'm not sure I agree with you. People like Lin-tu, and his leader, Sun Yat-sen, seek to change too much. Perhaps all China. But you . . . you will flee back to the United States now?"

She opened her mouth, and then closed it again.

"I hope you will not do that," Yuan said. "You have seen China at its worst, but I think you have also seen something of China at its best. And you must know by now that not only Chinese can act like savages. I know you hate the dowager empress, but she can never harm you now, and she is a very old woman, Constance. She cannot live forever. People like you"—he smiled—"and myself, may be of service to the new China that cannot lie so far in the future, if only by endeavoring to combat the Lin-tus and Sun Yat-sens of this world. And you are foster mother to a royal princess. Remember that, future Mrs. Wynne. Remember that."

He went along the corridor and down the stairs, leaving her staring after him, feeling a sudden surge of excitement such as she had not known since her first day in this tremendous land. Then she had felt she was beginning a new life. Now she felt the same.

She watched Harriet Bunting come panting up the stairs. "That Chinaman," Harriet said. "Ugh! Horrible people. He should have been hanged. My dear Constance, Mr. Bunting and I have passage on the *Robert Walkley,* leaving the day after tomorrow. Oh, that will be a happy day. But there is a cabin available for you and the children. And for *dear* Frank as well, I suppose, in all the circumstances. I have taken the liberty of reserving it for you. I know you are just as anxious to get out of this accursed land as I am.''

Constance looked out of the window again, inhaled the scents and listened to the sounds of Peking, and felt her excitement grow. ''But I'm not leaving, Harriet,'' she said. ''Didn't your husband tell you? Frank is going to take over his business.'' She smiled at Harriet's expression. ''I am going to live right here in Peking—for the rest of my life.''

Great Reading from SIGNET

(0451)

☐ **RAGE TO LOVE by Maggie Osborne.** (126033—$2.95)*
☐ **SEASON OF DESIRE by Julia Grice.** (125495—$2.95)*
☐ **THE DEVIL'S HEART by Kathleen Maxwell.**

(124723—$2.95)*

☐ **KIMBERLEY FLAME by Julia Grice.** (124375—$3.50)*
☐ **MOLLY by Teresa Crane.** (124707—$3.50)*
☐ **GILDED SPLENDOUR by Rosalind Laker.** (124367—$3.50)*
☐ **BANNERS OF SILK by Rosalind Laker.** (115457—$3.50)*
☐ **CLAUDINE'S DAUGHTER by Rosalind Laker.**

(091590—$2.25)*

☐ **WARWYCK'S WOMAN by Rosalind Laker.** (088131—$2.25)*

*Prices slightly higher in Canada

**Buy them at your local
bookstore or use coupon
on next page for ordering.**

## Fabulous Fiction from SIGNET

## More SIGNET Fiction

**Buy them at your local
bookstore or use coupon
on next page for ordering.**

## Fabulous Fiction From SIGNET